HEARTLESS

Heartless

ISBN: 978-1-7367707-0-2

Printed in the United States by Monponsett Press

For Mom

One

The white lines crawled across the green displays of the monitors, in rhythm with the steady sigh of the ventilator. The name 'Matthew Richardson' was written in black Sharpie on a piece of tape running at an odd angle below the squares of glass. The tape had been stuck to the machine in haste six months ago in the frenzy of the emergency room ten floors below. It had been put there during a desperate attempt to save the life of the young boy at the end of the tangle of the wires and tubes hanging between the machines and the bed. No one had seen any point in straightening it ever since.

Matthew's parents, Tom and Lisa, sat next to his bed. A knot of doctors and nurses hung at the back of the room. No one in the room paid the monitors any attention. The scrolling lines had not changed the hopeless story they had told in the six months since Matthew had been wheeled into the emergency room, a paramedic kneeling on his gurney and pumping air into Matthew's paralyzed lungs. And those six months had worn away any dreams that the story the lines could ever tell could ever be better one.

The medical team waited patiently for a sign that Tom and Lisa might be ready. Not that any parents could ever be ready for what they were being asked to do.

A scattering of posters and drawings were taped to the wall behind the bed, but Matthew would never see them. Lisa knew this; she had brought them from his room at home anyway, to remind everyone it was her little boy in that bed, not just a stack of fluorescent lines, mindlessly scrolling towards nothing

Her little boy lay still, as he had since the all-terrain vehicle he'd been riding flipped over. The thousand-pound vehicle had landed on top of him, dragging him down a muddy slope and into a small stream. He'd been unresponsive by the time his father and the other riders had found him, face down in the icy water. A thirty-minute wait for emergency help to arrive had turned into a six-month vigil, and the slow realization that no miraculous rescue was coming.

Lisa's blonde hair was pulled back in the same tight ponytail she'd been wearing since the day they started the daily treks to the hospital. Strands of identical hair peeked out from under the surgical cap on Matthew's head. They waved gently, pushed around by the draft of the air conditioning system. Lisa reached out reflexively and smoothed the rebellious tuft. Her hands were thin and bare. Her wedding ring had disappeared from her hand about the same time a four-figure donation had appeared on the website they'd set up to help with the medical bills. Tom had never asked her about it, and she'd never said.

Tom and Lisa didn't talk about much anymore, other than about the details of Matthew's care. And the endless stream of bills. And, once in a while, about their younger twins, when the cloud of grief raised enough for them to see beyond the inert boy under the white sheets.

Lisa had never directly blamed Tom, but she didn't have to. He'd bought the ATV for Matthew despite her objections.

And he'd insisted on bringing Matthew along for his rides through the lake country south of Pontiac, Michigan. He'd said it was a great father-son bonding experience. In the end, it had brought pain, debt, and the slow destruction of the family Tom had tried so clumsily to build. Sitting next to Matthew's bed, Tom consoled himself with the thought that soon things would be better. Not for Matthew or himself of course. But for Lisa and the girls.

On some unspoken signal, the small crowd in the back of the room shifted their positions. Two of them coughed, almost in unison. Tom knew what they were saying, without them saying a word.

It was time.

Tom met Lisa's eyes, and he nodded. Her jaw quivered but she did not argue. She had wanted to delay this inevitable moment for another two months, so they could celebrate Matthew's thirteenth birthday. But over the past two weeks, ever since he'd gotten that first impossible phone call, Tom had pushed hard to convince her that waiting was just more torture. The phone call had offered him a way out. A way to make things better for him family. But that possibility had not came without a cost. The arguments with Lisa had been part of the cost.

She'd been adamant. *Let him live to be a teenager,* she'd begged. *Even if only for a day.*

What about Matthew? he'd countered. *What if we are making him suffer, every day we wait?*

Lisa had relented at that terrible thought. Tom had hugged her, then gone into the bathroom, turned the water up high to hide the noise, and dry-retched into the sink. Because he knew it was a lie. Matthew was not in pain as far as anyone knew. There was no Matthew anymore, just a body on a bed.

But for Tom to give Lisa and the girls any hope for a future, the lie had to be told, because the procedure had to happen now. The man on the phone had made that very clear to him.

Tears burned down Tom's cheeks. He stroked Matthew's leg as Lisa sat near his head. Lisa began quietly singing the quiet refrain of "Hush Little Baby" to Matthew, the way she had when she rocked him in her arms so many years before. Even in this most terrible of moments, Tom marveled at how she could put aside her own agony to give Matthew even the faintest hope of comfort. Tom reached out to touch her arm. She did not acknowledge his gesture.

Two doctors moved forward, one to either side of Matthew's bed. They checked the monitors one last time, but only for protocol. The thinner, taller one standing on the far side of the bed spoke. "Time of death, 8:12 p.m." He recited the information in a monotone, like a bailiff announcing a verdict.

Despite those awful words, nothing in the room changed. The white lines kept crawling across the displays. But to Tom and Lisa everything changed. With that legal formality completed, Matthew was now considered dead, and his heart could be harvested for the benefit of a boy they'd never met, lying in a similar bed in a hospital a half-hour away.

Lisa buried her head in her son's chest and moaned, filling the room with a single, quavering note that held half a year's worth of pain. The sound of it made Tom want to crawl away. Instead, he buried his face in his hands and wept his own grief and sorrow. He and Lisa sat inches apart, each lost in their own personal misery. Tom did not try to touch her again.

The medical team gave them another moment to come to grips with the idea that Matthew was finally—irretriev-ably—gone. Then two orderlies unlocked the wheels on the bed and rolled it out into the hallway. "You can come with me," a nurse said. Tom and Lisa followed the bed as it was rolled down the hall towards the elevators that led to the surgery floor.

The scene made Tom think of the funeral procession to come in a couple of days.

The one he already knew he would be missing.

Two

Twenty years out of high school and a decade out of the army, Rick Morrow still stood like he was waiting for a quarterback to shout "Hike!" or a sergeant to bark "Dismissed!" Even the enormous stuffed lion tucked under his right arm was cradled in a way that fell somewhere between a football and a small child. But to anyone who looked closely, the deep lines creasing his face and the tightness of his lips hinted at strains that had aged him in ways years alone could not measure.

His back was still straight, but his biceps had thinned from lack of exercise. His legs were spread shoulder-width, but the knees of his jeans were shiny, worn to the very edge of their useful life, as were the scuffed work boots below them. His gaze was clear, but the circles under his blue eyes were cut deep by lack of sleep and uncountable bouts of tears and disappointment.

"You shouldn't be here, Rick," said the middle-aged woman sitting at the worn desk across from him, leaning her elbows on one of the stacks of papers that hid most of its scarred brown surface. "John's getting prepped for surgery and you've got a half hour ride to downtown to see him."

"None of us should have to be here, Rhonda," he said. "But it's nice to be here for something other than bad news about John."

She cocked an eyebrow, but there was sympathy in her eyes. "You know what I mean. You should be with your son."

Rick glanced at the stuffed animal. "I just want everything to be perfect. I didn't want to wait."

"I get it. But still…"

"Are you sure they won't change their mind?" he said. "Can't you talk to them?"

Rhonda shook her head. "It's the Richardsons' decision, Rick. I know how you feel. We'd rather have moved Matthew to Metropolitan hospital downtown and done both procedures there. But I guess this hospital is the closest thing to home they've had for Matthew for the last few months. They wanted to say goodbye here."

"Doesn't that make it riskier?" Rick shifted his balance as he spoke. The worry growing in his mind was channeling into a nervous energy that made him want to move, to turn his anxiety into some sort of action. The lion just kept on grinning at Rhonda from its perch against Rick's upper arm, its bright blue fur waving slightly in the breeze as Rick swayed back and forth.

Rhonda rose out of the chair and came around the side of the desk, facing Rick in the small open area of her office. The high ceilings and faded, ornate trim hinted at the room's origins, back when rooms like that were called parlors. The room had been the crowning feature of a Victorian house converted to administrative offices when they'd finished the gleaming new Saint Elizabeth Hospital Tower next door. Rick glanced out the drafty wooden windows towards that glowing tower. Rhonda followed his eyes, wondering if he thought he'd spot some sign of Matthew Richardson or his family. The Richardsons were lost in their own grief she imagined, up on the twenty-fifth floor of the tower, where the surgery units were located. In Detroit, half an hour from the Saint Elizabeth tower in Pontiac, Rick's own son John was being prepped for the surgery that could, with luck, give him a chance for a life close to normal for a ten-year-old boy. It was a drama that played out daily in hospitals around the country, Rhonda thought. One family submerged in grief, while another clung to hope. It was the cold calculus of the organ transplant process; a life lost for a life saved.

A life will *be saved regardless even now*, Rhonda reminded herself, fighting to keep her face neutral and her mind focused. *Don't forget that.*

"We've got everything covered," she told Rick. "We're going to fly the heart from here to Metropolitan. And we're using a new transport device we've developed here. It'll protect the heart far better than the way we've been doing it for the last twenty years. It'll go fine."

"Fly?" The color drained from Rick's face. "We can't afford that. We're still paying for the last flight to Chicago two years ago. Insurance didn't even cover half of it."

Rhonda shook her head. "Don't worry. The hospital will cover the costs."

"You can do that?"

"I'm the CEO. I can do whatever I think is right," she said. "All you have to focus on is John and your family." She reached back towards her desk and picked up an envelope with the *Detroit Lions* logo on the front corner. "I hope these tickets are a small step towards starting on that new journey. They're for the last game of the year. Four months should give John time to recover enough."

"Thanks." Rick took the envelope and shifted his grip on the lion to free up both hands, slipping the white rectangle under an elastic band he'd already put on the front paw of the stuffed animal. "I'm sorry you had to come all the way here for them," Rhonda said, relieved Rick's attention was on the tickets and not her face as she spoke. She was afraid her own feelings were becoming too much to hide. "The Lions' front office just assumed they should send them here. We would have gotten them to your home if you'd wanted."

"I appreciate that," Rick said. "I know it sounds crazy, but I wanted John to see them as soon as he woke up. I figured that way he'd have something to look forward to."

So he'd have something else to live for, was what he really meant, Rhonda knew. She glanced at the small, gift-wrapped box in the lion's opposite paw, also held in place with a rubber band.

Rick followed Rhonda's gaze. "That one's for Mary. It's a necklace. For all she's been through," he said.

"How's she doing?"

Rick shrugged. He tried to keep the gesture light, but Rhonda could feel the weight of it. "After what happened last time..." He paused, searching for words. "I think it's just hard for her to hope."

"That other heart should have gone to John," Rhonda said, as much to herself as to him. She knew if the heart everyone had expected to go to John nine months earlier hadn't been reassigned at the last minute, she and Rick wouldn't be in her office right now. And she wouldn't have faced the awful choice she'd made. It was a choice that she'd come to realize was really no choice at all. She'd always understood why Rick and Mary had been so resentful of the last-minute decision by the transplant board, giving the heart to a boy named Danny Cho instead of to their son. Over the past few weeks, she'd come to understand how much she resented that decision, too.

"I still wish I'd fought harder then," Rick said. "We never should have had to wait this long. We're getting lucky."

Fight NOW, she suddenly wanted to scream at him. *Demand to know why we're using the new heart container. Insist we drive the heart the twenty miles to Metropolitan. Make me undo what I have started.*

But he raised no objections. Asked no questions. His trust was the worst pain he could inflict on her, she realized. "It wouldn't have made a difference," she said to fill the void, still working to keep her face from betraying her thoughts. "The transplant board's decisions are always final."

"You shouldn't be able to buy your way into this country just to get on the transplant list. Nothing against that little boy, but it shouldn't work that way." Rick's words and his gaze trailed off into some unfathomable distance, reliving some of those terrible days, Rhonda guessed.

No, it shouldn't, but it always seems to, she thought. She took a deep breath. "The gift's a great touch. You all deserve something for what you've been through." She meant it, but that bit of empathy didn't keep the guilt from rising up in her chest. She pushed it aside and kept the weak smile plastered on her face.

"Mary more than me," Rick said, looking at the wrapped box. "It's not much, but I got some overtime hours lately." He smiled as well, a tired smile that still lit up his face and drove away the worry lines for a moment. "Don't tell the billing department. I can't give *all* my money to you guys, right?"

Rhonda forced a laugh in return. "Your secret's safe with me. But you should get going. They're going to put John under in about two hours."

"One more quick stop to make, actually." Rick said. "But it won't take long. Then I'm on my way."

Rhonda opened the tall wooden door to let Rick out. She closed it tight behind him, counted to three to be sure he was gone, and then collapsed against it, her cheek pressed against the cool surface. She closed her eyes and took a few deep breaths, then returned to her desk, her hands still shaking.

Three

Rick left the old Victorian house and jogged across the parking lot to the tower. The lion's head bobbed against his upper arm with every stride. The building's twenty stories of glass and steel rose in front of him, commanding the skyline over the stained concrete and brick buildings of downtown Pontiac.

He had read that the tower had been a bold gamble by Rhonda, half headquarters for her growing health network and half symbol of hope for a crumbling city. Washed by its lights now, Rick felt some of that hope seep into his bones. He made his way into the building and through the lobby. He avoided the flow of patients, visitors, and staff in the crowded hallways—almost without noticing them—as he followed the signs for the surgical floor.

He'd tried over the prior few weeks to put himself in the shoes of the Richardsons. He kept reminding himself that they were giving up their boy's heart so that a child they'd never met could have a chance for life. Rick had decided he needed to tell them how grateful he was, in whatever words he could muster. But he'd wondered how he'd feel if he were them, meeting the father of the boy who would hopefully live a long and happy life, after their son died a quiet, clinical death.

He'd decided instead to write a card to Tom Richardson. Rick had read the stories of Matthew and the terrible accident in the woods. He'd figured that maybe, father to father, he could say something that helped. Rick knew the anger he'd turned on himself at his inability to protect his own family over the years since John's diagnosis. He figured he could maybe help Tom Richardson forgive himself, at least a little bit.

Rick reached the surgical floor and spotted the orderly at the desk: a tall, thin and very young-looking man with dark eyes and dark curly hair. The kid's name tag said "Ashok."

"Are the Richardsons here?" Rick said.

Ashok motioned with his head towards a waiting room up the hall, near the doors that led to the surgical suites. He glanced at the stuffed animal under Rick's arm and raised an eyebrow. "That can't be for them."

Rick froze, realizing how thoughtless he would look to Matthew Richardson's parents with the whimsical gift under his arm. "Oh, God, no," he said, looking up and down the hallway, suddenly panicked that Tom or Lisa Richardson would emerge from the waiting room and see him. He took the card he'd written out of his pocket and slid it onto the desk. "I just wanted to leave this for Tom Richardson."

"And you are?"

"Rick Morrow. My son—he's the one getting the heart," Rick said.

"Oh" the young man said, some understanding and a bit of empathy in his voice. "That's cool." He took the card and leaned it up against the monitor in the reception station.

"How long before they're... done?" Rick said, trying not to sound eager for them to complete the task of ending Matthew Richardson's life. "I need to meet the heart at Metropolitan Hospital."

"They're pretty far into it," Ashok said. "The chopper's already here too. Pilot's downstairs getting coffee. He'll be in the air less than half hour after they're done in surgery. You're okay on time, but I'd get going soon if I was you."

"What kind is it?"

"What kind is what?"

"The helicopter. I used to work on them in the army."

Ashok shrugged. "It's not the usual one, but I don't know much beyond that." He seemed to wrestle with himself for a minute, then shrugged again. "You want to see it?"

"Really?"

"Sure. I don't think anyone would mind. I need to go check on the roof anyway. I make sure there's nothing in the way when they bring the stretchers... or coolers... up the elevator."

Rick checked his watch. He was already later than he'd told Mary. But even the idea of putting his eyes on the aircraft that would be ferrying the heart to John seemed to take away a bit of his anxiety. He nodded. "Sure, just for a second."

Ashok led him past the regular elevators to another, wider one further down the hallway. He used a key to activate the control panel and hit the call button. As they waited, the young man's phone buzzed.

"Damn," he said, glancing at the display. "I need to handle this."

The elevator doors opened. "That's OK," Rick said, starting to turn away. "I appreciate the thought though."

Ashok seemed to debate with himself for a second time, then smiled at Rick again. "You can go up if you want. Just please don't touch anything."

"Don't worry. I know what I'm doing around a helicopter," Rick said with a laugh.

Ashok hustled off down the hallway, putting his phone to his ear.

Rick stepped in through the open doors. There were only three options to choose from: Emergency Room, Surgery, and Roof. Clearly, this elevator was used only to get critical patients directly into the hands of the doctors or surgeons that might save them.

The elevator floor pushed against his feet as it started to rise, but it only had a few floors to travel. Then the doors opened onto the roof. Rick felt the shock of cool October air on his face. The helicopter was straight ahead, yellow straps securing it to the roof. It took Rick a second to recognize the model—a Canadian aircraft, manufactured by CeraGlobal out of Vancouver. He'd seen a few in the army, but they were more commonly used in the states as medical choppers and air taxis. Most pilots considered them the most advanced civilian helicopters available. The one in front of him was so clean it nearly glowed, the lights from the roof reflecting off the glass windscreen and the curves of metal along the sides. A LifeLift logo was painted on the copilot's door, with the words *CeraGlobal* underneath it. The rotor blades hung motionless, curving slightly towards the roof, but the aircraft still seemed to crouch rather than just rest there. It seemed as if the yellow restraining straps were the only thing preventing it from springing into the sky that very moment.

Rick felt his throat tighten at the thought that such an incredible piece of machinery was there for his family.

Seeing the sleek, powerful helicopter, and knowing what was happening in the surgical suite below, Rick started to let himself enjoy a feeling he'd not had in years—the feeling that, this one time, things were going to work out. And that ten years of hell would be behind him and his family.

Underneath those feelings was another emotion Rick tried not to acknowledge. It was one he knew he'd never share with anyone. It was a growing sense of relief. In the nine months since the transplant board had directed that heart to Danny Cho, nine months when John got increasingly weaker and no other heart became available, a quiet desperation had begun to throb in Rick's chest—the fear that his acceptance of the board's decision back then, his unwillingness to fight their authority, had doomed his son. But now, at the last possible minute, they'd gotten a second chance. Rick had begun to hope he could look at himself in the mirror and not wonder if his own weakness had cost John his life.

Rick looked out past the helicopter towards distant Detroit. The sky was brooding, with low clouds hiding the moon and stars. The dark sky made the lights from the skyscrapers, easily visible from the roof, seem even brighter. The bright lights made the city look close enough to touch, and that made Rick realize what a luxury the helicopter was, given it was only a twenty-mile ride to the other hospital. He realized he had not thanked Rhonda nearly enough. He found himself wiping away a tear.

Then, knowing he was already pushing the time, he pushed the "Surgery" button to head back downstairs. The doors opened a moment later and he stepped back out into the warm, brightly lit corridor. Ashok was coming out of a room further up the hallway, headed towards him.

"Cool, right?" Ashok said.

"Yeah. Thanks," Rick said. "The thing looks like it could get to Metropolitan hospital in about five minutes."

"It pretty much can," Ashok said. "But you can't. You ought to get going." He slipped past Rick and into the elevator, heading up to the roof himself to complete his work.

Rick nodded in agreement, found the regular elevators and headed downstairs.

Four

Rick felt his phone buzz just as he reached the parking lot. He pulled out the phone and saw Mary's face on the screen.

"Where are you?" Her voice was flat—if there was any emotion in it at all, it was disapproval.

"I'm heading to the car," he said.

"Why'd you even go there?"

"I had to get some paperwork." He knew his excuse would sound lame, but he wanted to keep both the tickets and the gift for her a surprise until he arrived. "It was on the way home from work anyway."

"Not really."

"I'm getting in the car now. Everything's going well here."

"They're getting John ready. He's scared."

"Tell him it's going to be OK." Rick made a conscious effort to put his growing confidence into his voice so Mary could maybe draw from it. "I mean that, Mary. It's all going well. They're even going to fly the heart to Metropolitan. It's going to be OK."

"Just get here. John should have his father here, too." It was clear what she thought of his decision to stop by the hospital in Pontiac, but there was no excitement or even real anger. It was a flatness Rick knew to expect. He fought the futile urge to try and convince her that this time was different, that this time luck was on their side.

The first raindrops, cold and hard, hit Rick's head as he reached the car. He cursed silently, knowing what could happen to Detroit traffic with even a little bit of rain. He dropped the lion onto the passenger seat, then jogged around to the driver's side, sliding in and starting the car with one motion. The lion flopped over to lean against the passenger doorframe as Rick took a hard left out of the parking lot and onto the busy road. Rick shot a glance at the giant stuffed animal, tickets to the game taped to one of its furry hands, Mary's gift affixed to the other. He fought the urge to let Mary's tone on the phone make him feel foolish for his gifts.

He nosed through the traffic, peering through the film of cigarette smoke fogging the rain-streaked glass, suddenly wondering if maybe he'd pushed his luck too far. He picked his way towards Route 75, which would take him from Pontiac to Detroit, then merged into the heavy traffic on the highway. Outside Pontiac the open spaces gave way to giant square office buildings scattered across the flat landscape like children's blocks on a table. The old Chevy bounced along on the broken, cratered roads that were a staple of Detroit driving. Rick had borrowed the car from a neighbor, since Mary would not be leaving John's side at Metropolitan Hospital. The one car they still owned was sitting in the parking lot there.

Thirty minutes later, as he neared downtown Detroit, the scattered office buildings were replaced by the endless rows of small brick homes that surrounded Detroit itself. The unfamiliar brakes seemed to grab or fail at random times, so he drove with extra care. He reminded himself that an accident at that point meant he'd never make it to the hospital in time. He tried to keep his excitement in check, reminding himself that a major surgery still lay between his son and a chance at a future. Hearts were not batteries, the doctors had told him, to be snapped out and in, and John was weak already. There was always risk. But at this point there was also really no choice. On the positive side, the surgeon, Doctor Mirchandani, had assured Rick and Mary that John was still strong enough for the procedure and had youth on his side. Doctor Mirchandani had operated on John twice before, the first time when the boy was only days old. Each time he'd given John a new lease on life, buying him a few more years. The doctor exuded confidence, and that confidence was infectious. At least to Rick.

Over the black outline of the buildings on his right, Rick saw flashing lights. It took only a second for him to know the lights belonged to a helicopter, chugging its way parallel to the highway. He'd gotten good at identifying helicopters by their profiles during his time in the Army, and the shape of this one was distinctive, even in the rain and dark. With a flash of excitement Rick realized it was the same helicopter he'd seen on the roof of Saint Elizabeth's less than an hour earlier.

He alternated between checking the road ahead and watching the blinking lights on the helicopter. He felt his glimmer of optimism build as he watched the powerful aircraft speed towards Metropolitan hospital. After all the fighting with insurance and doctors, all the heartbreak and pain for him and Mary, the layoff, the endless bills, he felt like he'd earned this quiet moment. He knew it was a sheer coincidence of timing, but he felt grateful to be able to accompany the heart on a little bit of its short journey. His own heart slowed and the frustrations and fears drained away, but the excitement remained.

He was on the way. The heart was on the way. Maybe this time, he started to think, he could live up to his promise to Mary that everything really would be OK.

After a few minutes it occurred to Rick that the helicopter seemed to be flying lower than the ones he usually saw on his daily commutes into the city. This helicopter was one of the best in the world; it would have instrumentation that made the darkness and rain a non-factor. The low altitude made no sense.

His hope turned a bit sour, as it had so many times in the past, and his mind started to creep back towards worry. *Climb a bit*, he thought, willing the machine to put a little more distance between itself and the buildings below. *Even just a bit.*

But every time he stole a glance out the window the helicopter still hung low in the sky. He realized too, as he watched more carefully, that it was not moving very fast. Rick was rolling along at thirty miles an hour in the wet weather, but he couldn't understand why the helicopter was not going much faster than that. As they got closer to the city limits, the aircraft grew closer to him, reducing the gap between itself and the highway. That move put even more distance between itself and the straight route it should be taking to the hospital.

His concern mounted, and resentment crept in. Even in what should be a perfect moment, he complained to himself, the world had to give him some reason to be stressed.

The rows of homes thinned out as he approached the Hamtramck exit, replaced by a stretch of semi-abandoned warehouses and factories. Traffic slowed to a stop again. As Rick watched, the helicopter, too, seemed to come to a stop, hanging in the blackness over barren fields and low buildings. Then he saw the lights of the machine start to descend. The helicopter dropped slowly, almost gingerly. The descent paused and the craft hovered just over the black outlines of some warehouses a quarter mile off the highway. He silently urged the pilot to forget about whatever was distracting him and bring the chopper back up to altitude. At this point Rick didn't even care if the helicopter beat him to Metropolitan by a mile, or even if the surgery started before he arrived. He just wanted the trip to be over.

Then, as if the pilot had made some kind of decision, the helicopter descended quickly again, dropping entirely out of sight behind the roofline of the distant buildings. It disappeared so suddenly that it seemed to leave a hole in the sky. There was no fire, no explosion; just blank sky where his son's new heart had been. The lack of any obvious sign of disaster didn't keep the terror from gripping Rick's chest, or the crushing premonition from welling up inside.

Once again, in what should be the best of moments, something was going terribly wrong.

Five

Rick stared at the space in the sky where the helicopter had just been floating, desperate for it to reappear. It didn't. The words in his head turned into a silent scream: *This can't be happening.* He peered over the cars in front of him. There was an exit a hundred yards ahead. Traffic began to crawl again, but Rick's panic was too much to let him wait. He pulled to the right and hit the gas. Drivers leaned on their horns as shot down the breakdown lane.

He stole glances out the window, trying to spot the helicopter. He took the ramp faster than he should, and the back end of the old car slid out a bit on bald tires. He kept his foot on the gas regardless, sliding around the right-hand curve of the exit. The lion was tossed across the seat, nearly winding up in his lap. He shoved it back towards the passenger door, his eyes still on the road.

He thought of calling Mary or the police or the hospital, but he didn't want to take the time. He knew had to get to the landing spot to see what had happened. It occurred to him that if there had been a mechanical problem he could fix it quickly or even drive the heart the rest of the way himself. He kept a mental picture of the helicopter's last location in his mind and roared down the wet road, flat brick walls pinned behind chain link fences flashing by his windows.

A few more blocks up, he calculated, *and one or two to the left.* He got to where he thought he'd be parallel to the location and turned left. He counted the blocks. Then almost on instinct, he slammed the brakes hard, screeching and skidding to a halt. A chain link fence sat ahead of him, a red and white *Caution* sign hung across its wires. He was staring at loading dock of some sort, only feet away from his front bumper.

He reversed course and got around the building, accelerating along its far side, close to where his mind told him the aircraft had landed. Suddenly, his windshield flared into a kaleidoscope of shimmering droplets. He couldn't see anything through the smear of water and reflection from the bright lights coming straight at him. He pulled as far as he dared to the right half expecting a screech of metal against the fencing along the road. A big SUV flashed by him in the opposite lane, barely slowing despite the rough, narrow road and the car it had almost forced into a building.

As his eyes adjusted from the glare, he hit the gas again. He rounded the same turn from which the SUV had just appeared. Ahead was a redder light, reflecting dully off the brick faces of the buildings. He pulled forward until he reached a break in the buildings on his right. Through the gap he could see an open space, with the red light flickering more brightly. The smell of smoke, acrid smoke, hit his nostrils. Terror growing in his chest, he spun the wheel, jumped the curb and bumped across the rough surface into the flat space beyond.

Then he saw it to his right. The helicopter. It sat perfectly upright on its skids, but the back half of the passenger compartment and the entire engine were engulfed in orange flames. He flung open the car door and leapt out, racing towards the fire. The car, still in gear, continued rolling unseen behind him, jumping a curb and slamming into the factory's wall on the far side of the open space. The force of the collision twisted the frame, popping the doors open. The Lion's mascot spilled out of the passenger seat and rolled onto the wet gravel.

Rick ran towards the fire, A man standing in shadows a few dozen feet away shouted "Get back!" But Rick barely heard him. The flames were crawling forward towards the cockpit of the helicopter. Rick grabbed the side door handle and yanked it open, not noticing the pain flare in his hand as he touched the hot metal. The interior was now nearly engulfed. Rick looked desperately around the passenger space, and then saw the red and white cooler, sitting on the floor between the two rear seats. He tried to reach it, but the heat was too much. Behind him the man still shouted, his words muffled by the roar of the flames. Rick pulled off his jacket and used it to shield his face and thrust his hand back into the conflagration. He held his breath against the heat and smoke. This time he got a grip on the cooler and pulled. It came out easily. The fire extinguisher stored behind the copilot's seat dislodged as the cooler struck it, the metal cylinder banging painfully on Rick's shins as it bounced out of the rear compartment. Rick stumbled backwards and fell to the ground, clutching the cooler to his chest. Then he felt hands on his shoulders and realized he was being dragged backwards.

The hands let go after a minute and Rick rolled over, the heart container coming to rest beside him. Through eyes watering from the fumes, he got his first look at the other side of the device and realized why it had felt wrong. The entire bottom third was opened like a wound. Piping and plastic fused were together by the heat. Rick could see the remains of the protecting fluid inside leaking into the damp ground. He could also see a lumpish, blackened shape inside, illuminated by the fire, and his gasps turned to sobs.

He dragged the ruined cooler closer and curled his body around it, trying to shield its contents from the rain and smoke. Sounds, more animal than human, escaped from his throat as his body shook. He pulled his jacket over the container, but he already knew the futility of his action. The heart he cradled was now nothing more than a charred piece of meat, fused to a plastic box.

Forty feet away the helicopter's fuel tank exploded. The heat washed over Rick, but he did not feel it. He passed out, sprawled in the dirt, wondering as he fell into blackness what he would tell Mary and John. Across the litter-strewn lot the lion lay still as well, its mud-streaked fur soaking up the rain, still clutching its pair of prizes.

Six

Mary Morrow pushed the speed dial button again. Rick's phone rang repeatedly. She hit the red button as soon as the voice mail message kicked in.

"Is that Dad?" John asked quietly. Mary was standing next to John's bed, trying not to do anything to make John worried.

She forced a smile. "I'm sure he'll be here any minute."

Why did he have to go over there today, of all days? She asked herself. But she knew the answer. That's what Rick did. Going wherever anybody needed him. Trying to control events, even when events had shown them time and time again that the things happening to them were beyond anyone's control. She'd realized that painful fact after the last heartbreak, nine months earlier. That's when she had made the choice to put her family's fate in God's hands. She remembered the day she'd finally made that powerful choice, sitting with her pastor over a cup of coffee, exhausted from the tears and the anger. *Hope is the enemy,* the pastor had told her. Because hope leads to vanity and selfishness. *We hope for things we think we deserve, whether they are part of God's plan or not,* he'd said. Acceptance meant trusting in God's plan.

Acceptance was the path to peace. He'd told her that, and she'd realized it was true.

Hope leads to selfishness. She knew that to be true also, all too well.

When she'd made the decision to trust God, she'd felt the peace the pastor had promised—a peace that had eluded her for years before. That peace had given her room to embrace her transcendent love for John's spirit, rather than just his flesh. It was a decision that let her get out of bed in the morning. When she knew John's spirit would live forever, it mattered less that his body may not survive another day.

But Rick wouldn't accept that peace. He kept plodding along, finding specialist after specialist, hoping for a miracle to come from science, not faith. She'd watched him, and helped him of course, even though she'd felt in her heart that none of it would really matter.

It wasn't that she wanted John to live any less than Rick did. She cherished every moment with her son. But she put her energy into heart-felt prayer, both for the life on earth John still lived, and for the afterlife he'd deserve, when God decided the time was right.

Now she was getting ready sing John to sleep, maybe for the last time. And Rick, who did not share her faith in the next life, was nowhere to be found, for what could be John's last day on earth.

They'd already been feeding John medicines for days. Antibiotics to fight infection. Other drugs to collapse his immune system. They'd had a dentist check his mouth for any signs of infection, too. Infection was the single biggest immediate risk to John, assuming he survived the surgery.

The next biggest risk would be his own body rejecting the new organ.

The staff continued their work, readying John for the most important four hours of his life. They worked quickly, with a sense of purpose, but joked with him as they finished their preparations. Some of them had known him for years. They had celebrated birthdays with him and played games with him when he was too weak to get out of bed.

This was a dangerous time for him. But it was a joyous moment too. Although nobody had ever said it, no one in the room truly believed would ever happen after the heartbreaking event in January—the one they all just referred to as "Danny Cho."

The organ donor list was an ever-changing thing. When a new heart 'became available' as they called it, a lot of factors determined who got it. Compatibility was chief among them, but distance mattered, too. Usually, a heart was only viable for a few hours after surgery, so the donor and recipient had to be geographically close. John's blood type was rare. The antigens he'd developed from all the transfusions made it even harder. And he was young.

Differences in age were not deal breakers in the selection process, but the doctors had made it clear that a youth's heart would be far preferable. When all the factors were put together, and although they'd never said it to Mary and Rick directly, everyone knew the odds of a compatible heart being available in the right place at the right time were not good. Twice they'd come close, only to have the crossmatching process disqualify John even though every other requirement had been met. And then, nine months ago in January, they'd gotten even closer. A near-perfect match had been found, a boy in Nevada who'd fallen, tragically, into a neighbor's swimming pool. He'd been an ideal fit and all odds said his heart would go to John. Mary had never been more excited.

But two weeks before the surgery, the transplant board had decided that a boy named Danny Cho in California was in greater need than John. Danny Cho—whose parents had moved from Beijing to Los Angeles only six months earlier, simply to get their son on the U.S. transplant list. There had been rumors of large donations promised, or test results rigged, but they had remained rumors.

All the close calls had been horrible rollercoasters of emotion for the family and the medical staff, but Danny Cho had been the final blow to Mary's trust in man or science.

That was why, even with the heart on its way from Mercy Hospital and the surgical team arriving as well, Mary kept telling herself that her son's fate was in God's hands, not her's or the doctors.' She kept up her silent prayer for John, while willing herself to accept whatever outcome the Lord had ordained.

The staff continued to bustle around the bed. Mary marveled at the nurses and aides as they teased and talked to John. Over the past few months, he'd been visibly failing. Every day the staff watched him inch closer to death, but it never showed on their faces or in their actions. They still helped him fight every step of the way, through dangerous fevers, emotional tirades, and nights of agony for a boy who was staring at death when he should have been starting to notice that maybe, just maybe, girls weren't so annoying after all.

The head nurse, Esther Williams, looked entreatingly at Mary. "We need to get John moving," she said. "They're getting ready in surgery."

"I know, Esther, it's fine." Mary said. She and Rick knew all the regular staffers by name. They'd spent enough time together, fought enough, cried enough, for them all to feel like family. But Esther was special even in that group. She had been caring for John since the first time he'd come here, and Mary knew the woman was almost as tense for this procedure as were she and Rick.

Esther looked at Mary one more time and set her jaw. "Okay, people," she said tersely to the team around her. "Let's get upstairs."

Seven

Rick fought his way back to consciousness, his brain clawing its way out of what felt like a dark, acrid-smelling hole. He forced his eyes open and found himself staring into a black sky, as fine droplets of rain cooled his scorched skin. A patchwork of red and blue lights bounced off the brick walls and jagged triangles of window glass that remained in the buildings surrounding the vacant lot. The colors refracted in the raindrops still falling from the blackness above, casting shards of light in all directions. Sirens wailed in the distance, growing closer. He tried to flail his arms, to reach out for the deformed plastic cooler, but they would not respond.

He thrashed again, trying to move his legs, his body, but they held fast. For a second, he wondered if the blast had paralyzed him. He had a moment of terror that he was falling into some kind of trauma-induced nightmare, unable to move as the news of John's death sentence reached his wife and son. After a moment, getting his bearings, he realized the truth was simpler, but far worse. He was strapped to a stretcher of some kind, on the hard-packed ground near where his car had finally come to rest. He turned his head to the side and saw the remains of the burning chopper being sprayed down by a crowd of firefighters. More figures in fire equipment and police uniforms milled about, most simply watching the action.

A young cop, tall with short hair under his soaked cap, stood near Rick, close enough for Rick to hear his words. He was talking to an older, taller black man in a raincoat who managed to look both completely bored and sharply alert. The cop gestured towards Rick.

"Hey Detective. The pilot says this guy came out of nowhere." The cop said. "Seems he tried to loot the damn helicopter while it was still on fire. Pilot said he never saw anything like it."

"That's about what this city's come to," the older man said, shrugging.

"No!" Rick shouted, struggling. The two men turned in unison.

Rick fought against the restraints. "You have to let me go. I need to get to the hospital."

"Settle down, champ," the detective said, "We'll get you to one soon enough. They'll need to patch your fool hand anyway." The two men turned away to continue their discussion.

"It's my son," Rick insisted. "It's his heart. I wasn't stealing anything."

The two men ignored him. The young cop was fidgeting with his radio. The detective was watching the last remains of the flames die down in the charred skeleton of the airframe.

"My son's going to die," Rick said, anguish in his voice.

At this the two men turned. The detective looked at the young cop, raising an eyebrow. The cop shook his head emphatically and said, "I asked the pilot, he said nobody else was here when he touched down."

"He's sure?" the detective said. "He must have had a lot going on right then to have seen everything."

"He seemed sure."

The detective looked at Rick. "Is your son here?"

Rick motioned his head towards the steaming, hissing remains of the helicopter. "He's not here. His heart is. The cooler. Did you see the cooler?" Rick had never felt more helpless, unable to move, trying to find words that would get through to the two men.

The detective turned toward the young cop again. The questioning look on his face deepened. "Yeah, there was a cooler," the cop said. "Crazy looking thing, with melted pipes and wires. This guy was holding it when we got here. It's what he stole from the chopper. It was a mess."

"What was in it?"

The cop shrugged. "Didn't look yet. Drugs is my bet." He motioned towards the car, still nose-up against the front of the building. "Bet he stole that, too. Different name on the car registration than his license. Different address, too."

"He has a driver's license?"

"Yeah, checked his wallet to get an ID. License matches his face. Credit cards, too. Not much cash."

The detective turned and studied Rick a bit more closely. "License and credit cards, eh? Probably has a job then. Or at least a place to live."

"Why?" the cop asked the detective.

"Son, how many homeless people or addicts have you picked up who had a driver's license, cash and credit cards?"

The young cop was silent. "Exactly," the detective said.

"My son's heart!" Rick shouted, desperate now. "That's what's in the cooler. My son's new heart." The two glanced briefly at Rick. The young cop just looked annoyed. But the detective's eyes tracked back and forth a few times between Rick and the helicopter and then came to rest on the cooler.

"Why do you think it's drugs?" he said to the young cop.

"Because it's a medical helicopter. Said so right on the side, before the fire got it."The detective's eyes went wide. "They don't go to that much trouble just to move some drugs. Go find out what's in that cooler, son. Now!" The young cop took off at a trot.

"You gotta help me," Rick pleaded.

"Just sit tight, sir," the detective said, more gently this time. He pulled out a cellphone and started looking at messages, shielding the screen from the rain with his free hand. After what seemed like an eternity, the young cop returned, running this time. He leaned in towards the detective and said something Rick could not hear. They both turned to stare at Rick. The older man mouthed the word "*Shit.*"

"Please," Rick said. "Let me go. I have to get to Metropolitan Hospital. I have to be there when they find out."

The detective seemed to turn the situation over in his mind, then motioned to someone Rick could not turn his head far enough to see. Two EMTs appeared and lifted the stretcher up to lock the wheels in place.

The detective leaned over to Rick. "Don't worry, that's where they're taking you."

Rick started to protest the restraints, but the detective cut him off. "They're for your own safety. Look, I really hope you're just making this all up," he said. He pointed to the flashing lights on the ambulance. "But even if you're not, you'll get there a lot faster in this."

The EMTs rolled the stretcher to the back of a waiting ambulance. In a final, desperate glance before they slid him in, Rick twisted his head around and spotted the cooler, still on its side in the middle of the courtyard, spattered in mud from falling rain and splashing boots. The young cop stood over it, peering down into the irregular hole carved by the heat from the fire, still not believing what he was seeing.

As the ambulance bumped its way over the rough ground toward the street, the technician in the back started collecting ointment and bandages. Once the vehicle reached the narrow road, she began cleaning and bandaging Rick's hand, which was now throbbing terribly. The siren started to wail as they picked up speed.

"Please," Rick said, raising his head to try and make eye contact with the EMT. "I need to make a phone call."

She just kept working on his damaged hand, clearly trained not to respond to the requests of restrained police suspects.

Rick felt a buzzing on his thigh. They had draped his jacket over his legs to make sure it went with him, and his phone was still in the pocket. It went still after a few seconds, then buzzed again a moment later. And again. Rick could picture Mary, dialing him frantically, her anger turning to panic. He could not move, could not answer. He also imagined somebody coming into the room where Mary was sitting. Some cop, or doctor, or administrator, who would invite her into the hallway to tell her the news that her son's hopes were gone. And she would be all alone to hear it.

Rick dropped his head back onto the stretcher, arms and legs still strapped to the frame. The phone buzzed one more time, then stopped, and for the second time that night, he wept.

Eight

Rick could tell from the sudden hard decelerations and the lurch of the stretcher as they nearly skidded around turns that the ambulance was moving fast.

"How long?" Rick asked the woman who had bandaged his hand. Every second that ticked by added to the chances of the news reaching the hospital before he did. She looked at him suspiciously, but decided this question was safe enough to answer. "At this rate, five minutes."

Her guess proved spot on. They pulled into the Metropolitan complex and went straight up to the emergency room entrance. The driver came around and the two EMTs guided the stretcher out onto the concrete and through the double doors. Two more cops, flanking a balding man in a sport coat and button-down shirt were waiting to meet them. Rick hopes rose as he recognized the bald man. He was an administrator at the hospital. Rick racked his brain for the man's name. *Todd*, he realized suddenly. And Rick realized something else, too. Todd looked terrified.

The cops immediately started undoing the restraints, and the EMTs helped Rick to his feet. Somebody must have radioed ahead about Rick, trying to sort out his story about the heart. Todd stepped up to Rick and surveyed him quickly. He started to ask if Rick was okay, but Rick cut him off. "What's happening?" Rick asked. "Where are they?"

The cops shifted a bit at the outburst, but Todd motioned them back. "They're upstairs," he said quietly to Rick. "Let's go."

The two men avoided orderlies and patients as they half-jogged down the hallway, Rick's bandaged hand throbbing in time with his pounding heart.

"Do they know?" Rick said.

"No."

"Where's John?"

"I'm not sure. He was on his way into surgery a few minutes ago."

Rick nearly stumbled. He had a vision of them removing John's heart, not knowing the one they were expecting was a charred lump in a field just a few miles away.

Todd saw his reaction. "Don't worry. They wouldn't start until the donor heart was here and they had confirmed it was viable."

They reached the elevators, and the car started its journey upward.

"Rick, I am so sorry," Todd stammered, now that they were alone. "Such a thing. We've never had anything like this. We take every precaution..." His voice trailed off as he realized Rick was not taking in a word he was saying.

They burst out of the elevator and into the hallway. Todd pointed down a few doors. "Mary's in there," he said.

Nine

Mary sat in a plastic chair that flexed uncomfortably as she shifted her weight. She was exhausted from stress and frustration. Adrenaline, and her anger at Rick, kept her alert and fidgety. After Esther Williams had snapped out her commands, the team had wheeled John upstairs to the surgery floor. One of the surgical nurses had come out and greeted them there, told them the heart was in the air and due in just a few minutes, and confirmed that the rest of the surgical team was close behind.

The anesthesiologist had readied the shot that would ease John into sleep. Mary had sat by his side and told him how much she loved him, and how everything would be okay.

"Where's Dad?" John asked. "We need to wait for Dad."

"We can't, honey," she'd said. "They need to keep this process moving along. We talked about this."

Rick and Mary had resolved long ago to respect and trust their son, and to tell him everything. They'd sat with him while Doctor Mirchandani had explained the whole procedure to John, and what the recovery would be like. And the risks. John always asked questions. Smart questions.

Only once, a few months earlier, had he asked them what it would be like to die.

"It's just another step," Mary had told him. "You'll be with God, and Gramma. And Aunt Jessica."

She had described to him a shining vision of the heaven that awaited all of them when the time was right.

Rick had stayed silent.

Now, as they prepped John for surgery, she'd just stroked her son's forehead. "Your dad will be here when you wake up," she said. "He'll be so happy to see you."

With those final words they'd slipped a needle in John's arm and asked him to count down from ten. His eyes fluttered shut before he reached five. Then they wheeled him away, and she was left wondering if she would ever see her beautiful, brave son alive again.

With John now in the hands of the doctors—and God— she sat in the uncomfortable chair, shifting back and forth. She'd given up calling Rick. Her battery was down to the red bar, and she wanted to have enough power to answer if he called her.

There were sounds in the hallway, and shouts. Then the door burst open, and Rick half-stumbled into the waiting room. Mary leapt to her feet, and gasped. Rick was soaking wet, and filthy. His pants were ripped. His right hand was bandaged. His hair was wild. And his eyes were red.

"There was an accident, Mary," he said, before she could speak. His voice was hoarse from the smoke. "A crash."

Mary tried to follow the rush of words. "The car? Are you OK"

"Not the car. The helicopter"

She saw the look of agony in his eyes. "Where is it?" she asked. Her voice rose, nearly breaking. "Where's the heart?"

He could not get out the words. He just shook his head.

In her shock she could only manage single disjointed words. *How? Where?*

Rick told the story of the car ride. Seeing the fire. The trip in the ambulance.

"I could feel the phone," he said, the feeling of helplessness still etched on his face. "I knew you were calling. I never should have gone."

She started to shake, the old terrible grief, the pain she thought she'd moved past, welling up inside. It was the pain she'd vowed never to feel again—the terrible emptiness when her vain, selfish hopes were crushed. "You told me it was going to be okay."

"I thought it was."

"You told me it was going to be okay," she said again, her voice rising and cracking.

He dropped his head. "I know."

She stumbled backwards. One of the nurses caught her and guided her to a chair. "Why did you tell me that?" she said to Rick through her tears.

"I thought it was true." Tears streamed down his cheeks, too—both for his own grief and the pain he saw on Mary's face. "It had to be true."

He searched the room with his eyes, then gathered himself. His next words were almost a moan. "Where's John?"

"We're bringing him back out now," a familiar voice said from the doorway. Esther Williams was standing there. She had clearly been giving them a minute to themselves, a brief chance together to try and grasp this new reality. She was shaking, and both Rick and Mary could see the pain on her face. But despite her own shock, Esther had sprung immediately into action, ensuring John's procedure went no further, even as she struggled to comprehend what had just happened. And then she had come to check on Rick and Mary.

"He'll be in recovery in just a bit." Esther remained in the doorway, suddenly uncertain of what to do, now that she had delivered that update. Mary stood up and held out her arms and Esther ran forward, her professionalism stripped away by her own emotions. The two women hugged, trying to console each other despite their own grief.

Over the next few minutes, the rest of the medical staff filed into the room. They hugged Rick and Mary. They hugged each other. Some cried, some just stared into space. Fifteen minutes earlier they had been a cadre of professionals, as close to playing God as human beings ever got, laser-focused on the miraculous procedure they were undertaking to save a boy's life. Now they were just a handful of people huddled together, reminded of their limitations by a set of events they could never have anticipated. Events that, even with all their technologies, training and commitment, they had no hope of undoing.

The scene reminded Rick of a wake.

From time to time, isolated words reached Rick as people talked in hushed tones to each other. *A crash. A fire. Maybe the rain. Maybe the engine.* They were all trading what little bits of information or speculation they had, trying to make sense of the senseless events.

The door opened again and Doctor Mirchandani stepped into the room, still wearing the surgical scrubs he'd donned for John's surgery. He spotted Mary first and moved towards her. "I'm so sorry," he said. He spoke in soft, measured tones, but his eyes darted about, as though looking for some different answer. "We prepare for every possibility. But this…?" His voice trailed off.

Esther motioned to one of the staff, who brought Rick a towel. "You'll be seeing John in a minute," she said gently. "You might want to clean up a bit."

It took Rick a minute to realize what she was saying. In the rush to get to John and Mary he'd never thought about how he looked. He found a public bathroom down the hall. Seeing himself in the mirror, he realized what Esther had meant. His hair was matted down and it both looked and felt like it had been soaked in engine oil. His face was ruddy from the heat and streaked with grime from the field and the helicopter itself. A stain on the right side of his shirt was impossible to identify at first. Then the image came flooding back to him. Him lying on the hard ground holding the cooler tight, the remaining protective fluid for the heart leaking out and soaking his clothing. His hands began shaking uncontrollably as he tried to open the faucets, but he forced himself back to steadiness.

He washed as best he could, using the small sink and hand soap, and made his way back to the waiting room. Esther spotted him and nodded encouragingly. Then her phone buzzed, and she checked the message. "Come on," she said to Rick and Mary. "John is just down the hall. They're going to wake him up." She straightened her back, her professionalism returning now that she had work to do.

Ten

Esther led Rick and Mary to the recovery room. The anesthesiologist stood next to John's bed. He, too, appeared shaken and defeated as he checked John's blood pressure.

After what seemed like an eternity, John's eyelids opened. He blinked rapidly and tried to work his mouth and his tongue. Esther dabbed a wet sponge onto his lips. His eyes focused and swept back and forth across the people surrounding the bed, trying to make sense of his surroundings.

He looked at his mother and father. Before either of them could say anything, he smiled slightly. "It worked," he said in a half-whisper, putting his hand over his chest, the relief on his face more evident than they ever would have expected. "I'm here."

Looking at his son's joyous expression, Rick realized now how scared John must have been before the surgery. John had never let on to his parents but clearly the boy had thought he was never going to wake up. Now, not only had he woken up—he thought the surgery was done. Rick felt a new kind of anguish. Neither he nor Mary spoke. Neither seemed to have the words to break the truth to their son.

John suddenly looked puzzled. "You said I'd have a breathing tube for a while when I woke up." Puzzlement turned to worry, as he studied his parents' faces. "Why don't I have one?" he asked, his voice quavering. "Why don't I have the tube?"

Rick realized this was one time he couldn't ask Mary to be the one to try and explain things to John. "Something happened, Johnny," he began, his own voice shaking like his son's. "Something nobody could have expected."

Rick told him the story in detail. John listened silently, but the panic grew in his eyes as his dad told him the final, horrible details.

"I'm going to die, aren't I?" John said quietly, after they'd dried his tears and their own.

"Don't say that, honey," Mary said.

"You said how lucky we were to get this chance. That it was one in a million. You *said* that."

"Those were just words, Johnny," she tried assuring him. "It's just a saying."

"There was this heart," Rick said firmly. "There was one before this. There can be others. And we'll talk to other doctors."

"There won't be another one. I know it." John said. The certainty in his voice was more heartbreaking than any tears.

They sat with him for another hour. At one point Mary said she was going down to the prayer room. When she came back, she seemed calmer. The tears were gone, replaced with a sort of stoic resolve.

Esther Williams and some of the other staff poked their heads in occasionally to offer words of encouragement, but mostly they left the family alone to deal with their shock and grief.

Eventually, John's fatigue and the lingering traces of sedatives in his body got the best of him, and his eyes closed.

Rick and Mary gathered their jackets and left John sleeping, his damaged heart laboring inside him and dying a little more every day.

Todd, the administrator who'd met Rick downstairs, was waiting for them in the hallway. The shoulders of his trench coat were still spotted with rain.

"Can we speak for a minute, before you go downstairs?" he asked. He was polite but there was concern in his eyes, even fear. Rick and Mary stopped and waited for him to continue.

"When you go downstairs," Todd said, "There will be news trucks and reporters. They'll want to talk to you. Usually in situations like this, we're happy to do the talking."

"Thank you," Mary said.

"That's not helping!" came a shout from down the hallway. It was Esther Williams, still in her surgical garb, walking quickly towards them.

"Esther, please," Todd said. "Let me do my job."

"If you want to help them, Todd, then tell them what they really ought to do." She turned to Rick and Mary, the anger clear in her eyes. "Listen," she told Rick and Mary. "I know this might not seem like the time, but I've seen this before. There's a lot of reporters down there."

"Exactly," Todd interrupted. "Which is why it's the worst time for them—"

"—It's the best time for them," Esther retorted, talking right over the communications director. "The best time for them to tell everyone how much they love John and how difficult this is for all of you."

"We don't need that attention," Rick said.

"But you will need the money," Esther said. "Get your story out there. People will care. Tell them how brave your son is. How hard he's fighting. They'll help. Trust me. There's still a road ahead for John. You need to be ready for it."

Rick looked at Mary, not sure what to do. She seemed to think for a moment and that same look of resolve came over her that Esther was projecting. She nodded. "I'll do it."

Rick turned to Esther. "Okay."

Rick and Mary pushed past Todd, who stood frozen, and moved into the elevator. The doors opened in the lobby and the two of them started towards the exit. They quickly found themselves surrounded by reporters, only steps away from the elevators. The throng started shouting questions about John and about the crash.

The questions overlapped, so Mary just began speaking and the reporters fell silent, tending to their cameras or microphones. "Thank you all for your concern," she said. "Our son is sleeping upstairs."

"Does he know what happened?" someone shouted from the back of the crowd.

"We've told him the news. He's being as brave today as he's ever been. He's been through more than any child should ever bear, but he's our strength through all of this."

When she had been attending the fundraisers with Rick, she'd still let him do most of the talking. Now, with a mass of cameras and microphones in her face, she spoke softly but clearly, looking from reporter to reporter in turn, as if each was the only person who mattered to her. Then she straightened her back and took a deep breath. "All of God's acts happen for a reason," she said, "and we have put our faith in the Lord. We will follow the path he has set out for us, and trust in him. We will be praying for our son, and we ask that you send him your prayers, too." Rick just stood still, keeping his face expressionless.

"Do you blame the hospital? Or the pilot?" asked a young woman, pushing her cellphone towards Mary.

"Right now, we're just focusing on our son, in the face of this terrible accident," Rick said, stepping in between the reporter and Mary. "Our family and friends have been there for us throughout this ordeal, and we are sure they'll be here for us now, too. That support means everything. We'll have some tough times ahead, but we know our friends and our love for John will carry us through."

More questions came, but Rick grabbed Mary's arm and pressed forward. They reached the exit doors and headed out into the rain.

Eleven

Half an hour later, Rick swung the car into their narrow, crumbling driveway. Their home was a small brick house built before the Second World War, at a time when Detroit was building houses faster than any other city in America. A sharp-pitched roof allowed for two bedrooms upstairs, with a simple living room, kitchen and dining room on the first floor. A small, detached garage sat at the end of the driveway. The layout of the house and garage were identical to nearly every other house on the street, and the streets beyond that, as were the steel bars that now protected the doors and windows.

When Rick and Mary had moved out of their bigger house in Oak Park they'd stored a lot of their furniture in the garage, unable to fit it all into the modest house. Everything in the garage had been stolen one weekend when they were in Chicago meeting with a heart specialist. They kept the empty garage locked, but now just to keep the neighborhood junkies from using it for shooting up or for shelter as the winter set in.

As they entered the house, they saw Rick's parents standing in the small living room. His mother's face was still red from crying, but she smiled bravely and hugged Rick and Mary in turn after they came through the door. His dad told them they'd put John's brother David to bed an hour earlier. They hadn't told him anything about the crash. Rick and Mary recounted the events of the evening once again. Rick's mother choked back more tears and fussed with the bandages on Rick's hands as she listened.

"We saw you on TV," his mom said. "All the reporters and the lights. It must have been awful."

"The TV station showed a picture of John and the Go-FundMe page," his dad said.

"Maybe Esther was right," Mary said to Rick.

"The phone's been ringing off the hook ever since," his dad said. "Reporters mostly. And some lawyers."

Like the rest of the house, the living room had the orderly but uninspired look of a space too small to allow clutter but occupied by people with neither the time nor energy to attend to the finer details that kept a house a home. A couch on one wall sat across from an older flat-panel TV. Two stuffed chairs filled out the seating in the room, separated from the couch by an end table. A small bookshelf next to the TV held some family pictures, along with the scrapbooks Mary had tried to assemble each year since the kids had been born. The bookshelf also held a small fish tank. A single goldfish paraded back and forth, as it had for three years. They'd bought it for John, to keep him company back when he'd been living at home, already too tired or sick to go to school. He'd named the little creature Ralph.

Rick's dad got a beer from the fridge for Rick and some wine for Mary. The four sat down while Rick's mom filled them in on David's day. When the clock showed 11 p.m., Mary picked up the remote and turned the TV on to one of the local news channels.

"I don't need to see it again," Rick said.

"I want to," Mary said.

Rick got up and walked into the kitchen. The aging fridge with its rounded corners was covered in pictures of the boys. A calendar hung on a magnetic hook on the side, displaying the family schedule, which mostly consisted of doctor's appointments and upcoming tests. A round wooden table with a scarred top occupied the center of the room. It doubled as dining table and workspace for whoever was cooking simple meals or heating up the Tupperware containers brought over by Mary's church group. A stack of medical forms and bills took up the center of the table. The pile of paper never seemed to get smaller no matter how hard Rick and Mary tried.

Everything on the counters was carefully placed by Mary to maximize efficiency in the small space.

Rick could hear the news come on. He couldn't make out the reporter's words but at one point he heard Mary gasp, and he knew they had come to the story. He waited a few minutes and went back into the family room.

"You should take tomorrow off," his mother said. "Everyone would understand."

"And give them an excuse to fire me?"

"They wouldn't do that," his mother said.

"Tell that to the people at my last company. I know they like me, Mom, but that will only go so far."

"Rick's right," his dad chimed in. "He just needs to do his job. Don't give them a reason to get upset."

His mother lapsed into silence. Mary said nothing.

Rick's parents started gathering jackets and hats. The news was still on in the background and a word, half-heard, caught Rick's attention. He turned to listen. The station had cut back to Saint Elizabeth's Hospital again, and Rick picked up the reporter's voice mid-sentence, "...the body found a few hours ago in the hospital's parking lot has been identified as that of Tom Richardson, whose son Matthew had been taken off life support only hours earlier in the very same hospital. According to early reports, he left his wife inside, went out to his vehicle, and took his own life. In a horrifying coincidence, his death at Saint Elizabeth's happened at almost the same time of the helicopter crash, only a few miles away, where his own son's heart was destroyed in a fire."

"What a tragedy for two local families," said the anchor as the station cut back to her. "And now let's see how long this rain will continue." Rick grabbed the remote and clicked over to another local station, but they were already past the story too.

"Rick, what happened?" Mary asked, watching his face turn ashen. "Was that...?"

"Yes, that was him," Rick said, trying to absorb one more shock at the end of the hellish evening. He thought about the card he'd left for Tom Richardson, wondering if it had ever been read. And how useless the words he'd chosen with such care had turned out to be either way.

"All of it for nothing," he said to no one in particular. "For us and for them."

Rick's parents left, and Rick and Mary forced down some leftover casserole. They looked in on David, who was sleeping soundly on one of the two youth beds in the room. The emptiness of the other bed was palpable. Rick showered, washing off the rest of the soot, grime, and sticky fluid from the heart container. Mary balled up the filthy clothes and put them in a trash bag down in the basement, then said her prayers. They crawled into bed as the clock approached midnight. Rick entire body was sore, and his hand throbbed. He and Mary lay side by side, the room silent but for the ticking of the clock on the nightstand.

"I'm sorry," Rick said into the darkness. "I shouldn't have gotten our hopes up. But everything was going so smoothly. The helicopter was brand new. It was a straight line to Metropolitan from Pontiac. The trip should have been nothing for that chopper."

Mary stayed silent. Rick kept talking, as much to himself as to the prone shape next to him in the bed. "I was watching it. Then the pilot just sort of put it down."

"He had to. It *was* on fire, wasn't it?" Mary said, finally, as if that should put any questions to rest.

Rick replayed the images in his mind. The visibility hadn't been great from the car, but he thought that if that was true, he'd have seen a trail of smoke, illuminated by the city lights below, as the helicopter hovered over the buildings. "It didn't seem like it was. Not while I watched it."

"It doesn't really matter," Mary said. Rick could hear the fatalism and the conviction of her faith creep back into her voice. "Now we just need to focus on John."

"It doesn't make sense, Mary."

"Maybe not to us. But that's just something we have to accept."

"Like Danny Cho?"

"I won't think about that. That's behind us."

Rick lapsed into silence, at war with himself. Part of him knew she had to be right, on both counts. There had to have been a reason the pilot put the helicopter down where he did. But the scene kept repeating itself in his mind—the helicopter picking its way above the rooftops with no sense of emergency, as if looking carefully for a place to land. In the

Army, he'd seen a thousand helicopter landings and more than a few crashes. What he'd seen earlier that night just didn't make sense based on everything he knew.

Danny Cho. The boy walking around right now in Los Angeles, with the heart that could have—should have—been John's. Back then, Rick had been too crushed, too confused, to fight the transplant board when they'd made the sudden change. *Those are the rules,* he'd said to Mary at the time. *There'll be another heart for John.* He'd said it more out of hope than certainty—and out of a desire to avoid a confrontation he felt they could not win. But as the months had gone on, and John had weakened, Rick had begun to hate himself for his compliance. In that moment, when John needed Rick to fight the hardest for him, Rick knew he had acquiesced, to the transplant board, to the hospital, to his own willingness to believe that maybe the other boy did deserve it more.

He'd vowed he would never do that again. But now, lying in the dark bedroom, he felt that same sense of helplessness closing around him. The world would go on just fine for everyone else, and he and Mary would be left staring at their dying boy, with no good answers.

His exhaustion finally caught up with him and he fell asleep, images of flame and the smell of burnt flesh threading through his uneasy dreams.

Twelve

Twenty miles away from the Morrows' house, Rhonda Marsh lay in bed, exhausted, with no chance of sleep ahead of her. Her bedroom was spare: a single dresser, a side table, no pictures on the walls. Piles of research reports and grant proposals were stacked near the bed. Clothes were scattered about the floor. She'd moved into the upscale townhouse nearly two years earlier, but she'd always been too busy at the hospital to pay much attention to dating or decorating, Now, in the silence of her bedroom, alone with her guilt and her terror, the lack of anyone or anything warm or comforting in the room was almost painful. The muted TV sitting on the dresser showed one of the late-night programs.

Her phone buzzed again. It was Murray, the head of finance for the hospital network. He'd called twice in the past half hour; she'd ignored both attempts. This time she answered.

"How are you?" he asked as soon as she picked up. "Not good," she said bluntly. "It's harder than I thought."

"I guess some of this has to be expected," Murray said. The media will be all over it for a few days, then they'll move on. They always do, right?"

"Tom Richardson kills himself in our parking lot and that's to be expected?" Her voice rose, nearly cracking. "Rick Morrow has to pull the heart out of a burning helicopter and then he and his wife are forced to talk about it on television? That's to be *expected*?" Rhonda could still see the blue lights of the police cars filling the parking lot after Richardson's body had been found. They'd needed to lock down the building for a half hour until they were sure there wasn't a shooter loose someplace in the hospital. Lisa Richardson had been stuck in a waiting room for that half hour, sitting next to her dead son.

"All we did was agree to shift the surgery to nighttime and use a helicopter service instead of an ambulance," Murray said.

"And use the AionOne."

"We might have chosen to do that anyway. We have the FDA approval for human trials. We had to test it sooner or later."

"I went into this to save lives, Murray. Now one man is dead. John Morrow will probably be right behind him."

"The boy could get another heart."

She snorted. "You know how unlikely that is. And how can all this *not* come out?" The press conference on both the shooting and the helicopter crash had been terrifying for her. She was dreading the follow-up questions tomorrow.

One reporter had asked why they chose a helicopter for such a short trip. The answer she gave—that speed matters, that traffic could have been an issue—flowed smoothly from her lips, but she'd felt nauseous saying it.

"How were the board members?" Murray asked.

"Fine. Most of them were concerned more about the negative publicity from the suicide than the fact John

Morrow's probably going to die soon. And they seemed to forget about both when I brought up the 25 million dollars we got to license the patent for the surgical clamp they'd already written off."

"I figured they would."

"And if it all goes okay nobody will ever know what I went through to save this hospital. The politicians will crow about Saint Elizabeth's being a sign of the new Detroit. The insurance companies will keep squeezing us. And the patients will think everything's just fine. And we'll have to look in a mirror every day and know what we did."

"They forced us to this point, Rhonda. But you still made the right call."

"*We* made the right call," she corrected him.

"Of course," Murray said. He paused for a minute. "There's one more thing."

"What?"

"I need to take a few days off. My dad's ill again. I need to head to L.A."

"Now?" Rhonda said in disbelief.

"I know it's terrible timing. But I don't have a choice. I'll stay in touch."

"I need you here. We don't know what will happen next."

"I need to go, Rhonda. It's my dad."

She sighed, relenting. "Stay in touch, okay?"

"Of course," Murray said.

They disconnected, and Rhonda went back to staring at a silent screen, where some young actress forced a laugh at the scripted questions from the late-night host.

In his own house, just outside Detroit, Murray put down his phone. A stack of cardboard boxes sat in the hallway, full of clothes and the handful of possessions he had left that still mattered to him. The boxes would be picked up tomorrow for shipment. All addressed to a destination far away from Detroit. Or Los Angeles. He'd follow the shipment a few days later, once he was sure the mess in Detroit couldn't catch up to him where he was going.

Thirteen

At 9 a.m. the next morning Rhonda and Murray sat side by side at the long glass conference table in the Saint Elizabeth boardroom, still nursing their morning coffee cups. A huge LCD screen was set into the far end of the room for presentations, and microphones dotted the table. Through the floor-to-ceiling windows on the far wall Rhonda could see out into the five-story atrium at the center of the building. Although she could not see them from where she sat, she knew kids were romping around in the play area 50 feet below.

As colorful and touching as she knew that scene was, not much sound reached into this room from the ground-level play area or the coffee shop that abutted it. It seemed surreal to Rhonda: the peaceful scene below contrasting with the storm she felt was swirling around the walls of the hospital.

The door opened. A short, brown-haired woman burst in, her arms wrapped around a stack of notebooks and an aging HP laptop.

"For god's sake, Rhonda," the woman said breathlessly.

"I know, Fiona." Rhonda cut her off. "I should have run it by you first, but things were happening fast."

"Not that fast," Fiona said, easing into a seat across from them, dropping the stack of materials in front of her with a

65

thump. "You make a decision to fly a heart across the city. You decide to trial the new transport container, and you don't think to run any of it by your chief legal officer?"

"I know we should have checked with you. But we do have the FDA approval for trials, and it was a golden opportunity."

Fiona shook her head. "So now you're a lawyer, too? And what about the dead man in the parking lot? I hate to say it, but I was thanking our lucky stars on the trip back here that all he did was shoot *himself.* If he was that unbalanced, he could have shot up the whole surgical floor." She was visibly whitening as she spoke. "He could have taken *hostages.*"

"We know," Rhonda said quietly. She'd had that same thought sometime in the middle of her sleepless night. "But that didn't happen. And we can't go back in time. We have enough else to worry about."

"Yes, starting with this visit from the police."

Rhonda had gotten the call asking for a meeting from the police commissioner himself just after she'd hung up with Murray. With the news coverage of the crash, the suicide in the parking lot and the spectacle of Mary Morrow on television, the commissioner had confessed that he wanted to show action quickly. He'd asked to send some detectives over and Rhonda had agreed. The last thing she'd wanted was a fight with the police on top of everything else.

"Okay," Fiona said. Her phone buzzed and she glanced at it quickly. "The detectives are here. And please, please, please let me do the talking this time."

Rhonda's assistant showed the two detectives into the conference room moments later. One was black, tall and thin with close-cropped hair. The other, a white man, was not as tall but far heavier, with a neck that spilled out of his shirt collar. He looked a few years younger than his partner. The black detective introduced himself as Kendrick Jones and took a spot a few open seats down the far side. His partner just muttered "Riker, pleased to meet you," and sat directly across from Rhonda and Murray. The two cops ignored the view out the windows entirely.

"Thanks for taking the time to meet with us," Kendrick said. "We're just trying to get a handle on what happened with the helicopter. Some other detectives will want to talk with you about the shooting."

Fiona jumped in fast, eliminating any chance Rhonda or Murray would ignore her advice. "I'm Fiona Esperanza, legal counsel for the hospital. Yes, we are all deeply shocked and saddened by what happened. On both counts. But shouldn't this be an accident investigation?"

"The Feds will look at the flight-related stuff," Kendrick said. We just got asked to make sure we know what happened on the ground, because it crashed in our jurisdiction and our officers were involved with Rick Morrow. We just want to know who had access to the helicopter while it was here. That sort of thing. We'll share it with the NTSB when they get around to investigating."

"We're certainly not aware of anything unusual," Fiona said.

"Well, the helicopter crashed," Riker said. "That's kind of unusual, isn't it?"

"And the father of the kid waiting for the heart." Kendrick flipped through his notes, looking for a piece of information. "Rick Morrow. He's the first guy on the crash scene, even though his son is about to go into surgery on the other side of town. That seems a little unusual, too, don't you think?"

"True," Fiona said. "But that has nothing to do with the hospital."

Riker shrugged. "It's a lot to happen in one night, don't you think?"

"As I said, we're shocked and saddened by it all," Fiona repeated.

Riker just scowled at her nonanswer.

"Does the pilot work for you?" Kendrick asked.

"No," Fiona shook her head. "We contract that service out to a company called LifeLift. They handle organ transfers and other urgent medical shipments around the country. The pilot worked for them."

"How's your relationship with LifeLift? Do you owe them any money? Have you made complaints about any of their employees lately?" Kendrick asked.

"No."

"Are they on shaky ground—financially—that you know of?"

"They're part of CeraGlobal. CeraGlobal is huge. They're totally solid."

"Anything else unusual happen that we might want to know about?"

"Not that we're aware of," Fiona said.

Riker leaned forward. "How about Rick Morrow? Would he have known the timing of the flight, or the flight path?" The two detectives seemed to alternate questions.

Rhonda was about to say "No," but Fiona spoke first. "He was here that night, so he might have known when the helicopter was taking off. You'd have to ask him."

Detective Kendrick looked at her in surprise. "Isn't that usual? I mean for him to be up here in Pontiac, if the surgery is happening downtown?"

"We had some tickets to the Lions for his son." Fiona said. "The team had dropped them off here. He came to get them."

"Did Morrow have any reason to be angry with you?" Kendrick said, turning his attention directly to Rhonda.

"No," Rhonda said. She was getting increasingly uneasy as the questions circled in closer to Rick Morrow and the accident. "I just filled him in on some changes to the plan."

"Changes…?" Kendrick raised an eyebrow as he drew out the question.

"About the use of a new transport device for the heart. And the decision to use the helicopter."

"Did those changes make him angry at all?"

"No. Of course not. He was excited, if anything," Rhonda said.

"Tell us about Rick Morrow," Kendrick said. "Did any of you know him?"

"We've been treating his son for almost a decade. And I had met him a number of times at fundraisers," Rhonda said. "We have events for potential donors, and we'd often ask him to speak for a few minutes about his son and how important our work is. And how important organ donation was. John's had an especially long wait for a heart. Rick was always glad to help."

"Why was it so hard to get this kid a heart?" Kendrick asked, sounding genuinely curious.

"Everything works against John," Rhonda said. "His blood type is 'O.' People with that blood type can only re-ceive an organ that is the same blood type," Rhonda said. "That's less than half the population right there."

"Still a lot of people though," Kendrick said.

"True. But that's not his only problem. He's had multiple blood transfusions. He's developed antibodies that will attack certain foreign tissue, including a new heart. Part of the transplant process is called crossmatching, which means checking his antibodies against the donor heart to see if he'll reject it. Twice we've had hearts that would otherwise have been ideal for John. But the risk of rejection was too high. Those hearts went to other recipients."

"But this heart was okay?"

"Yes, this one was okay."

"This kid really can't catch a break, can he?" Riker muttered.

"We've done everything we can for him," Fiona said. Rhonda and Murray stayed silent.

"Did Rick Morrow talk to anyone else other than you?" Riker said, looking at Rhonda.

She was about to say "No" when Fiona jumped in again. "I checked. He spoke to the floor nurse on the surgical floor. He dropped off a card for the Richardsons. They're the family of the donor boy."

Rhonda caught her breath. Rick Morrow had said he had one more stop to make. She hadn't realized it was in the hospital itself.

"What was his mood?"

"Ashok, the nurse, said he seemed to be in a good mood, actually. Excited."

"Okay," Kendrick said. "Was there anyone who had access to the helicopter on the roof?"

"Only Ashok would have," Rhonda said. "He'd operate the elevator and make sure the roof was clear. Otherwise, the elevator is locked. And the pilot, of course."

The police seemed satisfied with this, and Rhonda started to relax. Then Fiona spoke. "Rick Morrow did, too," she said. "I talked to Ashok."

"Say again?" Kendrick said. Rhonda and Murray just sat, frozen by that unexpected news.

"Rick Morrow went up to the roof," Fiona said. "Where the helicopter was. Just for a minute. He asked about the helicopter and Ashok said he'd let him see it."

The detectives settled back into their seats. "Who was with him?"

Fiona grimaced. "Ashok should have been. But he got called away. He let Morrow go alone."

Both detectives leaned forward.

"Ashok went up right afterwards," Fiona said, rushing her words to try and defend against the hospital's carelessness. "Everything looked fine. I just figured you should know."

"Is the heart insured? By the Morrows or anyone else?" Riker said.

"No," Murray jumped in. He could see the struggle on Rhonda's face as the questions continued, and he worried the detectives would notice it soon enough. He stood up and walked towards the glass, hoping to distract their attention. "We've done over a dozen heart transplants in the past two years. And many more lungs, livers, kidneys—even eyes."

Fortunately for Rhonda the cops kept watching Murray as he dropped into his fundraising mode. He gestured down towards the play area. "We specialize in pediatric cases. We're one of the best in the country. We've never had anything like this before. But to answer your question, the heart wasn't insured. It couldn't be, really. It would remain property of the transplant board until it was placed into John Morrow. The

Morrows didn't have any claim to it yet. And the transplant board would have no reason to insure it."

The detectives went through a few of the questions again, then excused themselves. Fiona offered to guide them to the elevators.

"My God," Rhonda said, once she and Murray were alone. "Fiona made Rick Morrow look like a suspect, not a victim. How many more ways can we make this worse?"

"We didn't make him look like anything." Murray thought for a moment. "It *is* odd that Morrow would want to go to the roof. And that he would be at the crash site so quickly."

Rhonda's eyes went wide. "You can't go there, Murray. He loves that boy."

"Think about it, Rhonda. All we know is that we agreed to use the new transport container and the helicopter. We don't know anything else. We don't even know why Tom Richardson killed himself. And if the media maybe starts wondering why Rick Morrow seemed to be around at all the wrong times…?"

Rhonda was aghast. "Don't even think it, Murray. We're not going to try and blame Rick," she said. "I don't care how easy that would make things." She locked eyes with Murray. "Don't you think we've done enough to him already?"

Murray dropped his gaze.

Rhonda stood up and opened the door. Murray trailed her out of the room, close behind. "That was the worst of it, Rhonda," he began gently.

"Don't!" Rhonda turned on her heel and held up her hand to him. Then she turned again and stalked off towards her office.

Murray headed back into the conference room, locked the door behind him, and sat until his hands stopped shaking.

Fourteen

Rick made it to work the next day despite the pain in his hand, a dozen other body aches and a knee that had stiffened up while he slept. The shop was busy, which was a relief. Most of the men stopped by his desk at one point or another during the morning, offering their gruff but heartfelt sympathies. But they quickly got back to work under the relentless stare of Luis, the floor supervisor.

Most mechanical repair work had left Detroit a decade earlier. But the low prices Morrow's company charged for its work, coupled with the high cost of shipping the heavy generators they specialized in out of country, still made it more economical to do the work locally. The company used to manufacture its own generators as well, but cheaper ones were now made in Asia, and they'd shut local production down three years before. Ironically, they now found themselves surviving by doing repairs for those same foreign generators. The imported machines were easy to work on—many sported designs clearly copied from the ones Rick's company had perfected over the years.

At four o'clock Rick cleaned up his workspace, punched his timecard, and filed outside with the rest of the crew. The company was housed in a run-down, one-story building surrounded by auto body shops, furniture rental companies, and other businesses that did well in communities when people were trying to make a dollar go further. The drab street was littered with papers, food wrappers, and plastic bottles. Rick stood with the rest of the crew, men who smoked and bantered in Spanish or Portuguese as they waited for the bus that came a few minutes past the hour.

He was relieved when he saw their blue Ford Focus pull around the corner. He didn't like Mary having to come here to get him; the neighborhoods around the shop were not good, and the car was not too reliable. Many of the men waved to him and wished him well again as he headed to the car. They were gruff, hard-edged men but he'd found them to be friendlier than a lot of the folks he'd worked with in the past, back in the shining offices near downtown Detroit.

"How's John?" he asked Mary once he'd buckled up. Those were nearly always their first words to each other these days.

"He's okay. He's off the antibiotics they gave when they were prepping him, but they'll watch him for infections anyway."

"How are you?" He said next.

She nodded in an odd way. Something between surprise and pride. "Did you check the GoFundMe page today?" she asked.

"No."

"You should."

He pulled out his phone and went to the page. For a minute he just stared. "That can't be right," he said quietly.

"It is," she said. "I checked it ten times."

He studied the screen again. Yesterday the account had shown a lifetime total of about nine thousand dollars, all that was left from the money donated by friends and family and a few kind strangers through a dozen fundraisers. Today it showed over twenty-two thousand dollars in new contributions. He refreshed the screen, just to be sure, but the numbers actually ticked up by another hundred dollars as he watched. He scrolled down the list of donations. They were from all over the country and even a few from outside the country. Mostly ten and twenty dollars, but more than a few were in the hundreds.

"Esther was right," Mary said, almost reverently. "I guess the national news put it on their websites this morning."

Rick nodded. "This is great," he said.

"People can be so amazing," she said. "Just when you least expect it."

"Some people." Rick said, fingering the bandage on his right hand. He'd skipped the painkillers that afternoon, and the burnt skin was throbbing again.

"We got so many calls today, too." Mary said. "Mostly our family, in the morning. But then in the afternoon it was mostly lawyers. It seems they all want to help us sue the hospital. Or the helicopter company. Or the city. Or anybody we want. Some even sent flowers."

"What did you tell them?"

"Nothing. Why would we sue any of them, unless we know they did something wrong?"

"They did do something wrong. Somebody did."

"You don't know that."

"I was there. I *know* it." He'd been thinking all day about the events from the prior night. He'd been around helicopters enough to know that when something went wrong in the air the result was usually a pile of smoking wreckage on the ground, not a perfect landing in a tiny field hemmed in by three story buildings. Something else nagged at him too from that night. He couldn't put a finger on it, but he couldn't let the thought rest either.

"Then the police will figure it out," Mary said. "Or whoever looks into those sorts of things. That's what they're there for."

"I guess," Rick said, adjusting the bandage again.

Fifteen

The police showed up at the shop at mid-morning the next day. Rick realized with a start that he recognized one of the cops. It was the tall black detective from the crash site. The other one was half a head taller than Rick, and twice as wide. There was a stir on the floor when their badges came out. Wages weren't good at the shop, and Spanish was more common than English. The tension went out of the air when the cops asked for Rick instead of looking for green cards.

Rick led the two men into the small break room. There was a plastic table with five chairs in the center and a few vending machines lining the far wall. Rick sat at the near end of the table. The white detective sat to his left. His frame seemed to barely fit on the narrow plastic chair, and his thick neck bulged out of his blue shirt. The black detective took a chair at the far end of the table and flipped open a notebook.

"I'm Detective Jones," the black man said. "Call me Kendrick. This is my partner, Detective Riker."

Rick just nodded.

"I'm glad to see you weren't more injured," Kendrick said, looking Rick over. "I'm sorry for the way we treated you there, at the crash. We just had no way of knowing what had really happened."

"I get it," Rick said.

"We know it's probably still not the easiest time to talk, but we're just trying to get a handle on what happened that night." Riker said. "Given how crazy things were, what with the 'copter crashing in our backyard, and you showing up on the scene and all, our boss asked us to just get a picture of things. Then the feds will take over."

"I didn't just show up on the scene," Rick said. "I'd been watching the helicopter while I drove to Metropolitan Hospital."

"Great, so then maybe you can help us understand what happened," Kendrick said.

"I was hoping you could help *me* understand," Rick said. "It didn't make any sense."

"Did you see the flames while it was still in the air? Or see the crash itself?" Kendrick said.

Rick shook his head. "There were no flames while it was flying. And no crash." He walked the cops through what he'd seen, from watching the helicopter's odd behavior through the sudden drop below the distant buildings.

"Are you sure you were watching the right helicopter?" Riker said.

"Of course," Rick said. "How else would I know where to find it after it landed?"

"We talked to the pilot and to the hospital," Riker said. "From what the pilot said, his alarms started going off as he approached the city. He figured out pretty quickly that the engine was on fire. He got away from downtown to avoid the tall buildings, spotted the open space between the old factories and aimed for it. He said he barely had time to radio for help before the engine failed."

"He said he had to do some sort of special landing.

Auto…" Riker said, thumbing through his notes.

"Autorotation," Rick said. "It's a way to land a helicopter even if the engine's not working. You have to dive fast to build up speed then pull up quick. The airflow forces the blades to spin. They sort of act like a parachute then."

Both cops just stared at him.

"I was an aviation tech in the Army," Rick explained. "I maintained helicopters. I know how they work. Which is how I know he didn't do what you just said," Rick's mood was quickly plummeting from hope into confusion. "I know what autorotation looks like, and that's not what he did. He came in low and slow. He did the *opposite* of what he'd have done if he was going to have to autorotate the blades."

Kendrick took over. "He tried to use the fire extinguisher once he was on the ground but apparently it was jammed, so he just got away from the fire. Then you came out of nowhere and ran right into the damn helicopter. He pulled you away just before the fuel tank blew up. Probably saved your life."

"I appreciate him saving me. I'd appreciate it more if he'd saved the cooler. Why didn't he grab it? Did you ask him that?"

"Yes, we did," Kendrick said, patiently. "It was strapped in so it wouldn't bounce around during transport. He couldn't get the straps undone before the flames got too bad."

"No, it wasn't," Rick said.

"Sorry?" Riker said, one eyebrow cocked.

Rick shook his head, his mind taking him back to the crash scene—the cooler in his hand, his flesh burning. "That can't be true. I pulled it out, no problem." Suddenly the nagging feeling from the other night came back. Rick ran through the events again in his mind: grabbing the cooler, yanking it, the pain in his shin when the fire extinguisher struck it.

The fire extinguisher, still sitting behind the copilot's seat.

"He didn't try to put out the fire," Rick said, almost to himself.

"Why wouldn't he try?" Detective Jones said.

Rick rocked back and forth a bit, trying to answer that question for himself. "I don't know. But the fire extinguisher came out when I hit it with the cooler. It wasn't stuck either. He never tried to grab the extinguisher. Or the cooler."

Rick looked at Kendrick. "You were there. You saw where the cooler was. If I got it out, why couldn't he?"

Kendrick stayed silent. Riker shrugged and leaned forward. "Maybe you just got lucky."

Rick leaned forward too, anger and confusion both rising up to heat up his face. "Lucky? Do you know what was in that cooler?"

Riker put up his hands towards Rick. "That's not what I meant."

"It doesn't make sense," Rick said, ignoring the apology, his mind working furiously to figure out how the pilot's story could hold together with what he knew he'd seen. "I told you. I watched it on the way from Mercy Hospital. I saw him change course and slow down. It was like he was *looking* for a place to land. He wasn't in any hurry."

"You went to the roof at the hospital, right?" Kendrick said.

"Why does that matter?"

"You were on the roof. You saw the helicopter. If you saw anything suspicious, I'd think you'd want us to know. Wouldn't you?"

"There was nothing odd. It's a new model. Canadian. It should have made that trip with no problems."

"You didn't touch it or anything, did you?" Kendrick's tone didn't change, but Rick could feel the shift in the conversation towards something that felt more like an interrogation.

"What the hell does *that* mean?"

This time Kendrick held up his hands. "We're not implying anything. We know how awful this must have been for you. We're just gathering facts. This will all go to the NTSB. I'm sure you want them to have anything that can help them figure out why it crashed and burned like that."

"It didn't crash," Rick insisted. "The pilot put it down perfectly. There was no panic. And it wasn't on fire when it dropped out of my sight."

"You saw it from a moving car, in the rain. You can't be totally sure of that, right?"

"No, not totally," Rick conceded. "But weren't there other witnesses?"

"We canvassed the neighborhood, such as it is," Riker said, rolling his eyes. "A few people said it came in slow like you said. A few said it came down in a ball of fire. One said it was towed in by a truck."

"Towed in by a truck?"

Riker shrugged. "Some junkie who lives in an abandoned house near the factory said he saw headlights from a truck right before the fire."

Rick's mind flashed back to the glare filling the windshield of the car as he'd searched for the landing site, and the SUV that had hurtled past, almost running him off the road. "There *was* a truck. An SUV, actually. I saw it heading away from the site when I was approaching it."

"Are you sure it was actually *at* the site? The pilot didn't mention it." Kendrick said.

"Why else would it be out there?"

"Drug deal. Guy getting a little work done by a hooker. There's lots of reasons people wind up parking by those old factories. The chopper landing probably just spooked them and they hightailed it out of there. Did you see the SUV at the crash site?"

"No."

"And then you tried to pull out the cooler."

"I tried to *save* it. What the pilot should have been doing," Rick said, his frustration growing, and the memories of that night making his heart race—it was as though he could still feel the hot plastic of the cooler in his hand, and the wash of flame that rolled over him moments later. It was obvious to him that the detectives were just going through the motions, and that they'd already written off his claims. Just like most people had written off his son.

"I know you're angry at what happened," Kendrick said. "I would be too. But the pilot said he did everything he could." He started to slide his chair back to stand, signaling that the interview was over.

"I get that things can go wrong," Rick said. "All I want is for him to be honest about it. For our sake. What he told you—that's not what happened. I'm not sure what he did, but I know he didn't do everything he could."

"You think somebody messed with the helicopter or something?"

"I don't know," Rick said. "More likely the pilot just screwed up somehow. Maybe he's embarrassed that he just panicked and ran away rather than save the heart. But *something* happened."

"We'll give all our notes to the NTSB. They'll investigate," Kendrick said. "But without a crime, there's not much else for us to do."

Rick realized with growing fury that they had already closed the issue in their minds. I want to talk to the pilot," he said, half shouting. "He's not being honest with you. You need to check it out."

"We already interviewed him," Riker said.

"A lot of good *that* did," Rick said, his voice echoing in the small room.

Some of the men on the shop floor glanced up as the raised voices reached them from the break room, but they quickly put their heads back down and focused on their work, trying to stay invisible.

"The NTSB report will take months," Rick said, throwing up his hands.

"It could," Kendrick acknowledged. "They don't work fast. Especially when nobody got killed."

"Nobody got killed? Are you kidding me?" Rick was fully shouting at that point but didn't care. He rose out of his chair, glaring at the two cops in turn. Riker stood too, his hand dropping to his belt.

"There might never be another heart," Rick continued. "My son's blood type isn't that common. And there are other issues, too. The odds of getting a heart that can work for him, this close to where we live?" Rick paused, and his shoulders dropped. "There won't be another one. This was it." He dropped back into the chair, staring at the table in front of him.

"The folks at the hospital told us how that works," Kendrick said quietly. "Your kid got dealt a tough hand."

Riker stayed standing but relaxed his pose. Kendrick put away his notepad and stood slowly. "I think we've got enough for now," he said. "Thanks, Mr. Morrow."

They left, and Rick slumped down into the chair, all emotion drained. Luis walked into the break room and eyed Rick. Luis was a short, wiry Mexican. They called him 'Let's Go' Luis behind his back, because he watched every break like a hawk, chiding the men to get back to work whenever they lingered in the break room. Rick took a breath, assuming Luis was going to usher him out of the room and back to his workstation.

"You okay?" Luis asked instead.

"Yeah," Rick said. He motioned towards the door where the cops had exited. "What the hell was that? The pilot is bullshitting them. But they come in here like I'm the one with something to prove." He looked at Luis. "They didn't give a damn about it at all."

Luis smiled a little at Rick's words. "Look on the bright side. If you were me, you'd be in handcuffs right now, the way you yelled at them." He turned to leave but looked over his shoulder. "Why don't you take off for the day?" he said, forming the words carefully, as though he may never have spoken that sentence before. "Things are slow. We'll cover for you."

Rick nodded his thanks. "If it's okay with you," he said to Luis, "I'll finish the day. Mary has the car at the hospital, and I don't feel like riding the bus anyway."

Sixteen

King Faisal Specialist Hospital rose like a small city of its own near the center of Riyadh, a small jewel offset by the main city's glittering new towers, all built by Saudi Arabian oil money and imported Indonesian labor. It was founded in the early 1970s and first operated by a U.S. healthcare company. It had grown to become one of the leading medical centers in the Middle East. And it was the only hospital in the region that had the facilities and expertise to perform the complex procedure happening at that moment in one of its shining new surgical suites. Three people waited anxiously for the results of that procedure. They were ensconced in a luxurious sitting room on the top floor of the hospital's private wing. The room was worlds away from its counterparts in Michigan in more ways than just distance. The furniture was plush and new, all glowing wood and brushed gold. A giant new model TV hung on one wood-paneled wall, and a variety of brand-new magazines and books were placed in racks and side tables around the room. The rug was hand woven, depicting scenes from the history and growth of King Faisal Hospital. A large oil painting showed the benevolent face of King Faisal himself. An attendant in a white jacket stopped in regularly to offer the occupants coffee, tea, or water, all served in porcelain cups.

The room was usually reserved only for use by the Saudi royal family, which itself numbered in the thousands. But the three people in the room were clearly not Saudi. Or even Arab. The two women had blonde hair, barely visible under head scarves worn in deference to their hosts. They both had donned traditional long abayas over their western clothing. The older woman, Lana Cera, was fit, with piercing blue eyes that missed nothing. Although most people would guess her to be in her fifties, her easy, quick movements, tailored clothing, and expensive makeup made pinpointing her age a difficult and probably dangerous proposition. Marie, the younger woman, shared the same cheekbones and nose as Lana, but without the same penetrating gaze or decisive movements. The man was darker-haired, wearing a green blazer and wrinkled khakis. He sat next to Marie on one of the deep, comfortable couches, holding her hand.

The three had arrived eight hours earlier, after nearly 20 hours in the air, flying straight from Vancouver. The CeraGlobal C8000 they had flown in was the flagship of the CeraGlobal aircraft division. It was designed to hold 12 people comfortably. But on this trip, it had been crowded in a different way, with both people and medical equipment. The couch in the aft compartment of the plane had been converted into a makeshift hospital bed and two doctors and a nurse had spent the flight tending to the young girl who'd occupied that bed.

That girl was now in the surgical room nearby.

The man was studying his phone, killing time. He let out a quiet whistle. "You won't believe this," he said to the two women. "A helicopter carrying a transplant heart crashed in Detroit last night. Nobody died, but the heart was destroyed."

Lana focused her sharp eyes on him. "Does it say what caused the crash, Phillippe?"

"It doesn't," Phillippe said. "But apparently, the father of the boy waiting for the transplant was first on the scene at the crash." He paused, swiping his finger down the screen to advance the article. "He was trying to get into the helicopter to save the heart. It says he was hurt when the thing blew up."

Lana's eyes narrowed. "Say that again?"

Phillippe repeated the information. "They had a video of him with his wife later on, at the hospital. That poor family."

Before Lana had time to process that news her phone chimed. It was a phone call she'd expected. If anything, it came a bit later than she'd thought it would. Then again, the man who ran the helicopter division always had been slow to deliver bad news.

"Lana, we've got a situation." The caller began. At least he didn't waste time with useless pleasantries.

"The crash in Detroit?"

"Yes. You know about it?"

"We get the news here too. We were just talking about it. Do we know yet what caused it?"

"No," he said. Well, apparently it was an engine fire that forced the pilot down. But we don't know what caused the fire."

"Who did the maintenance?"

"It was one of our subsidiaries. LifeLift out of Chicago. They do the medical transport."

"I run the company. I know what they do," Lana said impatiently.

"Of course, Sorry. We've already fielded calls from a handful of customers. They're wondering if they need to ground their own fleets." There was a tinge of panic on the edge of his voice. "We've prepared a statement for the media," he continued. "I've emailed it to you."

"Good."

There was a brief pause. Lana knew the man would save the worst news for last. It was a sign of the weakness that had already doomed his professional future in her mind.

"And the Saudis called earlier. They are totally freaked. They want to cancel their entire order. That's fifty helicopters, plus a five-year support contract. It's nearly a hundred million dollars."

"Don't worry about the Saudis," she said. "I just spoke to the Crown Prince himself." This last part was a bit of a lie. She'd actually spoken to the Prince a week prior, to ask for the use of his hospital and medical staff. And to offer him more than just her thanks in return for his favor.

"We'll give them a thirty percent discount on the deal," she said.

"Thirty percent. Are you serious?" The man's usual polite demeanor crumbled for a moment. "That's all the profit in the deal!"

"I know," she told him patiently. "But we can't afford the public relations hit if they pull out. Others might follow. Tomorrow, the Saudis will announce they intend to continue with the purchase. That will settle the stock market down until we can figure out what really happened."

"We already have their money in escrow. It will kill us this year, if we give them that discount," he pleaded.

She knew that's what he was really worried about. His divisional performance.

"I'll make sure the board readjusts your targets for the year. It's the only way."

She could feel his relief even over the phone line. "Okay, yes. Of course. Thanks, Lana."

They disconnected.

Lana already knew they'd complete the deal at the discounted rate. The remaining twenty-five million dollars would remain in escrow. Over time, Lana knew, the money would be blended with other escrow funds and eventually paid back out. Only it would not go back to the Saudi Defense Ministry where it came from. Instead, it would find its way into other accounts. Those less visible accounts would be controlled directly by the Royal Prince and his family. The Crown Prince's favor for arranging the surgery would be fully repaid.

She walked over to the windows and looked out over the lights of the city, replaying the last few days in her mind. Everything in Riyadh was moving along according to plan.

Things in Detroit clearly were not.

Seventeen

Phillippe was also staring out the floor-to-ceiling windows, having scanned the news coverage and run out of other ways he could think of to pass the time. The enormous panes of glass were framed by heavy ornate draperies of maroon and gold. He wondered if the gold was real; in that room, it wouldn't be hard to believe. The windows looked out over the entire hospital complex and the new spires of Riyadh, which rose like a crystal formation from the flat, endless expanse of desert surrounding them. The sun was setting and the lights from the city were starting to contrast with the blackness of the desert beyond.

He tried to keep his usual nervousness from showing, both to keep Marie feeling positive and to avoid a look of disdain from Lana. He ticked off the good things that had happened so far. The heart had arrived as Lana had promised. Another hurdle had been passed when Doctor Khalid, the chief surgeon, told them it was in excellent condition. *As good as any he had seen*, the doctor had said, *despite the long flight*.

The hospital had begun the surgery almost immediately after the heart had been inspected, and the procedure had been going on for nearly four hours.

Phillippe had added a search term for "heart transplant" to his news feed months earlier, when it had become clear that their daughter Annette would most likely require one. The news from Detroit had shown up in the feed an hour earlier followed by some of the national stories. He reread the accounts of the helicopter crash and came across the news of the suicide of the donor boy's father, too. From what he read, both families seemed nice enough: working class people caught in a rough spot they did not deserve. He clucked in sympathy for their misfortune.

Across the room, he heard Lana ask Marie if she'd checked email for work since they'd arrived. He kept his gaze focused on the dark horizon, hoping to stay out of the inevitable argument he knew was coming.

"No, mother," Marie said. "My attention's here, on Annette."

"You need to be able to do more than one thing at once," Lana said. "The business doesn't stop just because we're here."

"Maybe not for you."

Lana sighed. "You're a vice president. You have responsibilities."

"Nobody except Annette counts on me for anything. You know that."

"Maybe you should ask why that is," Lana said.

"You *know* why it is, mother."

Despite Marie's best efforts, her career at CeraGlobal had been a string of unsuccessful projects and disgruntled employees, to the point where now she was parked in an unimportant role in the communications department. She had a big title, compliments of her family name, but with no staff and no real accountability. It had been clear for a long time that Marie was not at all cut out for business, but her mother still prodded her on it. Philippe was never sure if Lana was hoping to rouse some latent talents in her daughter, or if she just wanted to remind Marie of her failure to live up to the family name.

Phillippe continued to ignore the two as they bickered. He had met Marie at McGill University. He was a professor of philosophy and ethics, and she'd been a graduate student, ten years his junior. They'd married a few years after. He'd certainly not grown up poor, but his family's comfortable home and regular vacations were nothing compared to the incredible wealth of Marie and her family, generated by CeraGlobal's twenty billion dollars in annual revenues. Still, even after a decade of servants, vacation homes, and private travel, he considered himself able to appreciate the suffering of those less fortunate. By all accounts the Morrow's son's blood type was as rare as Annette's, and the news made it clear the loss of the heart was probably a death sentence for their boy. Looking at them in the TV interview, Phillippe knew they didn't have the resources to jump on a personal jet and fly 5,000 miles on a moment's notice when a heart became available in some far-away land. Medical tourism was something Phillippe generally opposed, but in this case he'd found himself putting aside the ethical considerations and focusing on the fact that it was, at that very moment, saving his daughter's life.

The sun had dropped as he watched, and darkness had set in quickly over the flat desert. Beyond the pitch blackness of the horizon were some of the most desperate places on earth. Nations locked in the iron grip of dictators or terrorists, teeming with hungry refugees. Places where water was as scarce as human rights. They were the places Phillippe always used as examples in his classes to highlight discussions on the basic questions of human motivation and ethical obligation. Now he was here, in one of the most exclusive hospitals in the world, overlooking those very places. A few floors away world-class surgeons were saving his daughter's life while out there, kids her age died horrible deaths from hunger, violence, and disease.

Lana controlled the family finances as closely as she controlled CeraGlobal, the network of companies her grandfather and father had founded or acquired over three decades. A year ago, she'd named Phillippe chairman of the family charitable foundation. He'd been surprised by her decision. He also had to admit to himself that he wasn't sure whether she'd put him in charge of the organization because she thought he'd do a good job, or simply because she wanted to keep him busy and out of her hair.

Reading about the two Detroit families, Phillippe decided that regardless of her motivations, he'd put his position to good use. If Annette's surgery went well, he'd make a donation to each family on behalf of his own. Given the coincidence of the events, with Annette's surgery going on even as the terrible tragedy in Detroit unfolded, he felt a sort of affinity for the other two families. It was as if they were all in the same kind of difficult situation together. He debated letting Lana and Marie know about his idea but decided against it. Lana would tell him he was too caught up in the moment. And right now, Marie didn't have room in her heart for anybody other than Annette.

The attendant appeared in the room again. Phillippe asked for a cup of coffee, American style if possible. The man nodded and slipped out again, his feet silent on the plush carpet. Phillippe kept gazing out the window, watching the lights of the city brighten below.

Eighteen

At about 10 p.m., the bell on the waiting room door chimed and the door opened. Doctor Khalid was relaxed and smiling when he entered. The tension drained out of the room as he told them that the surgery had gone very well; Annette would be moved to intensive care shortly.

Phillippe and Marie fell into each other's arms and Marie cried softly. Lana smiled for the first time in days. She asked whether the heart had needed to be shocked. Dr. Khalid said no, it had started beating as soon as blood flow was restored, which was a positive sign.

He encouraged them all to go back to the hotel and get some sleep. Annette would be kept asleep for a few more hours at least, he said. He promised to contact them before they woke her up.

The hospital had called a car for them already, and it sped them the few minutes back to the Four Seasons hotel.

The hotel occupied 20 floors in the Kingdom Tower, one of the most iconic buildings in Riyadh. Once they rode the elevators up to the lobby, Phillippe and Marie found the hotel guest elevators to go up to bed. Lana waited in the two-story, stone and glass sitting area. A few westerners were scattered about, and a group of Chinese businessmen at a table were finishing their waters and fruit drinks. Even in this most cosmopolitan of hotels in Saudi Arabia, alcohol was forbidden. The lone Saudi man who wandered by glared in her direction without making direct eye contact. Lana chafed at the idea that he was most likely wondering why she was not accompanied by a male relative, as was law in the Saudi Kingdom. In the Four Seasons, she had bet she'd get a bit of latitude, but she knew she couldn't linger there alone forever. She'd texted Marco on the ride to the hotel and fortunately he met her in the lobby only a few minutes later.

"What the hell happened?" she hissed as soon as he arrived. "You were supposed to make sure nobody was there."

"We did." Marco said. "We got there an hour ahead of the chopper. Nobody was there."

"Clearly somebody was. And not just anybody. That kid's father, for God's sake."

"We passed a car as we were leaving," Marco said. "Nearly ran us off the road. It had to be him. He must have been following the chopper somehow."

"Jesus," Lana said. "Did he get a look at you?"

"No way," Marco said. "It was night, and raining, and we were going like a bat out of hell."

Lana calmed herself. "Okay. What's done is done. But you know what I think about things that start going bad."

"They usually keep going," Marco finished the thought.

"I'll keep the pilots on standby," Lana said. "Just in case you need to get back there. Be ready."

"Always am," said Marco.

Nineteen

Afternoon traffic was heavy, but Rick and Mary made it to the house by five o'clock. Rick's mother was there, watching David. The boy was playing with his Transformer toys as usual, playing out some sort of intense battle with rules only he understood.

"I've never seen anything like it," Rick's mother said as soon as Rick and Mary had stepped inside, pointing at the phone. She'd taken down a full page of messages on a yellow pad, in careful handwriting. "The lawyers are so pushy. Two even stopped by themselves to drop off cards. There were some reporters, too. It's a wonder David could get his homework done. Which he did like a champ." She said the last part loud enough for David to hear, but he stayed transfixed on the battle playing out in his hands and his imagination.

Rick just put the yellow pad to the side of the sink and helped his mother pack her things. A horn beeping outside told them when Rick's dad arrived to pick her up. Rick walked her out to the car, as he usually did. Their neighborhood wasn't the worst in Detroit, by far. The first-floor windows and doors in this neighborhood sported bars with scrollwork or decorative tips, not sheets of plywood or gaping holes. But the curves and points on the bars didn't hide their real purpose. And even in the daylight, things sometimes happened.

Mary made pasta and salad for supper. Rick asked David about his school projects, and told him about the calls from family members, gently trying to draw the boy out. Finally, he asked, "Did people talk about John today?"

David nodded. "The teachers did. And some of the other kids."

"Did the kids say anything bad?" Mary asked gently. John had carried an oxygen tank at school for a few months, and some of the bigger boys had been merciless about it. They'd called him 'scuba boy.' Now that John wasn't in school anymore, those kids sometimes used David for their entertainment. The teachers intervened when they could, but there had been a few scuffles. David did not back down to anyone when it came to his brother's defense.

"What did the kids say?" Rick asked, feeling his face heat up.

"They told me John was going to die. That God must hate us to make the helicopter crash."

"You know that's not true," Mary said. "Helicopters just crash sometimes. Like cars or planes."

"Which boys?" Rick said.

"It doesn't matter," Mary interjected quickly. Rick had confronted some of the parents before. It had nearly turned into a brawl when one of the fathers, as hulking and crude as the son who'd tormented John, had said, "Just tell your boy to toughen up."

"John is doing fine," Mary said to David. "And the kids at school just don't know any better."

They finished eating in silence. Rick helped Mary clean up, then headed over to the hospital. He visited John a few evenings a week, while Mary put David to bed. It was as though the family was a set of gears, always turning, and never all lining up in the same place at the same time for very long. It had been that way for pretty much the past two years. Almost long enough to seem normal.

He stayed at the hospital until John fell asleep. The staff was still reeling over the helicopter crash, and some of them had stopped into John's room to say 'hi'. Rick got home around nine.

Once in the house, he took a quick shower and climbed into bed. Mary was still awake. "We got two thousand more in donations," she said.

"That's good. Every bit will help."

"Yeah." She was quiet for a minute. "I was thinking, pretty soon, we'll need to get a van or something if we want John to be able to come home. Something for a wheelchair, and his stuff."

"Yes, we will," Rick said absently.

"I started thinking today that we'll need money for a funeral soon, too."

It took a minute for Rick to register what she'd said. He set his jaw hard. "We can't think like that."

"We have to. This was his chance."

Rick could hear her sniffle. She was turned away from him, but he guessed there were tears he could not see. But she didn't waver. "I think we need to start accepting the idea," she said after a minute.

"That sounds like giving up."

"It's not giving up. It's accepting things as they are and being able to enjoy what time we have with him. Some things are just beyond our control. It's God's will. Or you can call it bad luck, if that works for you. Either way, it's happening, and I don't think we can stop it. And we need to start think-ing about what happens after. For David. For us."

"We can talk about that in the morning," Rick said, turning out the bedside light. He lay on his back staring into the darkness, too tired to even consider Mary's words. Lost in his own thoughts, it was a few minutes before the quiet shaking of Mary's body beside him registered in his numb mind. Rolling towards her, he heard more soft sobs. He moved closer, draping his arm over her body, pulling her closer. She didn't acknowledge the gesture, but didn't pull away either. They fell asleep that way, silently, the way they had for more months than he could remember.

Twenty

Lana's phone rang at seven the next morning. She'd already been up for an hour catching up on the world news and the top messages from work. The hospital representative on the phone told her Annette had been stable through the night. They would be waking her up in an hour. The hospital was sending a car over to the hotel for her and her family. Lana called Marie to let her know.

Phillippe, too, had been up for an hour. He'd gone to the lobby for a coffee and used the time to make the two donations he'd had in mind the night before. He'd decided on ten thousand dollars for each family. When he clicked the "submit" button he felt a rush of kinship for both of those families, and pride in his ability to do something to make their life at least a bit more bearable. He made a note to himself to let Lana know he'd done it. When the time was right, of course.

The three met in the hotel lobby and made the second elevator trip to the ground floor. The car was waiting for them. They were at the hospital in a matter of minutes and were ushered into the same waiting room they'd occupied the night before.

After a short wait they were escorted to the Coronary Intensive Care floor. The corridors they traveled down seemed to glow, with modern halogen lights reflecting off gleaming stainless-steel hardware and perfectly waxed tile floors. This wing of the hospital had opened only a year earlier. It was as elegant as a five-star hotel in the U.S., and as well-equipped as any medical facility in the world.

Along the way to Annette's room the doctor reminded them that she'd still be on a breathing machine when they saw her, and there would be multiple IVs in her arms. He clearly wanted to reduce the shock of their first sight of Annette. He gave them all masks before opening the door to her room. For her parents' sake his warning turned out to be a thoughtful move; their daughter was almost indiscernible under the breathing mask and the forest of tubes and wires around her. Her parents and Lana were used to seeing her in a hospital bed, and IVs and monitors had been a part of Annette's life for nearly a year. But all three still sucked in a collective breath.

"Is she in pain?" Marie said.

"She'll be very uncomfortable for a bit, yes." The doctor said gently. "But there is no sign of internal bleeding. Or infection."

"Rejection?" Lana asked.

"Not so far," the doctor said. "The sutures are holding fine too. At this point we're watching for all those things." The family had been warned before the procedure that some level of rejection was inevitable. But full-blown rejection would be deadly. Annette would be on medication to manage that risk for the rest of her life.

They'd stopped the sedative drip earlier in the morning. After a few minutes, Annette's eyes fluttered open. Marie gasped in relief.

"Hi, Annie," Phillippe said, wiping tears from his eyes and leaning over her. "You're okay. You're really okay." He spoke tentatively, as though he was reassuring himself as much as he was his daughter..

He stepped back after a bit so Marie could reach Annette. Marie avoided the tangle of equipment as best she could and wrapped her arms around Annette's neck.

Phillippe wound up standing next to Lana. "Thanks, Lana," he said quietly, voice still husky, eyes still wet.

"Don't thank me, I did it for her," she said, turning away so Phillippe didn't see the shine in her own eyes.

Twenty-One

Every weekend for months Rick and Mary had alternated time at the hospital so that one of them could be home with David. It was small compensation to David for the huge amount of time they spent on his brother's care, but it was the best they could manage.

Rick was surprised to see a car parked out front when he arrived home from the hospital around five on Saturday. It was a Cadillac sedan; a few years old but clean and blemish-free. Mary was in the living room, sitting on the couch. As Rick entered, a tall, older man with ruddy skin and a full head of white hair rose from the chair opposite Mary. The man reached his hand out in greeting. Rick hesitated for a split second, then shook it. The man pretended not to notice the slight.

"Rick, I'm so sorry," the man said. His voice was low and smooth, polished from years of sermons.

"Thanks," Rick said, glancing over at Mary for some insight.

"Pastor Adams just stopped by to see how we're doing," Mary said. "He is going to dedicate tomorrow's morning service to John." She was trying to sound bright and cheerful, as if a positive tone could blunt whatever objection she expected Rick was already formulating.

"I've got to be going anyway," Pastor Adams said. In one motion he retrieved his coat from the couch and swept up an envelope that had been sitting on the glass coffee table. Rick caught the gesture and glanced at Mary again, this time more sharply. She just sat still, hands folded in her lap.

"God bless you," the pastor said. His eyes came back to Rick "I hope you both can make it to the service tomorrow. I hope to make it uplifting in this difficult time." When the door had closed behind the man, Rick turned back to Mary.

"He's been so helpful," she said, before Rick could ask the question already on his lips. "He didn't ask for anything when he offered to do the service for John."

"How much?"

She paused, steeling herself. "Five hundred dollars. He mentioned the pipes are leaking at the church. They need the money. And we have it now."

"*They* need the money? *We* need the money," Rick said. "You should have talked to me."

"Just like you ask me before you call up every new specialist you think might have an idea. Or tangle with some neighbor just for trying to be nice?"

Rick stayed silent. That fight was almost as old as John's condition. He wasn't up for reopening it again.

Mary waited a beat. "I guess you didn't see that we got a ten thousand-dollar donation in the account today. We're still way better off than we were yesterday."

"Ten *thousand*? We don't know anybody with that kind of money."

"I know. I couldn't believe it either. It was from a charity in Vancouver. They must have seen us on the news. We can share at least a bit of it with the people who are helping us. Don't you think?"

"People are giving that money to John. To help *him*. Not for plumbing at a church that you told me was renovated just couple of years ago."

A flash of anger crossed her eyes. "That church has done so much for me. It's about time I did something for them. They'd help you too. If you'd let them."

"I don't need their help."

"They'll be there for John and me long after all the reporters and other folks have forgotten about him. Unless you think the police are going to do something."

Rick shook his head. He thought of the cop delivering the stuffed lion to him, almost like an apology offered for what was going to happen next. "The police are done investigating," he said. "Next, it'll go to the federal people and the case will disappear forever. They're already moving on."

"What else would they do?"

"They could do their jobs and follow up on what I'd told them."

"What would it prove?"

"We always said John deserves to know the truth about everything, right?"

She nodded.

"He deserves to know the truth about this most of all. So do we."

Mary shook her head. "It won't change anything." She stood and faced him, speaking more gently. "It was raining that night. And dark. How can you be so sure you're right?"

"Maybe I'm not right. But even knowing *that* would be better than just hanging here in limbo. I keep replaying what I saw over and over in my mind, to try to make sense of it. It's driving me crazy." He put his hands to his head. "You don't understand. Everyone's telling me that what I saw didn't really happen. Which makes me wonder if everything else really happened. It's like I can't tell what parts of that night were real."

"The heart's gone. That part's real," Mary said, with a finality that shocked him into silence. Then she turned and disappeared into the kitchen.

Twenty-Two

The church was a modest building not too far from the Morrows' house. It was built of tan brick, with a small steeple
squared off at the top. The church's sign, on West Warren
Avenue, claimed "All Are Welcome." The plastic sign would
have been equally at home in front of a dry cleaner or bowling
alley. A small parking lot next to the church was protected by
a tall chain link fence. The windows and doors were covered
by steel grates.

West Warren Avenue marked an unofficial border between mostly black neighborhoods on the north side of the
road and mostly white to the south. From the variety of skin
tones on the people filing through the main doors, it was
clear the church drew from both.

Pastor Adams greeted them at those doors, taking both
of Mary's hands in his. He nodded a welcome to Rick and
ruffled David's hair before the boy twisted away, staring
sullenly at the ground. The three found seats halfway down
the aisle, a few rows from the front. Rick hadn't gone to
church with Mary for a few months. He was surprised by
the number of people who stopped by to hug her or squeeze
an arm in sympathy. She introduced Rick to many of them.
They all praised Mary for her courage and commitment to

John and the church. Rick had never considered Mary to be vain or self-centered, but he wondered briefly if that was why she found happiness in the church. There was a sense of celebrity about her from the people who knew her story. The thought crept into his mind that she actually enjoy their attention as much as their support. He dismissed that idea. It was petty. He knew her better than that. Or maybe he just hoped he did.

Pastor Adams began speaking. Rick had to admit that the man had a gift. Adams held the crowd's attention effortlessly, mixing his sermon with call and response refrains throughout the ceremony. Mary joined in enthusiastically. In hushed tones, Pastor Adams told the congregation the mass was being held in honor of John and briefly recounted John's story. From the knowing nods throughout the pews as he spoke, it was clear many in the room knew it already. There were gasps and murmurs of sorrow as the Pastor relayed the details of the crash, and what it could mean for John. Rick felt his face flush. He didn't like the idea of these strangers feeling they owned a part of John's story, just because they were nice to Mary or threw a few dollars into the basket now and again.

Then Adams began to talk about the hidden purposes of all God's actions, and the need for everyone to trust there was a meaning to every tragedy, a purpose for every pain. Mary nodded vigorously as the Pastor made his points. Rick realized it wasn't any sense of vanity that drew her to the church or the Pastor's message—it was the idea that John's condition had some sort of meaning, that there was a higher purpose to the pain they were all going through.

As they filed out after the ceremony ended a steady stream of people stopped Mary with more words of support.

Some tried to engage Rick too, but he just smiled thinly and nodded.

They stopped at Donut World on the way home. David loved the giant donut on the sign outside the tiny bake shop. Stopping there after they picked Mary up from church had become a part of their usual Sunday ritual. Once back home, David took his chocolate frosted donut into the living room to watch TV. Mary made tea for herself and coffee for Rick.

"That was a nice service," Mary said, picking at a blueberry muffin.

"It was," Rick admitted. He could see the impact of the support they gave Mary in the way she stood taller, more engaged than he ever saw her with the doctors or hospital administrators.

"You heard what Pastor Adams said about purpose," she said. "That's what I've been trying to tell you. I know you want to find reasons for everything, fix everything. And I appreciate that. Maybe in this case there aren't any reasons that we'll understand. Or any things that are fixable. But that doesn't mean there can't be a higher purpose."

"I'm glad you can believe that. I really am." Rick stood and paced around the cramped room. "But what happened to the helicopter wasn't an act of God, Mary. It was a screwup by somebody on earth."

Mary sighed. "We can't fight everyone, Rick."

"I don't want to. But we deserve honesty. John deserves it. And whoever caused this needs to face us and tell the truth. I won't let John just get swept under the rug to protect the pilot or anyone else."

"John won't get swept under any rug. You saw how people think of him at church. Maybe John just deserves to have us with him. As long as we love him, and they love him, he'll never be forgotten."

"Is that what Pastor Adams told you when you wrote him that check?" Rick regretted the words as soon as he said them.

Mary started as if she'd been struck. "Actually yes, that is what he told me." She turned and pounded up the stairs, leaving her tea behind.

Rick sat at the small kitchen table, his head in his hands. He hated himself for being so petty. Maybe he was jealous of how much the church meant to her. Maybe he just resented that the people there could seem to give her the comfort he couldn't. But despite his guilt he could not bring himself to leave John's fate in the hands of some unknown force, no matter how much she believed.

He thought of Masco's words in the office about the media. He decided that maybe he could still force the truth out of whoever was hiding it. Then maybe Mary would see what he meant.

The list of lawyers and reporters who'd called was still on the counter. He ran down the page until he spotted a name he recognized. A woman who headlined a news magazine show on local TV. She specialized in human interest stories. He dialed the number his dad had written down. He turned to face the back door as he waited for someone to pick up, so his voice wouldn't carry up the stairs in the small house.

Twenty-Three

The reporter had asked Rick a few questions on the phone in a rapid-fire sequence. She was clearly used to culling the cranks and crazies from real stories. When he'd told her the reason for his desire to do the interview, she was sold; the grieving father, accusing the police and hospital of a coverup would be great TV and even better clickbait for the website. She'd told him to come down to the studio around 4:00, and they'd tape an interview for her 7 p.m. show. He asked if he should wear a suit. She said no.

The segment aired as promised at 7:00. By 8:00, the interview and a print story based on her questions to Rick were both up on the local TV news website. The national affiliate picked up the print story an hour later, adding it to their own website.

Time in Riyadh was eight hours ahead of Detroit. So, Lana Cera saw the story about a half hour after she woke up in Riyadh, only a few hours after it reached the national news in the U.S.

She read it three times, then found the local affiliate site on the web and watched the video. She had to admit, Rick Morrow made for good TV: tall and rangy, with his short military haircut, well-worn clothes, and earnest face. Rick and the reporter sat in comfortable chairs with a small table between them, almost knee to knee. He called the woman "Ma'am," even though she was at most a few years older than him.

Rick talked about seeing the helicopter's odd behavior in the air and about the crash and the feeling of his arms around the ruined heart container. He choked up more than once, and his grief was clearly real. The reporter seemed visibly touched by his emotions, although Lana wondered if perhaps that was just good acting. Either way, it was effective. Rick told the reporter about his interview with the police, and his thoughts about the claims the pilot had made.

Are the police investigating your concerns? She asked, eyes wide, even though she must already know the answer to the question. But that was clearly the opening she'd prepped Rick for.

Not anymore, he said. *They don't seem to care at all.*

What would you want them to do? She raised her hands in a helpless gesture as she spoke, as though she was defending the police.

Find more witnesses for one thing. There was a car I passed near the crash. Find the driver. Push the NTSB to speed up their investigation. Don't just take my word for what happened. Don't just close the case on the crash. Or on John.

How can you be sure you're right? she asked, a question that sounded probing but was also just a softball for Rick.

I was an aviation technician in the army. Four years, Rick said. *I worked on helicopters. I know how they behave. I know what an emergency landing looks like. And I know the pilot's lying about what he did.*

Why would he lie?

Rick shook his head in response to the question. The reporter was good, Lana could see, and Rick and seemed to have forgotten about the cameras and was just opening his heart to her. He was entirely believable.

I don't know, Rick said finally, in a tired way that made it clear he'd asked himself that question a hundred times. *Maybe the pilot made a mistake. Maybe there was some sort of problem. I'm not saying he did anything on purpose. I know things can go wrong. I just want him to tell us the truth. For our sake. And for John's.*

The reporter let those final words hang in the air for a moment. Then she turned to the camera. *The truth. For a very sick little boy. That doesn't seem too much to ask,* she said.

And then the segment was over.

Lana saw that her hands were shaking with rage and even fear as she dialed Marco's number.

"I just saw it," he said, as soon as the connection was made.

"This is a disaster."

"It's just him making claims," Marco said. "He's got no evidence."

"Don't underestimate this. He's making claims on TV. He looks credible. This will come back to CeraGlobal in no time. And to us."

Marco spoke calmly. He'd spent over a decade in the military himself, under far more dangerous circumstances than Rick Morrow had ever faced. He knew when something was a disaster and when it was just a problem to be addressed. He'd already thought back to what Rhonda had told him about the interview with the police at the hospital. The outline of a plan was already forming in his mind. In the

TV interview, Morrow had mentioned seeing the helicopter in the air. Morrow hadn't mentioned being alone with it on the roof before it took off. An innocent detail if he'd added it. A crack in his story because he hadn't. A crack Marco could break wide open.

"This won't rebound on us—not if nobody believes him," Marco said.

"How do you make that happen?"

He laid out his plan for her. She agreed it made sense. "I'll need authorization from CeraGlobal for three million dollars," he said.

"Consider it done. The plane can get you back to Detroit."

"Give me a few hours to make some calls here, then I'll be in the air."

Lana put down the phone and leaned back in the plush hotel chair. *Focus on Annette,* she told herself. *Let Marco handle the rest.* That, after all, was what she'd hired him for, plucking him out of the Canadian special forces based on his unique skills and his reputation for a maniacal focus on the success of his mission, no matter what the costs.

She needed that focus from him now.

Twenty-Four

After hanging up with Lana, Marco set himself up at the small round table in his hotel room. He plugged in his laptop and grabbed a small notepad. His first action was a call, which he made while the PC was booting up. What he was planning wasn't technically illegal. But he was still happier having the conversation from a location far outside the U.S. or Canada. He found the contact he needed in his Signal account. The man he was calling only used the Signal privacy app, so that all his calls and messages were encrypted. It would be early afternoon in the Philippines, but Marco knew his contact there would answer no matter what the time when he saw who the caller was. A man answered on the second ring, his "Hello" tinged with an Eastern European accent.

Marco described what he wanted him to do. "I'll need some human engagement to post comments on the chat boards and websites. The rest your botnet can do."

"How big does this need to be?" the man asked. His business had two sides. His main business was creating the illusion of "trending" for various celebrities or advertisers. He advertised having a network of people constantly online that did the work. But the real impact was made by a botnet he'd built over years. He had nearly 50,000 unsuspecting computers at his disposal. They were personal computers, business servers, and even security cameras all over the world: anything run by a computer chip that he could infect with his own customer malware. He could use those processors and the dummy Twitter, Facebook, and Instagram accounts connected to them to make it seem like nearly any topic was capturing the world's attention.

His side business was working for people like Marco, deploying those same techniques to help muddy the water on topics his clients didn't want to see receive any thoughtful attention, or sometimes to destroy the reputation of their political or business opponents.

"It needs to be loud," Marco said. "Very loud. Centered around Detroit. I want this guy to see it wherever he goes and hear it from anyone he talks to. I'll send you sample tweets and comments for Facebook and the message boards. You'll need to keep an eye out for the original article when it runs and create a link to it yourself. I'll be in the air."

They agreed on a price and Marco told the man the money would be wired to him by the end of the day. The man said he'd begin the preparation immediately—he knew Marco was good for the money, and he did not want to disappoint one of his better customers.

Next Marco turned to the laptop, connecting to the internet via a private VPN to at least reduce the chance the local authorities could eavesdrop on his activities. He scanned the news from Detroit one more time, making sure Morrow hadn't made any additional statements that could screw up Marco's plan. Then he searched the web, getting a quick sense of the other local news feeds, blogs and websites that provided coverage to the Detroit area. The reporter who'd interviewed Rick seemed to generally slant her stories towards a sympathetic view of her subjects. Marco needed something different. He finally found it in a blog called "therealdetroit" that seemed to delight in revealing the hypocrisy and selfishness of government officials, companies and individuals.

He found the name and bio of the person who ran the website, a kid who clearly had not put a lot of effort into his personal photo on the "About" page. It showed him to be a wiry, bearded twenty-something, with unkempt and probably unwashed brown hair sticking out around a backwards baseball cap. His email address was simply truth@therealdetroit.com. His arrogant sneer in the picture reinforced what Marco suspected. The kid was one of the countless number of people who had no trouble using the web to throw mud at anyone and anything they saw fit, while keeping themselves safely hidden behind the anonymity of a generic email address and bogus screen name.

Marco composed a message and sent it to that email address, using one of the dummy email accounts he himself kept for just that sort of purpose. He sent an encrypted message with that website name to his contact in the Philippines using the Signal app. Then he called Lana's pilot, telling him to have the plane ready for an 11 a.m. departure.

Two hours later, he was signaling "thumbs up" to the pilot for takeoff. The back half of the big private jet was still crammed with the medical equipment and bed used to care for Annette on the flight from Vancouver. The metal IV poles and monitor stands rattled and swayed as the plane picked up speed on the long runway. The sound of the engines and the sight of the medical gear sent Marco back to a different time, in an open helicopter, screaming low over a jungle canopy, blood slicking the aircraft's floor as two medics worked feverishly to staunch the flow from the leg of one of his men. Marco had held an IV bag high, trying to will more fluid into the young man's veins as the medics tried to find and clamp the artery that had been severed by shrapnel from a rocket-propelled grenade.

They had not made it in time.

Marco tried to shake those memories out of his mind. He leaned the seat back and closed his eyes, calculating the time. It was a 12-hour flight nonstop to Riyadh, and an eight- hour time change, so he figured he'd land about three in the after-noon, Detroit time. But for now, he would be 42,000 feet up, far out over the Atlantic, far away from steaming jungles and the people and creatures that crawled through them, and the memories of his own men, wounded and dying in front of him. He hoped he could sleep soundly for a few hours at least, high over the featureless ocean below.

He'd learned over time that that was about the only place he could sleep soundly anymore.

Twenty-Five

As Lana was reading the coverage of Rick's interview from her hotel room in Riyadh, Mary was folding the basket of clothes she'd left at the end of the bed that morning. Rick could see her anger in the way she yanked the laundry out of the plastic basket, almost violently snapping the clothes as she squared them before slapping them down on the growing pile to her right.

"I know I should have told you before I did the interview," he said. "I don't know why I didn't."

"You didn't because you know I wouldn't have agreed." She kept her eyes on her task as she spoke.

"I'm sorry. I just can't let this go. I did that once before. I promised myself I wouldn't let John down again."

"It's not the same as Danny Cho."

"I know. But this time the heart should be in John right now. This one was his. I need to know why it's not."

Mary clenched her jaw as he spoke, her lips a thin white line. When she spoke, the words were clipped, a seething anger creeping through every syllable. "Who will that help, Rick? Will it help John? Will it help me?" She shook her head as angrily as she'd been shaking the laundry. "Maybe it'll help you, but it won't help anybody else."

"How can you just accept this and move on? It's like you're ready for John to die."

At those words she turned to face him, her face ashen. "Don't you dare say that! don't want him to die any more than you do. But at least I'm learning to be at peace with whatever happens. We can't control what's happening to John. We can't control the transplant board, or the hospital." She paused for a minute, and her voice dropped almost to a whisper. "When we try, we just make things worse." She wiped away a tear, but it didn't seem to be a tear of anger. "I think we need to be done fighting, Rick. At least I do."

She'd finished the laundry and picked up the basket. "These are David's. I'm going to put them away. Then I'm going downstairs."

The bedrooms were small, like all the rooms in their house. Mary did a masterful job keeping everything in its place, and that meant, even in the heat of an argument, not leaving a basket full of laundry out to clutter a walkway or bedroom. Rick heard the door to the boy's room open as Mary pushed her way in.

He finished getting himself ready for bed. A few minutes later he heard her footsteps descending the stairs. He knew he should follow her. But he didn't know what else he'd say. He didn't regret doing the interview. He wasn't sure if it would get the police to reopen the investigation, but at least he'd told people what he'd seen. Some part of the world knew that the crash that had cost John his chance at life wasn't just some act of fate. It was the fault of some human, even if Rick wasn't yet sure who that was.

Twenty-Six

Rick was at the shop by 8:00 the next morning. Several of the men stopped by his work area, some just squeezing his shoulders, some telling their own stories of the kind of treatment they'd received at the hands of police.

"You one of us after all," one of them had said, with a smile.

Rick spent the morning reviewing plans for upcoming projects. Part of his job was to handle scheduling and prioritization of the incoming work. He'd done that same task, on a much larger scale, at his prior company, coordinating multiple teams across several divisions of the company. Doing it with 20 people for a dozen or so projects a week was child's play to him, but it had been a huge problem for the shop. They considered him a hero for having solved it. They knew as well as he did that he was overqualified for his role, but it was the only work he could get. He'd been let go as part of a layoff at the automotive parts manufacturer he'd been at for nearly five years. He'd been warned by a few co-workers back then that they'd been looking for an opportunity to get rid of him no matter how good he was at his job. Sure enough, despite the supportive things his bosses said to his face, they'd lumped his termination in with dozens of others as they moved more and more of the work to Mexico and China. They got rid of the impact of John's expensive care on their insurance ratings and could explain it away as just one part of a larger action to avoid a union grievance.

Rick ate lunch at his desk, checking the news feeds to see if there was more coverage of the story or any comment from the police about reopening the investigation. Most of the headlines just repeated the one from the news station website, but one caught his eye. It read *"Hero Syndrome Behind Dad's Actions?"* He clicked on the link. It was to a website he'd never heard of called The Real Detroit.

We should all be sorry for the situation Rick Morrow's family finds itself in," the story began. *"But even as he demands honesty from the hospital and helicopter company that attempted to help his son, he may be hiding some important facts of his own. A closer look shows that the strange sequence of events around the helicopter accident that claimed the heart meant for his son may not have been an accident at all. Anonymous sources have confirmed to* therealdetroit *that Rick Morrow, who spent years working on helicopters in the Army, was alone with the aircraft in question in the moments before it took off from the roof of Saint Elizabeth's Hospital in Detroit. Morrow was also the first person to arrive at the scene of the crash, an unlikely event in any circumstances—unless one assumes that he had some knowledge that the crash would happen in the first place.*

The article went on to identify something called Hero Syndrome, and speculate that Rick, feeling jealous and powerless that he was not able to save his own son, had staged the crash in an attempt to become the hero himself, his plan to pull the heart safely from the flaming helicopter and drive it to the hospital himself going terribly wrong.

Rick read the story twice, in disbelief, his anger starting to boil. His trip to the roof had seemed irrelevant when speaking to the reporter. Now some jackass was making it look as though he had sabotaged the helicopter to give himself a chance to be some kind of a hero. Rick searched the web—no other articles seemed to be building on that one. But that story still sat there in his search listings. He thought about calling the reporter directly, but there was no phone number or even an address listed on the website. It seemed more like an amateur newsletter than some actual publication.

He felt suddenly exposed, almost naked, in a strange sort of way. He'd assumed when he did the interview that everyone would understand his concerns. He'd expected the coverage would be supportive; his son was dying, after all. It hadn't occurred to him that people might question his motives, or even his character.

Hero Syndrome. He typed the term into his browser and a Wikipedia listing came up. The definition fit the article's claim perfectly; a person with a history of failure and setbacks, manufacturing situations where they could become a hero to validate their own worth. It chilled him to think how well that description could describe the past ten years of his life.

He scanned the shop. Everyone was still heads-down, working on various pieces of equipment. Nothing had changed in the room around him. But he felt as though the world had tipped on its axis somehow, in a way that left him suddenly unbalanced and even a little afraid.

His next thought rocked him just as hard. *Mary might be reading it, too.*

He tried calling her, but she did not respond. That wasn't too unusual—she was probably at the hospital. He texted her as well, telling her to call him as soon as she could.

He heard nothing from her all afternoon, but just past 5:00 the blue Focus came around the corner, no different from any other day.

Mary stared straight ahead as he climbed into the car.

"Did you see the bullshit article that came out today?" Rick said, hoping she hadn't.

"Yes. Two of my friends forwarded it to me."

"How can they print something like that? They never even called me to hear my side."

She shrugged, keeping both hands on the wheel as she lifted her shoulders. "They didn't lie. You did go on the roof. And you were the first one at the crash."

"What are you saying? You believe them?" Rick had guessed she'd be angry. It had never occurred to him that she might see some truth in what the website reporter claimed.

"No. I'm just saying this is what I *didn't* want to happen. You wouldn't just accept that fact that the heart is gone. And so, you pushed. You talked to that reporter. And now you look like a crazy man. You think that's going to help John?"

"I never thought this would happen."

"Something like this was *bound* to happen. It always does."

"It's just one article on a bullshit website nobody reads. It'll be gone by tomorrow."

"Your mom saw it, too. She called me already."

"Nobody who knows me will believe this crap."

"John and David can read, too. So can their friends. And their friends don't know enough to know if it's a lie."

"*If* it's a lie? Of course it's a lie," Rick said.

"You just should have left it alone," Mary said, before withdrawing into a silence Rick knew better than to try and break.

He stared out the window, watching the oncoming headlights from the rush hour traffic stream by in the opposite direction, frustrated both by Mary's stubborn desire to move on and his own need to keep fighting. He knew Mary was probably right; they were victims of a series of random events that he needed to turn into a conspiracy to justify his own anger. But each pair of headlights flashing by reminded him of the SUV that had nearly run him off the road the night of the crash, barreling away from the helicopter. It just didn't make sense. And he wasn't ready to let that go.

That night was the first night for Cub Scouts. David came downstairs about 20 minutes after Rick and Mary arrived home, already in his Cub Scouts uniform. He had gotten the kerchief around his neck wrong, and Mary adjusted it, telling him how much fun he was going to have.

The three drove to the hospital to drop Mary off, with David speculating happily the whole way as to how the meeting might go and what the other boys would be like. His high, soft voice was the only thing filling the silence between Rick and Mary.

Rick left Mary off at the main doors of the hospital and drove back the way he'd come. The Cub Scout meeting was at a community center a few blocks from their house. Like most newer public facilities in Detroit, the building was mostly poured concrete, inside and out. Both for fire safety and damage resistance, Rick assumed. The interior walls were painted a pale glossy yellow. Rick guided David inside and down to the meeting room in the basement.

The Cub Scout troop leader introduced himself as Dan. He was lanky, with a scraggly beard and ponytail. He was about Rick's age and had two boys in the troop. Dan gave David a warm welcome and directed him over to a few banks of chairs where the other boys all sat in their blue uniforms.

Dan shook Rick's hand. "I saw you guys on the news last night," he said. "I know it must be tough." Even though Rick and he had spoken only once on the phone a few days earlier, the man seemed genuinely heartbroken for Rick and his family.

"Thanks," Rick said. "We're just hanging in there." "We'll say a prayer for you," Dan said. He pointed out the coffee and donuts in the back of the room and went over to organize the kids. A handful of other parents were milling around or sitting around the edges of the room. Some of them seemed to recognize Rick, but none of them made any effort to talk. Rick nodded hello and poured himself a coffee. Dan started the meeting. He had each boy say his name and his age. Dan made a point of highlighting David and three other newcomers to the troop. He began to describe

their upcoming projects and community work.

Most of the parents sat quietly, watching the proceedings or with noses buried in their phones. As the meeting marched on, Rick checked the GoFundMe page. He scrolled through the names of the donors, still wrapping his mind around the fact that so many strangers had opened their wallets to his family simply because of a news story. One donation caught his eye—it was from Tom Garner, his boss at his prior company. Tom had been the one who'd told Rick he was getting laid off. Rick had been angry and scared. *It's not my call,* Tom had said. *They're moving over a hundred jobs to the Mexico plant. I didn't have you on my list. Somebody upstairs added it. But I'm sorry. I know how much you've got to deal with.*

Easy for you to say, Rick had shot back. *You still have a job.*

I've seen the plans, Rick. Tom had said. *The Saltillo factory is big enough for four hundred people. We're all dead men walking here.* Tom had looked defeated, even then. Rick had stumbled out, leaving the man staring at his desk and waiting for the next one of his employees to be ushered in so he could deliver the same news.

Rick's phone buzzed, bringing him back to the basement room and the Cub Scout meeting. His heart skipped a beat, as it always did when he wasn't expecting a call. The unexpected ones usually meant trouble for John in one form or another. Instead, he saw an unknown number light on the screen. He hit the "ignore" button. He figured he could wait half an hour, and after the conversations with Mary since he'd gone on the news, the last thing he wanted was for David to be telling Mary that his dad had spent half the meeting on the phone.

His phone buzzed again two minutes later. It was another number he did not recognize so he hit "ignore" again. A few minutes later, he noticed two of the parents who clearly knew each other whispering, then darting glances toward him. He assumed they were talking about last night's news. He kept his focus on the meeting. As well-meaning as their intentions might be, he didn't feel like reliving the experience any more than he needed to.

Close to the end of the meeting, he saw his father's number appear on the screen. He started to wonder if it had been the hospital trying to reach him with those earlier calls. He stood up and sidled over to the door. He could feel eyes on him as he passed in front of several of the parents. He made his way upstairs and returned the call.

"Rick, what the hell?" his father said, clearly upset.

"Dad, did something happen with John?"

"John's fine. I just spoke with Mary. It's the internet, Rick. That article is getting talked about everywhere. People are commenting on it and retexting it like crazy." He meant retweeting it, Rick guessed, trying to think why that one two-bit website therealdetroit would suddenly get so much attention.

He hung up with his dad and went online. He was stunned by the volume of comments. Twitter was blowing up with tweets and retweets linking back to that website. Many linked to descriptions of Hero Syndrome or speculated on financial motives for him and Mary. He went to the therealdetroit website itself and saw the comments section under the article was full. He scanned the page quickly, but words kept jumping out. *Fraud. Liar. Coward.* Suddenly the looks he had gotten downstairs snapped into perspective. They weren't pity or curiosity. They were doubt—or suspicion. It was as though the steady stream of support they'd been getting onine since he'd done that TV story had somehow transformed into a flow of hate and criticism olmost instantly.

People were coming up the stairs with their coats on, and Rick realized the meeting was over. A few of them shot glances at Rick but none would meet his eyes. He went back downstairs and found David, who was talking to one of the other boys. Rick thanked Dan and walked with David back to the car.

David filled his dad in breathlessly about the meeting, buckled into the back seat of the car. Rick stayed in the parking lot for a minute and continued to look online, barely hearing his son's descriptions of the other boys, Mr. Dan, and the upcoming soapbox derby.

Rick put the car in drive and started the trip to the hospital. The discomfort that had started when he'd first seen the article came back to him, even stronger than before. He could imagine a buzz out there as people read the story and the comments and gossiped about what kind of man could do that to his own son.

As he passed the Ford Motor Company headquarters, the strings of chain stores and low-set office buildings surrounding the enormous campus gave way to street after street of small brick houses. The regular rows of homes were interspersed with garbage-strewn lots and abandoned structures where owners had just given up and left the properties to decay. Older model cars lined the cracked and uneven streets. Usually, Rick didn't even notice the state of the neighborhood. But now the sense of decay and despair seemed to be almost a physical thing, a heavy pressure in the air he could feel in his chest. Even though he and Mary had lived nearby for a few years, he'd always felt they were just visiting somehow—only there until things got better, until they got the one break they needed for themselves or John. Now he wondered if perhaps that was just what everyone in their circumstances felt. Did those people all keeping thinking that they were different from everyone around them, when the only difference was *how* they'd gotten there, and not whether they had a chance to ever wind up anyplace better?

Twenty-Seven

Rick and David got to the hospital around 8 p.m. Rick bought David a grilled cheese in the cafeteria and got coffee for himself and Mary. The woman at the register greeted him by name and told him how sorry she was.

They took the familiar route to the elevator and up to John's room. John was awake, but groggy, when they arrived. Mary was standing near the window with Rick's parents. David plopped into the chair in the corner of the room and pulled out his Gameboy. He talked almost constantly about John when they were at home, but at the hospital he usually buried himself in his games, rarely saying anything to his brother. Rick wondered sometimes if David didn't want to acknowledge his big brother's frailty when confronted with it face to face.

Rick headed straight over to the bed.

"Hi, champ," Rick said John, touching his son's shoulder. He could feel the bone and sinew through the thin material of the hospital gown. John had been losing weight slowly over the past few months and now was no bigger than David. "Hi, Dad," John said. It seemed like an effort for him even to get those words out. He raised his arm to point to the bandage on Rick's hand, ignoring the IV tube in his own arm. "Does it hurt?"

"'It's okay," Rick said.

"It's cool you saw a helicopter blow up," John said, smiling weakly.

"Yeah," Rick said, not meaning it, and amazed by John's ability to be so positive in the face of all that had happened. Rick told John about David's Cub Scout meeting, trying without much success to draw the younger boy into the conversation with his older brother. John's eyes started to flutter after a few minutes and Rick left him to doze off while David turned his attention back to his game. The adults stepped into the hallway, finding an open spot between the medical equipment, laundry hampers, and food carts.

"Rick, how could they write those things?" his mother asked.

"I don't know," Rick said. "It's some bullshit website. Half the stuff they put online is made up, if you ask me."

"You have to talk to the police," his father said. "They need to clear this up."

"They haven't done anything so far. Hopefully the TV news story will change their mind. And this will blow over." Rick spoke with more confidence than he felt. "This new stuff is just a bunch of comments on a bullshit website."

"It's everywhere," Mary said. "Even on John's page."

She held up her phone to him. It showed the *GoFundMe* page, which had a place for people to write comments of encouragement or support. Rick took the phone and scrolled through the recent comments. *With a father like that maybe the kid would be better off dead,* opined one of the writers. *I donated twenty dollars to this crackpot's kid. I want my money back,* said another. *Monsters,* a third one said simply.

Rick felt the anger that had started to build in the car rise up in his chest. "I'm going to find that reporter," he said, picking up his coat.

"Don't make this worse," Mary said.

Rick looked at her, the rage mixing with anguish in his voice. "If John winds up... If the end comes and he has to have even one brain cell stuck on the idea that his own dad might have had anything to do with it?" He shook his head violently, as if trying to fling those terrible thoughts from his own mind.

Mary didn't say anything.

"The pilot lied," Rick said. "I know that for a fact. He said he had to crash land the helicopter quickly. But that's not what happened. I saw it. And he said the fire extinguisher was stuck. It wasn't."

"You keep saying that. Why would the pilot lie?" Mary said.

"I don't know. Everybody lies, Mary." Rick said, bitterly. "The pilot. This website guy. Everybody."

"Mary's right," Rick's dad said. "Don't fan the flames on this. It'll die down quick enough. Picking a fight will just make it worse. The reporters don't care. They're just using you for tonight's news. They'll forget about it by tomorrow."

Rick turned on his father. "Just take it, Dad? Just bite my tongue and try and keep my head down? Do what's right? Just like I always do?"

"Rick!" his mother said sharply. "You don't want to mess with these people. Reporters. The police?"

Rick shook his head at her. "You don't get it. Yes, the reporters are using us to sell stories. And the hospital used us to test that new heart machine. Even Rhonda Marsh trotted us out to raise money for her new buildings. Everybody uses us. I'm done with it."

"Let's go say goodnight to John," Mary said, looking at Rick. "He's still the one really suffering here."

Twenty-Eight

Marie and Phillippe got back to the Four Seasons hotel around 5 p.m. Riyadh time for dinner. Lana met them in the main dining room, which was overflowing with staff. The crisp white linen and gold-trimmed china settings were already laid out for the evening guests. Spectacular arrangements of flowers spilled out of clay urns, breaking up the spaces in the giant room, adding warm colors and scents to complement the hard lines of the glass and metal fixtures. Smooth jazz played quietly through hidden speakers, completing the mood and ensuring privacy for the diners' conversations.

Annette was doing fine so far, Marie told Lana, but the next two days were still crucial. Phillippe had taken his phone out and was catching up on email and news as the women spoke. At one point he whistled quietly. "What is it?" Lana asked. His incessant web surfing was annoying to her even in the best of circumstances. He seemed like a high school kid to her, constantly distracting himself from anything going on around him.

"The Morrow guy. The news is implying he might have something to do with the crash. Who would have thought that?"

"Yes, I read that," Lana said. "But who knows for sure, at this point." She kept her voice neutral, but she'd been happy to see the social media backlash Marco had engineered against Rick Morrow. At least that part of the plan seemed to be going well.

"Yeah, but now I'm wishing I hadn't given him the money."

Lana froze. "What money, Phillippe?"

He looked up from his phone. "Oh yeah, I didn't tell you yet. I donated money to each of the two families in Detroit. Seemed like good karma, given everything they're going through. And how lucky we are." He left the last words hanging.

"You gave them money? From the *foundation*?" Her mind reeled again at the idea of a digital trail from her family foundation right to Rick Morrow and his family. And to the Richardsons? She felt a noose tightening around her neck.

She tried to stay calm, but Phillippe saw her distress. He interpreted it as disapproval and straightened his back. "Yes, Lana. You put me in charge of the foundation, and I felt it was a good use of money. It is a *charitable* foundation after all."

"Good use?" Lana said. "You don't know these people. You don't know what 'good use' is for them."

"They seemed like decent people, Lana," Phillippe said. "Just because they're not rich doesn't mean we shouldn't care about them. And just because there's no ROI, that's not a reason not to help them." He made air quotes as he recited the acronym.

"That ROI is what keeps you in fine wine and French vacations, Phillippe. And it's what got my granddaughter a new heart. We should be grateful for it."

"I *am* grateful," Phillippe said. "But I still don't see what's so wrong with what I did, unless Morrow does turn out to be a scumbag. Are we really so far above these people that we don't even want our name associated with theirs?"

"We *most definitely* don't want our name associated with theirs," Lana said. The words spilled out too quickly, her cool demeanor cracking for an instant. Philippe paused for a minute at her reaction. He was used to Lana being impatient with him. Even dismissive. But as she spoke there was a hint of something else in her voice too. Something beyond anger. It sounded like panic.

It took a moment for the pieces to come together. Then his eyes went wide. He dropped his fork with a clatter onto the glass table; he half rose to his feet, then sat down again, his body not sure what to do with itself as his mind processed the thought that had just exploded in it. The color drained from his face.

"Oh God, Lana. Tell me you didn't," he said.

"Didn't what, Phillippe?" she said, almost taunting him.

"The heart. It didn't come from around here," he said. "That's why the doctor said that, that the heart was in good condition after such a long flight. That's why we're here and not someplace near home for the surgery."

Lana stayed silent. In her frustration and anger, part of her was glad he was figuring it out. There would be some satisfaction in seeing how he handled the same truth she had to live with. And the same fear.

"What are you two talking about?" Marie said.

"The boy in Detroit. He had a rare blood type, too, didn't he?" Phillippe was almost speaking to himself now, the pieces coming together in his mind even as he spoke. "I bet if I looked, I'd find it's the same as Annette's, isn't it? That's where the heart came from, isn't it, Lana? Not from some dying kid in the friggin' desert out there." He waved his arm towards the towering glass windows that faced west. "It came from that crash somehow. You *stole* it."

Lana still did not speak.

"It was one of CeraGlobal's helicopters that crashed, wasn't it?" He sat back in the chair, dumfounded, the enormity of what he was thinking almost overwhelming him. "For Chrissake, it was even our transport company, wasn't it? You really did it, didn't you," he pressed. "You staged the fucking crash, and you stole the heart and flew it here."

Lana slammed down her phone. "Yes," she hissed. "I made this happen. I found a way to save my granddaughter's life while you were just sitting around hoping somebody else would take care of your kid, you sanctimonious hypocrite."

Phillippe shrank back, eyes wide in shock. Marie just stared at her mother.

"They are good people," Phillippe said. "You can't do this."

"I *did* do this, Phillippe. Yes, they are probably good people. That doesn't make them special. Nor does it give them the right to have their son live while Annette dies."

"What if people find out?" Marie said in a hiss, as the full scope

of what she was hearing set in. "You'll go to jail. We'll *all* go to jail."

"Maybe," Lana said. "The law's not that clear, actually. I researched it."

"My God," Phillippe said.

The three went silent for a moment as a white-suited waiter approached to take their order. Lana motioned him away without looking at him.

Marie was shaking. "What about Annette? People will know. She'll spend her whole life with people talking about her. Writing about her. It'll be awful."

"At least she'll have a life to spend reading it," Lana said. "What were you two going to do? Just watch her die?"

"It's tantamount to murder, Lana."

"We don't know that," Lana snapped. "Maybe the other boy would have died on the table. Maybe he'd reject the heart and be dead in a few weeks anyway. Who knows? Maybe another heart will show up tomorrow and he'll be fine. We don't know what will happen."

"Keep telling yourself that," Phillippe said. "He's got the same blood type as Anette. We know how unlikely that chance is."

"I *will* keep telling myself that," Lana said. "I didn't kill anybody. I just saved my granddaughter. It seems like you're forgetting that second part."

"There had to be another way," Marie said. "You put us all at risk."

"If there was another way, don't you think I would have found it?" Lana said. "I don't like this any more than you do. I know I put the company at huge risk. And our family name. But there was no choice." She leaned forward, hands on the table, her eyes boring into her daughter's. "Why do you think I work so hard, Marie? Why do you think your grandfather worked so hard? Sacrificed so much?"

"For the money." Phillippe said. "It's always the money."

Lana glared at him. "The money's not the end, you fool. It's just the means. Money gives influence. Resources. The money is for times like this." She looked hard at each of them in turn. "It's why other people's kids die in situations like this, and you daughter won't."

"That's not enough of a reason," Phillippe said. "It's enough of a reason for me," Lana said. "And I'm pretty sure it will be to Annette." She leaned back in the chair and looked at them each in turn. "I need to leave tomorrow. I have to see to some things back home. Will things be okay here?"

"How will you keep this a secret?" Marie said. "Annette can never know. Nobody can."

"I'll take care of that. We just can't do anything stupid." She locked her eyes on Phillippe. "Anything *else* stupid, I mean."

"What I did was the only decent thing that's happened here this week," Phillippe said icily.

Lana took a breath and let it out slowly. She continued quietly, almost contritely, "I shouldn't have said that. I know you meant well. And I know what I did is beyond what most people would ever consider. But I'm not sorry I did it. Annette was going to *die*, for God's sake. Now she's not. That's a decent enough thing for me. I thought it would be for you. And I need you to help me now, so we can get through it."

"How are we supposed to face ourselves ever again, knowing we did this?" Phillippe said, but his anger was gone now, too.

"I think the better question," Lana said. "Is how could we have faced ourselves if we didn't?"

"We'll do what we have to," Marie said. "But you have to make this work, Mother. Annette can never know."

Lana looked at Phillippe. He just nodded, without looking up.

Twenty-Nine

Lana was dressed and on the elevator by 7:30 the next morning. She caught up on the article at *therealdetroit* and the barrage of social media attacking Rick Morrow. Marco had done a brilliant job. Hopefully the onslaught of criticism would be enough to get Morrow to stay away from the media for a while. Marco was already on his way to Detroit to start the next phase of the plan and get Morrow to agree to be silent forever.

Sunday was a workday in Riyadh, but traffic gave way for the black town car, and she was at the hospital by 8 a.m. A hospital administrator met her in the lobby and ushered her up to the recovery floor. Doctor Khalid was waiting there.

"Are her parents not with you?" he asked, looking past Lana towards the elevator behind her.

"I wanted a few minutes with my granddaughter alone."

The doctor simply nodded; Marie and Phillippe might be Annette's parents, but the staff had seen very quickly who made the decisions for the family.

Annette was lying peacefully, eyes closed. A pair of tubes still snaked down to her forearms, but her color was already better, at least to Lana's eyes. With the door closed behind her, Lana finally let the stress and worry win out and the tears began to stream down her face. She fought back the sobs in big, wracking gasps, looking at the beautiful pink face of her granddaughter.

After a few minutes she composed herself and touched Annette's arm. Annette's eyes fluttered open. She smiled when she saw Lana looking down at her.

"I have missed that smile," Lana said gently. "How are you, Annie?"

"Okay," Annette said, her voice still raspy from the days on the breathing tube. "I'm tired, though."

"You should be. You've been through a lot."

"The doctor said we're in Saudi Arabia?"

"Yes, honey. We flew here three days ago." Annette had been drifting in and out of consciousness the days before the trip, but her total lack of recall made Lana realize just how close to death Annette had been. "You were pretty sick."

"I don't feel so sick now," Annette said.

"They operated on you. They made you better."

"What did they do?"

Lana touched her hair. "We'll talk more about that later."

"You brought me all the way here to see doctors?"

"I would have brought you to Mars if that's what it took to make you better."

Annette smiled weakly. "Will I be able to go back to school when we get home?"

"Pretty soon, yes. I think you will."

"I miss school," Annette said dreamily. Lana could tell fatigue was setting in again. "I like my classes."

"School's important, honey," Lana said. "Especially for a girl who has a big company to run someday."

Thirty

Monday morning, after breakfast, Rick told Mary he was calling in sick. "I just don't want to face the reporters today. Or the guys at work. Or anybody."

She nodded. "Okay. We can go to the hospital together."

"Sure," he said. "Let's go later, though. I want to run few errands first."

"I thought you said you didn't want to see anyone."

"I know," he said. "I just want to get some air. And pick up a few things at the hardware store. I want to finally get the closet door fixed in the boys' room."

"Okay," she said. She looked for a second like she was going to say something else but dropped it. The GoFundMe page and their Facebook page were littered with the worst possible comments from people who had been shedding tears for them only a day earlier. She decided she couldn't really blame Rick for not wanting to go to work. The prior day in the supermarket she'd felt it too. It was as though everyone was watching her. Judging her.

Once David was off to school, Rick took the car. He hustled to the hardware store and grabbed the screws and other hardware he needed. But instead of heading back to the house, he jumped on the highway again, heading north. He stayed on the highway until he was close to Dearborn, then reversed direction and headed back towards Metropolitan Hospital. He started glancing out his side window, picturing the helicopter's lights in the rain. In his imagination he could still see it hovering, moving slowly. He tried to find a reason for the pilot's actions, but nothing seemed to make sense. The mystery slithered around in his brain, with no facts to pin it down for resolution.

He retraced the turns he'd taken to the crash site, even picturing the headlights of the SUV as it sped past him, nearly running him off the road.

In the daylight, the wreckage of the abandoned factory was stark. Gaping holes, where windows or doors used to be, were either pitch-black or showed right through to the grey skies behind them. A line of rubble was piled along the length of the building, sloughed off the walls and roof by the years of neglect and vandalism. The only color came from the graffiti marking the building. Rick walked along the perimeter of the huge structure. He stepped past some bits of yellow warning tape that had been stomped into the ground by police and fire crews. Then, gathering his courage, he made his way to the spot where the helicopter had stood. The only other trace of the tragedy from that night was a charred oval of earth about seven feet long. A memory surfaced from deep inside; himself as a teenager, visiting a cemetery with his dad after Rick's best friend had been killed, hit by a car crossing a street near school. Rick had been too upset to go to the funeral. By the time he'd gone to the cemetery a few days later, all that remained to mark the burial spot had been an oval of disturbed earth and a few scattered flower petals, turning gray as they began to rot.

Now, staring at the burnt oval, he felt that he was staring at John's grave site. He pushed that image from his mind and tried to relive the sequence of events step by step. He could picture the pilot's surprised look, cellphone in hand, when Rick dove out of the car. The man had clearly been talking to somebody. But according to the police he'd already called in the mayday from the air.

Rick remembered pulling out the cooler. That would have been impossible had it been strapped down.

The pilot had lied about that.

And he remembered the pain flaring up his leg when the fire extinguisher struck his shin; the fire extinguisher the pilot had said was jammed.

Another lie.

Rick walked back to the car. He turned around one more time to look at the forlorn place where all their hopes had died. His eyes burned again, not from smoke this time. *I'm sorry, Johnny*, he thought to himself. Then he got back in the car and headed back to the highway.

He stepped into the house around 11:00. "That took a while," Mary said.

"Sorry," Rick said. "I just drove around for a bit, too."

Mary could see the mud on Rick's boots but stayed silent. She made lunch for the two of them and then they headed back to the hospital.

John was awake when they arrived. They chatted with him for a few minutes about nothing in particular. He was still pale and drawn, but his eyes were focused, and he even managed a smile. Mary did most of the talking. Rick always marveled at how she could sit with John for hours, telling him stories or filling him in on the littlest things that had happened, as though they were all still sitting around the kitchen table at home. John might not say 20 words the entire time, but it would still seem as though they'd had a rich conversation.

John asked about the Lions, who were off to an unexpectedly good start to their NFL season. He'd never been much of a sports fan, but that summer he'd met a few of the players when they visited the hospital as part of their community outreach. The players had taken pictures with the sicker kids and signed a jersey for John. Now he watched every game religiously.

As John and Mary talked, Rick thought about the tickets he'd picked up to give John after the surgery, when it seemed those worries would be behind them, at least for a while, and John could just be a 10-year-old boy at a football game.

One more dream broken.

It struck Rick that if he hadn't decided to pick up the tickets and drop off the card, he never would have seen what he'd seen and known to doubt the pilot's story. He would have just accepted the crash as another catastrophe in the line of setbacks that he and his family seemed to endure. It would still have been just as gut-wrenching, but at least he and Mary might have found a way to endure the pain together, rather than seeing it split them even further apart. Part of him wondered if that would have been better in the long run.

They said goodbye to John when it was time for his afternoon medications and headed home to greet David when he got off the bus. David's eyes usually lit up on the rare occasions when his parents were home early enough to meet him in the afternoon. But today he was downcast and there was dirt on his shins and knees.

It took a few minutes to get him to finally confess he'd gotten into a shoving match at recess with two older kids who'd told David that his dad was going to jail. The boys had finally held David on the ground while they taunted him.

"Did the teachers see it?" Mary asked.

David just shook his head. There were tears in his eyes, but it was impossible to tell if they were from shame, or anger.

"Did you tell the teachers?" Mary asked gently. David just shook his head.

"Why not?" Rick said. "They're there to help you. We've told you that."

David set his jaw. "Nobody helps us."

Mary tried to find words that could tell him he was wrong. That people like teachers were there to help. That they *did* care. But the newspaper articles and the awful words on the social media sites were still burning fresh in her mind, and no such words came, so she just hugged him instead. He patiently tolerated her embrace, then headed for the couch in the living room and curled up to watch TV before his homework time. Mary opened his backpack to take out his lunchbox. Balled up in the bottom of the backpack was a wad of green construction paper. Mary unfolded it. David had drawn a giant heart in red crayon, with stars shooting out of it. 'A super heart for my super brother,' was scratched out in David's rough penmanship. Mary put a knuckle to her mouth and cried quietly, trying not to let her son hear in the next room. After a minute she dried her eyes and refolded the paper, putting it back where she'd found it. Rick just watched her, unable to find words that could make any sense of their situation.

Mary's phone rang again on the table. She saw from the display that it was the hospital and grabbed it quickly. The call was short. She stood up as she disconnected, already reaching for the pocketbook hanging on the back of her chair. "Something's wrong with John."

Thirty-One

Rick knew the route to Metropolitan hospital by heart and had learned how to shave off every possible second from the trip. He'd even memorized the location of the worst of the potholes along the decaying roadway, to avoid the bone-jarring shocks that were a staple of driving in Detroit. It still took an endless half hour for them to reach the hospital complex. Rick knew fro experience that all but the farthest reaches of the parking lot would be full that time of day. He parked the car haphazardly on the access road that ran alongside the hospital campus. It was closer to the main entrance, and right then he didn't care if it got towed before they could get back to it.

They breathed a shared sigh of relief when they reached John's room and found him still in his regular bed, not wheeled off to a surgical room—or worse. His eyes were closed. His breath was uneven and shallow. Mary counted each breath. It was a habit she'd started when he was only three days old, his tiny life hanging in the balance, await-ing the first of many operations that might buy him a few months, or years. She'd found herself alone in the neonatal intensive care unit. John had been almost impossible to see through the web of tubes, wires and sensors connected to his body. He seemed more an extension of the sealed container he rested in, rather than the wriggling baby she had thought she'd be holding in her arms by then. Now, the ventilator pumping air into his lungs hissed gently, and she had found herself counting the quiet sounds, wondering how many breaths her little boy would have.

Esther came in just as Mary reached 100. Her smile was warm, but tired and business-like. She motioned them to the far side of the room, away from John's bed.

"We got him back," she said quietly. "But it'll happen again. John's organs are starting to fail. There's just not enough oxygen reaching them. The weak circulation causes other issues, too. His kidneys aren't draining enough fluids."

"Is he in pain?" Mary said.

"It's a slow process," Esther said. "He's okay right now."

"But eventually?" Mary said.

"You know we'll do our best to keep him comfortable, Mary."

"What happens next?" Rick said.

"Nothing for now. We'll keep monitoring him. As I said, it's nothing to worry about right now."

"What happens if you can't stop it? "

"It's a slow process," Esther repeated.

"How long is 'slow'?"

"A few months. Maybe a bit more."

Mary cried out involuntarily at that news.

"There's one other thing you should know," Esther continued quietly. "Once his organs reach a certain point of disfunction, he'll come off the heart list."

"They can't do that." Mary said. "He's waited so long."

"It's policy," Esther said. "Transplant is hard enough. If his body is too frail, it's too big a chance. They won't risk a heart."

"Too big a risk for the heart maybe," Rick said bitterly. "Not for John."

"We don't know exactly when that point comes," Esther said. "Maybe a month from now. Maybe more or less. For now, let's just focus on John. He's here today, and he'll be here tomorrow. And the next day."

Rick picked up Mary's hand and held it in his own for a moment. Then she slipped her hand out, walked over to the bed once again, and stroked John's head. They stood that way in silence for a few more minutes, listening to the rhythm of the machines that were keeping John alive.

Thirty-Two

Around noon Rick's phone flashed. He'd put it on 'silent' to shut out the endless stream of alerts driven by the social media storm that still howled around him. He glanced over at the screen just to be sure it wasn't Mary or the hospital trying to reach him. Instead, he saw the name 'CeraGlobal' sitting over the string of numbers on the display. He hesitated for a moment, half-suspecting it was one more lawyer or reporter calling on some kind of spoofed line. But that same name, turning to black on the side of the helicopter as the flames engulfed it, was still too fresh in his memory. He picked up the phone and hit the green button. "This is Rick," he said.

"Hi Mister Morrow. Thanks for answering," a man's voice said. The voice sounded perfectly pleasant, and neither young nor old. The caller seemed genuinely grateful to have reached Rick.

"Who's this?"

"My name is Marco. I represent CeraGlobal."

"You're a lawyer?"

The man laughed a bit, seeming genuinely amused at the idea. "No, not a lawyer. I work for the CEO, Lana Cera. I'm sort of her chief of staff I guess."

"Tell Lana Cera that her company killed my son."

"She feels personally gutted by what happened," Marco said. "Such an unfortunate accident."

"Unfortunate doesn't cover it," Rick said. "And I'm not sure accident does either."

"Yes, I saw your interview." Marco let a heartbeat or two of silence precede his next words. "And some of the terrible comments that followed it. People can be so... brutal. . . online."

"The comments are a bunch of lies."

"I'm sure," said Marco. "It always amazes me how people can have such different interpretations of the same events. You and the pilot, for example."

"I know what I saw."

"Those kinds of situations are confusing for everyone," Marco said gently. "But I'm not calling to debate your recollections."

"Then what do you want?"

"I want to help you. As does Lana Cera."

"It's a little late for that."

"Perhaps not. At least not in some ways."

Rick could hear a trace of accent in Marco's otherwise perfect English but couldn't place it. The man sounded almost too reasonable. Assured, but not arrogant, as though he thought no one could doubt the common sense of his words. Rick stayed silent.

"At least let me show you what I mean," Marco said after a moment. "Meet me for dinner. You and Mary, I can explain better in person. Then you can decide."

"We don't want to have dinner with you."

"Please," Marco said. "Maybe there's still a bit of hope that can come out of all this tragedy. And perhaps we can help clear up all those terrible statements about you that are sweeping the internet right now. I can only imagine how hard that is on your family."

Rick thought for a moment, playing back the look on Mary's face when she'd read some of the messages that had come into their social media feeds. "I'll ask Mary."

"That's all I could hope for," Marco said. "I'll text you the details."

Rick got the text with the restaurant details almost as soon as he disconnected. Clearly Marco had made the reservations before the call. Rick resented the man for seeming so sure he'd agree. But Marco had been right; if Rick could end the hatred streaming in on his family from the internet, he had to try. And if nothing else, maybe he could wring some real answers out of the man.

After a few minutes of debate on the phone, Mary had agreed to the meeting, with one condition.

Later that evening, Rick and Mary snaked down Jefferson Avenue in their rattling car, Rick carefully working his way over to the left-hand lane from the highway exit. The Renaissance Center, home to GM's headquarters, the Marriott hotel, and a host of retail stores and restaurants filled the sky to their left.

Their nephew Eddie sat in the back seat staring up at the view. Eddie was tall and thin. He was 28, but he had a quick, nervous way of speaking that made him look younger and less mature. Eddie was the one condition Mary had insisted upon.

"Remember, let this guy Marco do the talking," Eddie said. "Don't make any offers, and don't say yes or no to any of his. I'll handle that."

"I don't want offers. I want honesty," Rick said. He was still seething that they'd brought Eddie along. Law degree or no law degree, Rick still saw Eddie as the dorky kid who always trailed behind him at family events. But Mary had thought bringing a lawyer made sense, and Rick had relented.

Marco had made the reservation at Andiamo, which Rick knew faced lake Michigan, on the back side of the Renaissance Center. He'd eaten there regularly, years ago, when his company at the time had GM as a client, and Rick was an up-and-coming executive. Back then he'd never thought twice about tossing the keys to the valet and expensing the cost. Now he parked at the municipal lot a bit further up Jefferson Avenue, under Hart Plaza.

The trip back to the restaurant only took a few minutes, and the evening was warm enough. The tall buildings of downtown Detroit glowed to their left as they walked. The monorail connecting most of downtown Detroit rumbled overhead, full of shoppers and businesspeople. Rick had always liked this part of town, back when he'd worked nearby. Now he tried to avoid it. It reminded him of what he'd had to leave behind.

The restaurant itself was on the street level at the back of the giant complex, overlooking the water. The interior was glass and chrome, the polished surfaces reflecting reddish candle flames and whiter overhead lighting. When Rick told the maître d' that they were meeting someone she nodded and led them immediately through the dining room, her long gown sweeping behind her as she cut through the restaurant. As they passed the glittering tables, Rick couldn't take his eyes off the flowers. Red roses, a half dozen on every table, cut short and floating in crystal bowls. There had to be a hundred of them all told, he figured, just in that one room. He knew that Mary would be staring at them, too. She loved roses.

Rick's mind wandered back to Valentine's Day that prior February, and a florist shop where he stood agonizing over the cost of a dozen roses. Credit cards maxed, and more bills on the way, he'd finally turned and left the shop empty-handed, settling for a two-dollar card instead.

The maître d' gestured to a corner table. Marco was already seated, speaking quietly on a cellphone as they drew close. Marco spotted them and hung up quickly. He stood gracefully and greeted them. He wore a perfectly-fitting, light-blue sport coat covering a deep blue shirt that also looked hand-tailored. He was about Rick's height, with short-cropped hair. Marco couldn't hide a brief flash of surprise when Eddie introduced himself as their lawyer, but then he gestured them all to their seats and smiled. The table looked out over the water. The lights of Windsor glowed in the distance, reflecting on the river.

Marco was clean-shaven and his smile was relaxed and charming, just like his voice on the phone. He wasn't especially big, but he had an air of compact strength about him. He looked completely comfortable here among the sparkling glasses and flower arrangements, but still seemed incongruous somehow, like a tiger at a tea party.

The waiter appeared silently out of nowhere and took their drink orders. Rick and Mary got coffee. Marco asked for a glass of French white wine. Eddie ordered a Seven Up, which made Rick cringe inside a bit more.

"Thanks so much for meeting me," Marco began, "I can only image the pain you've been in for these past few days, and I just want to apologize on behalf of everyone at LifeLift and the whole CeraGlobal family of companies."

Rick and Mary stayed silent, as they'd agreed.

"My clients have suffered not only pain but significant, irreparable damage," Eddie began. He listed the insults and injuries they'd lived through, from the pain of the loss of the heart to the tarnishing of their reputation by the media.

Marco listened patiently, almost indulgently, to Eddie.

"Given those injuries, we do intend to sue not only Life-Lift but the hospital network and perhaps the police as well."

Marco nodded solemnly. "I can see why you would consider that course," he said. "I suspect I would, too."

It was Eddie's turn to look surprised. With all the possible responses they'd discussed on the car ride, sympathy and support was not one of them.

"As you know, LifeLift is part of a larger corporation called CeraGlobal, based in Vancouver, British Columbia," Marco said. The business is a family business, and it prides itself on its reputation. And on its community focus."

Vancouver, Rick thought. He felt a bit of deja vu but could not place it.

"And so that's why I've come today with what I believe is a very generous offer," Marco said. "Not that anything can truly compensate for what you have been through, but at least this should give you the means to do whatever you need to for your family. And for John."

"What are you offering?" Eddie asked, sounding genuinely curious, and more like the fresh-faced kid he was, not the razor-clawed injury lawyer he had made himself out to be.

"Three million dollars," Marco said.

The table was silent. In none of their discussions had an amount like that even been considered.

"Paid in installments every six months for three years," Marco continued. "As long as you honor the very fair and simple terms of the settlement. No court cases. No endless appeals. Just our gesture to make things right for your family."

"If you're offering that now, you'll offer more once we get to trial," Eddie said.

"No," Marco said. "The company's reputation is everything. Once we get to trial, the newspapers will be all over this story. The damage to the company will be done. At that point, we might as well bring all the considerable resources of our company to bear to win. And while I'm no lawyer, the ones we do have tell me that the law is not on your side here. You did not own the heart. There's no proof that John will suffer any damage, because another heart may be found. The hospital, not you, had the contract with the transport company." He paused. "And, of course, as much as it pains me to say it, there's no guarantee the surgery would have been.... successful." He shrugged, seemingly resigned to the inevitability of his own facts as he laid them out. "If you force us to trial, we'd probably win on those merits. The coverage you're getting in the media right now probably won't help much either. Or get any better. And in any case, we'd want to draw this out for as long as possible." He sipped his wine and paused to study the liquid in the glass, giving his words a moment to sink in. "I worry that time is the one thing you don't have, if you want to do everything you can for your son." He looked at each of them in turn, his gray eyes boring into each one of them. "This is a very fair offer. I really urge you to take it." He reached into an attaché case under the table and brought up a manila folder, which he placed carefully on top of his plate.

He stood again, a fluid gesture that seemed languid but somehow was almost too fast to follow. "I would love to resolve this while we are here today. Please take a look at the documents and discuss among yourselves. I have a call to make, so I'll give you a few minutes. And please feel free to order anything you like on the menu. It's our pleasure."

He left the three of them to stare at each other in silence for a moment. Mary spoke first. "Is he serious? Can he really do that?"

Eddie was scanning the documents quickly. "I think he can. CeraGlobal is a huge company. They probably settle cases like this all the time."

"It would make all the difference," Mary said. "We could get the van for John. We could move David to a new school where they wouldn't know to tease him."

She looked at Rick. "What do you think?"

"I think he hasn't told us anything about the crash."

"Maybe there *isn't* anything else to tell."

Rick just scowled at the table.

"I think we should take it," Mary said, into his silence.

"I agree," Eddie said. "It's a pretty great offer."

"What else is in there?" Rick asked, jabbing a finger at the documents

.Eddie continued to look through the agreement. As he flipped the pages, Rick stared at the roses, counting the loose petals suspended in the pool of water.

"It seems pretty standard," Eddie said, putting the papers down. "Method of payment, release of all claims against CeraGlobal. And agreement to drop any claims against any other parties or to speak publicly about the settlement or the case to anyone."

"What's that?" Rick said.

"It makes sense," Eddie said. "If they don't want bad publicity, they can't have us suing other people and putting the case back in the media.

"That means we can't sue the hospital? Or the pilot?"

"Right." Eddie said. "But even if we'd won against all of them, it'd take years, and I don't know that we'd get even close to this amount. These amounts are usually only seen in wrongful death cases. Or permanent injuries."

"You want to talk about wrongful death?" Rick said. "John is still alive now, but what they did...it might as well be called that. And this means we can't ever find out what really happened?" His voice rose as he spoke, but the room seemed to have a way of sucking up sound and no one around them seemed to notice his emotions. "We just have to move on with the money and let the whole thing disappear?"

Mary just stared at him speechless, tears springing to her eyes.

"Well, yeah," Eddie said. "But they're admitting guilt."

"They're buying their way out of ever admitting the truth."

The waiter appeared again but Rick waved him away. The man turned on his heels at the gesture, but not quickly enough for Rick to miss the hint of a sneer forming on his lips.

"John's probably going to die," Rick said. I can't stop that. *We* can't stop that. But doesn't he deserve to know the truth about what really happened? Don't we?"

"Can't you for once not think that the whole world is lined up against you?" Mary said, oblivious to Eddie's presence at the table, the frustration rising in her voice now. She spoke in a harsh whisper. "Maybe that's all there is this time. Maybe the pilot was confused about what happened. Maybe he is lying to cover up his own mistakes. But does it really matter? Can't we just put this behind us? Do what we can do for John with that money. For David." She was shaking now. She locked eyes with Rick but it was an entreaty not a challenge. "We're *broke*, Rick. The GoFundMe money will help for a while, but there will be more bills, plus the ones we already have stacked up. And with the stuff online, nobody's going to donate to us ever again. We're *sinking*." She paused for a minute. "*I'm* sinking, Rick. I don't want to fight. I just want to be with John and make him happy."

Rick was silent for a minute, his anger battling with his heartache as he watched the tears streaming down her face. She was right. He knew it. But he thought of every time he'd given in, accepted a decision, swallowed his pride, because somebody else was better educated, or had some bit of authority granted by some faceless institution. And he thought of Danny Cho.

"I'm sorry, Mary," he said. "I need to know what happened. I want *John* to know what happened. While he still can. I owe him that." His voice broke a bit as he finished.

Mary threw out her arms in frustration. "Sometimes things just happen, Rick. Sometimes it's nobody's fault."

He set his jaw. "And sometimes it is."

"Rick, you can't mean this," Eddie said, finally having gathered up enough courage to enter the conversation. "This never happens. I mean, I know I've only been doing this for a few years, but it never goes like this. Big companies always delay. They always fight."

"So then why aren't they doing it now?

"You heard what this guy said," Mary said. "They don't want the bad PR. That's all."

Rick shook his head. "They're hiding something. That's why they're settling."

Eddie started to speak but Mary shook her head at him. "Let's just tell him we need a day to think about it, at least," she said.

"Tell him whatever you want," Rick said. "But I'm not signing it."

Marco appeared again a few minutes later. He noted the still-empty plates in front of them.

"Nothing on the menu you liked?" he asked.

"Nope," Rick said curtly.

"Okay, then," Marco said smoothly. "If the menu was not agreeable, I assume the proposal, at least, is?"

"The money's fine," Rick said.

"Okay, terrific."

"But I want a public apology. And I want them to say what happened. For real. I want to talk to the pilot. And anyone else involved."

Marco shook his head. "That's sort of missing the point, Rick. Yes, they want to help make this right for you. But they have a business to protect, too. That doesn't happen if this stays in the news."

"I know how the PR works. That's why I want it. I want them to feel some of the pain. To read the headlines about themselves. To have to see their friends look at them differently, the way ours look at us now."

"You did that to yourself, Rick," Marco said, one eyebrow cocked. Then he sighed. "The money will make a lot of difference for John, Mr. Morrow," Marco said. "Any apology we make? In the end it won't make a bit of difference."

"It will to me."

Marco looked at Mary. "Is that what you think, too?"

"We both need to agree to whatever we decide," she said, keeping her face and voice neutral.

"Do *you* know what really happened?" Rick said to Marco, leaning forward. "Did they even bother to tell you? Or do you even care?"

"We appreciate the offer," Eddie interrupted, his voice shaking. "But we need a day to think it over. You can understand that, I hope."

Marco just pursed his lips. "I'm surprised. It's a very generous offer. Is it the dollar amount? I'm not sure I can do anything there, but I can try."

"It's not about that," Rick said. "It's about you people feeling some of the pain we feel."

Marco looked at Rick expectantly. Neither his posture nor his expression changed in the least, but suddenly the air around the man felt different somehow. *Dangerous* was the word that came to Rick's mind. "It doesn't matter," Rick said. "What you said to the media. What the pilot said. That's not what happened. Our friends, my parents, my *son*, had to read stories that said I might be involved. Your PR people shake their heads and call it a terrible accident and talk about their renewed focus on safety. It's all bullshit."

"What is it that *you* think happened?" Marco asked. His tone was mild, but his eyes bored into Rick.

"I think something happened that would make Cera Global look really bad." Rick said.

"Maybe you're covering up for the pilot. Maybe there was more wrong with that helicopter than you want to admit. Maybe they don't want to admit that the new transport machine started the fire because it'll ruin somebody's business plan. I don't know. But I was *there*. I don't know everything, but I saw a lot. And it's not what you all said it was."

Marco shrugged. "As I said, the alternative is not pretty. Years of legal battles. If you do win, we'll appeal. If we win, you may have to pay our legal costs, which will be more than you've made in your whole life. Best case, you won't see a dime for years. What would that mean for John?"

"Can we just have a few days?" Eddie cut in, before Rick could respond.

Marco appeared to think for a minute. "Two days. I realize this is a big decision. But no interviews, nothing public in the meantime." He drew a USB thumb drive out of his pocket and handed it directly to Mary. "Your lawyer can have the hard copy, but I have all the documents on here for you, just in case they're helpful. You were an accountant, if I recall? I think you'll want to look through them."

Thirty-Three

Rick, Mary, and Eddie rode in silence for a few minutes, Rick still fuming over the conversation with Marco, and Mary and Eddie simply too stunned to speak. They dropped Eddie off at his apartment in a triple decker near downtown and continued towards home.

Mary finally began. "You had no right to do that."

"No right to do what? To want the truth? To want some respect?"

"Three million dollars, Rick. The fact they'll pay proves they must know they were wrong. What sort of respect do you want beyond that?"

"I want this for John, Mary. I want everyone to know they were wrong and what it cost him."

"Really? For John?"

"For years, everybody else has decided what happens to us. Insurance companies that decided what treatments John could get." Rick's voice was rising now but he didn't care. "Researchers who decided what trials he could be part of. The transplant center that decides who gets which heart. None of them thought about John. They just thought about their studies, or their bottom lines."

"You're going to throw this chance away for John, just because you think somebody's not respecting *you*?"

She saw the hurt flash in his eyes as she spoke, but in that moment she could not bring herself to care.

"I don't give a damn if they respect me," Rick said. "I want them to respect John. His life isn't just a stat on a piece of paper." He thought of dozens of arguments with the people who represented the machinery of the healthcare system. So many times, he and Mary had been told "no." People always tried to look sympathetic, but there was an unspoken epilogue to every decision. *What does it matter?* Rick could almost hear them all thinking as they had picked up their papers or began clicking intently away at their keyboards, signaling to him that yet another door was being closed. *Your boy's probably going to die anyway.*

He continued to shout, some of the defeat from all those fruitless efforts fueling the anger in his voice. "I just want people to know what really happened to him. That his life mattered as much as anyone's."

"You want them to feel bad for what happened to him? Or for what happened to you?"

"Damn it, Mary. You know better than that. Or you should. He deserved for the world to stop for one minute and really understand what it did to him, for whatever reason those things happened. That's worth more than the money to me."

They had left the posh downtown areas and the streets were getting narrower and rougher. The cars around them started to look more like their own, dirty and dented. They were repaired as little as possible, then bought and sold from owner to owner, cascading down the income curve with each transaction until they reached people like Rick and Mary.

"I want the money," Mary shouted back. "I want us to call that guy Marco tomorrow and say 'yes.' I want to take the money and forget about the stupid helicopter and your stupid conspiracy theories. I want the money and then I want to forget about all this and just to go be with John. I don't need him to matter to anyone else but me."

They were nearly screaming at each other now, all the stress from the past days and years boiling out of each of them.

"I won't do it."

"I *will*," Mary said.

"Why do you want the money so bad? You think a bigger house will change anything? Or a new car? You think it'll cure John?"

"I want the money so I can get a divorce."

Mary's words came out uncontrolled, in a near scream, tears running down both her cheeks now. As soon as she said the words, she sat stock-still in the seat, shocked by the sound of them spoken so loudly in the small car. The final syllables seemed to hang in the air in the silence that followed. Neither spoke for what seemed like an eternity.

Rick stared straight ahead, hands locked on the wheel, trying to make sense of what he'd just heard. Three blocks went by before he spoke. "You can't mean that."

She wiped away the tears, and her voice dropped to a hoarse whisper. "I can't live like this, Rick. I can't be angry every single day. I can't keep hoping for some break that never comes, or even worse, gets pulled away at the last second, over and over again. I vowed that after Danny Cho. I told myself I'd never do that again. Then I did. And it hurt just as much. I just want to be at peace."

"At *peace*? John doesn't need us to be at peace. We should be hopeful. We should be angry. You *should* be angry every single day. We *deserve* to be angry every single day."

"That's the thing, Rick. I think we deserve to *not* be angry every day. John deserves for us not to be angry, every single day."

Rick was still stunned. "You decide to tell me this now? With all this going on?"

"I didn't plan on it. It just came out now. I'm sorry for that."

He shook his head, speaking in a whisper of his own. "You can't manage all this alone. Neither of us can. It's too much."

Her whisper grew hoarse. "Maybe it is. And maybe it's not. I wasn't always like this if you remember, just shuttling from the hospital to the house, arguing with insurance companies. I was a forensic accountant. I helped find criminals." She laughed, almost crazily. "I used to wear *suits*."

She shook her head at him. "You're not the only one who lost something these past years." She took a breath. "I'm willing to accept it. That it's going to be over soon. All the way to the hospital this afternoon, I thought it was going to be *today*, for God's sake. And I don't want to spend the rest of the time I have with John just being angry. About us or anything else. And afterwards? What else do we have Rick? Think about it; you proposed to me three months after we started dating. I was already six months pregnant and barely divorced. It was all such a rush. And then John was born, and we found out his condition. I'm not even sure there was a time we talked about anything else after that."

"I married you knowing John's condition. You know that's never mattered to me."

"I know you did." Mary said, some warmth creeping back into her voice at the memory. "None of my friends could believe you'd go through with it. But you did. It's not about giving up, though.

It's about accepting what's happening. For us. For John. For David."

They pulled into their driveway and Rick shut off the car. He turned to face her. "You were going to wait until after, weren't you. To do the divorce."

She nodded once without looking at him, a quick up and down motion.

"How long have you been thinking about this?"

"A while, I guess. Sometimes I convince myself everything will be okay, that I just need to have faith. But then I think nothing will ever change. Even afterwards—after John. And now all this, with the helicopter and the media—I can't go through that. I can't be there while you go through that."

"This isn't who we are."

"We never had a chance to figure out who we are. I'm sorry for that. For your sake. For bringing you into all this." Rick shook his head violently, fighting off her words. "Don't you dare say that. He's my son as much as David is.

I would never think of him any other way."

They sat in silence for a minute, the only sound the ticking of the cooling engine.

"It's the money, isn't it?" Rick said eventually. "You figure if you get the money, you don't need me anymore."

"It's not like that. I just want to be happy. I deserve better than this. So does David. So do you."

The car rolled to a stop in their tiny driveway. Rick turned off the engine. "You're right. We deserve better than this," he said. He climbed out of the car. "To me, that includes having somebody look me in the eye and tell me the truth, for once. Which I guess is more than you've been willing to do."

As he marched away, Mary saw him wipe a tear from the corner of his eye. She sat for a minute, until she realized he had paused by the front door, waiting for her, to be sure she got inside safely. She took a breath and opened the car door to follow him.

Thirty-Four

Marco left the restaurant and dialed Lana's number as soon as he was away from the staff lingering around the entrance.

"They said no," he said, bluntly. He knew by now not to bother to sugarcoat bad news to Lana. Those who tried just looked weaker in her eyes.

"They want more money?" she asked. "We can do that."

"It's not the money," Marco said. "The husband is dug in on this. He wants a public apology,"

"I can have LifeLift do that, if that's what it takes. They can put a letter in the damn newspaper if he wants."

"I don't think that's enough. He knows the story is bullshit. And he wants the truth. Or at least what he *thinks* is the truth. He's stubborn. And he's not stupid." Marco walked along the edge of the park as they spoke, staying away from any potential eavesdroppers and trying to burn off some of his own frustration.

"You sound like you're defending him."

"No, I just want to make sure we don't underestimate him."

"What does his wife think?"

"My sense is she'd take the money. They don't seem to be on the same page on too much."

"Okay, then. How do you convince him?"

Marco thought for a minute as he worked his way along the side of Renaissance Tower, which housed the Marriott hotel and GM's headquarters, as well as the restaurant he'd just left. Construction was starting to appear in Detroit again, after decades of decay, but the Renaissance center was still the new center of the city, rising high above the surrounding buildings.

"She wants it to be over. We need him to want it to be over, too. And to think that it is."

"How do we do that?"

"We turn up the pressure. Then we make a new offer. We will need to be able to say LifeLift will make that apology."

Marco hung up and made his way back to the hotel. He'd denied it to Lana, but he knew she was right; he *was* defending Rick Morrow. Until the meeting in the restaurant, Morrow and his wife had simply been abstractions, two minor factors in an overall plan he was executing. Now, seeing the pain on their faces, seeing Rick Morrow's courage in the face of the misery that Marco had helped inflict on him, it was harder to think of them that way. Marco was used to coming face-to-face with his enemies. But they'd always been men with guns, intent on killing him or somebody under his protection, or greedy, corrupt politicians and arms dealers. They'd deserved whatever they got from him. Rick Morrow, with his military haircut and steady gaze, seemed more like one of the men Marco would have been proud to go into battle alongside. He was not one Marco could get any satisfaction from destroying.

That was then, he told himself. *Your mission is different now.*

He put the sympathy aside. He had an hour's work to do before bed, and a few calls to make, to get the next parts of his plan in place. His room was on the sixtieth floor. As high as he could get in the hotel. It wasn't quite an airplane, but he hoped maybe he could get some sleep there anyway.

Thirty-Five

On Wednesday morning, Mary dropped David off at school and Rick at work. She was still drained from the day before. She wondered when she and Rick had become so calloused they could use John's suffering as ammunition in a fight.

She realized she couldn't bear to go back to the quiet house. Instead, she drove until a coffee shop caught her eye. Two days ago, buying a cup of coffee out like that would have been a luxury she would never have given herself. With the events of the past days, and the money that had flowed into the GoFundMe account, she decided she could indulge just one time. She found a seat inside and placed her order.

When the drink arrived, she gave herself a moment to lose herself in the smell and taste of an honest-to-goodness cappuccino. She couldn't remember the last time she'd had one. Then she checked the GoFundMe balance again. It was now well over $30,000, though new donations had nearly stopped after the hateful comments had started appearing online. The money was a drop in the bucket compared to the $3 million they'd been offered, but still more than she'd thought they'd ever have again.

Out of curiosity, she typed in the Richardsons' name in the GoFundMe search bar in her phone. She was hoping they hadn't been hurt by the press coverage. She considered that it might actually have gained them some sympathy, since their selfless act had turned out to been in vain. *Two funerals to pay for*, she thought. *And so much grief.* The Richardson's page was topped by a picture that Mary guessed must have been a year old. It showed Lisa Richardson holding her son Matthew, maybe in a park somewhere, or on a family vacation. His cheeks looked slightly sunburned, and mother and son were both smiling. She realized she'd never seen their faces before. She wondered, too, if there had been a different picture there before, maybe one showing Matthew's father, too.

She looked at the Richardsons' fundraising list and was happy to see there was a flood of recent donations, some anonymous, some not. One big one jumped out at her. It was for $10,000. She was surprised to see she recognized the donor's name, too. It was the charity that had put that same amount in John's account. The date stamp on the site showed that the two transactions had happened on the same day. She wondered who these people were, that they would be so moved to make such big donations to both families involved. Their generosity immediately made her feel selfish for her thoughts that morning.

Two funerals. An idea struck her. She typed "Matthew Richardson funeral" into Google, and sure enough, the responses showed a funeral service for Matthew at 10:30 that very morning in Pontiac. At the end of the short description was a one-line note that there would be a memorial ceremony for Tom Richardson the following day, for family only.

She said a silent prayer for Matthew and the family, and then decided she could do more than that. Mary wrote down the address for the funeral. She admitted to herself that maybe she was going more for herself as much as for anyone else, but it was still something gracious she could do for the Richardsons, she decided, even if they never knew she was there.

She arrived at the church just before the ceremony, having rushed home to put on appropriate clothing. The small Protestant church was only half full. Lisa Richardson and her twin girls were in the front row, along with a large man who seemed to be her brother or close family friend. An older couple sat with them. From the similarities in faces and mannerisms Mary assumed they were Lisa's parents.

The ceremony was short. Although the sadness was apparent, there was a sense of fatigue to it as well, and none of the raw, inconsolable grief that Mary associated with sudden loss—especially the loss of a child. Mary wondered despite herself if this was how John's service would be; just the final, exhausted chapter in a long tragic story, where everyone has known the ending for a long time.

The minister closed the ceremony by inviting everyone to the burial service. Looking around at the small crowd in the church, Mary decided she would stop at the cemetery, too. She was only one person, she knew, but she could not bear to think of Lisa Richardson looking around the gravesite and realizing that in the end, her son's tragic passing was marked only by a handful of exhausted relatives and bored funeral home employees.

The service at the cemetery was also brief, but somehow sadder than the church. Maybe it was the fact that it was the final goodbye. Maybe it was because the small group of mourners looked even more forlorn against the wide expanse of the graveyard. A few reporters stood on the edge of the grass near the road and snapped pictures, looking to wring one more story out of the Richardsons' ordeal.

Mary kept toward the back of the knot of people, making sure to stay out of the reporters' view. Tom's parents also hung to the edges of the small crowd. Mary never saw them speak at the church or the cemetery. She wondered if the guilt their son Tom must have felt for his own son's tragedy carried over to them as well.

At the conclusion of the service the small group began to break up. Mary turned quickly to walk away, not wanting to be noticed as the uninvited, and probably unwanted, guest. She especially wanted to avoid having a microphone and camera stuck in her face if the reporters recognized her.

She was too late.

"Excuse me?" a woman's voice called out. The words came from behind her, from someone still near the gravesite, but somehow Mary knew they were meant for her. She turned to see Lisa Richardson moving towards her. Mary had a moment of panic, and the thought of running for her car actually flashed through her mind, but she stood, frozen in place.

"You're Mrs. Morrow, aren't you?" Lisa Richardson asked as she got closer.

"Yes," Mary said. She decided to try and head off any anger. "I'm so sorry for intruding. I read about the funeral this morning and I just wanted to pay my respects."

"Don't be sorry. It's kind of you to come," Lisa said, to Mary's relief. Lisa Richardson was thin, almost gaunt. She'd made an attempt at applying makeup, but what looked like a half-hearted effort didn't fully hide the signs of exhaustion and grief Mary saw sometimes in her own mirror.

"I'm sorry," Mary said. "I can only imagine how hard it must be."

Lisa Richardson smiled wanly. "Yes, it's been hard. They always say it's something no parent should have to do, but until it happens to you, you can't really know what they mean. I wouldn't wish it on anyone."

"I know you did everything you could to keep us from that," Mary said, not sure where else to take the conversation. "We appreciate what you did so much."

Realization showed in Lisa's eyes. "Oh my, yes. I'm so sorry. I never should have said that."

"It's okay," Mary said. "Not many people can say they know what it's like, to have to live through this. You can, even more than us. And I'm sorry about your husband. To lose both, so close together..."

"Thanks. For Matthew, I guess I felt like I'd been saying goodbye to him every day for the last few months. For Tom, well, I guess we really said goodbye to each other a long time ago."

A few of the mourners stopped to kiss Lisa before heading to their cars. One glanced with obvious recognition at Mary, then turned and walked away quickly, saying nothing. Lisa seemed not to notice the silent snub. She turned back to Mary and brightened a bit. "You're lucky, at least in that way."

Mary smiled sadly. "Lucky isn't a word most people use to describe us."

"Your husband. The hospital gave me the card he'd left for Tom."

Mary shifted awkwardly, trying to hide her sudden surprise. "Rick didn't tell me he'd written a card."

"I got the sense it wasn't easy for him to write. I actually don't think he wanted anyone else but Tom to see it. But I read it. It was really nice. He told Tom to forgive himself, that he knew what it was like to feel so helpless, watching someone you love suffer when you can't find any way to help. To feel like a failure at the one thing that matters most." Lisa swallowed hard. "I do wish Tom had gotten a chance to read it, before..."

Mary just nodded, still wrestling with the idea that Rick had written such a note but had never told her about it. "You probably got a sense of it," Lisa continued. "But Tom never did much good for us. He meant well, most times, but he was probably never meant to be a dad."

"I'm sorry," Mary said.

"It's alright," Lisa said, "I really shouldn't be burdening you with that." She shook her head. "Although he did surprise me in the end."

"That he would do...that?"

"No," Lisa said. "Well, yes, that, too. But at some point, he'd taken out a life insurance policy. Five million dollars. He never told me about it."

"That's a relief," Mary said. "I mean for you and the girls." She paused. "But I thought that, you know, when somebody..."

Lisa nodded, not forcing her to complete the awkward sentence. "Yes, I thought that... dying that way... would not be covered. But the policy only excluded suicide for the first six months, and he took it out two years ago. How Tom paid for it I have no idea. He almost never had two nickels to rub together. And when he did, he'd buy another motorcycle or four-wheeler. I paid all the bills." She smiled sadly. "He was a lost soul, I guess. I think that's why I fell in love with him." Mary said nothing, but her eyes showed her curiosity, and Lisa came back to her story.

"Anyway, It's some Canadian insurance company. Vancouver, I think. I guess they're a little more generous up there."

"I guess they are," Mary said.

Lisa paused for a moment. " I owe you an apology, too, I think," she said.

"I don't see how that could be."

"We'd originally agreed to move Matthew to Metropolitan hospital for the surgery. I guess that's the usual way. But then Rhonda Marsh suggested we just leave him at Saint Elizabeth and do the surgery there, since that's where he'd been for the last few months. We weren't sure at first, but then we agreed. If we had said no, then the helicopter wouldn't have been used at all."

"We thought *you'd* insisted on staying at Saint Elizabeth," Mary said, carefully.

Lisa shook her head. "No, it hadn't occurred to us. But Rhonda kept pushing it. We pushed back, Then one day Tom changed his mind and said he wanted to stay there. Rhonda even offered to use the helicopter so we didn't have to worry about adding any risk for you." She bit her lip after the last comment, realizing how foolish it must have sounded in the face of what had happened.

Mary puzzled on Lisa's words for a moment. Rick had said clearly that Rhonda told him the Richardsons had insisted on having their final hours with their son at Saint Elizabeth in Pontiac. But Mary had no doubt Lisa Richardson was telling her the truth.

"Well, regardless," Lisa said, putting a hand on Mary's arm. "I hope that they can find another heart for your son. The idea of Matthew's death helping somebody else, it was the last hope that I held on to." She shook her head, and tears shone in her eyes.

Mary shook her head. "I try not to hope any more. It just makes it hurt more when things go wrong."

Lisa smiled, a sad, awkward expression on a face that clearly had almost forgotten how to make those muscles work. "For the first few weeks after the accident, no matter what the doctors kept telling me, I prayed every day that Matthew would wake up and smile at me. I had hope, even when they told me there was none. But I'll tell you, for the last few months, when I had to finally admit there was no hope at all for my little boy?" She shrugged, a gesture with more pain and sadness than Mary could fathom. "I'd have done anything for a chance at a little real hope. And to have something to fight for."

She squeezed Mary's arm again. "Having hope might be hard, Mary. But trust me, having none is worse." Then she turned and headed back to the handful of mourners still clustered around Matthew's grave.

Mary headed back towards the car. The cemetery was on a hillside on the edge of downtown Pontiac. The shining glass face of the Saint Elizabeth Hospital tower dominated the landscape, looming over the low, drab buildings that surrounded it. Thoughts tumbled through her mind: Rick in that building just a few days earlier; Rhonda Marsh telling him about the helicopter and the new machine; Tom Richardson taking his own life in the parking lot she could see from the heights of the cemetery; the huge, identical donations on the GoFundMe accounts; the dinner with Marco; strange insurance policies; and the CeraGlobal company in general. She'd not thought of Canada in years. But now it seemed to come up everywhere she turned. She was starting to feel she knew a bit of what Rick had talked about. The odd feeling that somehow there was some giant play being acted out around her family, and that everybody else knew the script but them.

She thought about the card Rick had written. For years she and Rick had worked as a team, maybe lost at sea sometimes, but navigating endless obstacles in their own lifeboat as they searched for a way to save John. It had not always been easy, but they had done their best to help each other survive the dark moments and, sometimes, even thrive in rare moments of calm. But then that lifeboat had been sunk without warning, broken apart when they'd lost that first heart to the Cho boy. Ever since then they'd each clung to their own broken remnants, doing their best to stay afloat as their separate pain and regrets pulled them further and further apart.

That's when she'd started thinking about divorce—they were already living in separate worlds, united in their love for John but increasingly separate in the ways they thought were best to help him.

Seeing Rick through the eyes of Lisa Richardson and learning about the card he'd written reminded Mary of how distant she and Rick had become. She felt an unexpected resentment that another woman seemed to know more about her own husband's feelings than she did.

Thirty Six

Mary got home around one o'clock. She had a few hours before David would get off the bus, and she busied herself straightening up the kitchen. Around 1:30 she was startled by the sound of the doorbell and a sharp knock on the front door. She went to the living room and peered out. The front steps were visible from that vantage point. In her neighborhood, it was never a good idea to open the door if you didn't know who was on the other side. She saw a grey Ford sedan on the street in front of the house and caught her breath. From the antennae on the car's roof and trunk, and the searchlight mounted above the drivers's mirror it was clear it was a police car. A look towards the front steps revealed a tall black man, looking to be in his fifties, standing at the door.

She opened the door but left the chain on. The man shifted a bit on his feet. "Mrs. Morrow?" he asked.

"I'm sorry, you are….? She gave him a quick look up and down as she spoke. His arms were by his side. She got a glimpse of something white swinging gently from his left hand but couldn't make out what it was through the narrow crack she'd created.

"I'm detective Kendrick, Detroit Police Department. Is your husband here?"

"Has something happened to him. Or my boys?" she asked, the fear rising in her voice.

"No ma'am. I have something for him. It was left at… the site." He glanced down at whatever he was holding in his left hand. He held up a badge in his right hand. "I was one of the detectives who spoke to him there."

Mary studied the badge for a minute then unlatched the door, motioning him in. He wiped his feet on the mat then stepped inside, still looking uncomfortable. Mary glanced down, and saw that the white object was a stuff animal. A lion. Dirty and matted. After another beat she saw the Detroit Lions logo on its chest.

"What is that?" She asked, confusion now mixing in with her receding fear.

"It fell out of your husband's car, at the crash site," Detective Kendrick said. "We kept it for evidence. I thought maybe he'd want it back. He said that's why he'd gone up to Pontiac. To get it. And these." He pulled a ziplock bag out of his jacket pocket. Mary saw some crumpled paper in it, and a small box in wrapping paper. "Do you recognize them?" he asked.

"No." Mary felt the confusion and a duller anger building as she her eyes went back and forth between the toy and the plastic bag. For the second time that day she was faced with learning something about Rick through another person.

"Can I leave them with you?" the detective asked, after a long minute.

"Yes, of course," Mary said. She took the items from him. She put them the stuffed lion on the couch under the window and kept the ziplock bag in her hand.

The detective stood for another uncomfortable second. "I'm really sorry," he said finally, "For what happened to him. And your son. And all the lousy stuff in the media."

Mary said nothing. Her mind was racing, all the painful memories of the past few days colliding together as she looked at the stuffed toy. *Why didn't Rick tell her?*

"I know we didn't make it any easier on him. But we didn't know. At the time." Kendrick continued, his voice trailing off at the last few words.

Mary just nodded, not trusting her voice.

"Anyway, good luck to you all," Kendrick said. He stepped back onto the brick landing. Mary closed the door. She opened the ziplock with trembling fingers and unpeeled the wad of paper. The ink had run but it was clear enough from the barcode on the long rectangles that she was holding tickets. The Detroit Lions logo was still recognizable at the top. Rick had gone to Saint Elizabeth to get the tickets, she realized. So he'd have them when John woke up.

She put the tickets back in the pack and took out the small rectangular box. It had been professionally wrapped. She hesitated for a second but realized she had to know what was inside. She undid the wrapping to reveal an elegant red box, slightly water stained. She opened it, already half-guessing what she'd see. The necklace inside still sparkled, having been protected from the rain and mud by the box and wrapping. She gasped. It was gold with a small diamond at the center. It was beautiful. *How could he have afforded this?* She thought. Tears sprang to her eyes as she realized what Rick had planned. Lion's tickets for John and David. And the necklace for her. And, she was sure, nothing at all for himself.

She put the necklace on the arm of the couch. She picked up the stuffed animal and held it against her chest. The white fur was stained with dirt and oil. *And with what else?* she wondered. The fur itself was matted. From the rain, she guessed, remembering the night of the crash.

Why didn't he tell me? she asked herself again. But she knew the answer. They hadn't been sharing much with each other in the months before the crash. Why would he share this, especially after what she'd said to him.

The flood of memories started to coalesce in a kaleidoscope of anger and pain. A simple stuffed animal. Some football tickets and a pretty necklace. For most families those things might represent a nice weekend or a birthday to remember. But to her family, they would remain as symbols of just one more futile attempt at joy: a crushed moment of love and hope. One more attempt by Rick to bring their family together had been destroyed by fate, or incompetence, or whatever forces kept driving her, him and their children further into misery.

Her dull anger built suddenly to a rage: at the police for their apathy; at the helicopter company for its incompetence; at the reporters and bloggers for their careless cruelty. And even at Rick for his stubborn insistence on trying to do the right thing. His keeping up hope, when she'd just wanted to give in to whatever came and let the pain that sprung from those endlessly crushed hopes fade away. The rage and the pain merged into an overwhelming flood. She pounded the lion's chest as her tears turned to sobs, trying with her fists to blot out everything the creature represented to her: the hopes, the failures, the future that seemed to have only one bleak outcome in store for her and her family. Finally, exhausting her anger, she slumped to the floor, her back against the door, hugging the stuffed toy close to her chest.

She didn't know how long she stayed on the floor, cradling the lion. At some point even the grief receded. But what was left behind was a clarity she'd not felt in a long time. Rick had never stopped fighting for John, she realized. Or their family. He'd never given up, no matter the cost to himself. But at some point, she admitted to herself, she had. Her faith had become a crutch, And a shield. If everything was in God's hands, she'd let herself think, no one could blame her for whatever happened to John.

No one, especially herself.

Thirty-Seven

Rick sat at his bench on Wednesday, his uneaten ham sandwich in front of him. He struggled to concentrate on the blueprints spread out on his desk. Thoughts of the past few days kept pushing their way into the front of his mind. He kept trying to find a way forward, but everything just led to dead ends. The pilot was now 5,000 miles away. Rick's attempts to convince the police and the media had gone horribly wrong. And then there was the terrible, lonely look on Mary's face when she'd talked about just holding John for his final days.

Rick's eyelids kept fluttering from exhaustion. The only thing keeping him moving was the anger that had been building since the previous night. It was deeper now, and somehow more powerful, because now it wasn't just for himself. His family was being ground up in a set of gears he still didn't fully understand. And he had no idea how to stop it.

Just as lunch break was ending Luis walked over to him. "Some folks want to talk to you," was all he said.

"More cops?"

He shook his head. "They're in the conference room in the back."

Rick made his way through the tables and benches to the back of the building, where a glass door led to a small hallway connecting a handful of cramped offices and a small conference room, usually reserved for vendor and customer meetings. Two men and a woman sat at the rectangular table that filled the space. All three were in suits: the men's were navy blue, the woman's a deep crimson. The three sat gingerly, as though trying to contact as few surfaces as possible.

Rick recognized the older of the two men. The man had thinning silver hair slicked back over his scalp. He was lean and sharp-eyed. He was the general manager for Rick's part of the company; he came and spoke once a quarter to the employees, droning on about productivity improvements and competitive pressures. Rick couldn't remember his name, but the man stood and offered his hand to Rick and said, "Jim Abbot. Pleased to meet you, Rick."

Abbot introduced the other two. The man was the communications director for the business unit, the woman was legal counsel. Both attempted a bright smile in his direction, but Rick could see the tight lines around their eyes and mouths.

Abbot motioned Rick to a chair and clasped his hands in front of him. "Thanks for meeting us, Rick. And first, let me say how sorry we all are at the terrible situation that occurred for your family."

The other two bobbed their heads in unison.

"We're here because we value you as an employee," Abbot said earnestly. "We're glad we've been able to do our part to help your family, in terms of some flexibility in your work hours."

Rick nodded. He didn't point out that because he was paid by the hour, the flexibility simply meant they'd let him leave early once in a while and not paid him for the time he missed.

"We hope you value us as an employer, too, Rick," Abbot said. "Because we need your help."

"What sort of help?" Rick could feel the urgency in their stares, and their tense postures. He could almost feel some unseen force pushing on them, driving them to whatever ask they were going to make of him.

"Thomas Hospital Systems is a big customer of ours, Rick. Do you know them?" Rick nodded. He'd seen their name on some of the work orders that crossed his desk. They built and maintained hospitals.

"That's great," Abbot said, nodding vigorously, as though he and Rick were already part of some great collaboration. "Well, we've been notified that we're in the driver's seat for a major contract with them. We could get all their installation and maintenance work for their backup generators and power systems. It would double the size of the business here."

"Great," Rick said, feeling tendrils close in around him somehow, even though he couldn't quite yet piece together the connections.

"It *would* be great," Abbot said nodding vigorously. "It would guarantee work for the people here—for your friends—for years."

Rick nodded again, waiting for the punchline.

"The thing of it is..." Abbot leaned in closer to Rick. "Thomas Hospital Systems is owned by CeraGlobal, and as you can imagine, it's hard for them to do business with us when one of our employees, you know, seems to have a sort of grudge against them."

And there it was, Rick thought. The connection he'd known was there somewhere clicked in his mind. Of course, it was CeraGlobal. "My son may die because of them," Rick said, bluntly. "I guess you could say I do have a grudge."

"I don't blame you a bit," Abbot said. "I'm sure I'd feel the same way, in your shoes. Especially with what happened with the media. That was a bum deal." He pushed himself to his feet and walked to the end of the table. "But that won't help you or your family. Or any of these people out there," he swept an arm around the room, out towards the shop floor. "We've got a chance together to help everyone. Our whole company. Your whole family."

"I just want to know what happened," Rick said. "And I want CeraGlobal to admit it. No PR spin. No power plays. You call it an accident, but I don't think it was. At least not the way they say it was." Out of the corner of his eye, he saw the lawyer trade a worried glance with the communications director.

Abbot nodded as if in sympathy, but Rick caught a flash of frustration in his eyes. Abbot put his hands on the back of a chair and stared down at Rick. "They've told the truth, Rick. They took it on the chin publicly. I read the stories. I hear they're offering you a major settlement even though legally there's no requirement for that. They screwed up, and they know it." He shook his head sadly. "You can do a lot of good for a lot of people here, Rick. But if you decide not to," he splayed his arms out to his sides. "I'm not sure how long we can keep this facility open. Business is tight. We've been considering a layoff already, but we hoped this order could swing things the other way."

"It's completely your call, Rick," the woman said. "We aren't forcing you to do anything. I want that to be clear.

And as Jim said, we've done our best for you, with your... unique...circumstances." She dwelled on the word unique. "But in a layoff like that, nobody's safe. No matter what their situation. We'd really rather avoid that."

Rick stood, too, and looked at each of them evenly in turn. "Who called you?" he said. "That guy Marco? Or did he delegate this one to somebody else at CeraGlobal?"

He saw the fear in Abbot's eyes. He could feel the pressure weighing down on all of them; their own hunger for the order and the profits it would bring, pinned hard against the threat from CeraGlobal.

"On the flip side we'll need more managers if we get that order," Abbot said, ignoring the question. "I looked at your background. You've managed teams before in your past jobs. I'm sure we'd have a need for you in a bigger role. This could change everything for you."

"Everything's already changed for me," Rick said. "You know that."

He turned and left the room, leaving the three of them to stare at his back. He walked straight back to his bench, ignoring the curious stares of the men around him. He guessed from their looks that the management team had already spread the story that Rick's decision was the key to at least a few years of financial security for them all. Some of the men glanced at him hopefully, no doubt praying he'd agree to whatever deal they were demanding of him. He knew how desperate the situation was for most of them. A few years of stability, even just a bit of a raise, would mean a lot to them. And to his own family. He'd met some of the wives and kids when they came by the shop. He thought of them now. And Mary's words still rang in his ears.

He got up and walked to the back of the shop. Luis was in his office, pecking away at his ancient computer with his gnarled index fingers. He looked up as Rick filled the doorway. "Tell them I'll think about it," Rick said. "I just need a few days."

"Works for me," Luis said gruffly, and went back to his work. Rick returned to his station and plowed through a few more blueprints, lost in thought, the sandwich getting stale in front of him.

Thirty-Eight

Mary waited for David to come off the school bus, then the two of them piled into the car to pick up Rick at work. She'd spent the afternoon at the hospital, with John slipping in and out of consciousness. The infection was fi nally under control, Esther Williams had reported, and the new medicine had stabilized his heartbeat. Mary tried not to think about all the drugs that were fed into John's body every day. They might be keeping his heart alive a bit longer, but she knew from her own research that they were slowly destroying his liver and kidneys.

Once they were back home and David was set up in front of the TV, Rick and Mary threw together some dinner. Meals had become simpler and simpler affairso ver the months, as both time and money became harder to come by. Mary reported on the information from doctors as they ate, and they ran through the usual small talk about David's day.

"I went to the funeral for the Richardson boy today," Mary said finally. She offered it almost as a question, testing to see how Rick would respond.

"How was it?" he asked. He seemed preoccupied.

"Sad, of course," she said. "Fewer people than I thought there would be."

Rick just nodded.

"It was strange. Sort of like looking into a mirror. Or into the future." The last words came out without thinking. It was a feeling that had been playing at the edges of her mind all day and now it had just sort of crystallized. That was the feeling she'd felt, like the guy in *A Christmas Carol*, standing on the edge of the scene from his own future, terrified of what he was seeing, powerless to change it. But Lisa Richardson's words still rang in Mary's ears. Faced with that feeling, hope might be hard to cling to. But not having it was worse.

"Some people came to work today," Rick chose his words carefully. "They told me there was a big contract in store for the shop. But I had to agree to stop talking about the crash and everything."

"Why would they care about that?"

"Why else?" Rick said. "The customer is part of Cera-Global. The same people who own the medical transport company. They pretty much said that if I don't agree they're going to have to do a layoff. They're holding all those guys at the shop hostage to make me agree."

Mary stopped eating for a minute and looked up sharply. "CeraGlobal. The Canadian company?"

"I guess so," Rick said. He sat quietly for a minute, not noticing Mary was suddenly sitting still, blinking the way she did when her mind was working rapidly.

"I was thinking a lot today," Rick said, filling the silence. "About the money. And the guys at the shop. And you." He looked up from his plate. "I think we should take the deal…"

Mary looked up again, stunned.

"…If that will make things better for you and for John," Rick continued. "And for David afterwards. I get it. I don't know why I get so stubborn about everything. You're right— none of that really matters. I really do just want you to be happy."

"What about the pilot?" Mary said. She knew she should feel relieved, even glad. Instead, she felt a surprising rush of fear at the notion that Rick was suddenly giving up, just when she was starting to think his instincts might have been right all along.

"I still think he's lying. Maybe they are all lying. But so what? It's what big companies do, right? It's what people do. We can't stop it. For once, we can get something out of it. Something that matters."

"I'm sorry it came out that way, last night," Mary said.

"That's not the same as saying you didn't mean it," Rick said.

Mary stacked the dishes in the sink. "The Richardson woman, Lisa, said something to me. She said she and her husband had really said goodbye a long time ago. I guess I worry that's true for us, too."

Rick made a cup of coffee for himself and tea for Mary. It was a part of their after-dinner ritual, a bit of caffeine to give them enough energy to pay the bills, or pore through the insurance documents, or help David with his homework before they all collapsed into bed.

"I know you're right," he said. "Maybe we never really said hello the right way to begin with. But that doesn't mean I don't love you."

"Lisa Richardson said something else, too," Mary said, suddenly wanting to change the subject. "It turns out that the husband had a life insurance policy."

"Did you hear what I said? About the money?"

"I did. But listen to me first. It turns out, it pays out even though he committed suicide. Five million dollars."

"That's great for them."

"Turns out it's from a Canadian company. I also went to the Richardson's GoFundMe page. They got the same donation we got. Ten thousand dollars. Same charity. The charity is from Canada, too."

"Canada's a big place," Rick said with a shrug.

"I know," Mary said. "But both are based in Vancouver. Same place as the people who visited you are from, I bet. Maybe Canada's a big place, but I bet Vancouver's not. Anyway, it seemed odd to me. It makes me wonder."

"Jesus, Mary." Rick said. "You were the one telling me to let it go. I am agreeing. We'll take the money, and you can get the van and a house and whatever else you think you need. The shop will get the new work. I might even get a promotion."

Mary could hear the capitulation in his voice. Despite their arguments she knew he had thought he was fighting for her and for John. Now he was agreeing to eat his pride, even his deepest beliefs, if that was what it took to make things better. She studied him across the cramped room. He looked older to her suddenly, hunched over his dirty dinner plate. And smaller, too—his broad shoulders now hardly filled out the worn cotton shirt. She thought of the lion and the necklace, and felt a grief for him she had not felt in a long time. And a sudden shame that her own arguments had helped the CeraGlobal company—and whoever else was involved in this whole horrible mess—finally do to Rick what John's illness, the insurance companies, and the greedy bosses never could: defeat him.

"We can call Eddie in the morning," Mary said. "We don't have to talk about it right now. We'll sleep on it."

Rick collected the empty cups and Mary got David ready for bed. She felt another pang of guilt tucking him in, realizing she couldn't recall if they'd said a word to him all evening.

Rick went to bed around 10:00. Mary told him she wanted to pay some bills, now that they had the money from the GoFundMe account. She made another cup of tea and turned on the aging desktop computer perched on a small desk in the corner of the dining room. There was a stack of bills there, and she thought about getting out the checkbook and working her way through the pile. It would be satisfying, she thought, to see the stack of bills and late notices that had plagued their life for so long gone with just a couple hours of scribbling.

Instead, her mind kept coming back to the conversation with Lisa Richardson, and the dinner with Marco. And to Rick, strapped to the stretcher, treated like a criminal simply for trying to save his son's chance at life. And to the odd offer he'd gotten at work, from yet another company somehow tied to CeraGlobal. But mostly she thought of Rick from just a few hours earlier, staring down at the remains of his four-dollar supper, agreeing to take the scraps being offered—even if they were scraps wrapped in gold—to give up on the one thing he thought he had left to offer John.

Her conviction from earlier in the day still thrummed within her. She started a Google search on CeraGlobal. The company, or what was really a collection of companies, was dizzying in its complexity at first. But her training as an accountant, long before John needed full-time care, quickly came back to her . Follow the money, her boss had always told her, and you'll get to the truth. She traversed the company website, recent articles, and financial websites, and learned that CeraGlobal was one of the world's largest private companies, run largely by Lana Cera, the granddaughter of the man who had founded it. Mary realized now why the PR issue was such a big deal. CeraGlobal not only owned the company that did the medical transport, but the company that made the helicopters as well. The giant company was based in Vancouver, but its operations were scattered all over the world. It had businesses in transportation, medical devices, military equipment, construction…and insurance.

She saved the links to the pages about CeraGlobal that mattered most and turned her attention to the charity. Their website was sparse but it did list their board of directors. The executive director was a university professor named Phillippe Gaumond. The other directors were various businesspeople and civic leaders from the Vancouver area. It wasn't until she started scanning press stories that she found the link: the charity was the family charity for the Cera family, and had been started by Gregoire Cera, the prior chairman of CeraGlobal and Lana's father.

Mary wondered if that had been part of their original plan; donate some money to her family and to the Richardson family so CeraGlobal could come off as good corporate citizens? Would the company have just walked away at that point, had Rick not gone on TV and made them worry that a PR disaster was looming?

She felt her anger grow at their cynicism and her own naiveté. She felt foolish too, for the guilt she'd felt earlier when she'd been humbled by the generosity she thought she had seen in the donations the Cera Foundation had made. She clicked on one more business site link, to a Canadian publication. They had a few stories on CeraGlobal's growth, and a recent deal with Saudi Arabia for helicopters. Nothing that had anything to do with her, or Rick, or John. She was about to close down the site when a familiar name at the edge of her fatigue-blurred vision caught her eye and she wondered why the Saint Elizabeth's Health Network was being discussed on a Canadian business news website.

She clicked through to the article. The headline read "Is CeraGlobal Losing Its Focus?" It was from Tuesday morning, and it was by a financial analyst questioning Cera-Global's rumored purchase of the patents of a failing medical device company. CeraGlobal was apparently buying out all the previous investors, including Saint Elizabeth's Health Network. According to the analyst, the company was paying many times the market value, and the analyst questioned the continued diversification of the company, at a time when companies such as General Electric were selling businesses and getting back to what they did best.

Mary rocked her head from side to side to work the stiffness out of her neck. She felt the feeling from earlier in the day return. The feeling of some distant entity reaching out tendrils to touch more and more of the world around her and her family. Was this one more angle CeraGlobal wanted to protect? It made sense; the cash would buy her and Rick's silence. The investment would buy the hospital's compliance. The tragedy would fade and CeraGlobal would go on its merry way. It made no sense otherwise; every other article had painted the company as a calculating and ruthlessly efficient competitor that simply did not make mistakes or emotional decisions. Why overpay? Wouldn't bad PR for the hospital make the price for the assets go down?

She retrieved the USB thumb drive Marco had given her from her purse. She slipped it into the computer and clicked open the file, looking at it almost as if to test her own memory. There it was in black and white; three million dollars, paid over three years, as long as Rick and Mary stayed silent. Enough money to take care of John. To send David to college. To move, when the time came, to a different city maybe, where they could start a better life, together or apart.

As these thoughts floated through her sleep-starved brain, her computer's hard drive chattered away in the background. Mary closed the files, oblivious to the sound. Meanwhile, the file Marco had loaded on the thumb drive did the rest of its work, downloading another piece of software onto Rick and Mary's computer. It was a program Marco had gotten from a friend in the Canadian intelligence service. It embedded itself deep into the operating system of the aging Window's PC—where none but a skilled computer expert could ever spot it—and began to do its work.

Mary left the computer running and headed upstairs, figuring the machine would put itself to sleep mode in a matter of minutes. David and Rick were both sound asleep. She crawled quietly into bed, realizing only afterwards that she'd not even thought of doing her prayers. *Maybe in the morning*, she thought.

She closed her eyes, but sleep wouldn't come easily. For a while, she played back images of the CeraGlobal website, and recollections of Marco with his perfect suit and deadly eyes. She thought of Rick hunched over the dinner table, defeated. The thoughts blurred together as she passed into sleep, the company and the man Marco both poised and unblemished, but with hearts of ice. And she dreamed of John floating out to sea in a rowboat with no oars, Rick swimming desperately behind him, unable to catch him, too far out to return safely to shore. And her just standing in the sand, watching them disappear.

Thirty-Nine

Lana's jet touched down in Vancouver just after 11 p.m. Once the plane's altitude dropped below 5,000 feet, her phone had buzzed and blinked as a day's worth of emails and text messages caught up with it. She scanned the list, but all she was looking for were two voicemail messages. She spotted the first and hit "listen." It was Marco, relaying that the social media onslaught was still on track, and that Rick should have already received both a carrot and a stick by his management team.

She played the second message, from Marie: Annette's temperature was up a bit, but overall she was still doing well, and the doctors had said they would just watch things for a bit. Lana breathed a small sigh of relief.

Once settled in the back seat of the car, Lana dialed Marco's number. He filled her in on the attempt to pressure Rick through his job.

"Will that work?" she said, when he'd finished the update.

"I don't know. This guy is stubborn. But if everybody around him is pushing him to give in, maybe he'll come around." Marco paused for a minute. "Plus, I don't think he's the kind of guy to hurt people he cares about."

"That's a weakness we can exploit."

"If you say so."

"I *do* say so." Lana's voice was cold. "Are you having second thoughts again?"

Marco said nothing. Lana took his silence for capitulation. "Three million dollars," she said almost to herself. "Jesus. Does he know they don't even have a case?"

"It's not about that with him. It's about fairness. My sense is that life has kicked the crap out of him and his family for the past few years, and he's just had enough. But they agreed not to go to the media or the courts until we talk again. And I was told he said he'd think about the offer at work. So maybe we're getting to him."

"Well, he might think that life kicked the crap out of him, but that's nothing compared to what we'll do if he doesn't come around."

"I think if we sweeten the pot, maybe be willing to publicly acknowledge some mechanical problem, he'll give in."

"That won't help our helicopter sales. But okay, if that's what gets this done," Lana said, then ended the call.

Marco thought back to Rick Morrow. The idea of breaking Morrow's spirit should have felt like a clinical exercise to Marco. It was something he'd done to Lana's adversaries a dozen times over the past two years. Instead, the pain and determination he'd seen in Morrow's eyes kept tugging at him. He realized he was desperate to get the Morrows to take the deal. It was more money than they'd ever get in a lawsuit, but just as importantly it would get them out of Lana's sights. And hopefully out of his own conscience.

He shook those thoughts from his head and headed down to the hotel bar for a drink.

Fourty

Rick, Mary and Eddie turned off Route 75 onto Jefferson Avenue the same way they had before. Rick started to pull past the side street that led down to the restaurant, but Mary tugged his arm.

"Let's use the valet," she said.

Rick shrugged but took the left turn and pulled up to the curb in front of Andiamo. The valet was a young blonde woman in a perfectly pressed brown uniform. She eyed the car suspiciously before getting in, as if wondering whether the decrepit vehicle would burst into flames before she could dump it in an out-of-sight spot in a dark corner of the garage.

"Don't forget to leave the key," she said.

"It's in the ignition," Rick said.

She looked at him quizzically. Rick pointed at the metal keychain dangling from the steering wheel stem.

"Oh," she studied the key with a distant curiosity, as if it was brontosaur bone. "We don't get many of these."

Mary grabbed Rick's arm before he could respond, and she gave the young woman a ten-dollar bill.

"Thank you, sweetie," Mary said.

Rick stared at Mary but let her guide him toward the stairs.

Marco was waiting at the same table in the corner. Mary started to wonder if this table was always reserved just for him, or maybe just for people like him.

A feeling had been building in her all day. She couldn't quite describe it, but it was some combination of terror, anger, and wild abandon. She had not slept much the prior night, and the jitters from lack of sleep just added another kind of energy to her jangled nervous system. The closest feeling she could remember was when she'd started to see the odd patterns in a set of financial statements. That suspended place, with certainty in her gut that something was wrong, but with her mind still buzzing as it tried to see the patterns in the noise.

She had told Eddie that morning to set up the meeting but had not told him or Rick about her research the night before. She had also told Eddie to demand five million dollars, not three. Marco had called back an hour later and agreed to the number. *Another wild overpayment,* she'd noted, *from a company that was legendary for fighting for every penny.* She'd added that to the stack of odd coincidences and behaviors she'd assembled the night before. The stack wasn't tall, but it was getting bigger with every question she asked.

Even when she set eyes on Marco, Mary wasn't sure what she intended to do. But looking at his even teeth and hand-made shirt, her anger and resentment just grew stronger. And so did that sixth sense that told her she was on a path to something important.

They sat down, and the same waiter appeared, hiding whatever shock he felt that these people had been allowed into his restaurant twice in one week.

"I'd like champagne," Mary said, catching Rick and Eddie by surprise.

Marco nodded. "Champagne for the table," he told the waiter, then he turned to the group and grew more somber "Before we start, I have one piece of news I thought you'd want to hear, as unfortunate as it is," Marco said.

"LifeLift has discovered some discrepancies in their maintenance records. I can't swear to it now, but it's very likely they installed a faulty fuel pump in the helicopter. The pump could very likely have failed, leading to the fire that brought the craft down."

Rick sat, stunned by the words. He'd never expected them to admit anything like that.

"It's not certain, and of course our discussions right now are confidential. But if we do reach an agreement, I suspect one thing I can commit to is that they'll issue a public statement to that effect. The truth will be out there. Assuming their investigation holds up, of course."

"We certainly would love to resolve this, "Eddie said. "And we appreciate your flexibly on the amount. And your increasing honesty in the matter."

"We're not getting more honest," Marco said. "We're just getting more information." His eyes flashed that danger signal Rick had noticed, but it was gone in an instant. "We've always wanted this to work for everyone. So, to reiterate, although we see no legal obligation here, CeraGlobal feels deeply for the pain you are going through. We do care."

Mary felt such revulsion at his words that she almost laughed. She felt she was seeing him and, through him, Cera-Global, more clearly every second. And with every layer of veneer that peeled away, she felt her own fear fade and her mind become more focused. The champagne arrived and the waiter poured each glass with great ceremony. He took their order and seemed to just fade from sight.

"So, how is your son?" Marco asked.

"He's okay," Rick said, tentatively. "He could be better. But we all know what happened there."

Marco nodded, accepting the barb. "Yes, I understand. You can't imagine the soul-searching happening inside Life-Lift now with what they've discovered. They are looking at every process, every training regimen. They are committed to learning from this, so nothing like this can ever happen again."

He looked at Rick. "I understand you've got a background in engineering and quality, don't you? I'm sure they'll be looking for qualified people to help them with that effort. And they'll pay top dollar."

"I'm happy where I am," Rick said tersely. "I've already had one job offer this week. But I'm guessing you already knew that."

Marco ignored the comment, and made more small talk during the meal, asking about David and Rick's work. He knew an awful lot about their family, Mary noted. She wondered who had done that research for him. The thought sprang into her mind that there could be a private detective waiting outside even now to follow them home. A chill of fear crept into her chest, resolving itself as a feeling of violation that only fueled her anger even more.

After the meal was cleared away, Marco reached down to his briefcase for the papers with a fluid motion that looked more like a shark striking a seal than a man rummaging for documents. "So, are we ready to get this done?" he asked.

"If I may," Mary said. "I do have a few questions first, and maybe a request or two that are not in the documents. I'm sure they are nothing major." She said the words casually, but the frost in her tone was unmistakable.

"Of course," Marco said, more slowly.

"Thanks." Mary said. "First, as a part of any deal, we'd like an opportunity to speak to the helicopter pilot."

Marco just smiled at her. "Mrs. Morrow, the entire point of this settlement is to eliminate that sort of drama, for us and for you."

"I understand," Mary said. "It's not for any sort of investigation. I just think for our sake, it would be good to clear the air on what really happened."

"I just told you what we think happened."

"Still, we'd like to talk to the pilot."

Marco sighed in frustration. "Are you still accusing him of lying?"

Mary felt the anger start to seethe in her chest, but she kept smiling.

"Not at all," Mary said. "It was a rainy, stressful night for everyone—I'm sure there's some explanation for what Rick saw, even if there was a problem with the fuel pump. Which of course you're not yet certain of. I think for everyone's sake it would be good to understand that."

"Yes, it was stressful for everyone. The pilot knew how important that trip was. And let's not forget, the crash nearly killed him. In fact, LifeLift gave him six months leave to get himself settled."

"That's generous," Rick said. "He gets six months to chill out. I got the whole weekend off. Except, of course, for becoming a suspect in the crash he caused."

"We had nothing to do with that," Marco said. "And for the pilot, I think he's decided to spend time exploring Australia and Asia. I believe he's already on his way there. So, it would be impossible to get him back for that meeting."

"You actually *make* planes, don't you?" Mary said.

"Still," Marco said. "He deserves a chance to get his life back together."

The waiter appeared again, and Mary asked for tea this time. Rick and Eddie ordered coffee. Marco just sipped his water, studying Mary. "I am sorry to be rude, Mrs. Morrow, but are we going to be able to get this done now?" he asked. "I really need to be heading out."

In that moment, the fragments of emotions, thoughts, and uneasiness that had been flitting about in Mary's mind snapped into place so hard she almost felt she could hear them click. Her heart still pounded from fear, but all her doubts were gone, and she knew exactly what she wanted to do.

"I'm sorry to be rude, too, but you can take your money and stick it," she said, her eyes boring into Marco's, all restraint gone now.

Marco froze, but his own eyes flashed brightly. Rick and Eddie also froze, not believing what they'd just heard.

"Mary, what are you doing?" Rick said, recovering first. "I meant what I said yesterday."

"We don't need your money," Mary continued, ignoring Rick, each word a dart fired right at Marco's face. "We've gotten this far without it, and we'll do just fine tomorrow." Her own anger started to boil over. "And the day after. And every day that God gives us with John."

Marco turned to Rick and Eddie. "You're letting her make a terrible mistake," he said.

"No." Mary shook her head, her eyes still locked on Marco's. "We might not have your money, or your power. But we have our pride. And we aren't going let you sweep this, and us, under the rug just to save your precious brand, or your pilot's reputation. Or whatever it is you're doing. I deserve the truth. John deserves the truth." She glanced at Rick. "My husband deserves the truth. All of it." she sat back in her chair and picked up her champagne glass.

"You think I'm lying?" Marco said.

"I think you're full of shit," Mary said. "Or to be more polite, yes, I think you're lying. Maybe you could tell us about the insurance policy Tom Richardson took out. Or the business deal between the hospital and CeraGlobal. Or why the hospital insisted on using your helicopter."

Marco willed himself to sit still as she reeled off her insights. *How could she know all that?* he thought. But part of him was impressed. Everything he'd felt about the Morrows after the previous meeting was proving even more true than he'd realized. They had a sort of courage he wasn't used to seeing in the people Lana sent him after. A sort he hadn't seen in a long time. A part of him was almost glad they'd figured those things out. But he knew Lana would be far from glad, and he knew the Morrows had no idea what Lana was capable of doing next.

As deceitful as the reasons for the offer were, Marco knew that money was still the Morrows' best bet at a future. "I don't know what you're talking about," he heard himself saying. "CeraGlobal is a conglomerate—they do all sorts of deals all over the globe. And yes, they sell insurance—to millions of people. This offer won't last, Mary," he said, almost pleading. "Please take it, for your own sake."

Mary just stared at him, resolute. Rick and Eddie just sat stone-faced, trying to get their heads around everything she'd said. Marco realized he had no chance of changing her mind. He dropped a pile of hundred-dollar bills on the table. "I'm sure this will cover dinner," he said, rising from the table. He paused and met Mary's eyes again. "Please reconsider. It's really better if you do."

Rick watched Marco finish the sentence and turn away. Rick had a fleeting thought as Marco spoke that, at the time, the man had seemed to actually believe in what he was saying.

"Mary, how, why?" was all Rick could muster, once the three of them were alone. Mary just shook her head.

They sat for a few minutes, finishing their drinks. The waiter came and collected the money with a sniff. The three worked their way through the crowded dining room and into the fresh air. Rick gave the valet the tag for the car. As the valet came back around with the vehicle Mary walked over to the dormant flower bed that fronted the restaurant between the sidewalk and the road, put her hands on her knees, and vomited into the leafless bushes.

Despite his own shock, Rick felt a bit of satisfaction as the pretty face of the valet twisted into a mask of revulsion and disbelief. He gave her another $10 bill and said, "Bad shrimp. You might want to tell the chef."

The young woman just stared at him as Mary made her way to the car and got in the passenger side. They pulled out into traffic. Mary blew a long breath out of her mouth and leaned back. From the back seat, Eddie switched his gaze back and forth between Rick and Mary. "We really ought to talk more before we have these meetings," he said.

Forty-One

"Please go through it again. And think hard if you may have left anything out." Lana said the words slowly, almost gently. She was sitting in the back of a town car, gliding through Vancouver, heading home from the CeraGlobal tower in the early evening dark. She'd spent the day reconnecting with the various businesses that made up CeraGlobal, making sure her general managers knew her absence from the office wasn't a chance for them to relax in any way.

Marco walked her through the dinner discussion again, detail by detail. Anticipating her desire to know everything, he'd even broken his own rules and jotted down some notes.

"Okay, based on what they said, what do you think they actually believe?" She said when he finished his debrief.

"I think right now they still believe we're just a big company covering its ass," Marco said. He knew there was no point in couching his phrases at this point. "But I think they'll keep pushing until they feel they get some sort of answer they trust. They're clinging to that."

"It seems all your other plans have failed; how do you suggest we stop them?"

"I'm not sure we can," Marco said. Part of him was just stating a fact, but part of him was still resisting the idea of punishing the Morrows any further, despite their own stubbornness. He realized he was still frustrated with the Morrows for not taking the deal. He could imagine the sort of misery Lana would want to rain on them now. That potential was starting to bother him as much as any retribution he'd face from Lana for his inability to win the Morrows over.

"I pay you to say you can."

"I told you this whole plan had risks."

"You didn't say that your failure was one of them."

He bit back his retort, even though he was starting to think he wouldn't care if she fired him on the spot.

There was silence on the line for a moment.

"Well, maybe you don't have any ideas, but I have one," Lana said, finally. "Although it's not something I want to do. I'll call you back in a day and fill you in."

They hung up. Lana leaned back in the comfortable back seat of the town car, looking out over the night sky of Vancouver. The vehicle reached the water, and the driver eased his way onto the road along the water, working his way towards the Cera family home, which was carved into the cliffs at the far end of the harbor. She was furious with Marco, but she'd already started to consider the idea that the Morrows might not fold. She knew from her experience selling weapons in regimes across the world that zealots with nothing to lose were the hardest people to negotiate with.

She chewed her lip thoughtfully, then sent an email to her assistant to arrange another call with the Crown Prince in Riyadh. She needed to set her final option in motion. She knew it would cost her far more than she'd had to put up for the use of the hospital. But she could not let CeraGlobal go down in ruins. And she would not let her granddaughter go through life as the girl with the stolen heart. Any price she could think of would be worth it. She started thinking through the pieces she'd need to make the one offer even zealots like the Morrows couldn't resist.

Forty-Two

"Why didn't you tell me you were going to do that?" Rick asked. He filled a cup of coffee for himself from the plastic carafe on the faded linoleum counter. Then he poured hot water from the kettle into Mary's teacup and brought it to her. She was sitting at their kitchen table, in sweatpants and a sweatshirt, waiting for David to stumble downstairs for breakfast. Rick was already dressed for work.

"I honestly didn't know I was going to," Mary said, repeatedly dunking the teabag in the steaming water as she always did. "I still can't believe I did."

"But the research you did, everything you said to him, that must have taken hours to put together. You didn't even tell me you were doing that."

"I just did it the night before. It actually wasn't that difficult." She smiled. "Old habits die hard, I guess. They're a big company. There's plenty of evidence, if you know where to look. And I do,"

Rick stayed standing, almost pacing in the tiny kitchen, his long legs covering the distance in the small room in two strides. "But what made you even do the research? I'd thought you were dead set on taking the money. Then you come of out nowhere and start dropping all this stuff on Marco. I had no idea what to think."

Mary got up and disappeared into the living room. Rick heard the closet door creak on the hinges he was always meaning to oil. She came back holding the stuffed lion he'd gotten for John, and a small box. Rick just stared for a moment. The sight of the toy sent his mind back to the night of the crash. The rain, the mud. And the smell of burning rubber from the flaming helicopter.

"How?" was all he could manage.

"A detective brought it by. He told me you'd gone to the other hospital to get the tickets."

She placed the lion on one of the kitchen chairs. Its head peeked comically over the edge of the table, as though it was waiting happily on its next meal. "I'm sorry." She said.

"You don't need to be."

"I am. For what I said that night. Thinking you were being selfish. I was the one being selfish." She sat down at the table and took a sip of her tea. "I was so mad at you for fighting everyone for everything. I think I was mostly mad because the more you fought, the more I had to admit I'd stopped fighting in ways.

"You never stop loving John. Or David."

"Or you." She said.

He smiled. "I thought you decided all of this is in God's hands."

"I still believe that's true," she said. "But I also realize that doesn't let me stop doing my part."

She set her face in a way Rick wasn't sure he'd seen before. It was a combination of love and determination that made him catch his breath. "If God does intend for John to die," sher continued, "Then so be it. But He'll have to go through us to make it happen."

They were quiet for a minute, but it was a communal quiet.

"So, what does that mean about what you said in the car? About a divorce." Rick said finally.

Mary shrugged softly. "I don't know, Rick."

"Then why'd you say it that night?"

"I felt like one of us had to," she said. She stared into her teacup for a minute, gathering her thoughts. "You're a good man. The best I've ever known. I think the only reason you stay with me is that you'd never abandon me and the kids with things being so difficult. I'm afraid you've confused obligation with love. No matter how hard things are, that's not a reason to stay together. I guess I wondered when you went through with the wedding, after John was born, if it was already becoming that."

"It wasn't."

She nodded at the question. Clearly it was one she'd been wrestling with for a while. "You were right, what you said the other night. I was afraid. I was pregnant. And alone. I'd never been alone before. Yeah, I had my degree. And a job. But in some ways, I'd always had somebody to look out for me. My parents. A boyfriend. A husband, such as he was… You were a lifeline. I grabbed it."

"So then why did you say yes?"

"I admit, maybe at first, I wondered if I loved you for loving me. But I grew to love you even more, for you, watching how you threw yourself into everything. It's not about not loving you."

They both sipped from their cups. The house was silent, except for the creaking of the floorboards upstairs as David made his way to the bathroom.

"And now you think with the money, you can just go your own way."

"The money's not the reason. I told you, I've been thinking about it for a few months."

"I'm not that shallow, to marry you just to be a hero," Rick said.

Mary smiled. "I know. I think being a hero comes naturally to you."

"I don't feel like one."

"I don't think the real ones ever do."

"So you did all that stuff because of a fake lion?" Rick asked again, smiling.

"Not entirely. When I talked to Lisa Richardson, something clicked. The things she said, and things you'd said. They all just started to seem like too much to ignore. My old forensic instincts started to kick in. And the way that guy Marco talked. Like you said, it just felt like everybody was using us somehow. Like everybody was in on some plan but us. I didn't like that feeling."

She didn't tell him about her dream. Or that she knew about the card he'd written to Tom Richardson.

"I know we should have talked ahead of time," she said. "But I don't even know what I would have told you. It wasn't until I saw his face, and everything from the day before, and the days before that it all came rushing together in my head. I was just...so angry!"

"That's how I felt at the first meeting with Marco." Rick said, smiling despite himself. "You should have seen Eddie's face when you lit into Marco. I don't know who was more freaked out, Marco or him."

Mary smiled, too. "I'll tell him I'm sorry. I'm sure he's already gotten to know our side of the family way better than he'd ever expected."

They sat quietly for a minute. In the silence some of the invisible weight that always seemed to press down on them seemed to leave the room, at least for a moment.

"If I heard you right, you're saying the pilot set the helicopter down carefully. Not at all like he was in a hurry." Mary said the words more as confirmation than challenge.

"Yes."

She nodded in acceptance. "And the cooler wasn't strapped in, like they said it was."

"Right."

"And the fire extinguisher was not stuck."

"Right again."

"You think the fire got started *after* he landed the heli-copter, and that he didn't even try to put it out or save the cooler?"

Rick nodded. "And I also think he made the distress call after he landed. I was watching the clock, to see how long it was taking to get across town. The police told me the time of the distress call. I'm positive it was *after* I saw the helicopter land."

"But why?" Mary shook her head. "Who would want to do that? The only thing in there was the heart. Who'd want to destroy that?"

Rick just shook his head. "I don't know. Rhonda said the device they'd put it in was experimental—they were testing it. Maybe somebody wanted to ruin it."

"That doesn't make much sense either."

"What does, in this whole mess?"

Mary continued. "Then the foundation for the same family company gives us a big donation. And gives Lisa Richardson a big donation. And the company buys some patent the media seemed to think was useless from the hospital for zillions of dollars. And Tom Richardson winds up with a life insurance policy with the same company that gives his wife millions of dollars, that pays out even though he kills himself. Then Marco agrees to admit they were faulty on their maintenance. And they offer us a few million dollars more, if we'll stop asking questions."

"They really want this crash to go away," Rick said.

"Actually, no. They really want *us* to go away," Mary said. "Admitting the fire was their fault will be a big hit to their business. They're willing to take that hit if it means we'll back off."

"Your complaining in the media was the only thing that kept the story alive." She put a hand on his. "I'm sorry for what I said before. I'm glad you did it." She thought for a minute. "What's next. Do we sue them? At least then we can do proper discovery like we used to do in my accounting cases. I don't know how else we learn more."

Rick shook his head. "That will take years, Eddie said. They'll just delay and delay. We don't have that..." He trailed off into silence.

"...that sort of time. I know." She said gently. "So, what do we do? The pilot's so far away now. Isn't he the one we need to talk to?"

"He'd just lie again."

"Who else would know?"

Rick thought. "Rhonda Marsh, maybe. She insisted on using the helicopter company. She made the business deal with CeraGlobal. Maybe she would know why they'd want to hide this so badly. Assuming it was them."

Mary nodded. "We need to talk to her. But I bet her lawyers have told her not to say anything."

"I can be pretty persuasive," Rick said. "I convinced you to marry me, didn't I?" He smiled wryly. "You, all pregnant and tired and mad at the world. I had to ask you three times."

Mary couldn't help but laugh at the memory. Newly divorced, throwing up every morning, lower back already aching; a marriage proposal had been the last thing she'd expected or wanted from anyone. "Yes, you know how to talk people into doing things," she said.

They both kept smiling. They sipped their drinks, each thinking about how long it had been since the air in the kitchen had felt that light. Neither one mentioned it aloud, both afraid any further words would ruin the moment.

Rick's smile faded after a bit, as he looked at the notepad in front of Mary. "But you're right. You don't need me. You've figured out more than I ever could have."

Mary looked at him, more tenderly than she had in months. "And you don't need to prove anything to anybody. Both boys are lucky to have you."

He smiled at the compliment, but only for a moment. "What am I supposed to do now, move out?"

Mary shook her head. "Let's just get through the next few days. I honestly don't know what happens next for us. But now I want to know as much as you do about what happened the other night. We *all* deserve that."

They heard David's feet popping the treads on the creaky stairs well before he came into sight. Mary got up to pour him a bowl of cereal. David shuffled into the kitchen, eyes still puffy from sleep, but already dressed for school.

His pants were already getting short on him, and the elbows of his shirt were shiny from wear. Rick thought for a moment how proud he was of David, who never complained, never demanded attention. The counselors at the hospital had always reminded Rick and Mary that David deserved a childhood too. They'd said that it was not healthy for David to have his brother be the center of the family's life all the time. But that was easier said than done. David had seemed to find a way to create his own world, in his toys and video games, often curled up in the chair next to his brother's hospital bed while doctors and nurses bustled around him. David could be there for his brother, and not there somehow. Rick just hoped the 'not there' part wasn't taking over and pulling David further away. Rick always meant to find more time for David. More activities to get him involved in. But somehow things always got in the way.

David dropped into a chair and started shoveling cereal into his mouth. Mary went upstairs to change out of her sweatpants.

"Anything big going on at school today?" Rick said to David, trying to sound more cheerful than he felt.

David just shook his head.

Rick paused. "I'm proud that you fought for your brother the other day," he began. "But you know you don't need to get yourself in trouble."

"Those kids are bullies," David said. "I don't care."

"I know. But you don't have to worry about what they say. It's just words."

"You told mom we have to fight for everything."

"I know. And I meant it. But that's for us grownups to worry about."

"So, I should just let them say those things about John?"

Rick could see the anger and hurt in David's eyes. He swallowed hard. "No, not always. It's tricky, I know. It's just that maybe you don't have to be angry all the time."

"You are."

Rick felt the stab at his heart. "I know it looks that way. It's different for grownups. Sometimes we have to fight for what's right. But you shouldn't worry about that."

"I heard you talking to mom. She said Johnny was going to die. Is he?"

Rick's heartache grew as he wondered for a minute what else David must have overheard in the past few years. When the stress was high and all the focus was on John it was easy to forget the house was small, and that David was never far away. "We were just upset after the crash."

"But she meant it."

"The doctors are doing everything they can. We can't give up hope."

"He can have mine."

"What?"

"My heart. He can have mine."

Rick smiled. "You can't give him your heart, buddy. It doesn't work that way."

"I'm not a moron. I *know* how it works. But he can have it. Then he'll be okay. You and mom will be happy."

Rick shook his head, horrified. "We would never want that, David. I know sometimes we have to focus on him, because he's sick, but that doesn't mean we love him any more than we love you. "

"It's okay if you do." David met his dad's gaze. Rick found himself staring back into a pair of eyes that looked harder and older than any ten-year-old's should. David got up and put his bowl in the sink, oblivious as only a child can be to the milk that splashed on the counter as he moved, then went into the living room to fetch his backpack.

Rick sat alone for a minute, lost in his anger at the seemingly endless pain his family was asked to endure. And more convinced than ever that he had to find a way to put a stop to it all.

Forty-Three

"My mother leaves town and now you're all ethical again?" Marie said. She picked at her dinner in the Four Seasons restaurant, stabbing quickly into the dish. Her entree was a perfectly-prepared steak from a halibut that had been caught less than a day earlier on the other side of the world.

Phillippe gritted his teeth. "That's not fair, Marie. Ethics have been my life's study for years. I *teach* them for god's sake."

"I know what you do," Marie said. "But let's face it. You've never had to live with the outcomes. You've never had to take a stand and give something up for them."

"You were one of those students once. You felt differently about them then."

"I didn't know anything about *anything*, back then." Phillippe sipped his tea, gathering his courage. "So now I do have a chance to act on them. We both do."

Marie sighed. "Oh, come on, Phillippe. This is the real world. You can't take ideas from your classroom and make them work here."

"If I can't, then what good were they to begin with? People have died defending those ideas throughout history. They aren't just classroom chatter."

"Maybe mother's right. Would we honestly let Annette be one of those people? What do you want to do, give the heart back?"

Phillippe was quiet.

"Exactly," Marie said. "I can't believe mother made this happen either. But she did. And Annette's going to live because of it."

They were silent for a few minutes. The wait staff floated around the dining room, eyes attentive for the slightest indication that a diner required attention. Groups of businesspeople, a mix of Arab robes and western suits, sat and enjoyed western steaks and local dishes, or huddled over thick, sweet Turkish coffees.

"But what Lana's done," Phillippe said finally, letting his voice dropped to a whisper. "That Morrow boy. He's probably going to die because of this."

"What my mother did was take a terrible risk to save Annette," Marie said. "I've been thinking about what she said. She has to live every day making tradeoffs most of us would have nightmares about. Like my grandfather did."

Philippe shook his head. "Just because we have the means to save our daughter, does that mean we have the right to, no matter what? Don't we have an obligation that's bigger than that?"

Marie dismissed his question with a shrug. "Those other people? Don't you think they would do the same if they could? *We* can. *They* can't. That's the only difference. That's always the only difference." She put down her fork with a clang on the mahogany table. "I think Mother's right."

They paused for a moment as the table was cleared. The waiter asked what else they'd be needing. Phillippe ordered more tea. Marie just shook her head, and the man disappeared back to the edges of the room.

"I'm still glad I made the donations."

"Jesus, Phillippe," Marie said. "Don't you realize how dangerous that is? If they start to even *guess* at what happened, you gave them a trail right back to us." She softened her voice. "It's great that you care about those people. But right now, we can't think that way. This is about our daughter. Is that how you want Annette to be known for her whole life? The girl with the stolen heart?"

"No. But how do we look ourselves in the mirror after this?"

Marie shrugged again. "Why would we have to? We didn't do this. My mother did. Annette will be alive. We're her parents. We're just protecting her. It's what we're *supposed* to do."

"Is that really all we are? Just another creature protecting our offspring at all costs like any other animal would do?"

Marie slammed her knife down on the table. The wait staff all turned in her direction at the sound but did not intrude. "All we are?" she said, her voice low, but full of anger and hurt. "You have your students, Phillippe, who hang on your every word," she said. "Mother has her business, and the power to do... whatever she wants. I've got none of that." She smiled bitterly. "Having Annette was the only thing I've ever done that my mother could be proud of. Hell, she's the only thing I've ever done that *I* could be proud of." She stood up. "I love her. And I will save her. At any cost."

Forty-Four

Murray Weiss strode into Rhonda's office in the tower building Thursday morning, holding two Starbucks cups.

"You're a hero," she said, reaching for hers.

Despite her fears from just a few days earlier, the hospital felt like it was starting to return to normal. The media had stopped calling, the surgical floor was back in operation, and the money Marco had promised had arrived via wire into the hospital's bank account. The hospital was safe. And solvent.

She had a full diary of appointments and meetings, including two interviews for a new head of nursing. She loved interviewing. Seeing the organization she'd built through the eyes of people that wanted to join it renewed her own sense of purpose. Plus, she had to admit, the ego stroke that came along with the compliments she always got from candidates was more than a little gratifying. She and Murray ran through their usual morning checklist, bouncing through topics ranging from bed utilization, cash flow, and operating costs to fundraising. They'd worked together long enough that they could speak in a form of shorthand, hitting key topics quickly and anticipating what the other would want to know. Today, those mundane topics seemed almost blissful to Rhonda. Murray, too, seemed more upbeat to Rhonda than he'd been in weeks. Being CFO in a company that was running out of money couldn't be much more fun than being its' CEO, she knew.

"The money is a real weight off your shoulders, isn't it?" she asked.

"You have no idea."

"When are you leaving to see your dad?"

"Two days probably. I just need to get a few things arranged."

"I'm sorry I pushed you not to go. I just wasn't sure what to expect."

"No worries. Neither of us was."

They finished their work around nine and Murray stood, saying he had another appointment to get to. As the door closed behind him Rhonda reached for the resume of the first candidate. Her desk phone buzzed.

"Doctor Mirchandani called for you while you were with Murray," her assistant said. "He needs to speak to you."

Rhonda sighed, frustrated that her moment of peace was being interrupted so soon. "Let him know I'll call him at lunch."

"Okay," her assistant said, doubtfully. "But he didn't seem to want to wait that long. He was...upset."

"Upset?" Rhonda had seen many sides of Kunal Mirchandani over the years while he built his reputation as a world-class heart surgeon and helped the hospital build its own. "Upset" had never been one of them.

"Yeah. Really upset. He said it was about the transplant from the other day, and the device they put the heart in. I couldn't follow all of it."

Rhonda's annoyance instantly blew back up into the quiet terror she'd just been hoping she'd left behind for good.

"See if he can come over now," Rhonda said, her own heart racing. "And see if Murray can come back, too."

She slid the resume back to the far corner of the desk and took another sip of her coffee, the surface of the liquid shimmering in time with the shaking of her hand.

Fortunately, Murray had not yet made it out of the building. He was back in her office ahead of the surgeon. Rhonda filled him in quickly.

"What could he know?" Rhonda said, fear evident in her voice. "What if he figured something out?"

"Take a breath, Rhonda," Murray said. "Let's not get ahead of ourselves." He smiled reassuringly, trying to hide his own concern.

Kunal arrived five minutes later, carrying a laptop under his arm. When he noticed Murray at the conference table he paused, clearly taken aback. Rhonda had another moment of panic when she thought Kunal would ask Murray to leave.

The doctor's urgency seemed to trump whatever concerns he had about Murray's presence. He sat down next to Murray. "Something is very wrong," he said simply. "I need to get the AionOne back from the police."

Rhonda wondered if her skin looked as flushed as it felt. The AionOne was the longevity extension system they'd used to transport Matthew Richardson's heart. "Why, Kunal?" she managed to get out.

"The data," Kunal said, nodding to himself as though that answer should have been obvious to everyone in the room.

"What data are you talking about?" Rhonda said.

"The AionOne tracks data about itself and the heart inside it." Kunal said. "Things like temperature, oxygen levels. We needed it to get FDA approval and for our own diagnostics."

"Those probably won't be too useful, now. Unfortunately," Murray said.

Kunal shook his head. "No, it is still useful. And there's more. We incorporated a lot of the same technology you'd find in your smartphone. It has an accelerometer to show if it's been dropped. A GPS, so we can track its location. Altimeter for altitude. Pretty much everything your phone tracks, it tracks. Even when we have hundreds of these in operation, we will be able to monitor each unit; where it is, how it's performing. If something goes wrong with one, we can be on it before the organs it is carrying are damaged."

"I didn't think those capabilities worked yet," Rhonda said, trying to hide her dawning horror.

"I didn't make them active on the prototypes," Kunal said, turning to face her. "But once you decided to use it to transport the Richardson boy's heart, I had my team enable them."

Kunal put his PC down on the edge of the conference table and flipped it open. "Come, look," he said to Rhonda. She came out from behind her desk and the three of them crowded around the small screen. It showed a map of the Detroit area. Kunal clicked a few keys, and a series of red dots started to appear on the map. "Those are the locations of the AionOne," he said. He pointed to the first dot, then traced his finger along the line formed by the small red circles. "It starts where it should, at this hospital. And it heads toward Metropolitan hospital, as you would expect. The dots get further apart as the helicopter gained speed."

Kunal took a breath. Rhonda could feel her heart pounding in her chest. Murray locked eyes with her for an instant. His eyes were wide. Kunal was oblivious to the two of them as he continued his narration. "But then this is when it gets odd." A series of dots appeared in a tight cluster, about halfway between the two hospitals.

"The helicopter seems to slow down, and even circle around for a bit. Then the altimeter data shows it landing."

"That makes sense," Murray said, a bit too forcefully. "That's probably when the pilot detected the fire."

"Yes, I'd think so," Kunal said. "Interestingly, he seemed to take his time landing, according to the data. That is what Rick Morrow said on the news. But that's neither here nor there for this purpose. What happens next seems to be impossible."

Rhonda waited with dread for whatever that was.

"I expected that the data would stop around this point from the fire damage," Kunal said. "And the first few times I looked at the data, I actually stopped the recording here. But last night I played it again and happened to let it run a bit longer. And saw this."

The dots started appearing in a line again, this time moving away from the crash site. They meandered a bit but then started to form a mostly straight line, getting a bit further apart. After a bit they clumped again in a small cluster some distance away from the first grouping.

"I've mapped these dots," Kunal said. "That second cluster is the airport. It seems the device was on the ground there for about ten minutes."

Rhonda stared straight ahead, not even daring to sneak a glance at Murray as Kunal fiddled with the PC. The dots might just seem like curiosities to the doctor, but to Rhonda it felt like she was seeing her fingerprints highlighted at the scene of a murder.

More dots appeared in a straight line, quickly getting very far apart, heading east. Then the line of dots ended.

"The distance of those last dots, and the altimeter data, indicates that it was on a plane that took off heading east. Once it got high enough and fast enough to make cellular reception difficult, the radio would have stopped transmitting, to save power. But the AionOne still stores that data locally to transmit once it gets back in cell tower range."

"Wouldn't it just turn back on when it landed, and tell you where it was, if that was the case?" Murray said, desperate for anything to challenge what he was seeing on the screen. "Yes, and no," Kunal said. "I haven't enabled it for all the global cellular networks. It would work in some countries, but not in others."

"But Kunal," Murray said, trying to sound reasonable. "The AionOne was in the helicopter. It was recovered. It's in an evidence locker somewhere at the police station. What these dots showed is impossible. It *has* to be bad data."

"That's why I need the machine back. It's possible the data on it can still be recovered. Maybe I can reconcile the data sets and see. If we can't prove the telemetry is reliable, it'll put our FDA approval at risk."

"The device is evidence now," Murray said. "I am sure the police have to keep it." His voice cracked a bit but the doctor, still engrossed in his own argument, didn't seem to notice.

"Evidence of what?" Kunal said. "I read the news. The police said there's no crime."

"This makes no sense, Kunal." Murray shook his head. "I hope you're not telling people about this. It could set the project back months, as you said, if the FDA thinks the AionOne is not reliable."

"No," Kunal said. "I haven't told anyone. I just asked the person at the police department if I could have it back for research purposes. I want to have the design technician look at it to tell me if maybe I am just missing something obvious."

"Let's hold off on that," Murray said. "No reason to get everyone worked up if it's just the machine going haywire from the fire, right?"

"Either way we should get it," Kunal said stubbornly. "In the worst case it will still tell us something about how the device performed after the crash. We can use it to improve survivability."

He pointed to the screen. "And if the data is still good, we'll be able to figure this mystery out. We are lucky Mr. Morrow was able to get it out of the helicopter. At least it gives us a chance."

"Yes, quite lucky," Murray said. "But let us get you the thing back first, before we start sharing this, okay?" There are competitors out there who are working on their own designs. We've got a six-month lead on them now, and let's not make them any smarter."

Kunal looked at Rhonda, clearly hoping to get a different answer from her.

"Murray is right," Rhonda said weakly. "I'll see what I can do with the police."

"Okay," Kunal said, reluctantly. Rhonda saw the distant look on his face that appeared when he was working through some complicated or unexpected problem, but then he turned and moved towards the door. In the doorway, he turned back and looked at her for a long moment. "When will we be getting the other unit back?" He asked quietly. "The one we loaned to the potential investors. I'd like to look at that one also."

"The investors might need it a while longer," Rhonda said.

Kunal set his jaw. "When did our investors become more important than our research?"

"Without the investors, none of our work would be possible, Kunal," she said. "You know this."

Kunal turned again and left the room.

"Kunal won't rest until he figures this out. You know how he is," she said, her voice shaking.

"We'll call Marco," Murray said. "This one's on him. If Morrow hadn't been able to get the AionOne out of the helicopter, there'd be nothing left for Kunal to analyze. The rest we could just chalk up to bad data. Let's let Marco fix it."

"How can he possibly do that? Sooner or later there's no reason for Kunal not to get the thing back. Do you think Marco can get the police to destroy it or lose it or something?"

"He's going to have to. Or figure something else out."

"We're not cut out for this," Rhonda said. I want to be running a hospital, not a crime ring.

"It's just a bunch of dots, Rhonda. It doesn't mean anything."

"Kunal won't agree. Neither will the police."

"I'll make sure Marco understands that," Murray said as he pushed his chair back from the table.

"I'll call you later."

Rhonda's assistant slipped in behind him as he left the office . She put a resume on Rhonda's desk, "Your interview is on the phone," she said. "Oh, and Rick Morrow has called for you twice already this morning. Do you want me to put him through next time?"

Rhonda just shook her head numbly. Her assistant looked at her oddly, then swept back out of the room.

Forty-Five

Kunal Mirchandani sat in his perfectly ordered lab, staring again at the computer screen. The dots made their familiar walk across the map, from the hospital to the crash site, to the airport, and then off into the ether. It made no sense to him. To him, things that made no sense were not things to be tolerated.

He debated for the second time calling the police to see if he could get the device himself or getting one of his technicians to doublecheck his findings. But he'd told Rhonda he would not, and so he sat tight and fumed.

He already regretted his promise to Rhonda. He could tell Murray had pressured her into her decision, putting money above medicine. Kunal was not naive; he knew that funding was essential for his own work. He was grateful to Rhonda for giving him the chances she had even when he was a young resident. She'd put him on the global stage as the hospital grew. She'd had the courage to let him pursue techniques and ideas no one else would have supported. But lately he felt that things seemed different with her. More remote. More about the business than the medicine.

He stared at the screen again, this time pulling up tables of data marked by three-minute intervals. He tried to identify where the data had gone bad. But a part of his scientific mind refused to discard other possibilities until he could get enough data to eliminate them. That included the idea that Rhonda and Murray seemed unwilling to even consider—that the data was right.

The thought that someone would have taken the AionOne and flown away with it was ludicrous of course. Rick Morrow had pulled the ruined device from the helicopter, according to the news. And even as he ran through the data, he knew the remains were sitting at a police station only a few miles from his office. He wanted to eliminate the idea as crazy, but the evidence so far would not let him. He needed to get his hands on the unit from the helicopter. For some reason, neither Rhonda nor anyone in the police department seemed eager to help him.

Then it occurred to him that even if he could not get his own hands on it right now, there was one other person who *had* handled that container after the fire. Somebody who had seen at least some of the events in real time who could help decipher the data. He opened the contacts list on his computer. He was as fastidious about his phone directory as he was anything else: if he'd seen a patient or spoken to a parent, the number would be in there. And he was closer to John Morrow than any other patient he'd had over the years.

As he'd hoped, he had a cellphone number for Rick Morrow. He'd told Rhonda he wouldn't share the data with any of his technicians. But, Kunal reasoned, a few innocuous questions to Rick Morrow couldn't cause any trouble.

Rick was at his workstation at work when the phone buzzed. He always left it on the table in case it was the hospital or Mary. He felt a little comfort when he saw the name 'Mirchandani' appear on the screen. Dr. Mirchandani had saved John's life for the first time when John was only 36 hours old. John had turned blue in the hospital nursery, and it had become apparent that his heart was unable to sustain him. Mirchandani and his team had rerouted one of the major veins in John's heart, returning the oxygen-poor blood from his upper body directly back to his lungs. It was something Rick had later learned was called the Norwood procedure. Doctor Mirchandani had operated on John again when he was three, doing something called the Fontan procedure which rerouted another major vein, basically hacking John's dysfunctional heart in ways that at least kept some amount of oxygenated blood flowing through his body. Both procedures had kept John alive and let him live a childhood that, although by no means normal, was rich and loving. But it was always clear that John's pieced-together heart would not be enough to sustain him into his teenage years, and that a transplant was always going to be needed.

Rick remembered the calm, quiet, precise voice as well. Mirchandani spoke softly, but his words had a way of being heard even in the loudest of settings. Mirchandani explained the reason for his call. He described the AionOne and asked if the black rectangular device attached to the side had looked damaged to Rick.

"There wasn't one I saw," Rick said.

"I'm sorry," the doctor said. "It would have been on the side. Black metal."

"I'm telling you, it wasn't there," Rick said. "I remember every second of that night, doctor. I can still feel the thing in my arms." He paused for a second, trying to control his emotions. "I can still see the opening on the side, and the heart inside. I can smell the fumes from the fuel. The cooler was smooth on the sides except for the tubing. There was no black metal box."

"I see, Rick. Well, that's a surprise, but helpful. And if there's anything else you can tell me about the condition of the device…"

"…How about somebody tells *me* something, for a change?" Rick shot back.

"I am not trying to anger you," Doctor Mirchandani said. "I realize how difficult all this must be. I feel some responsibility for this."

"Why did you use the damn helicopter in the first place, doctor? And why won't people just be honest about the crash?"

"I don't lie," Dr. Mirchandani said, sounding almost curious that Rick would propose that such a thing was possible. Rick took a breath.

"I know that, Doctor. But you know I was there that night. I saw what happened. The helicopter didn't crash suddenly like the pilot said. It hovered. It landed in control. Maybe there was something wrong with the engine, and the fire started on the ground. I don't know. But then why make up a story? Why attack me just for saying what I saw?"

Kunal thought back to the dots on the screen, showing the helicopter stationary over the crash site.

"Everybody thinks I'm crazy," Rick said. "But I'm not. I'm sorry to take it out on you, but I'm just pissed."

Kunal took a breath, processing everything Rick was saying, which perfectly matched the data he'd seen on the screen. "I don't think you're crazy. "He thought for a brief second and came to a decision. "I have something I think you should see."

Forty-Six

Lana waited on hold for several minutes, on an encrypted line provided to her by the Saudi intelligence agency. Waiting was not something she was accustomed to, but even she was not above a bit of inconsideration from the crown prince. His world moved at whatever pace he wished it to. Finally, he came on the line.

"Hello, Mrs. Birkhart." Engaging with her, a divorced woman, at all was out of the ordinary for a Saudi male, and so even now he pointedly used her married name. Curiously it was one she never used and had, in fact, never told him.

"It is gracious of you to take the time," she said, continuing the formality.

"Your granddaughter, she is doing well?" the prince said.

"Yes, she is. Thank you again for your help with her procedure."

"Of course," the prince said. "Nothing is more precious than our family, yes?"

Lana felt the first vibration of an undefined fear at his too-casual words. She'd learned from her past dealings with the prince that the more reasonable he sounded, the less reasonable his negotiating terms were likely to be.

"I have looked into your request," he said. "It is a difficult one, as you can imagine."

In other negotiations, she'd test his own urgency, acknowledging the difficulty of the task and making clear that her request wasn't so important to her that she'd put him out in any way. They'd do that dance for days, maybe even weeks.

But now she had no time for subtlety. "But it can be done?" she asked.

There was a pause, and she winced. Suggesting anything was beyond his abilities was tantamount to just giving him the finger. Coming from a woman, it was nearly unthinkable. "I meant, can it be done within my means of repaying you, Prince Nassir."

"It can be, of course, I believe," he said, apparently mollified by her recovery. "But it's highly unusual, even for us. Of course, only you can decide if the price is a fair one."

She felt the fear ratchet up in the back of her neck but pressed on. "I realize that. I am willing to keep our same terms for the next two contracts. You'll get twice the equipment you would otherwise receive."

He sighed. Lana could picture the shrug; the uniquely Arab gesture that somehow embraced both the prince's total subservience to the will of Allah and his complete comfort in the unlimited power he wielded over all around him.

"That is a very nice gesture, Mrs. Birkhart. But for what you are asking, we require something more. This is a big undertaking, even for us. If it were to become public, you can imagine the consequences to our reputation."

Lana gritted her teeth. In a kingdom that routinely tortured and killed its own citizens, what she was asking did not seem that far out of the ordinary. "What is it you wish, Prince Nassir?"

He explained in great detail what he wanted. Lana listened silently, terror and anger growing in her as he spoke.

"You know I cannot do that, Prince Nassir," she said, more forcefully than she intended. "It would be treason. It would mean the end of my company. Surely there must be something else."

"I'm afraid that's what I require, Mrs. Birkhard. The stakes are high for both of us, I realize that. We will be sharing the risk together. I trust you would be good with that."

"Please," Lana found herself saying, through clenched teeth. She felt herself falling into a bottomless pit as they spoke. "You can't require this of me, your highness."

"Of course, I cannot require it," the prince said smoothly. "We each make our choices. You may choose to say no and live with the consequences if you cannot control the situation you yourself have created. I can choose to move on, too. I'm sure I can find another vendor for my aviation needs. And, I'll have avoided a very real risk that I'm only considering taking because of my family's long-standing relationship with yours. I knew your father and grandfather quite well, you recall. We had a great deal of ... trust between us."

"They always spoke highly of you," she said. She'd come to know over time the secret deals the families had made in far corners of the world. Those past deals had been the foundation of CeraGlobal's growth. She feared this one might be the cause of its demise.

Lana weighed her options, which were really no options at all. Annette's face swam in front of her as she sought desperately for a way out of the noose the prince was closing around her neck.

"Thank you, your highness. I'll do what you ask, but only if my needs require it when the time comes." She knew it was dangerously cheeky to put in that qualifier, but felt she had to try and save face at least a little.

"Yes, of course," he said. "These are choices only for the most difficult of times. I am sorry you find yourself in such a time now."

Lana hung up, thinking bitterly that the prince clearly was quite happy for her 'most difficult of times.'

Forty-Seven

Marco stayed in the shadows as he followed the doctor. His instinctive concealment was the result of years of training and still more years spent in some of the most dangerous places on earth.

Doctor Mirchandani, on the other hand, strode blithely along the sidewalk, never glancing once into the alleys he passed or stopping to see if he was being followed.

Marco kept his eye on the backpack slung over the doctor's shoulder. Every few minutes the doctor shifted its weight on its shoulder, seemingly as much to reassure himself that it was there as to reduce any discomfort.

Marco had had only had a day to plan, and he didn't love all his options. It was a busy neighborhood. Open shops everywhere. Regular police patrols. Very little intel on the target's patterns. It'd be called a shit-show in the military, and it smacked of one here, but time was his enemy. He'd only learned the prior night that the doctor insisted on walking the blocks from the hospital to his condominium. The route was largely lined with apartment buildings with a few restaurants and retail stores mixed in on the first floors of the three and four-story buildings. A few minutes online had confirmed to Marco that despite the luxury cars on the street and the designer brands in the store windows, people still got robbed from time to time in the area. That fact would certainly help create the story he hoped the police would buy into after he was long gone. The doctor's route took him through an older section of Detroit. Although the sidewalk was fairly well lit, there were some odd corners, narrow alleys, and blind spots Marco could use to his advantage.

The spot he'd chosen was still a few blocks up, where the buildings thinned out and a bit of hedge shielded the view from the road. He was about to take a left to cut over to a parallel street and get ahead of his target when the doctor stopped, looked around briefly, then entered a coffee shop, working his way around the metal tables on the open sidewalk.

Marco cursed at the unexpected event. He debated using the extra time to get himself into position up ahead. But despite the doctor striking him as a man of routine, Marco hadn't had his usual days or weeks of intel to really confirm the man's habits. Marco decided to make sure this disruption didn't signify anything important.

A minute or two later, a city bus unloaded its occupants onto the pavement at the corner. Even from this distance, under the bright streetlight marking the bus station, Marco could make out Rick Morrow's long frame and short-cropped hair.

Now the doctor's change in route made sense to Marco. And now things were far more complicated.

Sure enough, as soon as he had his bearings, Morrow headed straight for the coffee shop. Marco considered his options. Morrow would recognize him if he saw his face. But Marco was in a pair of nondescript jeans, a hooded sweatshirt and baseball cap—hardly the thousand-dollar blazer

Morrow was used to seeing him in. Marco decided to take a chance.

He took out his cellphone and held it casually as he approached the coffee shop. He kept his back to the window and held the phone as though checking an email. He stopped in front of the metal tables, turned on the selfie mode and angled the lens to point into the shop. Reflections from the streetlight and passing cars didn't help, but the bright lights inside did. What he saw was enough to confirm his fears. Morrow and Mirchandani were sitting at a table against the side wall. As Marco watched, Mirchandani reached into his bag, pulling out his PC.

Marco figured he'd tested his luck enough. He put away the phone and retreated to his original vantage point. His choices were now more limited than ever but waiting did not seem like one of them. He decided he should still follow through on the plan for tonight. At least he knew for sure that the doctor had the computer with him. He'd talk to Lana in the morning to figure out what she wanted to do about Morrow.

Ten minutes later, still inside the coffee shop, Rick was wishing the doctor had chosen a bar instead. Mirchandani had walked him through the data, showing him the red dots and explaining the significance of their spacing and timing. Rick told him about the SUV that nearly ran him off the road, heading away from the crash site even as he approached it. And he confirmed again that there was no black metal box affixed to the container.

The two men sat in silence for a bit, trying to comprehend the possible implications of what they were seeing.

"Have you told the police about this?"

"No. I showed Rhonda Marsh and Murray Weiss. Rhonda said she would try and get the AionOne back from the police so I could study it more. I was going to show the data to my lab tech, since she wrote the software, but Rhonda asked me to hold off on that."

"It seems crazy. Who'd take that device?"

"First off, this is still just a possibility, Rick. That's why I wanted to know what else you saw."

"But still," Rick said, hanging onto his prior question.

"Well, distance is one of the biggest constraints on organ donation," Mirchandani said. "Organs can't last too long even on ice. Donor and recipient need to be pretty close geographically. The AionOne eliminates that. Twenty-four hours gets you anywhere on the planet, with the right plane. Rhonda's plan was to partner with a medical device company and share in the profits—it will be highly valuable." He shrugged. "Maybe someone wanted to steal a functional one, to learn how it worked. We're in clinical trials with it, so it's not a secret we've developed it. There are countries that don't worry much about patent protections. Possibly it was taken to one of them to reverse-engineer."

A group of high schoolers piled into the coffee shop, all puffy coats and brightly colored backpacks, chatting and laughing as they ordered their lattes and cappuccinos.

Rick leaned in closer to Doctor Mirchandani to avoid shouting. "It will be valuable for you, too, right? Rhonda said you're the inventor."

"Yes, it could be lucrative for me."

"I talked to Rhonda the day of the crash. She said you'd agreed with her decision to use it."

Rick stated it as a fact, not an accusation, but the doctor shook his head vigorously regardless. "My only priority was John," he said. If I'd had my way, we'd have done both procedures in the same hospital. But Rhonda said the Richardsons objected, and that we'd just fly the heart between the hospitals." He seemed to disappear inside himself for a moment, apparently reliving his debate with Rhonda. "I told her it wasn't clinically necessary. But she was stubborn. So, I relented." He looked at Rick sadly. "I wish I'd fought harder."

"I know that feeling," Rick said. He took a breath. He already thought he knew the answer to his next question, but some part of him demanded he ask it anyway. "For that theory to be true, they had to have transferred the heart to some fake version of the AionOne and put the fake in the helicopter. I guess the idea would be that it would get destroyed beyond recognition by the fire?"

"No, the heart was still in the original, functional device," Mirchandani said. "The data would have shown if it had been disconnected from the feeding tubes."

"But I saw the heart, at the crash. In the thing."

Mirchandani shook his head. "You saw *a* heart. But the data is clear. The AioOne was still monitoring a healthy heart before it went out of tracking range. There was no way anyone could have replaced Matthew Richardson's with another working heart.

"Then the heart I saw?"

"I hesitate to think where that came from."

Rick's own heart skipped a beat as an impossible hope flitted through it. "Could the real heart still be out there somewhere. Could it still be ... okay?"

Doctor Mirchandani shook his head. "I'm sorry, Rick. There's no way. Even in the best of circumstances, the

AionOne could only keep it healthy for a day or so. I was so excited for John. You know he's always been special to me."

Rick swallowed hard at those words, even though he'd expected them. But another question occurred to him. "If the AionOne that you were tracking went somewhere else, where did the one in the helicopter come from?

"There's only one other functional unit. Rhonda Marsh sent that to some potential investors who'd wanted to see it first-hand, about a week before the crash. Either someone would have had to use that one, or create a fake one based on the few pictures that have been shown to the media."

"Where were those investors?" Rick was betting he already knew the answer to this question, too.

Doctor Mirchandani searched his memory for a second. "Someplace in Canada, I think."

Forty-Eight

A few minutes later, Marco watched Rick Morrow leave the coffee shop and took a left toward the bus stop another block away. Morrow exited the shop alone, leaving the doctor inside. Marco turned his attention back to the coffee shop. Moments later, the doctor exited the coffee shop and walked quickly in the same direction as the bus stop, away from Marco's location. Marco sighed in relief when he saw that the doctor was back on his expected route.

Marco decided to continue with the plan. It was pretty clear the doctor had shown the tracking data to Morrow, but Marco had to hope he hadn't given him a copy of it. Either way, the doctor, with his PC, was still the target. Marco let the doctor get a a bit further away then stepped out onto the sidewalk. He decided he'd trail the man for a few blocks, then cut left to sprint around the narrow block using a parallel side street he'd located. That route would let him get ahead of his quarry without attracting much attention and be in position to execute the plan.

Fully focused on spotting Mirchandani ahead of him, he didn't note the passing traffic or hear the growing whining of the city bus as it picked up speed from its most recent stop.

Rick had dropped into a window seat on the sidewalk side of the half-full bus. The passengers on this route were a mix of professionals going home from the hospital and medical center, and hourly workers from the few factories that still ran on that side of Detroit. Some of the young professionals had eyes glued to their phones, faces painted a deathly white by the bright screens. Most of the others sat silently in the semi-comatose state that made the tedious bus trip and proximity to total strangers a bit more bearable.

The bus lurched into traffic and Rick watched the storefronts roll by. He saw Doctor Mirchandani stepping out of the coffee shop and turning up the road, facing the approaching bus. Rick could see into the warm-looking shop, where Doctor Mirchandani had shown him the data. What the doctor had showed him had seemed impossible. But it still screwed tight the certainty in Rick's heart that the helicopter crash was no accident at all. What Rick couldn't stand to think was that the heart itself might not have mattered at all. That the organ that could have saved John's life had just been a piece of useless flesh in a new high-tech container that could spell millions of dollars in profit for some subsidiary of CeraGlobal.

Rick tried to push away images of the heart being tossed out on the side of the road from a speeding car or left in the trash in some tech lab. Anger and grief washed back and forth over him.

His mind went back to the bright lights of Metropolitan Hospital in the distance from the rooftop landing pad, and the cool air on his face. He'd been so excited to see the helicopter waiting there. Now he felt foolish once again, thinking the destruction of the craft was just a rounding error in somebody else's plan. He thought of going to the police himself. Mirchandani may have promised otherwise to Rhonda, but he hadn't. And he realized he was frustrated that once again Rhonda Marsh had taken such a gamble with the helicopter and the device, putting herself and the hospital ahead of him and John.

Then realization came over him like a flood. So many pieces of information snapped into place at once. The helicopter. The money flowing between between CeraGlobal and the hospital. The payout offers.

Rhonda Marsh wasn't just working after the fact, protecting the hospital from whatever had happened. She had been a part of it from the start.

Even as that implication hit him, a figure caught his eye on the sidewalk. A man walking quickly along the uneven concrete, a baseball cap pulled low over his eyes. Something about his smooth, almost cat-like walk drew Rick—a familiarity he couldn't place. Then as the bus drew across from him, the man stepped through the light spilling out of a laundromat. For a moment the glare reached under the ball cap and Rick caught a glimpse of a profile. It was Marco, hooded sweatshirt bunched around his neck, head down low, tracking Doctor Mirchandani's route. With dawning horror, Rick realized that was why Rhonda Marsh had told Doctor Mirchandani not to go to the police. It wasn't to buy time to help him learn more. It was to buy time for Marco to get rid of whatever the doctor already knew.

Rick pulled out his phone and dialed Doctor Mirchandani's number, but the call went straight to voicemail. He jumped to his feet, startling the passengers nearby from their stupor or text exchanges. "Stop the bus!" he yelled. The driver looked up into his mirror at the commotion.

"Next stop a few blocks up, sir. Not safe to stop here."

Rick stumbled his way forward as the bus bounced over a series of potholes. "No. I need to get off now."

The driver shook his head emphatically. The other passengers slumped down further in the slick vinyl seats, resigned to the idea that the ranting man at the front was likely to delay their trip home even further.

"There's going to be a crime!" Rick shouted.

"Okay, Nostradamus, settle down," the driver said. "Two blocks up and you can throw on your cape and go take care of it." The bus continued to roll forward, even as Doctor Mirchandani and his stalker moved further in the opposite direction. Rick could feel the distance growing between him and the two men on the sidewalk, and between him and any chance to stop whatever Marco intended.

"Let me out now," Rick begged. "I can still stop it."

"Sit down now, sir," the driver ordered. "I can't let you off here." He gestured towards the door-side of the bus. A steel guardrail flashed by; they were on an overpass that spanned the train tracks. There was no sidewalk or shoulder on the side of the road. No way out for Rick, as the distance between him and the impending disaster behind him kept growing and growing.

Forty-Nine

Marco crouched behind the trash barrels in the narrow alley between two brick-faced apartment buildings. His heart was pounding from his sprint around the block to get ahead of the doctor. He'd silently moved the metal barrels so that he could remain out of sight in the shadows but still see a good bit of the sidewalk. He slipped on the tight leather gloves he'd adopted for this sort of work and pulled the balaclava up over his face.

The ground underfoot was cobblestone, covered in grit and bits of broken glass. He'd need to be careful not to make noise with his first step.

He saw the wiry doctor approach. The backpack was slung over the man's right shoulder leaving it facing the road, not the alley side where Marco waited. That would make things a bit trickier but not impossible, Marco thought. As the doctor passed in front of the alley, Marco covered the ground in two quick, noiseless strides. Mirchandani barely had time to turn before Marco was on him. Marco grabbed the doctor's right shoulder with his own left hand and spun the man back into the alley, out of sight of the road. After two quick punches from Marco's right hand, the doctor dropped to the rough ground.

Marco wrestled the backpack from Mirchandani's shoulder. Even in his stunned state, the doctor tried to paw at the pack. "Take my money," he begged. "There's nothing else in there you want."

Marco tore the shoulder strap from the man's hand. From the weight he could guess the laptop was still in it. He'd considered rifling the doctor's pockets for the wallet to add to the story but had decided against it. The quick grab of the backpack was a better imitation of the addicts who caused most of the crime in this neighborhood.

He turned and sprinted back along the alley to the far end. He'd chosen his escape route to hopefully make it several blocks away from the crime scene without seeing a soul. He checked for cross traffic at the end of the alley and then walked quickly but casually across the street and towards another alley on the opposite side. He'd just reached the second opening when he heard a shout behind him. He turned to see doctor Mirchandani stumbling into the road, dazed but still doggedly pursing him. Marco barely had time to process the image before the shout was drowned out by the screech of tires on pavement. An enormous pickup truck struck Mirchandani full-on just as the doctor gestured towards Marco. Mirchandani flew through the air, arms pinwheeling, and rolled to a stop in the middle of the street. Marco froze in horror. He stepped back towards the scene as the driver of the pickup got out and rushed towards the motionless body. Marco saw the driver frantically calling emergency services.

Marco hesitated, his desire to help his unintended victim competing with his decades of training to put the mission above all else. His training won out and he turned back into the alley before the driver could spot him.

In the shadowy corner of a small, wooded park he took a leather satchel out of the gym bag and slipped the PC into it. He took an expensive leather jacket out of the gym bag too, and stuffed the backpack, hat, gloves and hoodie into the gym bag. He'd located two unlocked dumpsters along this route in the short time he'd had to plan the action. He continued his route, dropping the backpack into one of the dumpsters, covering it with cardboard, and dropping the gym bag into the other, three blocks away, also covering it to be sure it wasn't visible to any casual observer. As he worked, the image of the doctor kept trying to fight its way into his mind. He pushed it away, but the sick feeling growing in his stomach kept getting stronger. He'd probably killed the man. That was something he'd vowed he'd never do again.

Finally, wearing the leather jacket and satchel and rid of the bags, he'd completed the transformation from local gym rat to stylish businessman. He kept up a brisk walk for three more blocks, hearing sirens in the distance. He had no doubt they were responding to the driver's call. He reached a busier main road where he could hail a cab. He had the cab drop him off four blocks from the Marriott and paid with cash, hands still trembling.

Fifty

"Call 911," somebody said tiredly from the seats behind him. Rick wasn't sure if the suggestion was meant for him to call in the crime he was shouting about or for the driver to call in about the crazed man on the bus, but he didn't care either way. He thought for a moment about calling the police himself, but what would he say? Once again, he had no evidence, nothing to give them other than his own beliefs.

`Instead, Rick eyed the controls in front of the driver, looking for a lever that would open the door. He was willing to jump out of the moving vehicle, despite the narrow space between the door and the metal barrier. Nothing stood out at him. The bus approached a traffic light as it turned yellow. For a minute Rick thought the driver would stop at the light, trapping him even longer, but the man hit the gas instead, speeding through the intersection then immediately slowing down hard as he pulled to the curb in front of a bus shelter. Rick was nearly thrown into the windshield, but he managed to grab an overhead rail. The driver opened the door and Rick dove out, knocking aside two young men as they waited to board. They shouted obscenities but he was already running back through the intersection towards the coffee shop. Cars beeped as he sprinted across the overpass.

The space between the vehicles and the guardrail was even less than he'd thought when he'd seen it through the glass of the bus door. He had to twist sideways once to avoid the extended door mirror of a pickup truck. Once across the elevated road, the sidewalk reappeared. He ran hard, mind racing. Rick couldn't imagine that Marco and the doctor had a planned meeting, unless everything he'd thought about Mirchandani was wrong. His lungs burned as he passed the gleaming lights of the coffee shop. His tireless focus on work, John, and his family left little for anything else, including exercise. And the cigarettes he's been sneaking didn't help.

Two blocks after the coffee shop, he saw a handful of people gathered at the far end of a small alley. He saw that the alley seemed to connect the avenue he was on to a parallel road. One man was kneeling next to a figure lying in the middle of that other road. Even at that distance Rick recognized the jacket of the man on the ground. It was Doctor Mirchandani.

Rick pushed through the group to the doctor. The kneeling man was in his sixties, dressed in jeans and T-shirt. He was explaining to the people around him how the man on the ground had just stumbled out of the alley in front of his pickup truck, without even looking to either side.

"Probably on drugs," somebody muttered.

There was blood on Doctor Mirchandani's face, and his eyes were rolled back in their sockets. But Rick could hear labored breath over his own gasps. Mirchandani was alive.

"Doctor," Rick said, putting a hand on the fallen man's shoulder. There was no response.

"You know him?" the kneeling man said.

"Yes," Rick said, still fighting for breath.

"Police are on their way," the man said, holding up the cellphone. "I didn't even have a chance to stop. He came out of nowhere."

Rick turned to the growing crowd. They ranged in age from twenties to seventies, mostly with thrown-on jackets and hats. All drawn from nearby apartments by the commotion, Rick figured.

"Did anyone see what happened?" Rick shouted to the group.

They all shook their heads, some muttering various disclaimers about watching TV or doing dishes.

Rick saw blue lights flashing off the windows above, signaling the approach of the police car. The image of the crash site rose up vividly in his mind; the blue lights flashing off gaping, broken windows and wet concrete. The hard ground and the smell of the burning helicopter. And his own total helplessness once again.

The police arrived seconds later and took control of the situation. The ambulance followed just a few minutes later.

The police began quizzing the crowd looking for witnesses or details, as the paramedics hovered over the Doctor. Rick heard one of the EMTs say "severe head trauma," to his female partner. The cops asked the driver of the pickup truck if he'd take a breathalyzer test. He nodded. "I'm just coming from work," he said. "I ain't had a drink in two days. Not sure about this guy though," he said, pointing toward the doctor. "He stumbled out into the road from the alley. Didn't even look."

"He wasn't drunk," Rick said, starkly, when he could get the attention of one of the cops.

The officer doing the bulk of the questioning, a stocky young woman with blond hair pulled tight behind her head, paused in surprise. "How do you know?"

"It wasn't an accident. It was a robbery. He must have been chasing the man who robbed him. I know who did it."

"You saw?" she said, readying her notepad.

"No," Rick said. "I saw the man earlier, following this guy."

"Where'd you see this?"

Rick recounted the bus ride, and his glimpse of Marco through the window.

"You sure?" the cop said. "You saw him from across the street, while you were on the bus?" Rick could see the skepticism on the young woman's face, and he felt his anger rise.

"Yeah, I'm sure. Ask the bus driver. I told him to stop. I told him something was going to happen." The cop turned to the driver of the pickup, who was still clearly shaken up from the incident. She asked him if he'd seen anybody with the doctor or on the street.

He just shook his head.

"The victim still has his wallet. And his watch and phone," the cop said to Rick. "Doesn't look like a robbery at all."

"He had a backpack," Rick said. "That was taken."

The cop looked at Rick skeptically. "But you weren't here. You didn't see any of that."

"No," Rick admitted. "But he had it when I met with him. Now he doesn't."

"And you say you know who did it."

"The guy you want is here on business. I think he's Canadian. I don't know where he's staying. Someplace downtown. Someplace nice, I'm sure. I know his name. And where he works."

"He's here on business, staying in some swanky hotel, but he rolled the doctor in an alley out here, and left his watch and his wallet?" Rick could see her skepticism grow.

"I know it sounds crazy," Rick said. "The doctor had a laptop. I think the guy who attacked him wanted what was on it. I have a cellphone number." Rick pulled out his phone and found the number from when Marco had called him to set up the meetings. Rick recited it to the woman. She wrote it down but then flipped her notebook shut.

"Aren't you going to call it?" Rick asked.

The cop glared at him. "We'll wait for this guy to wake up, and we'll ask him what happened. Then we'll go from there."

The paramedics loaded Doctor Mirchandani into the ambulance, and sped off, lights flashing and sirens wailing. The sound of the sirens reminded Rick of his own ride to the hospital two weeks earlier, strapped in the back of an ambulance, consumed by helplessness and grief. He'd been too late then to save the heart. And he was too late now to save the only person who may have known what actually happened to it.

Fifty-One

Once back in his hotel room, Marco changed his pants and swapped his sneakers for loafers. He opened the minibar, pulled out a nip bottle of scotch and downed it in one motion. The image of the doctor was still seared in his mind. He'd vowed years ago never to let another man die because of his own carelessness or poor judgement. But he'd seen enough violence done to men to know there was almost no way the doctor could survive the impact with the pickup truck. He paced around the room, replaying the event moment by moment, trying to make the outcome change. In the end, the doctor still wound up lying broken in the road. Marco was left wondering why a man like that should die for Lana Cera. And how he himself had gotten to the point where he could be the one who made it happen.

He called down to the valet to have his car brought around. He headed out of his room, the satchel over his shoulder. His mind was forcing itself into autopilot, back in the mode from years ago where he knew he'd drive himself to complete his mission, pushing aside the cost to himself or others. But part of him couldn't help but think that back then at least the missions had felt worthwhile, even if the cost was high.

He collected the car from the valet then worked his way through the city to Route 96 and took it a few exits out of the downtown area. Once off the highway, he found a deserted lot in one of the area's many decaying neighborhoods. The houses around were mostly boarded up. He scanned quickly but thoroughly for security cameras regardless.

Confident he was not being watched or recorded, he tossed the PC on the pavement and ran it over multiple times with the rental car, hearing the snapping and crunching as the device was crushed under the tires. After he'd reduced it to a tangle of circuit boards and scattered bits of plastic, he tossed the wreckage into a nearby sewer drain and made his way back to the hotel.

Marco was back in his room by 9:30. Despite the gut-wrenching guilt he felt about the doctor, his discipline still held. Mostly. He ran through his evening again, trying to think of any places where he may have been seen, or may have left evidence tying him to the actions in the alley. He came up with none, so he pulled another small bottle of scotch out of the minibar. He finished it and one more. After an hour, he felt tired and drunk enough to go to bed.

He woke up to pitch blackness, hands clawing at the air around him, the covers tangled around his legs, the cotton sheets cold and damp. He clicked on the bedside light and sat until his heart slowed down. It was the usual dream. The spiders and ants, crawling on his filthy skin. The smell of rotting leaves and his own sweat. But now a new image was there, too: the slim form of the doctor catapulted through the air by the pickup truck, arms spinning from the force of the collision.

Marco knew he wouldn't get back to sleep. He had no desire to try. *Move forward*, he told himself. That's what had been drilled into him all those years in the field; no matter what happens, no matter who dies next to you, or how bad the situation looks, keep moving forward. It's how he'd survived three days lost in the jungle after that night, with shrapnel from an RPG lodged in his thigh. Walking one agonizing step at a time toward the east, until he'd wandered out into a field near a UN aid station. Remembering the cries of his two squad mates when the guerrillas had tripped over them in the dark and dragged them away for a night of torture and a horrible death that, by the end, probably couldn't come fast enough.

Right now, Marco knew moving forward meant stumbling out of bed to the small desk and firing up his computer. The lock screen showed a cabin, high in the mountains of Canada. Above the tree line. Above the spiders and the ants. And the smells of wet earth, rotting vegetation. Away from selfish people and ambiguous morals. He stared at the image for a minute, then went to work.

First, he checked on the social media campaign. The first wave of retweets and posts were dying down now, but the effort had done what it was meant to. Rick and Mary no doubt felt like the whole world had turned against them. Marco added one more bit of new information to the mix, sending a few new Tweets and posts to his contact in the Philippines. Another wrinkle to the coverage would light the internet back up again, just when the Morrow's thought that maybe they'd gotten through the worst of it.

Next, he opened the command-and-control software that ran the malware embedded in the thumb drive he'd given Mary. As he'd hoped, the malware was beaconing, letting him know it was installed and active. He scanned the information provided by the malware; the PC Rick and

Mary owned was many years old. He shook his head in disbelief; had the operating system been one version older, his software would not even have worked. The hacker that supplied it to him must not have imagined anyone could still run a computer that outdated.

He continued to scan the data and found what he was looking for. One of the things the malware did was log all the keystrokes entered via the keyboard, tracking every word any user wrote. It also parsed that data, looking for certain kinds of information. It was an elegant piece of software and in only a few minutes Marco had what he needed. He began copying all the email traffic from Mary's accounts, and all the emails saved on the computer. The malware would even scan the hard drive for emails Mary thought were long-since deleted. It was amazing, Marco thought, how little people know about the digital devices they entrusted with their most important secrets. He typed in a command to kick off another utility that would scan the emails for keywords, names, addresses and phrases that he thought could be useful; that would filter out all the spam traffic and inane crap that filled most people's mailboxes.

In a few minutes the program had winnowed the file down, but it was still hundreds of emails. Marco started scanning them in chronological order. The communications started almost immediately after John's birth, as Mary reached out to friends in panic and grief, responding to notes of congratulation on the birth of her son with carefully worded, hopeful responses about complications and tests. They devolved over time into grinding narratives with insurance agencies and doctors over bills, treatment regimens, and John's tenuous hold over life. Marco started to get a sense of the slow downward spiral of the Morrows into a constant state of stress, worry, and dashed hopes.

Some of the emails were commiserations between Mary and her close friends over the pressures on her marriage and family. They spoke about Rick's single-minded effort to fix an unfixable situation at the exclusion of almost all else in his life. And Mary's loneliness as she tried simply to make sure her son felt loved, even as she and Rick were drawn further into their own private wells of grief and pain, unable to help each other or themselves.

Marco had seen families destroyed by rockets raining down from the sky. He'd seen men have limbs hacked off by warlords, simply to punish them for the way they voted in elections. Women raped by bands of soldiers as the ragtag militias swept through ruined villages.

But those had been moments in time. Awful moments, but moments he'd witnessed from a distance, or events he'd interrupted with rifle fire of his own. The glacially slow, unyielding crush of events that was destroying the Morrow family day by day was something different, he realized. It was free of the bloodshed and searing imagery he'd witnessed first-hand in Africa, but somehow, even though he was seeing it through a string of stolen files, it felt more personal, almost intimate to him as he read email after email.

He realized when he got to the end of the file that he'd been lost in the documents for almost two hours. He stretched out his neck and shook himself out of his reverie. He felt even dirtier now, he realized, knowing he was a main contributor to the latest chapter in Rick and Mary's sad and lonely story.

Fifty-Two

By the time Rick got home, Mary had put David to bed. The remains of a pot of spaghetti sat on the narrow electric stove. He ignored it and told Mary about the meeting with Mirchandani, and the questions raised by the data from the heart container. Mary put a hand to her mouth as he told her what had happened after. Of all the doctors they'd encountered, Rick knew she had also felt he was one of the few who'd not just worked on John, but who'd actually cared about him.

"Marco did it. I know it." Rick said. "I keep thinking about how he played with the knife at the table that night, like it was so natural he didn't even think about it,"

Mary said. "You need to tell the police. This time they'll have to do something."

"I did tell them." He thought back to the look of doubt on the officer's face, standing over Doctor Mirchandani's body. "They won't do a damn thing. At least not anything serious. I could already tell."

Mary paced. While she usually moved around the kitchen with an unconscious competence and grace, gained from years of perfecting the location of every utensil, every jar and box to maximize the use of the tiny space, now she seemed trapped by it. "Can this really be happening?" she asked. "Things like this? They don't actually happen in the real world, do they?"

"Everything that's happened to John is something that shouldn't happen," Rick said.

Mary's eyes were blazing. "Lisa Richardson told me Rhonda was the one who suggested leaving their son at Saint Elizabeth's in Pontiac. It wasn't the Richardsons' idea at all. That's why Rhonda convinced them. So she and whoever she was working with would have an excuse to use the helicopter."

"I don't think she would do it alone. She already had the transport container. And the heart. What did she have to gain for herself?"

Mary thought for a moment. "A lot of money from the CeraGlobal companies. I saw that in the news reports. Maybe there was something about that device she didn't want anyone to know. Maybe it wasn't going to work after all, and she wanted to hide that fact for a little longer? Maybe they were going to sell the device to somebody else, too."

Rick searched for a beer in the half-empty fridge, pushing aside a few containers of leftovers and the odd container of milk or juice. He thought of the doctor's eyes, rolled up in his head. "Doctor Mirchandani might be dead. It was that bad."

Mary trembled. Rick couldn't tell if it was fear or anger. She seemed to gather her courage. "There's one more thing," she said. Rick just looked at her, wondering what else could get piled onto the mountain of difficulty they were already facing.

She took a breath. "The websites. The really nasty ones. Now they're saying John's not your son."

"He *is* my son," Rick said reflexively, but he felt the blood drain out of his face.

"I don't know who told them, but they figured it out. Now they're saying that the only reason you'd adopt a kid with his condition is because you knew you'd find a way to cash out sooner or later."

Rick slumped back in the chair. "Who thinks of things like that?" he said. "Who hates anybody so much they'd say that?"

"And they're saying worse things, too, about how maybe I lured you into it. To give me help with John. They've made up whole stories about us that aren't true."

"Screw that. We need to get to what *is* true then," Rick said. "Something that can prove things Mirchandani showed me are true. Something to make the police pay attention. Or make Marco back off."

"We're not cut out for this, Rick. Without the data from the PC, what can we do?"

"There's one more thing we can try," Rick said. "Doctor Mirchandani said he had an assistant."

Fifty-Three

Rick found a woman named Shreya Kim listed as a research assistant for Dr. Mirchandani on the hospital's website. He dialed the number listed for the lab.

What sounded like a young girl's voice answered after two rings. For a moment Rick thought he'd dialed the wrong number, but the display on the phone showed otherwise.

"Hello, is this Shreya Kim?" he said, into the long pause he'd left.

"Yes," said the voice at the other end of the phone. Rick could hear the question in her voice.

Rick explained who he was and his meeting with Dr. Mirchandani in the coffee shop. "He said the only copy of the data was on his PC. But I'm hoping maybe there was some possibility of a backup or something?"

"I'm sorry," she cut him off. "There's nothing I can do to help."

"You're his assistant."

"I am. But I can't help you."

From the finality in her voice Rick guessed the next thing he'd hear was silence as she disconnected. He took a chance. "I'm glad Doctor Mirchandani never thought that way," he said. "Or my son would be dead already."

There was silence on the call for a moment. Rick held his breath. "I got a call from the hospital legal administrator," Shreya Kim said, finally. "I'm not supposed to give you any information."

"Please," Rick said. "You're our only hope. Dr. Mirchandani showed me the data, before the accident. He clearly wanted me to have it."

"I'm sorry," she said. And hung up.

Rick relayed the conversation to Mary as they sat at the kitchen table.

"Is there anyone else who worked with him?" she asked.

"I can't find any more names," Rick said.

Mary thought for a minute. "Then let's talk to her again."

"She just hung up on me."

"Let's not give her that chance," Mary said, reaching for her coat.

An hour later Rick and Mary were sitting in the car, watching people file out of the low hospital annex building. The structure was far simpler than the graceful hospital building that loomed over it. It was clear that the small number of donors who actually understood the unglamorous but essential purpose of basic research wanted their money to go to the work, not the trappings around it.

They waited until just after 6 p.m. They had decided that was late enough when the building would be close to empty, but early enough the lab assistants would still be there. Rick and Mary were betting Doctor Mirchandani tended to hire assistants who worked the way he did—meaning, all the time.

They entered the lobby area and followed the directory on the wall to the second floor. Doctor Mirchandani's lab was partway down on the right. The door was locked, and Rick looked at Mary, exasperated. Mary pushed the buzzer mounted next to the door. After a minute they heard activity on the other side of the door, and it swung open. A diminutive, 20-something Asian woman was staring at them. Then her eyes went wide.

"Shreya Kim?" Rick said.

"You're trespassing," the woman said. "I told you I can't help you."

"You're the only one who can," Mary said. "Please."

"I'm going to call security." The woman started to push the door shut.

"Doctor Mirchandani would tell you to help us," Mary said.

The woman glared at Mary at the sound of the doctor's name, but the door stopped moving. "It doesn't matter," Kim said. "The only copy of the data you want was on the PC. And that's gone. And Kunal didn't tell me anything else about it."

"He saved our son's life. Twice," Mary said.

Kim's exterior cracked a bit. "He saved a lot of lives," she said. Mary thought she spotted a sparkle of a tear at the corner of her eye.

"It wasn't a coincidence," Rick said. "He got hurt because of that data. I know it."

"Tell the police. The hospital told me I'd lose this internship if I spoke to you." She started to close the door once again.

"They won't help. But you can," Mary said. "Our son is dying. We just want to do what we can to save him. I think Kunal would want you to help us with that, don't you?"

The arc of the door stopped for a second time. The woman paused and thought for a moment. "I'll look," she said. "Then you leave. And you never tell anyone you were here."

She let them into the lab area. Rick was surprised to see no test tubes or beakers. It was all computer screens and electronics.

"It's Dr. Kim, right?" Rick asked, as she led them further into the lab space.

"I'm a doctoral student, but in engineering, not medicine. Call me Shreya."

"I thought this was a medical lab," Rick said, taking in the glowing screens and hanging wires. "Looks more like a computer repair shop."

"It *is* a medical lab," Shreya said. "We model most of the body's structures and simulate the tests with programs. It's way easier than cutting dead people up all the time. I write the programs."

"So much for donating my body to science." Rick muttered.

The woman eyed his body critically. "My way is better," she said. "I like to help fix people. It doesn't mean I want to touch them."

She stopped at what appeared to be her workstation. "What did you want to see exactly?" she asked.

"Doctor Mirchandani was working on a device, to keep organs alive for transport."

"The AionOne. I wrote the software that managed the device and maintained the optimum environment for the heart."

"This AionOne, it sent data back to Dr. Kunal's laptop?" Mary asked.

"Yes. Eventually it will use a web portal so different people can log in and view it, but for now we just used his

PC. The patent lawyers told us not to keep extra copies of the data or designs until the FDA approval was complete."

"The data was on the PC that was stolen." Rick said.

"That's right."

Rick felt his heart sink. "Is there a backup of his PC maybe, from last week?"

Shreya shrugged. "I doubt it. His PC gets backed up automatically, but it has to be connected to the lab network for that. He's been working up at the hospital mostly, so I don't think he'd have had a chance to back it up."

Rick looked at Mary, then at Shreya, dejected. "That means there's no other record of whatever the transport device sent?"

"Look," she said. "I want to help. But this seems… pointless." She said the last word with disdain, as though random thought was the most abhorrent thing she could imagine. "The AionOne was toast, in the accident. The heart was too. What's the point of the data?"

"The heart in that thing was for our *son*," Mary said. The words were simple, but the tone in them was enough to cause Shreya to recoil a step.

"I know about John," Shreya said. "I am sorry about that. Kunal talked about him sometimes. He really liked him."

"He showed me the data," Rick said. "He seemed to think the heart, or at least the container, might have been taken from the crash and flown somewhere. It sounds crazy, but he was pretty sure something was wrong. Is there any chance? Any way the data could still be out there?"

She thought for a moment. "There is one possibility. We used his PC as the target device, but there was a staging server in the DMZ." She stopped at Rick and Mary's confused look. "A DMZ is a part of our network where we can put stuff that has to connect to the outside world but where we don't want it to be a doorway into our own network. It helps with patient privacy rules. I designed the software so his PC would pull the data from the server in the DMZ once a day."

"So..." Rick said.

"So the data is possibly still on the server, unless it refreshed the cache. I can try to grab it there. It's a bit of a break with our security policy. I'll try it once and then shut it right down."

Shreya sat down at her keyboard and started typing, her slim fingers flying across the keyboard. "Just give me a minute and I can get to the server in the DMZ."

She stared at the screen as lines of text cascaded down it. Eyes locked on the display, she spoke so quietly it was almost a whisper "I meant what I said before. He really had a thing for your son, you know."

"We just figured it was him being a good doctor," Rick said.

"He is a good doctor," she said firmly. "A *great* one. But he was really excited for your son when he learned about the heart. He always seemed to think of him as special."

"We do, too," Mary said."

"We're sorry for what happened to him," Rick said. "I'm sure he'll be okay."

"They both deserve better," Shreya said. They watched a few more seconds of her slim fingers tapping on keys. "Okay, I've got it. Here's the folder where the data was cached, and… " She looked up at them, shaking her head. "…it's empty. It got cleared automatically, like I said."

"There's no backup for this?" Rick asked, already guessing the answer.

"Once it's gone from here," Shreya said, gesturing toward the screen, "It's gone forever. I'm sorry."

Rick had never felt less in control or more impotent. It seemed all the pieces they needed to figure out the truth were scattered all around them, but somehow it was impossible to put them together. The ones they needed the most seemed to keep slipping away the fastest. Or were yanked away, by Marco and CeraGlobal.

"There's got to be another way," Mary said, as much to make herself and Rick feel better as anything else. She was still trying to process everything she'd seen, and everything he'd told her.

"The heart can tell you," Shreya said.

"It's ruined," Rick said. His mind flashed back to the crash scene. The gaping wound on the container, still smoking from the heat. And the charred lump of flesh inside. "Ruined" seemed like far too simple a word for what had happened that night, but it was all he could muster.

"A DNA comparison will tell you whether it's the same heart as the one that left the hospital. Heck, a blood test or tissue match might even do it. There's plenty of tissue and blood samples from the donor. If it's the same heart, the data's wrong. If it's not the same heart?" she paused and shrugged. "Then I have no idea what to tell you."

"Can you help us with that?" Mary said.

Shreya shook her head again. "It's more complicated than you think. The DNA from the donor is private health data...the hospital or the family would need to release that. The DNA from the heart though—that's something the police can give you. Or maybe the hospital can. It's hard to know who owns the heart now. Or whatever heart was in the helicopter when you found it."

"How can that be?" Mary said.

"There is not a lot of law on who owns an organ once it leaves the body. The transplant board technically gets to decide what happens to it. It's sort of public property and they're in charge of it. But neither the donor nor the recipient gets a say in that. Organs aren't personal property once they're signed away."

She looked at each of them in turn, shrugging. "There's nothing more I can do. I'm sorry."

Rick and Mary thanked her and left the lab. They made their way back to their car silently. The hospital loomed over them, all bright lights and gleaming steel. Rick remembered reading that the architect had designed it to evoke an oasis of hope. To Rick it looked like a fortress. And increasingly, it seemed the answers they needed were locked somewhere inside it.

Mary slumped down in the car seat. Her voice was frayed with fatigue. "How do we get the DNA samples then? Why would they give them to us?"

"We have to do something. We can't wait."

Mary thought for a moment. "We could call Esther," she said.

"She'd be breaking the law, I think."

"You know Esther. She's got her own laws."

Fifty-Four

"I want to go to a Lion's game."

John said it firmly, almost defiantly. The tone and the content both caught Mary off-guard. She'd been playing checkers with him, the board spread out on the table extended out over John's bed.

She sighed. "I know you do, honey. But you know the doctors said the risk of infection was too high. It's too risky."

"They said they were worried about infection because they wouldn't be able to do the surgery. That doesn't matter anymore. I want to go."

"But it will matter, John. If you're sick and another heart becomes available..."

"It won't."

"You can't think that way."

"It's true."

"We agreed, honey. Once you were better, we'd go together." Mary kept her voice calm, even though her heart was breaking.

"I won't be better, Mom. You know it. Everyone here knows it. I can tell in the way they look at me. I want to go to a game. Who cares if I get an infection?"

"I'll talk to your dad about it."

John sighed. "That means no."

He was quiet for a minute. Mary realized he'd started to cry softly. She choked back her own tears. "I promise I will, honey. I promise you'll get to see them play."

He nodded through his tears, giving up the argument.

After the checkers game she walked with him up and down the hall for a few minutes while the orderlies changed the bed linens. The doctors wanted to give him as much exercise as he could take, to keep the fluids moving in his body. He pushed a tree of IV fluids on a triangular stand. Mary guided the oxygen tank as they shuffled along the hallway.

Once they were back in the room, she helped him back into bed. One of the regular nurses came in and checked his IV tube, chatting with John about some TV show he'd been streaming. Mary cherished the moments when she could watch him like that, without him realizing it. He smiled at something the nurse said. His earlier tears gone now, his smile was slow and wise, almost sublime. It was look she saw on him sometimes, and one she'd seen on a few of the other long-term patients on the floor. It was a sort of peaceful, transcendent seperateness, as though his constant closeness to death let him see the world through different eyes, and possibly from a different place. It seemed to Mary in those moments that one part of her son may be in this world, but one part of him was already looking into the next. Her lip quivered as she watched him, equal parts love and anguish threatening to drown her where she sat.

Once he was asleep, she headed downstairs to meet Esther in the lobby. The two women found some chairs and sat side-by-side in a corner of the large open space. Esther's eyebrows kept crawling further and further up her forehead as Mary told her the story. The inconsistencies from the crash. The settlement offers. Rick's meeting with Dr. Mirchandani. She left out what Rick had told her about seeing Marco before the doctor was injured. It still seemed crazy enough to her, even with the image of him flipping the knife casually in his hand, and she could only imagine how it would sound to Esther.

"I know it sounds insane, Esther. And it probably is," Mary finished. "But it's all been driving Rick crazy since the night of the crash. And now it's driving me crazy. We just want to know what happened. And the hospital should, too."

"Hearts don't just disappear, Mary. I check the waiting list at least once a week just to see whether anyone's come along that might bump John down the list. There's only two people on it now with his blood type and antigens. And both are still on the list as of this morning."

"Dr. Mirchandani told Rick he thought it might be that machine they were after. The AionOne?"

"Even that's crazy," Esther said.

"People do crazier things every day. Don't you want to know if John's going to die so somebody could steal that machine?"

Esther glared at her. "I don't intend to see John die at all, Mary."

"I'm sorry," Mary said quietly. She realized her earlier conversation with John was still playing on her own emotions. "But if it's possible that he might, because of something somebody did. For money? For whatever reason? Wouldn't you want to know that?"

Esther sighed and thought for a moment. "I can't get the DNA sample that easily, Mary. But I guess I can do a tissue match. John and Matthew's hearts were a close match including antigens. If the heart tissue from the crash isn't that same match, we'll know. That would mean the heart was switched, which means the container was, too."

"Will you get in trouble?"

Esther smiled. "Trouble never bothered me, honey. But no, the tissue match isn't something that's considered personal information. It's already in the donor files. And as for the heart in the crash, I can't imagine anyone would care about that now. I'll call the coroner's office."

Fifty-Five

The Wayne County Medical Examiner's building was a low brick building, nicely landscaped with a pleasant-looking wooden sign in front of a curved driveway. From its appearance, it could have been an office building or even a daycare. Nothing on the outside would lead anyone to imagine the dozens of corpses inside, stacked on cooled shelves, awaiting their turn on the autopsy table.

Over the years Rhonda's hospitals had sent its share of bodies there, mostly crime victims who died in the ER or were pronounced DOA after a short and hectic ambulance ride. She'd never been there herself. She'd made the arrangements for this visit through her senior contacts at the police station. She left the large cardboard box in the back of her car and went into the front entrance. The waiting room was pleasant, with modern furniture and muted still-life paintings on the walls. She wondered how many parents, husbands, wives, and children had sat in those seats, waiting for their turn to identify another statistic in the Detroit crime annals. Thankfully the area was empty right now.

She announced herself to the receptionist, who asked her to wait a moment. Rhonda walked around the room, unwilling to sit in one of those chairs where so many people had waited, hoping against hope that the identification had been wrong and it wasn't their loved one on the other side of the glass. She tried to remember how old the building was. She knew her mother had come to this building, or one like it, when they'd gotten the news that Rhonda's brother had been shot in a revenge act by a rival gang. Rhonda had only been twelve at the time. She tried to picture her mother sitting in this lobby, waiting for the terrible moment when they'd show her the body of her boy.

Rhonda realized she was glad her mother was not alive to see her today. Rhonda had always thought of herself as a fighter for all those people who had no one else to fight for them. But not today. Today she couldn't escape the reality that she was there today to commit a crime of her own, in service of other worse crimes already on her personal balance sheet.

After a few minutes a young black man in a white lab coat came out through locked doors to greet her. He introduced himself as Tony. He wore a badge with the title "Assistant Coroner." He ushered Rhonda back through the locked doors into the chrome and tile of the lab areas. In some ways, it looked much like the workspaces of her own hospital. But it felt different. Here, the fight between life and death had already been decided.

They walked down a hallway lined with small square doors, a checkerboard of temporary tombs. Tony found the one in question and slid it open. A large orange plastic bag with the word "Evidence" stenciled onto it sat on the sheet of stainless steel. It was too small to hold a body but still bigger than she expected. She hoped the cooler she'd brought would be big enough to hold it.

"That was quite a story," Tony said pointing at the bag. "The crash, the whole thing about the heart. I can't imagine what it was like for those families."

"They'll never be the same," Rhonda said, numbly. "None of us who were part of it will be."

"I wondered what would happen to this," Tony said, as he matched the tag on the bag to the work order he'd been given. "The police said they don't need it. We weren't sure what to do with it."

"It's the hospital's responsibility. We'll incinerate it," Rhonda lied.

He offered to meet her at the loading dock to help her get the bag into her car.

Her grisly cargo on board, she drove for an hour, far outside the city. She went southwest, through Dearborn and past the gleaming Ford Motor complex. She headed towards the Pinckney Lake recreation area. Outside of Dearborn, she found a deserted rest stop. She pulled into a parking spot near the dumpster. She put on latex gloves and opened the trunk. She cut open the plastic bag and got her first glimpse of the AionOne that Rick Morrow had pulled from the burning helicopter. The metal tubing was bent from the heat. The melted opening on the side was larger than she thought it would be. Her mind went to Rick Morrow, his arms wrapped around the plastic container, his son John's hopes as much turned to ash as the lump of meat inside. She steeled herself for the next part. She reached into the opening and removed the heart itself. It was still cold from the coroner's refrigeration. She put the heart in a large Ziplock bag and put the cooler itself into a nondescript black plastic bag. She tossed the cooler into the dumpster, as Marco had instructed, and piled some other loose cardboard on top of it.

She put the Ziplock bag into the Styrofoam cooler she'd packed. There was no need to keep it cold, other than to help avoid the smell. Charred meat, death, guilt. She wasn't sure she'd ever get the smell off her skin or out of her thoughts.

She drove for another hour, far into the wooded hills. She followed narrower and narrower roads into the park and then found a remote parking spot. It was midafternoon now, early enough that the kids were still in school and the park was empty. The air was cold, and a bit of rain was falling. She took the Ziplock bag and a small shovel that she usually kept in the trunk in case of snow. She followed a rough path for a few hundred yards and then stepped off into the forest itself. She weaved between the trees over uneven ground for what seemed like forever. She picked a spot behind an old, rotted tree. It seems as good as any. She dug down a foot or so, then took the heart out of the bag and dumped it into the hole. It landed with a splatting sound like a pound of hamburger dropped on a table. She felt her stomach do a half- flip. As she looked into the hole a vague recollection came to her; somewhere in this area was where the Richardson boy had had his accident, rolled over by the ATV his father never should have let him drive. And now she was burying the heart that the world thought was his. It seemed to her like some sort of twisted full circle. But none of it felt like closure. She filled in the hole and smoothed the ground as best she could.

She knew she should head back to the path but could not pull herself away from the spot at first. She felt tears flowing down her cheeks. "I'm sorry," she whispered. And she realized with relief that she had at least enough humanity left to feel that way. She grieved for Matthew Richardson, whose conscious life had ended in an icy creek in these woods. And for John Morrow, who would die soon, probably thinking of the chance he almost had, and wondering what God or luck had had against him for his whole life. And for Kunal, still struggling for life with a swelling brain and a crushed skull. She tried not to think any more about the heart she had just buried. Or to consider that she didn't deserve the privilege of mourning any of them.

As soon as she'd picked the heart up, she knew without a doubt it was human. Her medical training told her that.

She did not want to guess where it had come from.

She took a different route back to Detroit, as Marco had insisted. On the way she got rid of the shovel, the bag, gloves and Styrofoam cooler. She was back home by dark. Her cellphone showed eight missed calls and almost 60 unread emails. Two of the calls were from Murray. One was from Marco. She ignored them all and poured herself a glass of wine. Then a second.

Fifty-Six

The CeraGlobal C8000 touched down smoothly at Vancouver International Airport. The tangle of tubes hanging from the special hooks in the plane's ceiling swayed and bounced a bit, but Annette's bed barely moved. The pilots were the best in the world, usually recruited straight from the Canadian Air Force. Lana always saw to that.

The ambulance was already waiting in the circular driveway at the private terminal exit. They never even saw a customs officer as they walked through the small waiting area that separated the runway from the street.

Anette's medical team was also waiting. They transferred her stretcher from the airplane to the ambulance. Phillippe and Marie watched the process. While the medical team focused on Annette, the family's bags were transferred from the cargo area in the back of the plane into the trunk of a town car. Phillippe caught a flash of red and white and saw them load the heart transport container into the trunk as well.

"We brought that with us?" he shouted to Marie over the whine of the idling engines.

"Mother wanted it," Marie said. "She wants to have it studied. She thinks there might be a business opportunity in it."

"There *will* be a business opportunity in it," Phillippe said, as they moved towards the car. "With this thing organs can be shipped anywhere in the world. They'll just be one more natural resource, taken from the poor parts of the world for the benefit of the rich. Only this time the resource will be the people themselves. That's the business Lana will create." He turned to Marie. "Who knows? Maybe Annette will get to run it someday, if Lana has her way."

"You can argue with my mother about the state of the world all you want next time you see her," Marie said, moving toward the town car as the rear doors to the ambulance swung shut. "I'm taking Annette home."

The ambulance was working its way into the heavy Vancouver traffic before the jet had even taxied to its hangar. Marie and Phillippe's driver followed behind. An hour later, they pulled into the Cera family home. A specially configured room was already waiting, complete with the most modern medical equipment in the world. Annette's regular doctors could take care of her at home now, Marie thought with relief.Once Annette was safe in her new room, Marie called Lana and told her they'd arrived safely. She could hear stress in her mother's voice. A lot of stress. But her mother told her everything was okay and that they'd talk later.

For the first time in weeks, Marie started to feel that maybe life could get back to the way it was supposed to be.

Fifty-Seven

Work had fallen into a grim routine for Rick. Clearly the men he worked with had been told that Rick wouldn't agree to their deal. That meant their jobs were in jeopardy and they knew it. None of them confronted him directly, and there were no threats or messages left on his desk. They were good men, and Rick felt almost more guilty that they didn't stoop to those sorts of actions despite the hardship he knew they might be facing. But some of the camaraderie was gone. They spoke more often in Spanish around him, and Rick could only imagine what some of them were saying.

He worked in silence and ate alone.

After noon on that Tuesday, Rick glanced down at the phone on his desk, his only companion, and saw a text notification. The number looked familiar but there was no name attached. He opened the phone and checked the message. It simply read "Call me. Shreya Kim."

He dialed the number, heart pounding. The young woman answered after one ring.

"You know the data you were looking for?" she said, sounding out of breath.

"Hard to forget," he said.

"After you left, I forgot to close the window to the server, so I was still connected to the data file."

"Did the data show up?" Rick asked hopefully.

"Nope," she said. "But the AionOne did. It called home."

Rick's heart sped up even more. "How?"

"I can only guess that it got back into range of a cellular network it recognized."

"Here?"

"Nope. Vancouver. I'll text you the location."

Rick got the image a few minutes later. It was a pointer on a Google map, as innocuous as a restaurant or bus station marker. He zoomed in on it using the Google satellite view. The image dove in and the pointer settled on a large square building. The words "Cera Tower" were on the map next to it.

That was the proof, Rick thought. The CeraGlobal company had stolen the container. They were the only ones who could have faked the crash. If the fake AionOne had been destroyed by the fire as planned, nobody but the pilot would have been able to say what happened.

Except he'd showed up.

He wondered what had happened to the heart itself. Had it simply been tossed in the trash somewhere on the way to the airport? An inconvenient bit of flesh, just messing up the precious container that could make them millions? Or was the heart itself useful in some way the doctor hadn't imagined?

The $5 million Marco had offered was chump change, Rick figured. Chump change for the chumps Marco must have figured him and Mary to be.

He thought of Jim Abbot's lackeys nodding in unison as the man tried to bully him into silence. He thought of the police ignoring him to his face and probably ridiculing him over their morning coffee. He thought of all the times he'd been told there was nothing that could be done, whether it was over a prescription bill that was bigger than a car payment or a clinical trial that somehow John was just never right for.

But mostly he thought of Marco, manipulating every situation, every angle, on behalf of CeraGlobal.

Fifty-Eight

Mary got to the hospital in time for a late lunch with John. He ate lightly, slowly, oxygen feeding into his nostrils from a harness below his nose. The harness got in the way once in a while and she'd help him sort it out. She reveled in watching every bite he took. Eating was such a normal activity. When she watched John eat, she could forget for a minute what was happening inside him, as his heart continued to fail a bit more each day in its struggle to keep him alive.

He'd finished his lunch around 2:30 and still had some energy, so she talked to him about David's school, and about little things around the house. Anything to keep him engaged and distracted.

John was starting to doze off when Esther Williams slipped into the room. Mary wasn't sure if Esther had been watching, not wanting to interrupt her quiet time with John, or if it was just another example of the woman's sixth sense for the rhythms of her patients.

Esther's face, however, was not set in the professional calm Mary was used to seeing. She looked angry. Very angry. She motioned for Mary to join her in the hallway. Once outside the room Esther led her to an empty patient room down the hall. She closed the door behind them.

"I did what we talked about," she began.

"Oh my God, did you get in trouble?" Mary said. "I'm so sorry we asked."

Esther shook her head impatiently. "No, not that. It's the heart. The guy at the coroner's office told me Rhonda Marsh had picked it up herself. He said she was taking it to be incinerated."

Mary felt her legs go weak, and she grabbed the end of the bed for support. "Does it make sense that they'd do that? It never occurred to me."

"I guess sooner or later they'd do that. The coroner wouldn't keep it forever without a criminal case to require it. But Rhonda herself going to get it? That makes no sense. I called the waste management department at the hospital. They're the ones who package the biological waste to send to the incinerator. I was hoping maybe the heart would still be at the hospital. But they said no one had brought them the heart or the device it was in.

Mary's mind was racing. Once again nothing was ever straightforward. Even the simplest of events seemed to have angles that just didn't make sense. "Maybe we're thinking about this all wrong," she said. "What if Matthew's heart was never put into the container? Maybe she kept it at the hospital. For some other patient?"

"Impossible, Mary. Kunal—Dr. Mirchandani—did the procedure himself. Rhonda wouldn't have touched it. And there's no way Kunal would do anything to hurt John." Mary wasn't satisfied. She was sure there had to be a reason Rhonda wanted the heart to be gone. "And the transplant list hasn't changed? Those two boys are still on it?"

"Yes. I checked again this morning. It hasn't changed since a Canadian girl came off it a few weeks ago."

Mary froze. "Canadian?"

"Yes. There was a girl who came on and off the list in a matter of weeks. She was Canadian. The notes said her doctors were pursuing an alternate treatment. I remember because I figured it was some new treatment available there that we haven't approved yet in the States. I've been meaning to look into it to see if it was something that might help John."

"Do you remember her name?"

Esther thought. "Annette something."

"Annette Cera?" Mary felt a combination of dread and rage start to build in her chest.

Esther shook her head.

"No. It started with a G, I think."

The floor felt like it was falling away under Mary's feet again. "Gaumond?"

"Yes, that's it. Annette Gaumond." Esther saw the look on Mary's face. "Does that mean something?"

Mary steadied herself. "I don't know. But I'm more sure than ever that the heart Rhonda took from the coroner wasn't Matthew Richardson's. Did you ask Rhonda about it?"

"Not yet. I wanted to talk to you and Rick first. I suddenly don't trust Rhonda very much."

"Without the sample from the heart, we can't prove that it wasn't Matthew's?"

"No, we can't. We need some tissue from the heart that was in the cooler at the crash. Or even a blood sample. But that's all gone now."

Mary thought back to the night of the crash and Rick rushing into the hospital room, hand bandaged, bruised and filthy. She stood up straighter, the beginning of an idea forming in her mind. "How much do you need?"

"Not much. Just enough to get a DNA sample or blood type."

"I think I know where to get it," Mary said. "Give me a couple of hours and I'll be back."

Fifty-Nine

Rick got up from his desk. He found Luis huddled with another man over a workbench in the back of the shop.

"I'm sorry, Luis. I got a call from the hospital," Rick said. "I gotta go."

Luis just nodded.

Rick cleaned up his work area and grabbed his lunch cooler. He was on the street in a matter of a few minutes. He took out his phone but didn't call Mary or the hospital—neither had called him. He dialed Marco's number instead.

After the third ring Marco picked up. "Hello Rick," he said, his voice neutral.

"I know what you did," Rick said, without preamble. "I know it was you."

"You need to stop this, Rick." Marco continued, evenly. "I understand your frustration. But you can't just keep trying to take it out on me. All I did was offer you a settlement at the direction of my employer. A very generous one, too."

"You took the picture in the restaurant."

"Everybody there had a phone, Rick."

"You followed the doctor and me. And you took the PC. I saw the map."

"Map?"

"The map from the data the AionOne kept. It had a tracker on it. You knew that, too, didn't you? That's why you took the PC."

Marco's voice got more urgent. "I don't know anything about that. And I know you have no reason to trust me, Rick. But I'm telling you. Take the money. Help your family. This won't go well for you."

"You're here to give me advice now? Or threaten me more?"

"Call it advice. I know you have no reason to think I'm in your corner on this, But I am. This fight's not worth it," Marco said. "Trust me. End this. Go back to your son. That's where you need to be. The heart's gone, Rick."

"I know that. But tell me then, why's the container it was in now sitting someplace at CeraGlobal's headquarters in Vancouver?"

"I told you, I don't know anything about that," Marco said. But Rick spotted the slight pause in the reply. He'd struck a nerve.

"I know enough to go to the police now," Rick said. "But if you do want to end it, I'll tell you how."

"I'm listening."

"Twenty million dollars," Rick said. "And a verbal apology. Nothing needs to be in writing. Do that and we'll never go public. CeraGlobal will keep its precious reputation. You can even keep the damn container and make as much money off it as you want."

"I thought it wasn't about the money," Marco said.

"It's not. We'll take the original five million you offered for ourselves and donate the rest somewhere. I just want it to be enough to hurt. Even a big company like CeraGlobal will feel that."

"You're crazy," Marco said. "But I know the CeraGlobal leadership team does want to end this."

"Meet me tonight at 6:00," Rick said. "Where the helicopter crashed. That's where I want the apology."

"I'm not sure I can put all that together so quickly. Like you said, that's a lot of money, even for a company the size of ours."

"Make it happen," Rick said. "Otherwise, I can still make the eleven o'clock news with what I know."

Rick got home around 3:00. He'd guessed Mary would still be at the hospital with John, and he was right. David was with his grandparents at their house for another few hours. His own small house was silent except for the ticking of the kitchen clock. He went down into the basement, to a tall safe he hadn't opened in two years. The first thing he saw when he opened it was his hunting rifle. It was a remnant of a hobby long forgotten since the term *hypertrophic left heart syndrome* had entered their lives. On a small shelf above the rifle was what he was looking for. A Sig Saur 9mm pistol. He'd shot it back at the range with his buddies long before he was married. Almost too long ago to remember.

He took the pistol down from the shelf. He'd forgotten how heavy it was. He checked the action and filled two clips. He slipped the pistol into his jacket pocket and locked up the safe. He lifted a length of rope from a nail near the doorway and wrapped it around his waist, under his jacket, hidden from sight like the pistol.

He walked the long blocks to the bus stop. There was a rental car office a few miles away, on the bus route. That was his first stop. He'd already reserved a full-size sedan. American made and inconspicuous in Detroit. And with a trunk big enough to hold a body.

Sixty

"How the hell could he know that the AionOne is here?" Lana asked once Marco reached her.

"The bigger question is *why* is it even here?" Marco said. "It should still be in Saudi Arabia, where nobody can find it. Who said to bring it back?"

Lana was silent.

Of course she did, Marco thought to himself. "You never cease to amaze me, Lana. Even in the middle of all this mess you couldn't resist a chance to make a buck?"

"So what if I did?" she said. "Somebody's got to get you paid."

"Do you know how risky that is? The thing has a location tracker in it, Lana." Marco said exasperated. "That's how the doctor figured out something wasn't right."

"Do you think Morrow is serious?"

"I don't know why he'd want to meet me otherwise, do you?" Marco could hear the sarcasm in his voice, but he didn't care. He was getting tired of being the buffer between Lana and the messes her greed and selfishness were causing.

"He knows so much," Lana said. She sounded stupefied, as though such a threat to her goals should be impossible to even consider.

"If you think I'm going to make him disappear, you're crazy," Marco said.

"You did it for the doctor."

"That was a mistake. I never intended for him to get hurt. He didn't deserve it."

"I'm sure knowing that would make him feel better."

"Don't push me, Lana."

"I'm just saying. Morrow can cause a lot of trouble. For *both* of us. But mostly you, I'd say."

Marco ignored the implied threat. "It's not like we haven't caused enough trouble for him, or his family."

There was a pause. "Since when did their feelings start mattering to you?"

Marco wasn't sure why the anger was welling up inside him, but it was. "There are some parts of my life I wanted to leave behind. You know that. That's why I took this job instead of another tour of duty."

"What I expect is that somebody who takes a job, and to whom I pay as much money as I pay you, does what they're paid to do. Do you really think I pay you this much just to track down pictures of diplomats with hookers or deliver a bribe to some bureaucrat in a customs department? And it's not like this is the first time you've made things miserable for somebody I wanted. Get real."

"It's the first time they didn't deserve it. I even found out the kid wasn't his biological son. I tossed that out to the media, too. Morrow adopted the kid *after* he was born. He *knew* the life he was signing up for. That takes guts. He deserves better."

"I don't pay you for your moral judgements, Marco. Unless getting paid doesn't matter anymore to you. My whole company is at stake here. I need to know I can count on you." Marco bit his lip, thinking about the cabin in the mountains. "I've got my end under control, Lana. But you're right, he knows a lot. Hopefully he's serious about this offer. Otherwise, I think we're out of options."

"No, we're not," Lana said. She filled Marco in on the final offer he could make to Rick, if nothing else worked. Marco made Lana repeat every word. As astounded as he'd been at her audacity in taking the AionOne to Vancouver, he was still almost unable to believe what else she was considering. He took a breath and cleared his mind, but the images kept coming back to him of the Morrows at the restaurant, and on TV. He tried to focus on execution of the plan, and not the human consequences. That's how he'd been trained, and how he'd trained other men. For a minute he found himself thinking that that training felt dirty, somehow, and wrong. But he knew in his heart it wasn't the training that was wrong: just who he was using it to help. And hurt.

Sixty-One

Lana continued cursing the Morrow family to herself even after she hung up with Marco. The news cycle around the crash had died down. But in the past few hours she'd learned she had something even bigger to worry about. The doctors had told her Annette was starting to show signs of rejecting the heart. They were managing it aggressively, they said, but they were getting concerned. She told them not to inform Marie or Phillippe yet, and to keep her posted hourly.

She stood up from the mahogany desk and paced around the open space in her home office, footsteps muffled by the rich pile of the maroon and gold carpet. The risk of Annette rejecting the heart had been Lana's silent, personal nightmare before and after the procedure. It had been, until Rick Morrow showed up at the crash site, the one thing she knew she couldn't control. Or fix.

Tall French windows opened onto the landscaped back yard, with the roofline of the pool house just visible in the distance, over a line of decorative trees. The early afternoon sun was pale and already getting low in the sky for this time of day, as winter approached. Photos of her father and grandfather lined the wall in the office. They were serious men who had built CeraGlobal through sheer will, brains, and fearlessness. Those were the photos that reminded her every day of the responsibilities she bore to carry the family name forward. That reminded her to be the sort of people they had been.

On the desk itself sat a single picture in a wooden frame. It showed a happier scene. In it, a younger version of herself, arm around a tall, smiling young man. The young man shared her spare frame and piercing eyes. Nobody would doubt they were brother and sister. The photographer, her father, had captured the pair on the deck of their sailboat in Vancouver Harbor. It had been a sunny, fall day more than three decades past, on Lana's twenty-fifth birthday. Lana had always had the brains, but her brother Dan, two years older, had an easy charm and an irresistible smile that Lana could never master. Different in so many other ways, they both shared the intensely competitive nature that seemed to come with the Cera name. Her father had always said they'd make the perfect pair to run the company, when the time came.

She could not look at the picture without the memory coming back of the day Dan and her father had died together. Their small plane had crashed on a mountainside in Chile. They'd been in the country to close a deal for construction equipment. They had died a few years after the picture had been taken. Dan had gone along to handle the difficult negotiations with the Chilean government. Lana had stayed in Vancouver to manage the business side of the transaction. The plane had hit the steep face of the mountain during a thunderstorm. No distress calls. No warning. Just a terse message of condolences from the Chilean government that told Lana she now had all CeraGlobal to carry on her young shoulders.

Usually, the pictures renewed her determination. Today they seemed to mock her.

She did the math on the time zones and realized she'd need to wait a few hours before she could call the crown prince. She scolded herself for procrastinating on the one thing she knew she had to do in the meantime, and so she sat back down at the desk. The only three things on her desk besides the photo were a laptop computer, a Polycom conference phone, and a leather blotter. She turned on the laptop and logged onto the company network. She navigated to the subnet she was looking for, and was challenged for a second login, this time requiring a six-digit number that was displayed by a specific app on her phone. Only a few dozen people in the company had access to this part of the network. All of them had security clearances with the Canadian government.

Once into the subnet, she found the folders she was looking for and began copying them onto her local hard drive. She ignored the warning screen that reminded her that she was downloading confidential documents.

She knew her actions were being logged by a security system that was part of the network, but she figured she could claim an urgent need to audit the Northern Eye program after her unexpected time out of the office. A joint project with the U.S. and several other NATO countries, Northern Eye was, on paper, an updated early-warning system for Russian (and now North Korean) ballistic missiles. But its underlying purpose was to capture even the faintest glimmers of digital communication emanating from Western Russia, including Moscow. CeraGlobal had a key role in designing the listening equipment that would be deployed across Northern Canada, as well as the encrypted communications channels that would funnel all the data back to the NSA's new facility in Idaho.

She copied the files onto a USB drive and placed it into the drawer of her desk, then deleted the files from her computer. She knew enough to be aware that any decent digital forensics person would be able to retrace everything she'd done. She hoped that there'd be no need for that. Somehow erasing the files seemed to make her feel better, as though it erased the guilt for the treason she was in the process of committing.

Three hours later she called the crown prince and told him she'd accept the offer of his help. She confirmed she'd provide the information he'd requested as a sign of her appreciation. How he had even known to ask about the Northern Eye program was beyond her ability to guess, but he'd known enough to ask for specific information. Either he was well informed, she figured, or well-coached by a third party who had a direct interest in the capabilities of Northern Eye. A third party sitting somewhere in the Kremlin, no doubt.

Regardless, she knew she was committed to this path as she disconnected the call. In reality, she knew she'd been committed as soon as the virus had found its way into Annette, and begun eating away at her heart valves a year earlier.

She'd done what she could to save Annette. The rest was up to the doctors, and the antirejection medicine they were pumping into Annette at an enormous rate. But Lana knew she had to set about preserving the company's reputation too.

She hoped Rick Morrow was serious about the money and the verbal apology. But if he wasn't, she now had her final card to play to force his hand. She looked at the pictures on the wall and wondered if her father and grandfather would approve of the risk she was taking. She knew her brother would not.

Sixty-Two

Mary tried Rick's cellphone again as she drove from the hospital to the house. He didn't answer. He hadn't been at the shop waiting for her, and the men there had just shrugged and turned away when she asked if they knew where he'd gone. She alternated between bouts of tears and anger as she drove. The thought of the heart meant for John beating in the chest of someone else, or simply tossed away as rubbish, was more than she could bear. It was hard for her to imagine the audacity and the power it must have taken to make such a thing happen. It seemed impossible on the one hand, but completely obvious as she thought through everything she knew.

She started shouting for Rick as soon as she unlocked the door to the house, but nothing but silence greeted her. She took a quick look upstairs to see if he'd fallen asleep, but there was no sign he'd even been there. She headed to the basement and found the plastic bag she'd tossed there the morning after the crash. She took a deep breath. She'd vowed the morning of the crash that she'd never set eyes on the items inside again. But now she ripped it open and pulled out Rick's windbreaker and jeans. The stains were still visible on them. Dirt. Grease. And another bigger stain on the jacket from where Rick had held the cooler close to his chest. She tried not to think of what that stain represented. But it was exactly what she needed. Her hands shook and she fought back tears regardless.

She turned to head back upstairs. Her eyes passed over the far corner of the basement, and she froze. There was no room for messiness in their small house, so everything had a place. A set of cheap metal shelves against the wall held old files and extra clothes, and the basement corners were crowded with the dusty artifacts of their individual lives before John: golf clubs, snow skis, and a pair of old bikes with tires sitting flat on the concrete floor. It was all where it should be—but now the cardboard boxes that had been stacked in front of Rick's gun safe were pushed out to the center of the room.

Her heart started to climb into her throat. She ran over to the safe and started spinning the lock. It took her a few tries but she remembered the combination eventually. She felt a bit of relief when the door swung open and she saw Rick's hunting rifle sitting snug in its rack. But then she noticed the open space on the top shelf. She knew Rick had kept a pistol of some sort up there. Now it was just an empty space.

She closed the door and ran back up the stairs in a panic. Images of the headlines about Tom Richardson sprang to mind. She knew Rick had been frustrated, angry, and even despondent since the crash. But would he really do that to himself? Or did he mean the gun for someone else. She tried to swallow the terror she felt and called Esther. She relayed her fears to the woman in a tumble of words.

"Okay, Mary, where would he go?" Esther asked, already in problem-solving mode.

"I don't know. Not the hospital. Not his parents." She thought hard. If he was really going to end his own life, where would he do it? Suddenly she knew without a doubt. "He'd go back to the crash site. That's where all this started."

"I'll be there in twenty minutes," Esther said. "Keep trying his phone. And call the police."

Mary disconnected from Esther and started to dial 911 but stopped before the third digit. She could imagine a couple of young cops, showing up at the vacant lot, nerves on edge, to find an agry Rick with a pistol in his hand. She hung up the phone.

Sixty-Three

Mary knew she had a few minutes before Esther got to the house. She needed the time because there was one more idea she needed to pursue based on what Esther had told her. She took a deep breath and tried to put everything out of her mind as she waited. She had no idea if Rick was getting ready to kill himself. She didn't know if John could last another week. And she didn't know whether Esther would get anything useful from the jacket stains. But despite all that, Mary knew she needed to sound relaxed now if her hunch was to have any chance of working. She'd located the number for the Cera Charitable Foundation on their website. She dialed it.

"Cera Foundation," a cheerful young male voice declared once the call connected.

Mary forced a smile onto her own face to help with her act. "Phillippe Gaumond, please."

There was a pause. "Mr. Gaumond is not available. May I help you?"

Mary knew the next part was the crucial part, where she'd find out if her guesses were correct. "I just wanted to check in with him, to see how his daughter Annette was doing."

"I'm afraid we don't release personal information on the Cera family," the young man said. "Of course," Mary said. "I just wasn't sure if they were back in the country. He'd asked me to ring him when he got back. I just forget what date that would be."

"Oh, yes." The man said, relaxing a bit at Mary's apparent familiarity with the Gaumonds' schedule. "They got back yesterday, I think."

"Our son has a similar condition to Annette," Mary said, as though confiding in the young man. "We all sort of stick together for support."

"Of course," the young man said, now totally disarmed. "Annette's back home, I believe. And I guess everything went well. Mr. Gaumond said he'd be back in the office next week."

"I'm glad she's okay," Mary said warmly, even though her anger was rising as the man confirmed what she had suspected. Now she had to try for the final piece. "After all, it's a long flight from Saudi Arabia."

"For sure," the man said. "But it's a sweet plane to do it in."

"Okay, well, thanks for the update. I'll try him again next week," Mary said, as brightly as she could. Then she hung up before he had time to ask for a name or phone number.

She sat still for a moment, trying to grasp what she'd just heard. The audacity of what had been done was almost beyond her imagination. But now she had no doubt. The Cera family had stolen John's heart, and someplace in Saudi Arabia it had been transplanted into Annette. What had happened to John was no act of God. Or human error. It was cold and calculated beyond belief.

Her shock turned into anger. And the anger into a desire to act. To do something to fight back. But she knew that before any of that, she needed to find Rick. She went outside and was standing in the driveway when Esther arrived. "Get in," Esther shouted through her open window. "No," Mary said. She thrust the jacket and jeans, wrapped in a new plastic bag, through the open window. Esther stared at the bundle in confusion. "That's what Rick was wearing the night of the crash. He said the cooler leaked all over him. The fluid from the cooler might have what you need, right?"

Esther thought for a second. "It might."

"Find out," Mary said. "I'm going to go find Rick." Esther started to argue but Mary cut her off. "Please, Esther. It's the one shot we have left. Test it."

Esther nodded. "I'll bring this to the lab myself. We'll have our first results in a few hours." She backed out of the small driveway and sped back towards the hospital.

Mary got back in her own car, and headed off in the opposite direction, towards Saint Elizabeth's Hospital.

Sixty-Four

Rhonda stood in her tower office, watching patients and staff m illing a bout i n t he a trium f ar b elow. S he'd n oted a while back that the white and green coats of the staff always clustered together away from the play area on one side. The patients and their families grouped together on the other. It was as though each group had retired to their neutral corner in the atrium. It seemed to her to be part of some unspoken treaty that, in that one space, patients and staff would give each other a respite from the battles they all faced together on the floors above. She realized, looking down on the scene, how much she resented the fact that none of them would ever know what she was sacrificing to let them fi ght that battle for another day.

She turned at the noise of her door opening, wondering who of her staff would still be in the building that late. She froze halfway when she found herself looking at Rick Morrow instead. He closed the door behind him and took out a pistol. Rhonda had been around enough guns as a young girl in Detroit. It felt different, though, knowing someone was holding it to use on her. Even so, she found herself oddly calm, as though part of her had expected this moment over the past few days. Maybe even wanted it.

Rick just studied her. But the gun barrel didn't waver.

"What's wrong, Rick?" was all she could think to say, her mind racing as she tried to guess how much he knew. She walked slowly towards her desk, keeping her eyes on his.

"You lied to me," he said.

"We shouldn't have used the helicopter. That was my decision and I'm sorry." She reached her desk and let her arms dangle. Her left fingers found the edge of the panic button under the desktop. It was there in case a violent patient or family member decided to confront her directly. She'd never had to push it for real before. Her finger hovered under the button. "But it was an accident," she continued. "No one could have predicted that."

Rick stepped forward and gestured at her with the pistol. "None of it was an accident. *You* convinced the Richardsons to stay at this hospital so you'd have a reason to use the helicopter and stage the crash. *You* decided to use the new container so they could take the heart a longer distance. *You* told Marco about the doctor so he could steal the computer. *You* took the heart from the coroner's office so nobody could test it."

Each sentence was like a blow to her chest. She spoke, but her words sounded desperate now, even to her. "I can have security here in two minutes. You'll wind up in jail for sure this time. Is that going to help your family?

"*You* were supposed to help my family. We *trusted* you."

Rhonda's finger touched the button. A single push and help would be on the way.

Rick saw the motion. "Go ahead. Bring security. Maybe they'll shoot me. Maybe I'll shoot you. Either way you'll be back on TV. And all this will be public."

Her mind raced for a response, but she knew there was no point in refuting him. He was right. And she realized she was tired of lying. She dropped her hand to her side.

"Just to sell a patent, Rhonda?" Rick said. "To make some money for the hospital? For yourself?"

She shook her head. "Not for me. For the hospital. To keep all this going. We needed the money. Somehow those people knew it. They knew everything they needed to know."

"Marco."

She nodded, a tremor going through her as she heard the name said aloud. "He knew all our money problems. He said he could make them go away."

"We trusted you," Rick said. "You told John you would do everything to help him."

Rhonda pointed down at the figures in the atrium. "They trust me, too. They deserve my help too."

"They're not my son."

"I know he's the only kid in the world that matters to you. But he can't be the only one to me." She wasn't sure if she was trying to convince Rick or herself, but she put as much force into her words as she could.

"He was supposed to be the only one that mattered that day. *We* were supposed to be the ones that mattered that day." Rick's face flushed and his teeth flashed in a snarl as he spoke. "After everything we went through. All the dinners I went to and the speeches I gave at your fundraisers. That was supposed to be *our* day. You traded us for something you thought was better."

"It wasn't that simple."

He stepped closer again, the pistol now only inches from her chest. "It was to us."

"If you're going to kill me, please don't do it here," she said. "There's been enough bad news here for one week."

He motioned to the closet on the walled side of the office. "Get your coat. Leave your phone on the desk."

A minute later they were walking side by side to the elevator and down to the lobby level, Rick's right hand on the pistol in his coat pocket. They passed a few nurses and orderlies from the night shift in the hallways, and Rick kept waiting for one of them to raise an alarm. But they all just nodded at Rhonda, and she just acknowledged them and kept walking. He led her out to his rental car and opened the trunk.

"You don't need to do that. I won't cause trouble," Rhonda said.

He considered her promise for a minute, then unlocked the passenger door and waited until she was inside with the door closed. He jogged around to the driver's side. Once his door was closed, he picked up the rope from the floor. Rhonda's eyes went wide as he wrapped it around her wrists, but she didn't resist.

He pulled out into traffic. "Where are we going?" she said.

"I'm going to show you what you did," he said. "You and Marco."

<h1 style="text-align:center">Sixty-Five</h1>

Rick drove through the busy traffic, following the route he had taken the night of the crash. Once they passed Nine Mile Road, he took the same exit he'd used to chase the helicopter and weaved his way through the same dark streets. His anger built as he remembered every minute of that night. They passed abandoned houses and the shells of the old factories until they rounded the last turn and came to the old Fisher Body Plant building.

Marco was already at the lot, standing casually in the semi-dark. He watched carefully as Rick got out of the car. His eyes went wider when Rick went around to the passenger side and hauled Rhonda out, hands tied in front of her. Marco took a step forward and Rick pulled the pistol out of his pocket. Marco stopped his advance and shook his head. "That's not going to help, Rick," he said. He glanced at the gun but didn't seem afraid of it.

"You know who this is?" Rick said, tipping his head towards Rhonda.

"She didn't have a choice," Marco said. "We pushed her into it."

"She had the easiest choice,": Rick said. "All she had to do was do her job."

Marco shook his head. "I'm the one who's behind this, Rick. Let her go."

"It was you that night, wasn't it, on the street? With the doctor."

Marco nodded.

"Doctor Mirchandani never hurt anyone," Rick said.

"I never meant to hurt him, either." Marco said. "You have to believe me."

"But my family. You *did* mean to hurt us."

"It was my job."

Rick pointed towards a spot on the ground a few feet ahead of Marco. "Kneel down there. Face me."

Marco considered the instruction for a moment, then complied.

"You, too, next to him," Rick said, pushing Rhonda into the lot.

"This is where it happened?" Rhonda said, suddenly realizing where they were.

"Yes. Get down."

Her voice started to rise as the reality of the situation struck her. "Please, don't."

"Just do what he says," Marco said. He was still eyeing Rick, but sitting back on his heels as requested.

Rhonda walked over next to Marco and carefully lowered herself to her knees. She stared up at Rick in terror.

Rick felt his rage building. "Look around," he said. "What do you see?"

He waited while they took in the roofline, with its angular, jutting water tower. The wide dark maws of the missing windows. The rubble and garbage littering the ground. "This is what I saw that night," he said, once he felt they'd seen enough. He pointed with his left hand, keeping the pistol in his right. "Over there was where the helicopter sat. Where the pilot lit it on fire. Or maybe you did, Marco. You were in the SUV I passed, weren't you?"

"If you'd been driving a foot more towards the left, this all would have ended right then," Marco said.

Rick pointed at a spot a few feet from Rhonda. Tears were running down his face now, outrage and grief both washing over him, "That is where I was lying. Watching John's chance at life leak out of that goddamn machine of yours." He walked over and squatted a few feet in front of them, where he could look into their eyes. "What happened to the heart?" he said to Marco. "Did you just throw it away someplace?"

"Does it matter?" Marco asked.

"Did you give it a proper burial? Like I'll have to do for John because of you? All for that damn machine?" Rick's finger closed tighter around the trigger.

"It wasn't about the machine," said a voice from behind Rick. He spun towards the sound. Mary stepped into the gray light of the open space.

"It was the heart, Rick. They wanted the heart, not the machine."

Rick stared at her, uncomprehending.

Mary turned to Marco. "Annette Cera. Or Gaumond, I guess technically," Mary said. "That's her name."

Marco shrugged. "You might as well stick with Cera. Her dad doesn't have much to say about what happens in that family."

Rick flipped his gaze from Marco to Mary, confused. He let his right hand drop to his side as he tried to make sense of their words, the pistol dangling loosely. Marco eyed it but made no attempt to move.

"Annette Gaumond. That's who got John's heart. She was dying, just like John." Mary said, as she walked up beside Rick. "Her family put her on the transplant list for a while. But they took her off when they realized that there wouldn't be enough time to wait. They heard about Matthew Richardson. They realized John was in the way of what they needed."

"She'd gotten an infection in Africa that damaged her heart beyond repair," Marco said, "She only had a few months to live at best. Same as your son."

"Is she in Vancouver, too?" Rick asked, trying to make sense of what he was hearing. "Is that why the device is there?"

"She's there now,' Marco said. "I guess Lana Cera wanted the container brought there. To re-create it. Sort of a bonus to the whole thing." He snorted derisively. "Lana never misses a chance to turn a profit."

"She'll be trying to turn that profit from prison," Mary said. "Her whole family will."

"You can't prove any of it," Marco said. "The police can't help you. We can work this out together."

"Easy for you to say after what you did to Dr. Mirchandani," Mary said.

"I never intended for him to get hurt. But it's true. Without his PC, without the heart, there's no evidence. You can't prove it wasn't Matthew Richardson's heart that was destroyed in the crash."

"Yes, we can," Mary said. She pointed to the spot where Rick had been lying a week earlier, the AionOne and the heart clutched in his arms. "The fluid from the container had soaked Rick's jacket. There is blood and DNA from the heart in it. Enough to test. A friend at the hospital called me a few minutes ago. She already knows it's the wrong blood type. And she's sure the DNA match will confirm it."

Marco nodded as he considered the news. "I guess that would do it." He stood up and started brushing off his knees.

"Stay down," Rick said.

"You won't shoot," Marco said. "I know how angry you are. But you're not that kind of guy. Besides Mary would be an accessory to murder. You won't let that happen." He reached down to help Rhonda to her feet. She looked nervously at Rick but stood slowly.

"Don't try me," Rick warned, raising the handgun again.

"I don't plan to. I'm done hurting you," Marco said.

"All this is going to be public," Mary said. "You'll all go to jail."

"And then John dies," Marco said.

"Keeping you alive won't change that," Rick said.

"Don't be so sure," Marco said.

"You have no right to say that," Mary said. "You can't save John."

"No, I can't," Marco said. "But Lana Cera believes *she* can."

"No more bullshit," Rick said. "Even she can't do that."

Marco pointed towards the spot where the helicopter had burned. "Would you have thought in a million years she could have done *that*?"

"How?" Mary said. "There's no heart for him. We'd know."

Marco reached into his jacket. Rick raised the gun at him. Marco slowly withdrew his cellphone and showed it to Rick.

"Agree to meet Lana, and you can ask her yourself," Marco said.

"It's a trick," Rick said.

Marco shook his head. "Not much point in tricking you. You already know the truth. Lana told me she can be here in the morning. You might as well hear her out. You said yourself there's nothing more to lose. Maybe there's something to gain."

The empty lot was silent for a moment, except for the distant, omnipresent thrum of cars on the highway a few blocks away.

"We'll go to where she is," Mary said. "Annette will be there. I want to see her too. I want to see the girl who has John's heart."

Rick glanced at her face. There was determination there, but also something more—a deep anger of a kind he wasn't sure he'd ever seen in her before. He turned back to Marco. "Call her," he said.

Sixty-Six

Against the dusty tan of the flapping tents and the merci-lessly blowing sand of the Al Kharaz refugee camp in the south of Yemen, the giant black SUV looked like an intruder from another planet. Despite its incongruous presence, none of the camp residents lifted their eyes to stare. The dirty, hungry occupants of the camp were mostly Somalis who had fled a nightmare in their own country only to wind up in different one in Yemen. They knew from hard experience that it was best not to attract the attention of people who rode in vehicles like that.

The Al Kharaz camp was 100 kilometers from Aden, the last stronghold of the Yemeni government, which was backed by the Saudi military with quiet support from the United States. Saudi jets had been bombing the country for years, trying to beat back the Shia rebels. The civil war had destroyed nearly all the infrastructure in the once-beautiful country. As desolate and dangerous as Yemen was, thou-sands of Somali refugees still found it to be a haven compared to the worse conditions in their own native lands, and Al Kharaz was one of two refugee camps set up to house them.

In addition to its military forces, the Saudi General Intelligence Directorate, which was directed by the crown prince himself, was active in Yemen. The agency had made inquiries with various camp doctors looking for a young boy or girl with good health. The only twist was that the child needed to have a very specific blood type. The agents offered a high reward for success. A camp doctor in Al Kharaz had responded that he had just such a child in his care. It was a boy who'd been treated for a knife wound to his arm suffered somewhere on the dangerous journey from Somalia to Yemen. He was otherwise remarkably healthy, considering the circumstances.

The SUV worked its way through the camp along a gravel track. Children moved around the camp in packs, unsupervised. Almost half the camp's 17,000 residents were children. Food was not plentiful in the camp, but starvation was not even the worst issue. Cholera swept through the tents almost constantly, and other illnesses were inevitable with so many people packed into a space only slightly larger than a square kilometer.

The vehicle reached a larger structure with wooden walls and a metal roof. A red cross flag flew from a makeshift pole lashed to a corner of the building, barely upright in the hot, steady wind. Four people stepped out of the vehicle. The two young men who had been riding in the front were dressed in army fatigues, with submachine guns slung over their shoulders. Their shoulder patches marked them as part of a Saudi Arabian special forces unit. They studied the space around the building with the relaxed but thorough glances of combat veterans. The other two men lifted medical bags out of the rear of the SUV and then all four headed toward the building. One of the two carrying the medical bags was a tall, thin man with thick black hair and a beard. His companion was older and heavier, with graying hair under a headscarf. The soldiers treated the two men with the medical bags with great deference. The soldiers were surprised to see the *Mahabith* operating outside the borders of Saudi Arabia. Even though both young men held decorations for valor, they had no interest in getting on the dreaded secret police agency's list of interest for any reason.

A pale, sweating man in a stained white doctor's coat met the group at the door. He looked around furtively even though there was no one to see him other than the four visitors.

"You are the doctor who contacted us?" The tall visitor said.

"Yes." The doctor spoke with an accent the tall man could not place. Most of the doctors and medical teams in the camp were outsiders, in the country for a matter of months through the Red Cross or Doctors without Borders.

"Where is the boy?"

"In the back," the doctor said, gesturing with a turn of his head. "He's been told he needs special treatment. His mother is worried." The doctor led them down a narrow hallway lined with sheets of plywood. Doorless openings along the way revealed treatments rooms packed with sick, hungry, and injured men, women, and children. The heat in the building was almost unbearable, and flies entered and exited with impunity.

The room at the end of the hall held an examination table. A Somali boy, 9 or 10 years old, sat on the table, shirtless. A clean white bandage was wrapped around his left bicep. His mother sat on a flimsy folding chair in the corner, rocking slightly back and forth.

The two men from the Mahabith opened their bags and took out the tools they needed. The heavier one took blood from the boy and began running tests on it. The tall one examined the boy and quizzed the camp doctor at the same time. He asked about known illnesses, how long the boy had been in the camp, and so on. The doctor relayed some of the questions to the mother. She answered when asked, but otherwise continued to rock back and forth and spoke softly to herself.

"He's in good shape, mates," the doctor said, as though talking about a used car he had for sale, not a young boy. "He meets all the criteria you sent me. I even did the virtual crossmatch."

The visitors continued their work while their security detail stood outside in the hallway. They worked with intensity. After an hour they nodded to each other, satisfied.

The pale doctor spoke quietly to the mother, who began to cry. She asked him some questions in Arabic, and he answered as best he could with his crude knowledge of the language. She was clearly not consoled by his responses.

The tall Saudi looked at the doctor impatiently.

"I told her earlier that her boy needs special attention that we cannot provide here, and that you'll take him to a better hospital in Aden," the doctor said. "I have told her she cannot go along but that her son will come back in a few days."

One of the men took clean trousers and a shirt out of a bag and handed them to the boy. He looked over at his mother, confused, but the camp doctor told him in his halting Arabic to put them on. The boy stood up from the examination table and put on what were probably the first new clothes he'd ever had in his life.

The tall man shouted through the door and the two soldiers came in. The mother's eyes went wide at the sight of the weapons. The two soldiers simply took the boy by the arms and led him quickly away down the hall. The mother, realizing this was no ordinary medical mission, began to wail, but the doctor held her back. The visitors gathered their bags and turned to leave. The tall one turned back and handed an envelope to the doctor. "This is what was promised," he said.

The doctor nodded quickly and shoved the envelope into his shirt. The boy was loaded into the SUV and the vehicle sped off. Nothing was recorded. He'd just be one more nameless boy who disappeared without notice in the overcrowded, barely-regulated camp.

The SUV drove the two hours back to Aden in near silence. The boy stared straight ahead, either too terrified to speak or overwhelmed by the quick transition from the squalor of the camp to the air-conditioned vehicle.

A few minutes out from Aden, the tall man gave the boy a pill and a glass of water and told him to drink it. He resisted at first, but a glare from the man was enough, and the boy swallowed the pill.

In Aden, they drove directly to the airport. A small jet was waiting, engines turning. The boy was drowsy by now from the medicine. The two soldiers guided him onto the plane, strapping him into the leather seat. Five minutes later, the plane was in the air, arcing north up the coast of Yemen. The heavy-set man put a saline drip in the boy's arm once he was asleep. Their instructions had been to get him as healthy as possible, as quickly as possible. Why the crown prince wanted this particular boy was something neither of them needed or wished to know.

Sixty-Seven

Of all the unbelievable things around her, it was the couch that kept drawing Mary's attention. She'd only been on an airplane twice in her life. Once was on her honeymoon, and once during a brief, wonderful window of time after John's second surgery when his health had stabilized and they could live, for a bit, like a normal family. They'd gone to Puerto Rico for a week, letting John sit on the beach and even walk in the water. Those plane rides had been cramped, the four of them stuffed into the cheapest seats they could find. She'd brought leftovers from home for their inflight meal to save a few dollars.

The idea that an airplane could have a couch was somehow almost impossible for her to grasp, but it was just one among a long list of things that had been beyond belief over the past few days. It had started with Esther telling her that Annette Cera had been on the heart transplant list only to have her name removed suddenly. It had ended with Marco claiming that there still could be a way to save John's life. And in the middle of it all, her reaching the crash site and seeing Rick standing in front of Marco, a pistol pointed at the man's forehead. The look she'd seen on Rick's face still made her shiver.

And now here she was, sitting next to Rick on a private jet streaking towards Vancouver. Marco had moved to the second seating area in the plane and was lying on the couch, eyes closed. Every inch of the plane reeked of money and power, from the gleaming wood inlays and plush carpet to the CeraGlobal company logo imprinted in the paper napkins. When they'd boarded, Marco had moved around the plane casually, like he was in the living room of his house, offering them water and soda and showing them how to work the TVs.

She'd asked Marco if this was the plane they'd used to whisk the heart out of Detroit. "That one was bigger," he'd replied simply. The fact that the family could own an even bigger version of a plane like that made her feel small. It also fueled her resentment. The only thing that seemed to be as limitless as their resources was their selfishness.

She looked at Rick. His eyes were shut. Neither of them had slept much since the events at the crash site.

Marco's words still rang in her ears. He'd refused to provide many details at the time on how Lana proposed to save John, but he'd insisted it was true. Somehow, he believed Lana could do what the entire medical community of the world's richest nations could not.

She felt the plane decelerate a bit. The slight motion of the plane was enough to rouse Marco. He went into the bathroom in the back section and then came forward. He took a seat opposite her and Rick, who continued to doze.

"Twenty minutes," Marco said. "Use the bathroom now if you need it."

They sat in silence for a minute, the only noise the whisper of the air rushing over the wings and the steady, faint drone of the engines. Marco stared straight ahead, seemingly lost in thought.

Mary took out her phone and opened the photo app. She thrust it towards Marco, the screen side pointed at his face. "This is him," she said. "This is John."

To Mary's surprise, Marco reached out and took the phone. He studied the photo for a minute. "He looks like you," he said finally.

"You should know what he looks like. That's the boy you've been killing."

"I know what he looks like," Marco said.

"How would you know? You've never seen him before," Mary said. Then a horrible thought crossed her mind. "Did you go to the hospital? Did you see him?"

Marco looked out the window at the light cloud cover below. "No. I did some...research. As part of my job."

"Why?"

Marco's smooth veneer cracked, and he seemed embarrassed suddenly. "It doesn't matter now. I won't do anything else with what I found."

"John understands what's happening," Mary said, ignoring her first glimpse an almost-human emotion on Marco's usually stoic face.

Marco just studied her. He was an odd mix, she realized. He was clearly uncomfortable, maybe even ashamed in some way. But he made no attempt to avoid her stare, or her judgement.

"He understands he's dying," Mary continued. "You should know that, too. His organs are starting to struggle from lack of oxygen. Fluids are building up in his body. He doesn't say it directly, but I know he can feel it. Every day he dies a little bit. And we die with him."

"I had no interest in hurting you or your son."

"What did you think you were doing?

Marco shrugged. "I got taught a lot of unusual skills in the military. Those skills aren't that useful in too many other places. But they were to Lana Cera. I was in a bad way near the end of my last tour. She recruited me. Offered me a ton of money and a chance to get far away from my old life. Or so I thought. So, I do a lot of…" he paused, seeming to struggle to pick the next words. "…*unusual* things for Lana."

"Awful things," Mary said.

"Usually to awful people," Marco said. "Powerful or wealthy people, but still, some of the worst you can find, in their own ways."

Mary's eyes continued to bore into him. "We weren't. We aren't. We didn't hurt anyone. We just wanted to save our son's life. You took his chance away."

"At least he had one to start with. Most of the rest of the world I've been in, a kid like him never has much of one to begin with."

Mary wasn't swayed. "What do you think that's like, Marco? For a little kid to lie in bed every day wondering what it will feel like to die? What do you think goes through his head as he watches the sun come up and go down each day outside his hospital window, knowing he's a little closer to finding out that answer?"

"It has to be terrible."

"This…" Mary waved at the plane around her. "This money; this power. It doesn't give them the right to do what they did. But at least *they* have a reason I can understand. You?" She shook her head. "You're just a thug. With a nice smile and an expensive jacket maybe. But a thug all the same."

"I understand why you'd think that," Marco said. "But it's more complicated."

"You might have studied us. But you don't understand anything about us," Mary said. "And no, it's not more complicated than that." She leaned in closer, her voice dropping to a hiss. "Until you've had to sit by your own child's bedside and tell him the one hope he had to live was gone? Don't tell me you 'get it.'"

Marco's eyes sparked. "There are different kinds of suffering, Mary. And a lot of ways to feel like you let down the people who counted on you. And we all do things that don't look so good in the daylight. Different motives maybe, but the same result."

"It isn't fair," Mary said. "Money shouldn't just get you everything."

"I've learned that only people who don't have money think that way."

Mary glanced over at Rick. His eyes were still closed. She felt tears in her own eyes. "I thought Rick was going to that lot to kill himself. I thought you'd driven him to that."

"He wouldn't do that," Marco said. "He's tougher than that."

"Would you have killed him if Lana told you to?"

Marco shook his head. "No. But kneeling in that lot, I did wonder for a minute if he would kill us. I know the look. What does that say about him?"

"It says he loves his son."

"Marie and Phillippe Gaumond love their daughter. Lana Cera loves her family. I've seen them together. They're no different in that way."

"You're all going to hell," Mary said.

An odd sort of pain passed like a shadow over Marco's face. "Already been there," he said. "I'm just looking for a way back out."

A pleasant chime sounded in the cabin.

"That means we're on approach," Marco said. "Time to wake up your husband. It's going to be a busy day."

Mary roused Rick and looked across him out the window. They were landing from the south. The Strait of Georgia glistened in the distance off the left side of the plane, with Vancouver Island below them. Sharp-edged mountains rose up in the distance ahead of the plane, their tops already bright white with snow sparkling in the clear air.

The landing was smooth. She felt another wave of disorientation when they simply walked off the plane, through a small reception area and into a waiting SUV, their bags offloaded and put into the car by two polite men with overalls and earmuffs. There were no customs lines. No security checks. Marco took up the passenger seat and nodded to the driver, who looked like his younger, beefier double. The driver circled the small roundabout in front of the private jet terminal, and they sped off along an access road that paralleled the runway, only separated by a chain-link fence, and headed into Vancouver.

Rick and Mary were silent in the second row of seats. Marco made occasional comments about Vancouver and the landmarks around them. Mary guessed he'd grown up near this city from the way his eyes lit up when he pointed out the mountains in the distance or named the famous buildings along their winding route. They worked their way through the city, finally picking up the highway after passing over what Marco told them was the Kingsgate Bridge.

Mary checked her phone every few minutes. There were no new messages. Finally, she realized the reason. "I can't get a signal here," she said quietly, to Rick.

Rick winced. "We don't have international calling," he said. "I forgot."

"I told Esther to keep in touch," Mary said. "About John."

"I'm sure everything will be okay," Rick said. "Maybe we can borrow a phone to call later."

The car picked its way along the coastline west of the city for half an hour or so. There was dark blue water on their left and mountains climbing ever higher on the right. The homes got steadily larger and further apart as they worked their way along the winding road. Eventually they pulled into a long cobblestone driveway that curved to the right and then the left, obscuring most of the property from any traffic. They passed a perfectly manicured lawn that appeared as though no human had ever walked on it and came over a small rise. The house sat in front of them. The main part of the building was two stories high and seemed to stretch as wide as David's elementary school. One-story wings spread out from either side of the central structure. The house was cedar-shingled, and the roof seemed to be slate. The driveway ended in a circle, like a hotel. The car came to a stop halfway around the loop, under a portico that led to a set of brick steps.

"Welcome to the Cera residence," Marco said. "Well, at least to the Cera family home. They own a few other properties scattered around the city."

"It's so big," Mary said, despite her commitment to herself to show no deference, no sign of intimidation.

"Wait 'til you see the water side," Marco said.

The driver led them to the front door and held it open while they entered. Mary held back a gasp. The house was built into the steep cliffside, so while the roadside appeared to be an enormous but traditional lodge-style house, the ocean side extended down at least another two stories. Opposite Mary, fifty feet away across shining hardwood floors, windows that had to be two stories tall opened onto Vancouver Harbor. A handful of islands dotted the water a quarter mile out, off to the left side of the view. Couches and coffee tables were perfectly scattered around the room, which stretched almost the width of the main structure. A cluster of comfortable chairs formed a semicircle around a massive stone fireplace to her left. Mary calculated that the chairs in that one sitting area would have overfilled her entire living room. Here, she thought, they simply looked like a cozy island in the huge space. A wide staircase curved up to her right, to a mezzanine that ran the length of the room. The room dripped with a sense of casualness and luxury that balanced perfectly somehow, as though everyone in the world had a room like this.

"Have a seat," Marco said. "I'll go find Lana."

Sixty-Eight

Rhonda reached her office in the main hospital building around 9 a.m. She didn't know what was going to happen in Vancouver. She knew that—depending on the outcome up there—her days at the hospital could be numbered. She didn't want to waste any one of them.

"Esther Williams has been waiting for you for an hour," her assistant said. "She's angry."

Rhonda stepped into her office. Esther was at the glass wall, looking down into the atrium. She didn't turn when Rhonda greeted her.

"Mary told me everything that happened. Who else knows?" Esther asked.

Rhonda knew lying was pointless. Everything depended on what happened in Vancouver and whatever plans Marco and Lana Cera had concocted. "Murray Weiss knows," she said. "But he left to go see his dad in L.A. His dad is ill."

"His dad doesn't live in L.A. He lives in Cleveland," Esther said. "I know his doctors. He's fine."

Rhonda felt a pang of betrayal at the words, but not nearly as sharp as she'd thought. Murray's job was to create contingency plans. Part of her had suspected he'd have one for himself in this situation. She turned to Esther. "Did you come to tell me to resign? Or that the police are on their way?"

"You need to keep John on the transplant list," Esther said. "No matter what. You don't leave town, and you don't quit. You need to do whatever you need to do to give him a shot."

"There's no shot. You know that."

"I'll decide that. You just do what I tell you to. I don't know what Rick and Mary are going to do or what Lana Cera thinks she can pull off, but if it's for real, then John deserves that chance."

Rhonda nodded. She joined Esther at the window. "You know what I was thinking, when I was kneeling in that lot?" she asked.

Esther shook her head.

"I was thinking how my brother Tony died in a lot like that. And my uncle died on a sidewalk not too far from Metropolitan Hospital. I'd vowed to myself that I'd be different. *I'd* be the one that changed things in this city. *For* the city. Instead, there I was, kneeling in a vacant lot in Detroit with a gun to my head. No different at all."

Esther shook her head again. "You're different than that," she said. "At least you were. What you built here is amazing. Impossible even. But Rhonda, it would have survived even if the money ran out right now. You *know* that. Somebody would have bought it. The city would have stepped in. It's too important for it to fail. You didn't have to do what you did."

"Maybe it would have survived," Rhonda said. "But it would have survived without me. I wouldn't have survived that." She went to the interior windows, taking in the same view Esther had been seeing. She let her eyes wander from the courtyard below to the patient floor across the massive open space of the atrium. "I wouldn't be here to see it."

"Kunal may not be here to see it, either," Esther said quietly.

"I never thought that could happen. I just wanted to save the hospital."

"Will you do what I asked?" Esther said.

Rhonda nodded. "I've got no place else to go. I'll do what I can."

Rhonda nodded again. This close to the glass she could hear the faint laughter of the children playing far below, floating up on the warm air of the atrium. She wondered how many more times she'd get to hear that sound.

Sixty-Nine

Marco returned to the massive entrance hall after a few minutes. He led Rick and Mary out of the great room and down a set of stairs as wide as the Morrows' living room. The hallway was narrower on the level below. They passed a few closed doors on either side of the wood-lined passage, feet silent on the plush carpet. Marco opened a doorway at the end of the hall and ushered them into an oak-paneled room.

The large space was lined with perfectly organized bookshelves topped by a series of oil portraits. A gleaming wooden table sat in the center of the room, big enough for a dozen upholstered chairs to fit comfortably around it.

Lana Cera was at the head of the table, on the left side of the room from where Rick and Mary entered. Marie and Phillippe were to her left along the far side of the table, the expanse of polished wood separating the pair from Rick and Mary. Lana, Marie, and Phillippe had stood in unison as the door had swung open.

Rick had only seen a picture of Lana, but there was no doubt it was her. She was taller than he expected. As tall as him, he guessed. But the short hair, lean frame, and piercing eyes were exactly what he'd pictured somehow. Phillippe seemed older than Rick would have thought, given Annette's age. The man had unkempt, greying hair, a bit too long for his age, and reading glasses dangling from a chain around his neck. He had a glass in front of him, ice cubes floating in a golden-brown liquid. Marie had her mother's face, but on a stockier, shorter frame. Worry lines and fatigue creased the corners of her eyes.

No one made a move to shake hands.

"Hello," Lana said, once the door closed behind them. "Thank you for coming." Even her greeting sounded more like a command to Rick.

"We didn't have a lot of options," Mary said bluntly.

"Of course," Lana said. "Sit down, please, and we can talk." If she was put off by Mary's tone, she did not show it.

Rick and Mary took seats opposite Philippe and Marie. Marco moved to the side wall, away from the table, and settled into a hard-backed chair next to a reading lamp. Apparently, this was not his show, Rick thought.

"I trust the flight was good?" Lana said.

"Where is she?" Mary said.

Lana smiled thinly.

"I assume you mean Annette. She's in a room at the other end of this hallway."

"I want to see her."

A hint of irritation flashed across Lana's eyes. "I promised you would. She's getting some medical attention right now."

Rick caught Marie's glare at her mother. Apparently not everyone in the Cera family agreed with the decision to let him and Mary see Annette.

Lana pointed to a set of silver carafes in the middle of the table flanked by white porcelain cups. "There's coffee and tea. And water. If you'd like anything else, please just ask."

"We're good," Rick said.

Phillippe stood again. He went to the bar at the end of the room and filled his glass from a bottle of whisky that looked half empty already.

Lana watched him return, pursing her lips in disappointment, but saying nothing. She turned back to Rick and Mary. "I can only imagine how you feel about us right now. I'm sure I'd feel the same if the situation were reversed." The words were said gently, but to Rick it was clear that Lana could not imagine a world where the situation could ever be reversed.

Lana continued. "But then again, in many ways our problems are very much the same, so maybe you can understand a bit. I am sure we have the same desire. The willingness to do anything to save our children. To use any means we can think of."

"We fight for John. But we follow the rules," Rick said. "We're nothing like you."

"The rules are the only chance people like you have," Lana said. "I understand that. You needed the system to come through. For the process to work." She stood up and walked over to the far wall, flanked by the oil paintings. The subjects of the paintings were either men or couples. From the vague resemblances many of them had to Lana, Rick guessed they represented her family tree.

"Time wasn't going to be there for Annette," Lana said. "The damage to her heart was too severe. She only had a few months at best. Our doctors said she may not have been approved for a transplant anyway, given her condition. Following the rules wasn't going to save my granddaughter."

Lana turned back to face them and shrugged. "So, I made my own rules." She stood defiantly. The paintings behind her seemed to add to her conviction, as though the entire Cera history was evidence of her own rightness.

"You took our son's only chance," Mary said, the fury clear in her voice. Is that part of your 'choice'?"

Lana shook her head. "I didn't do this to hurt your child. I did it to save my granddaughter. The rest was…" Her voice trailed off for a moment. She gathered herself. "The rest was just what it needed to be. I'm sorry, but your child just wasn't part of my thinking."

"Our *child*?" Mary's lips curled back in a snarl. "What's his name, Lana? Do you even know his name?"

Lana stared at her for a moment.

"You'll kill him, but you won't even bother to learn his name."

"His name is John." The words came quietly, almost mournfully, from the far side of the table. It was Phillippe.

"Okay. *John*," Lana said, after another disapproving glance towards Phillippe. "No, John was not part of my thinking. Again, I'm sorry, but that's just the way it is."

Rick looked at Phillippe and Marie. "And you agreed with this?"

"We didn't know what was happening, at first," Phillippe said. Marie said nothing.

"But you know now. And you still go along." Phillippe hung his head.

"We couldn't let Annette die," Marie said. "She's everything to us."

"Marco said you could save John," Rick said. "That's why we came. Not to hear your bullshit excuses."

Lana's phone buzzed and she glanced at the message. "We'll talk about that. But if you want to see Annette, the doctors are saying we should go now."

Marco stood and glided to the door in that liquid way he had. He held it open. The rest of the group walked back down the hallway to the far end. Lana opened a door there and led them into a windowless sitting room. A long side table was filled with prescription bottles. A stainless steel refrigerator had been placed in a corner, incongruous against the paneled walls and velvet drapes. What looked to have been a makeup table now held other medical supplies and instruments.

Plastic sheeting covered a set of double doors at the far end of the room.

Rick studied the labels on the drug vials. He recognized most of the names. He'd researched endlessly the drugs John was taking, and the ones he'd need to take after the transplant, to prevent his own body from rejecting the heart and to balance his body chemistry and to stave off life threatening infections. But there were some that he didn't expect to see. IV antibiotics. In huge doses. He started to ask about them, but a nurse handed him a surgical mask. He looked around and realized everyone else had been given one, too.

He knew by now that Lana was not one to leave anything to chance, but the masks and the plastic sheeting seemed like a bit much, Rick thought. He put those observations aside as Lana moved forward. There was a rustle as she pushed aside the plastic and opened the double doors, revealing a large bedroom filled with state-of-the-art medical equipment. The blinking, buzzing machines lined the walls and hung over the single hospital bed centered on the wall to the right. The bed faced a massive picture window that looked out onto the sound to the left. Two women in medical scrubs were gathering up their equipment. Annette was nearly lost in the bed, surrounded by machines and a pair of tubes snaking down from IV bags and disappearing under her bedsheets.

Rick watched Mary from the corner of his eye. Her own eyes had gone wide, but she made no attempt to move into the room.

Marie was standing to Mary's left. "Is she comfortable?" Mary asked.

"Yes," Marie said. "As much as we can expect. The suture site is still very sore."

"Is she able to walk?" Mary said.

"Yes, she walks a bit every day. But she's been more fatigued the last two days." Marie nodded her head. "The doctors say that can happen sometimes."

The group was silent for a minute. The monitors in the bedroom beeped and sighed in a pattern so familiar to Rick he almost didn't notice it.

"She's pretty," Mary said.

"Yes," Marie said.

Rick felt his heart begin to race. Even in the face of this awful crime, Mary's first thought was of the little girl in the bed beyond. And Rick knew that somehow, Lana and people like her counted on that. Those kind of people took for granted the goodness in people like Mary. Marco had it wrong, Rick thought; most people in the world would do the right thing given the chance. People like the Ceras counted on it. He felt the heat in his face. He realized he was leaning forward, starting to take a step towards the room beyond, toward the little girl who held John's heart inside her own chest. From the corner of his eye, he saw Marco shake his head, almost imperceptibly, his eyes locked on Rick's. But it wasn't a challenge or threat; it was almost like advice from a friend.

Rick took a deep breath. Lana had promised there was a way to save John, he reminded himself. Although he did not believe even she could make that possible, he knew he had to listen, in case there was even the slightest chance she was right.

"Okay," Mary said. "Thank you."

They all turned without a word and made their way back down the hall to the library, returning to their original seats. Rick poured glasses of water for himself and Mary.

"That was always her favorite room because of the view," Marie said, her mind still on her daughter. "She loves to watch the whales in the sound. She gives them names."

"We have a goldfish at home. John named him, too," Mary said.

"We can turn you in," Rick said, looking at Lana and her family members in turn. "We have the proof despite everything you did to destroy it. We can ruin you and your company."

Lana nodded. "You could. But Annette will still have her heart. You won't have gained anything."

"What's left to gain?" Rick asked.

"I said earlier we have more in common than you think. I have no desire to see your son die. To see *John* die. Or to see my family's company ruined. Or for Annette to spend every day with the media in her face, asking her how it feels to live life with a stolen heart."

Lana leaned forward. "I can do for John what I did for Annette." She looked at Rick and Mary in turn. "I can get him a heart."

The words hung in the air, almost too impossible to have been formed or spoken, never mind heard or comprehended.

"There are none available," Rick said. "We'd know."

"There are none available in the transplant system—you're right," Lana said. "But the transplant network is not the whole world."

"How would you know what else is out there?"

"I have contacts. All over the world. Many of them are powerful people. They can make inquiries to their hospitals. I can scour the whole world for a heart. And with the machine that doctor of yours invented, I can get it here in time. For John. If we reach an agreement."

"From where?" Mary said. Her voice was neutral, but Rick could sense something deeper behind the question.

"That doesn't matter quite yet," Lana said.

"It should," Mary said, coldly.

Lana ignored the rebuke. "We'd need to agree to a few things first. I want to see each of our families walk away from this terrible situation in one piece. So, we'll need to build some trust with each other."

"What do you want?" Rick said.

"Silence," Lana said. "You agree never to go public with anything you know, or think you know. No lawsuits. No interviews."

"And if we agree?" Rick asked, eyes raised. He found himself relaxed in an odd way. He started scanning the faces, trying to understand the dynamics that mattered most—the ones that would never come out in words or questions. Marie's eyes were burning. He could feel her resentment and stubbornness; she did not care if John, Mary, or Rick lived or died. She clearly just wanted this meeting over so she could go back to Annette. Phillippe looked lost, some sort of despair written all over his face. As Rick watched, Phillippe took another deep drink of whisky. Marco sat motionless in the corner, eyes tracking from side to side, missing nothing.

Mary was oddly still, too, as though her mind was working through some problem he couldn't identify. And Lana sat at the head of the table, spine straight, eyes boring into him as they spoke. But there was worry in the way she held her hands. Something else was going on in her mind too. Rick couldn't place it, but he knew it mattered.

"I'll make a phone call, and a lot of things will go into motion," Lana said.

"The heart?" Mary asked, quietly.

"It will meet him at the hospital here."

"What keeps us from turning you in, once John's okay?" Rick said.

Lana nodded seriously. "Now we're to the crux of it. This comes back to the trust we talked about."

"Why would you trust us any more than we trust you?" Mary said.

Lana ignored her question. "What will you do to save John's life?" she said to Rick.

"Anything." Rick said. He didn't hesitate with the answer, but his mind was racing, wondering what she could possibly want him to do that she could not do herself.

"You probably think you're nothing like us, don't you?" Lana asked the question gently, almost kindly. "Especially after what we did to you."

Rick said nothing.

"Would you have done the same thing? If you had the money, and the means?" Lana said. Now she kept her eyes on Mary. "Wouldn't any parent, Mary?"

"We did everything right," Mary said. "We waited and waited. We saw hearts go to other kids. You're right. We're nothing like you."

"You did everything right?" Lana asked. She seemed almost amused by Mary's answer. She stood and walked over to the bookshelves again. "Do you remember Danny Cho, Mary? What you did then?"

Rick saw Mary turn ashen.

"That wasn't like this," Mary hissed.

"No?" Lana said.

Rick saw that Mary was reeling, suddenly. He could hear the anger in her voice, but there was something else, too. Shame.

He looked around the room for any clue to help him rescue Mary from whatever was happening. Marie and Phillippe obviously didn't know any more than he did. Marco, though, was staring at Lana. There was fury in his eyes.

"Do you remember Danny Cho, Rick?" Lana said.

"His parents moved to the U.S. from China," Rick said.

"His dad invested in a U.S. company to get the visas. He had the same blood type as John. When that girl drowned in Nevada, they crossmatched him and John to save time. John had been on the list for years, but the transplant board said Cho was more urgent. So, he got the heart."

"Do you know anything else about Danny Cho?" Lana said, almost taunting him.

"I know his family and yours would get along just fine," Rick said. "Why does he matter now?"

Lana smiled. "He's the boy your wife was willing to see die, to get John back to the head of the line."

Seventy

Esther sat in a cramped office, scowling. A small prefab desk piled with medical journals jutted out from one wall. There were four other people in the small room with her. That number was easily two more than the space was meant to hold. Two were men in their forties, wearing the long white coats of doctors. One of the two, seated behind the desk, had reading glasses perched on his nose. The other, still wearing surgical scrubs under his hospital coat, held a paper cup of black coffee. Both looked tired. Rhonda stood at the end of the desk. Fiona Esperanza leaned against the far wall in a black skirt and blue blouse, arms crossed. She was silent but shaking her head rapidly as if already rejecting what she was about to hear.

"I'm sorry," the doctor with the reading glasses said. "The charts are clear. His kidney function is way down. Fluid is collecting in his lungs. We need to take him off the transplant list."

"Can't we wait a bit longer?" Fiona said. "There is still a question of lawsuits, and the media will get wind of this. We'll look like we're abandoning him. We don't need another news cycle around this whole mess."

The other doctor cut her off. "This is a medical decision, Fiona. We don't make those for PR reasons."

"Of course not," Fiona said. "But there must be some gray area. For the family, too. The media hasn't exactly treated them kindly through all of this. We shouldn't make it worse."

"I've seen the charts, too," Esther interjected. "John's still got most of his kidney function. He's young. He'll recover fast. It's too early to do this. And his parents are…" She tailed her voice. off, remembering her promise to Rick and Mary. "They're not available right now. We have to wait."

Both doctors shook their heads. "It's not fair to do that," the one with the glasses said. "We could jeopardize the chances of the next child in line, if a heart becomes available suddenly and we're caught in paperwork. The data is clear. And so is the prognosis."

"What does 'clear' ever have to do with this?" Esther said. "We make arbitrary decisions all the time about who's on the list, and who moves up or down the stack. There's as much art as science to this. I'm just saying let's have a little consideration. He's a tough kid. He's worth betting on."

The doctors both shook their heads, clearly unmoved. "Doctor Mirchandani would bet on him," Esther said bitterly, knowing immediately that she'd crossed a line.

"Kunal is my friend, too, Esther," the one with glasses snapped back.

Esther looked down, not trusting herself to speak as she thought about Dr. Mirchandani, who was being wheeled into surgery somewhere on the floors above her at that moment, to try and alleviate the swelling in his brain.

Fiona nodded in defeat. She scrawled her name on the document on the desk. "Rhonda needs to sign as well."

"I'm sorry, Esther," Fiona said as she passed the documents over to Rhonda. "I know how close you are to John Morrow."

They all looked at Rhonda. She looked at Esther hard, then nodded. "Okay. I'll sign the papers and forward them to the transplant organization."

Esther's eyes went wide. "You can't, Rhonda."

Rhonda avoided her glance and walked quickly out of the office, the documents under her arm.

Esther scrambled to her feet, pushing her way out of the office, and started to follow Rhonda down the hallway, her anger building. A knot of residents got between them, clustered around an attending physician to head downstairs on rounds. Esther worked her way around them and picked up her pace, trying to close the distance to Rhonda before the woman made it to the elevator and disappeared upstairs. Esther was still trailing Rhonda by ten steps when Rhonda approached a janitor's cart jammed against the wall. Eyes fixed straight ahead, Rhonda dropped the paperwork casually in the trash bin strapped to the end of the cart and kept heading towards the elevator without breaking stride. Once there she turned back, waiting for the doors to open. She spotted Esther and gave her a faint, sad smile.

Esther nodded, then turned back towards her own wing, already mentally running through the list of patients she needed to check on.

Seventy-One

"Ani? That's your name?" the man in the lab coat asked, reading off a clipboard.

The Somali boy in the hospital bed nodded. The remains of a huge dinner were still spread out on the tray that spanned the bed. He'd eaten every bit of the food and looked ready to eat more if they offered it. It was probably more food than he'd had at any one meal in his life, the man in the lab coat thought.

"How are you feeling?" the man asked.

"Cold," Ani said.

The man nodded and made a note to raise the temperature, which was already a few degrees above normal. Air conditioning was another thing the boy had probably never experienced before.

"I am not sick," Ani said.

"We are just running some tests. To make sure."

"I am not sick," Ani repeated, gesturing to the IV taped to his left forearm. "I want to go back."

"You will soon enough," the man said. "We just want to make sure you are okay. Your mother asked us to be sure you are okay. We should do what she asks, right?"

Ani dropped back into a suspicious silence at the invocation of his mother. The man checked off the final vitals on the sheet. The boy was well-hydrated from the saline drip in his arm. There was no sign of dysentery from the camps, or infection from the wound on his arm, and he was otherwise in the ridiculous good health of a 13-year-old boy, despite a poor diet and life in one of the world's worst war zones.

"Would you like anything else to eat?" the man asked.

Ani nodded. The man made a note for another dessert to be brought up, even though it was late in the evening. After all, given the call he'd gotten earlier, it was probably the boy's last meal. They might as well give him a good one.

Seventy-Two

The boy Mary was willing to kill? The idea almost couldn't register for Rick, except for the fact that the words clearly stung Mary. She was ghost white and tears sprang into the corner of her eye.

"How do you know about him?" Mary hissed at Lana.

"You really should be careful what you keep on your computer," Lana said. "It's amazing what hackers can find these days."

"Danny Cho," Rick said flatly. "So what?" He looked around the room, trying to gain insight from the others.. From the look on their faces Phillippe and Mariewere as confused as Rick about where Lana was going with her questions. But Marco's face had changed entirely; he was staring at Lana, his jaw set and anger still burning in his eyes.

"You really didn't know, did you?" Lana continued blithely, turning to Rick. "It wasn't clear from the emails if you were involved or not."

"Stop," Mary said. "That doesn't matter now."

"Sure it does, Mary," Lana said. She turned to Rick. "You didn't know about the emails Mary sent to the transplant board? And to your congressman? She claimed the Cho boy had an infection they were hiding, and that he wouldn't be a good candidate. That America shouldn't be saving the lives of foreigners when their own citizens were in need. That the Cho family were frauds. She said terrible things would happen to their boy, once he got out of the hospital. That he did not deserve to get the heart. That *John* did. The Cho family even called the police at one point."

Lana looked at Mary. "You would have been happy to see Danny Cho die back then, wouldn't you, Mary?"

Mary shook her head, but Rick saw some of the earlier anger rising inside her again. "It wasn't fair. America builds the health systems. We pay for the transplant network. And then somebody waltzes in and jumps the line, just because they can. Yes, it made me angry. And I did things I regret."

"I'm sure that was *so* frustrating, Mary," Lana said, almost soothingly. Rick could feel the sarcasm in her voice, He clenched his fists but stayed silent, trying to figure out what Lana was up to.

"But I stopped the emails," Mary said. "I dropped it, and Danny Cho got the heart."

"We noticed you stopped," Lana said, glancing at Marco, who looked away. "I was wondering why you did that."

"I got better advice," Mary said.

"Enough," Rick said, rising to his feet and putting a hand on Mary's shoulder. "We came here because you said you could save John. Not to get a lecture."

Lana glanced at Marco again, but he stayed coiled in his chair.

"I did say I could," Lana said. "And I can. Please sit down and I'll tell you how this works."

Rick sat down slowly and reached out his hand to cover Mary's. She was still shaking a bit, but her composure had returned.

"The AionOne is on its way to a location in the Middle East right now," Lana said. "There's a boy there, roughly your son's age. Perfectly healthy. He's a match in every way from his blood type to his antigens. Everything you could hope for. You agree to my terms, and his heart will be here in less than a day. We'll fly John here in the meantime, and a surgical team in Vancouver will perform the surgery. They've been briefed already that the surgery is happening here because the Cera foundation is paying for it. There will be paperwork showing the heart donation was legitimate. John can recover here for as long as he needs to."

"You said this boy is healthy," Mary said. "Then why is his heart available?"

Lana's look was almost pitying. "Nothing's wrong with him. He was just born in the wrong country in the middle of a civil war." Then she smiled at Mary, so sweetly it was clear she was mocking her again. "And no, Mary. I don't know his name."

The room was silent.

"You can't do this," Phillippe whispered.

"Shut up, Phillippe," Lana said, without even looking at him. She kept her eyes on Rick and Mary. "Yes, he's a healthy boy right now. But once the recruiters in the camps get ahold of him, the odds are his miserable life will end in a shopping plaza somewhere, with dead tourists all around the remains of his body. Or if we're lucky maybe at the end of a U.S. drone strike before he has a chance to make the world an even more miserable place. That boy's life was over the day he was born. It's not even his fault. But why not make something good come from it?"

"That's how you think you get our trust?" Rick said. "We share a crime, so nobody can turn anybody in?"

"We share two living children who have a chance to do something useful in this world, each with parents who love them," Lana said. "And yes, we share a secret that keeps us all safe."

She cocked her head as though just remembering something. "Oh, and yes, you'll receive a $10 million settlement from the CeraGlobal Corporation. And a public apology for the troubles you went through because of the negligence at the LifeLift company. The LifeLift CEO will be fired as well. You will have everything you wanted, Rick."

Rick felt Mary's hand shake under his. "Why didn't you just do that for Annette?" she asked. "Why go to all the trouble to steal John's heart? You could have left us out of this entirely."

"It's not that easy, Mary," Lana said. "This option doesn't come without a different kind of price. But it's one I've agreed to pay. If you want me to."

"What price could be higher than our son's life?" Mary spat.

For a moment everyone in the room could see a different emotion cross Lana's face; it looked like shame. "It's something I'll have to live with," she said. "But not something I will share with you. But I agreed, and here we are."

"Say yes. Please," Marie said, leaning forward in her chair. "How can you not say yes?"

Time seemed to stop for Rick as the offer hung in the air. He knew he and Mary were poised between two worlds that could not be more different from each other. To say "yes" was to step from one to the other, with no way ever to return. He'd felt up to this moment that he and Mary were only partially present— next to but not fully in this impossible environment of power and wealth. They were suspended from entering it fully by their disgust for the selfishness and moral blindness of the people at the table. He knew that to say "yes" to Lana was to break that barrier and to land fully in this world. To be, as Lana had said, just like them.

He knew that to say no was to kill John again, for the second time in a few days. He and Mary had given up nearly everything to care for John. Was it so wrong, he wondered, to give up some abstract sense of morality too, to finally save him? Was there really any other choice?

He drew in his breath to say "Yes," but felt a firm hand squeeze his wrist before his could speak.

"I need to talk to my husband," Mary said, her hand still on his arm. "Alone."

"There's a room down the hall you can use," Marco said to Mary. "I'll take you there."

"Twenty minutes," Lana said. "I can't make this offer last forever. And let's face it, John doesn't have that much time, either."

Seventy-Three

Esther was only part way through her patient visits when her phone buzzed. It was from a friend of hers who worked on the surgical floor.

"Surgery 5, now," was all it said.

Esther's heart started pounding. She did a quick catalogue of the floor around her. No alarms were sounding, and the nurses and aides bustled around with their usual purpose and calm.

It hit her as she strode towards the elevator that Kunal was still in surgery.

She broke into a trot and slapped hard at the elevator call button. It arrived quickly, and she was on the surgical floor in a matter of a minute. She pulled on a mask and gloves and pushed through the door to the viewing room overlooking the surgical suites.

Three people were staring down into Suite 5, including the friend Stephanie who had texted her. Esther saw the worry in her eyes as she greeted Esther silently. No one else in the viewing room moved. But down below them in the surgical suite was near pandemonium. The sound from the surgical suite was piped into the viewing room so surgical residents could listen in as part of their learning. A tangle of voices overlapped each other, shouting commands and relaying information. The two surgeons who'd been working to relieve the pressure on Kunal's brain were moving faster now, huddled over the opening in their patient's scalp.

"It looks like blood clots got dislodged during the surgery," Stephanie whispered. "He's suffering a series of strokes."

"How bad?"

"He's not bleeding out, but they can't seem to get blood to his brain. They're trying a shunt now, to hopefully get around the blockage."

"How long has it been?"

Stephanie shook her head. "Too long."

"Oh, Kunal," Esther said, looking down on the controlled chaos below. The surgical team worked furiously, performing the complex task at almost reckless speed. Doctor Mirchandani was loved by all in the hospital, and the people in the surgical suite were no exception. Esther knew they would do anything to save him.

The group upstairs watched for a few more minutes, trying to follow the dialogue from below. Finally, the surgeons stepped back from the table. One of the two put her hands on her hips and shook her head in frustration. Esther could see the traces of the heartbeat and other vital signs on the monitors which were replicated on the wall of the viewing room. Kunal was still alive, but there was no telling yet what the loss of oxygen would have done to his brilliant mind.

Esther gave Stephanie a quick hug and made her way back to her floor. She knew from experience that getting back to work could help keep her mind off the fight for Kunal's life. She held back her grief and sadness. She would not let her patients see those emotions on her face. They had enough problems of their own.

Seventy-Four

Esther's phone buzzed again a few minutes later and she stole a look at it. This time it was a call from Fiona Esperanza. She washed her hands and decided to go straight to Fiona's office, which was in the administrative building. Moving and working were the only things keeping her from breaking down and crying. She'd gotten the text a few minutes ago from Stephanie that the damage to Doctor Mirchandani's brain seemed catastrophic. Had he not been in surgery and on a ventilator when the strokes happened he'd have died in a matter of minutes. As it was, he was only kept alive by that breathing machine and a raft of other devices.

She found the dark-haired lawyer in her office, staring at the phone as Esther entered.

Fiona stood up when Esther entered. She handed Esther a document without saying a word, a haunted look on her face. Esther recognized it quickly as a living will. She skimmed the handful of pages quickly, then read it again carefully. She looked up at Fiona for confirmation.

"It's authentic," Fiona said. "I'm his medical proxy."

"But he could still recover," Esther said. "You can't execute this."

Fiona shook her head. "I spoke to the surgeons—they've done multiple scans. The damage...it's like a bomb went off in his skull."

Esther winced.

"I'm sorry," Fiona said. "But that's how the surgeons described it. He's gone, Esther."

Esther read the key passages again. "He even did his own crossmatch to be sure John could take his heart if it ever came to it," she said with admiration.

"You know Kunal," Fiona said. "He wouldn't leave anything to chance."

Esther took a deep breath and cleared her head. She thought of John and Mary Morrow in Vancouver. "I need to go," she said.

"I'm going to execute Kunal's wishes, Esther." Fiona said. "But I'm sorry we can't change the decision we made earlier. The transplant board is firm on this stuff. They won't let us reverse our diagnosis."

"The transplant board doesn't know anything about the discussion we had earlier," Esther said. "Ask Rhonda."

"You didn't!" Fiona said, a horrified smile curling the edge of her lips.

"I didn't do anything," Esther said. "Rhonda did. All I did was ask. You should have known I wouldn't let anything take away John's chance." Esther grabbed her phone. "But I need to send a message. Right now."

She texted Mary, typing furiously as she left Fiona's office. She still wasn't sure what Mary and Rick were doing in Vancouver, but she was sure they needed to know what was happening in Detroit.

Seventy-Five

Marco didn't speak as he led them to a room halfway up the hallway. He followed them in and closed the door. The room was a game room, big enough for a pool table, ping-pong table and several smaller tables. One of the smaller tables held a chessboard; another one, octagonal in shape, had chip holders and markings for poker or other card games. A giant TV was mounted on the short wall at one end, surrounded by mesh rectangles that Rick guessed hid audio speakers.

"You can talk in here. Nobody will hear you," Marco said.

"Did you arrange this part, too?" Mary asked. "This boy she's talking about?"

Marco's eyes hardened. "No."

"Is it really possible?" Rick said.

Marco nodded. "One of my guys is on his way right now to...where the boy is. He has the functional AionOne. Lana's got some sort of agreement with the government there. I don't know exactly what it is, but given how insane her ask was, I can guess." Rick could see a hint of disgust on Marco's face.

"You read my emails," Mary said to Marco. "That's how you knew about Danny Cho."

"Yes. It was part of the job."

"Then you know I stopped fighting against him. I apologized to the family."

"Yes."

He started to leave the room but turned back. "Make whatever decision you want. I'll make sure you get home safe, no matter what you decide. Remember that."

He slipped out and closed the door behind him. "These people are monsters," Mary said.

Rick shrugged. "Monsters whose kid has a new heart while our son is dying."

Mary looked at him sharply.

"I always tried to do the right thing, Rick said. "Then I look around this place and we see that girl. It makes me feel like a fool. I bet Annette doesn't think her grandmother is a monster."

"Don't be too sure about that." Mary sat down at the octagonal card table and picked up a red poker chip, turning it in her fingers. "I'm sorry I didn't tell you about Danny Cho and what I tried to do."

"I don't blame you."

"You should. I had no right to do that to that boy."

"I'm sorry I didn't fight harder so you wouldn't have to even think about that."

Mary shook her head. "It wouldn't have mattered. The board wouldn't change their mind." She put down the chip, stacking it carefully on a pile of white chips and picking up another red one. "Do you know why I stopped fighting?"

"I figured the police made you."

She shook her head, a flash of old anger moving across her face. Then she laughed a bit, but it was a sad laugh, tinged with disbelief at the depths of her own feelings and where they'd taken her. "The way I felt then, I wouldn't have stopped for the police. I was in John's room when I made one of the calls to the transplant board, lying about Danny Cho's condition. I thought John was asleep. But he wasn't. When I hung up, he asked me who Danny Cho was, so I told him that he had cheated to get in line ahead of John and was going to get the heart we'd talked about."

"What did he say?"

"He just smiled and said he was happy for Danny. And he meant it. John knew what it meant for himself, but I could see he was truly happy for that other boy. And then he asked me why I was trying to hurt Danny and take the heart away from him."

"You weren't trying to hurt Danny Cho. You were just trying to get John what he deserved."

Mary met his eyes. "That's exactly what Lana would say." She put the second red chip on the white pile and repeated the process. "This other boy, the heart they are talking about. They're going to kill him to get it for us."

"That's not our problem, Mary. He's not our problem."

"Maybe he should be," she said quietly.

"John's our only priority."

"Sure, we can say that," Mary said. "And those people can say that Annette's *their* only priority. And so it goes. Why shouldn't that other boy be our priority, too? Doesn't he deserve to be *somebody's* priority?"

"You heard Lana. Life doesn't mean the same thing where he's from."

"But it means the same thing to me." She looked at Rick. "To *us*. We owe John everything we can give him. But part of that is a world that's worthy of him living in it, for as long as he gets to."

"He could have a whole life in front of him. We can't take that away," Rick said, dropping into a chair across from her.

Mary studied her handiwork with the poker chips. "I know you spent a lot of time with John. But sometimes I don't think you really *saw* him. You were so focused on making him better you didn't always see who he actually is. I used to do that too. I thought of all the things I dreamed for him: him going back to school, running on the beach, having a *girlfriend*." Her voice caught with the final word. "But I realized those aren't things he dreams of. He's spent his whole life sick. We dream of those things for him, but that's not the life he knows."

"Why can't he know a different one. Even just for a little while?" Rick said, but the force was gone. A tear trickled down his left cheek. "Just let the poor kid win, even for once."

Mary realized she'd been wrong, He had seen the same boy she did after all, Mary realized. And she thought again how much she'd underestimated her husband. She stood and smiled. "We are winning, Rick. We've had ten amazing years with John. He's had ten years of life that even a decade ago he never would have had. And when the jerk I was married to bailed on me, you stepped in to become his dad, even knowing what that meant." She swallowed hard. "That was the bravest, and stupidest thing I've ever seen anyone do." She stared down at the table. "And we have David. Look, I know I said what I said in the car. But even if life, and marriage haven't been perfect for us, we have had some great times together, all four of us. Maybe that has to be enough."

Rick stared at the table for a minute, then nodded—slowly at first, then more firmly. "Let's go talk to Lana," he said.

Seventy-Six

Esther got the frantic voice message only minutes after texting Mary: it said Dr. Mirchandani had crashed twice after surgery. He was in the intensive care unit now, but the team there was unable to stabilize him, the strokes and brain hemorrhage had been devastating, and his body was on the verge of shutting down.

She checked on John Morrow quickly. He was sleeping soundly, which he did more and more each day as his own body fought to survive, as the blood flow from his heart failed to provide everything his cells so desperately needed. Once she was sure he was stable, she headed up to the ICU. The nurse there was an enormous black man Esther knew only as KC.

"He's hanging by a thread," KC told her now, when she picked up the chart.

"How long?"

The man shrugged his massive shoulders. "Hours, I'd say. Not days, for sure. The ventilator is keeping his organs alive for now, but his autonomous brain functions are all but gone. We can only do this for so long."

"I need one day," Esther said.

KC shook his head. "I doubt you have until sunset." Esther checked her phone again to see if Mary had replied. Instead she saw the red "undelivered" text under her previous note. She re-sent the message only to see the same note appear. She cursed and started to dial the phone, to see if she could reach Mary directly. KC cleared his throat politely. Cell phones were not allowed in the ICU, even for Esther.

Esther nodded and made her way out to the hallway, but it didn't matter. The call went straight to voicemail without so much as ringing. She cursed and put the phone away. She couldn't do anything until she spoke to Rick and Mary. And she had no idea why Mary's phone would be off, today of all days.

Seventy-Seven

The group gathered again in the library where they'd first met. Marie stared stone-faced at Rick and Mary. Philippe had his hands on the table. His gaze was unsteady, and remorseful. Marco took his seat in the corner, but another man joined him, too. Rick recognized him as the man who'd driven them from the airport. The young man remained standing, hands clasped in front of his body. To Rick he looked more like a guard than an observer.

Lana picked her cellphone up from the table and held it out for Rick and Mary to see.

"Should I make the call now?" she asked, as though the last 10 minutes were only a formality.

"Yes, call your friends," Rick said. Lana started to smile slightly.

"And tell them to let that boy go home," Rick added, staring at each of them in turn. Lana froze, one eyebrow arching up. Phillippe let out a breath that sounded more like a silent scream.

"You can't mean that," Lana said. "You're signing a death sentence for your son."

"We're giving him the life he deserves," Mary said. "Even if it's a short one. We won't let his life be based on a crime.

And we won't be part of letting another little boy die for any reason."

Lana started to shake visibly. "The money, then. Even if you are going to cling to some virtue about your son's value, I'll still give you the money, if you agree to stay silent."

"We don't need the money," Rick said. "We'll get by just fine."

"You can't do this." Marie said. "Annette deserves to live her life in peace."

"She deserves to know the truth," Mary said. "Maybe she'll even decide to make the most of the heart she's been given. She might be the only one in this family who's got one."

"Truth?" Marie said. "We gave you a chance to do the right thing. Now you'll bury your son in some shitty little grave in some shitty little cemetery. And you'll rot away in your shitty little house in Detroit until that gets taken away, too. Is that the truth you want?"

"We'll be just fine," Mary said. "We'll see how you do when this story is all over the papers. And you're all in a courtroom for what you did." She stood up. "Now we want to go home and see our son."

Lana seemed to calculate for a second. "Of course. But I'm sorry to say, the plane won't be ready for a few hours. We'll give you someplace to relax until then."

"We want to go now," Rick said.

"I'll see what we can do," Lana said. "Anton, please take them back to the game room. Get them something to eat, too."

The young man standing next to Marco moved forward. Rick glanced at Marco who nodded almost imperceptibly. Rick debated for a moment and decided to trust the assurance he seemed to be getting from the man, rather than try and fight his way out of the room.

Anton led them out of the room and down the hall. Lana closed the door behind them and turned to Marco.

"They cannot get back to Detroit," she said. "You need to make sure of that."

"It's over, Lana," Marco said. "Annette got her heart and now you all have to deal with the price you paid to get it. I thought you said it would be worth it regardless."

"I know what happened to the doctor in Detroit," Lana said. "You'll be paying the biggest price of all."

"I'll take care of myself."

"They won't change their minds," Phillippe said, hoarsely. "They're better than that."

"You need to fix this, mother," Marie said. "I will not let Annette grow up with the world knowing those things about her. You're supposed to protect her."

"Yes, I'm supposed to protect her," Lana said, "And I'm supposed to protect the company. And I'm supposed to protect the family name. I don't need you to lecture me on that, Marie."

Lana turned back to Marco. "They can't leave here unless they change their minds."

He shook his head. "We're done here Lana. You took your shot, Lana. I know them. They aren't changing their minds. Your money doesn't buy everything."

Lana stared at him coldly. "You're missing my point. They don't leave here, unless they change their minds. On all of it, not just the money." She turned and stalked back to the windows.

Seventy-Eight

Esther and Fiona stood nose-to-nose in Fiona's office. "We cannot do this, Esther," Fiona said.

"We have to, Fiona. We don't have time to wait."

"I'm not cutting a little boy open without his parent's consent."

"You know they'd approve."

"Then where are they?"

"I can't reach them right now."

"What if he dies, Esther? Do you want them to come back to find that out?"

"He's dying already. This gives him a chance to live."

Fiona shook her head. "We'd be risking the whole hospital. We'd never be allowed to do another transplant again. Never mind the liability issues. I can't approve this."

"Then what do I do?" Esther said.

"Find his parents," Fiona said. "Haven't they heard of cellphones?"

Esther's phone buzzed. She reached for it, hoping it was Mary, but then saw the text. "Oh God, "she said. "Kunal's crashing again."

She bolted out of the lawyer's office and back up to the ICU. Four people huddled around Doctor Mirchandani's bed. KC looked up as she entered. "We got him back," he said. "But he's down to a few hours."

Esther racked her brain. If Kunal died, they'd only have a few more hours before the heart would be useless.

"I need more time," she said.

"At least you won't have to worry about transport," KC said. "That buys a few hours."

The word "transport" brought Esther up short. She thought back to the helicopter crash that had started this nightmare only a week or so earlier. "Maybe I can buy us a few more hours," she said, bolting for the door. She went through her phone directory as she half-jogged down the corridor. She found the number for Doctor Mirchandani's lab and dialed, hoping that somebody was still there. A woman with a young-sounding voice answered after a few rings.

"Shreya Kim," the woman said flatly, as a greeting. Esther explained who she was and what she needed. "There were only two prototypes. And they are both gone," Shreya said,

Esther's heart sank.

"Why does it matter anyway?" Shreya asked. Esther explained what she was trying to do.

"Hold on," Shreya said. The phone was silent for so long, Esther thought she'd lost the connection or been hung up on. But then the woman came back on.

"We have some parts. But no batteries. And no shell. It can't go anywhere."

"It doesn't need to," Esther said. "Could it work?"

"I don't know. We'd need a container of some sort. And power."

"I'll take care of that," Esther said. "Just pack it up." She told Shreya where to go once she arrived at the hospital and hung up, still walking quickly down the corridor. Moments later she reached Rhonda's office, breathless and sweating. She barged by Rhonda's assistant and walked straight into the office. Rhonda was sitting with her back to her desk, looking at the pictures on the wall. She spun around as Esther pushed through the door.

"I need to talk to Mary and Rick," Esther said. "Do you know any way I can reach them?"

Rhonda stared blankly for a minute then focused on Esther's face. "Why?"

"We might still be able to save John. But they have to agree to the procedure."

Rhonda collapsed deeper into her chair. She knew if she connected Esther to anyone in Vancouver it would mean the end of her role at Saint Elizabeth's. And probably a jail sentence as well.

"Come on, Rhonda," Esther pleaded. "If there's anything you can do, now's the time. You're still a doctor. At least I thought you were."

Rhonda finally nodded. "I have a number. To a man named Marco. I can call it and relay a message."

"Do it," Esther said.

"I will."

"*Now*, Rhonda," Esther stood with her arms crossed. Rhonda nodded numbly and took her cellphone out. She made the call, and Esther listened to be sure the message was delivered accurately. Then Esther hustled out of the office, and back to the clinical wing. She had a lot to do in the next few hours. *Come on, Mary*, she thought to herself. None of it would matter if the Morrows didn't get back in touch in the next few hours. Already on to her next challenge, she was not in Rhonda's office when Marco called back ten minutes later with his own set of instructions for Rhonda.

Seventy-Nine

Marco left the library and let himself out onto the deck that paralleled the full length of the hallway. The deck reached from the library on one end to Annette's room on the other. It was eighty feet of rare mahogany, with wire railings to avoid obstructing the view from inside.

A splash in the bay caught his attention. A killer whale surfaced to breathe, its black body outlined against the blue water and the impossibly bright sparkles of the sun off the tops of the waves. It occurred to Marco how seldom he, or anyone except Annette for that matter, ever really looked at the view here. Lana's grandfather had built a house that was a monument to the sea. As far as Marco could tell, almost nobody who lived in it seemed to care.

He heard the swoosh of the door opening behind him and the unsteady scuffing of footsteps as someone approached him from behind.

"Hi, Phillippe," he said without looking back, his eyes still on the prowling Orca in the bay.

"I hate when you do that."

"Old habits die hard."

Phillippe came up next to him, his hands on the railing.

Marco could smell the whiskey on his breath. "You're okay with all this?" Phillippe said.

"Not my job to be okay or not," Marco said.

"I just figured... it seems wrong to me still. What Lana's doing. Even though it's my daughter."

"What *you're* doing," Marco said. "You could have said no."

"I can't imagine how the Morrows view us."

"Yes, you can," Marco said. "That's why you can't do this sober."

"I didn't know, at first." Phillippe said. "What you two had planned."

"It's not my plan. And you didn't ask Lana."

"Annette is my daughter. Most people would understand why I went along. But you? What's your excuse? Money?"

Marco thought of the cabin high up in the mountains. "Just looking for a little peace and quiet," he said, still not looking at Phillippe.

"I'm going to make another donation to the Morrows," Phillippe said. "I don't care what Lana thinks."

"No, you won't," Marco said.

"She can't stop me."

"She won't need to. You'll stop yourself. You won't cross her. Or risk your family's reputation."

"They deserve better than this," Phillippe said. "The Morrows, I mean."

"Yes, they do," Marco said.

Phillippe left him, swaying slightly as he made his way along the long deck, towards Annette's room.

Marco took a piece of paper out of his pocket. It was a printout of the image on his lock screen. The cabin in the mountains. The closest he could get to the clouds, where the air was pure and cold. Out of reach of the dank smell of jungles and the terrible things people did to each other out of greed, or fear, or love. Out of the reach of memory, he'd hoped. He stared at it for a minute, then crumpled it up and released it over the railing. He watched as the wind from the bay caught it, bouncing it against the rocks below, until it disappeared into the surf.

"Yes, they do," he repeated to himself.

Marco was still watching the spot where the paper had landed when Rhonda's call came in. Rhonda delivered the message Esther had recited to her. When she finished, Marco just said, "Okay," and disconnected. But the edge of a smile curled his lips for a moment.

He headed back into the building, leaving the whale to its business in the sound. He found Lana in the library.

"There's no point in keeping them," he said to her. "The law's sketchy on organ ownership and right now the worst thing you're guilty of is blowing up your own helicopter. But you keep these folks much longer, and you've got a kidnapping charge around your neck."

"I'll decide how much trouble I want to be in," she said, not even bothering to look at him.

"And what about the other boy? Are you really looking for a murder charge, too?"

Lana smiled grimly. "They don't define murder quite the same way where he is. And if I have to live with that one, too, I'll do it. It's only the Morrows who don't have the guts to own that for their son."

"A conscience can be a terrible thing," Marco said. Lana didn't reply. Marco couldn't tell if she was ignoring his sarcasm, or if she was agreeing with his point. After a moment he realized her calculating mind had been at work again. She turned to him. "You're right, it can be. Get the Morrows back in here."

"They won't change their minds," Marco said.

"Maybe they will," Lana said. "As you said, a conscience can be a terrible thing. So, I'll remove it for them."

"We'll see, Lana." He padded down the hall. Anton, the other security guard, was standing outside the game room door. Marco knocked before entering. Rick and Mary were near the card table. They both took a step toward him. Both looked frightened and angry.

"We want to go home," Rick said. "Now."

"I know," Marco said. "I promised you'd be safe, and I meant it. But Lana wants to talk to you again. I don't know why, but after she's through, I'll get you out of here."

"Our phones don't work," Mary said. "They're both dead. I want to check on John."

For a second, Marco debated sharing what Lana had told him about keeping them in Vancouver, but he thought it would just make them more upset. And if one of them did something crazy now, they'd most likely wind up in a Vancouver jail cell, not on a plane back to Detroit.

"I'll find a way for you to call home," he said. "But first go see what Lana wants."

The pair made their way back to the library. Marco walked to the far end of the hall and retrieved Marie and Phillippe, who'd been sitting outside Annette's room. Everyone gathered in the library again.

"We want to go home, now," Mary said.

"I understand," Lana said. She held up her phone. "But I'm going to make this really simple for you. I did call my friends. And I told them to go ahead with the surgery."

Mary gasped. Phillippe took another drink from his glass.

"We said no," Mary said.

"I know you did," Lana said. There was an odd fire in her eyes now, and she almost chewed off her words as she said them. "But it's going to happen anyway. In an hour, they'll cut the heart out of that boy and put it into the AionOne. Like the one you saw, Rick. And they'll send it back here."

Rick recoiled at the memory of his arms wrapped around the melted plastic case, the fluid leaking out into the ground in front of him. The heat of the fire burning his skin.

Lana pressed on. "You can't stop it from happening."

"Why?" Mary said.

"I'm making it easy, Mary. Now you've got no decision to make. Either the heart goes into John, or it goes into the trash. That's your only choice. The boy's life? That's on me. You get your son, and I take the guilt. What's easier than that?"

Mary just stared at her. "You wouldn't."

"I would," Lana said. "'I will. And you can just sit here and wait while I do it. I'll let you know when the heart's in the air. Then you have one hour to decide if you want me to send a plane for your son."

"You're kidnapping us," Rick said, standing. "We're walking out of here now."

"No, you're not," Lana said. She looked at Anton, who moved to block the door.

"I promised them safety," Marco said. "This is crazy."

"They are safe," Lana said. "And in a couple of days they'll thank me for this."

Marco turned and stalked out of the room, trying to think of a way to get Rick and Mary back to Detroit without having to shoot his way out of the house. He was halfway down the hall when the idea hit him. He redialed Rhonda's number and this time he gave *her* very specific instructions on what to do.

Still in the library, facing Lana, Rick and Mary sat dumbfounded. "Let us go home. We said no," Mary said again.

"Then you can stand here and watch me get ready to toss the heart into the ocean tomorrow morning," Lana said. "Who knows? Maybe one of Annette's favorite whales will get a free breakfast." She smiled at the look of horror her words brought to Mary's face, then took a sip of water. "We'll see how much conviction you have then, Mary," she said.

Marco came back into the room and sat at the far end of the table, tucking his phone back into his pocket.

"For God's, sake what's wrong with you two?" Marie shouted across the table. "My daughter's down there right now. Needles in her arms and plastic on her doors, but she's alive. She has a chance. Your son John could have the same chance. All you have to do is agree to leave us alone."

Rick shook his head.

"Marco told me about you, Rick," Marie said, her voice softening, but a note of desperation creeping in. "He said did everything you could for John. Let my mother save him now. Is there really anything more important than that?"

For a minute all the old anger welled up inside Rick as he thought about the battles he and Mary had fought, the slights they'd endured, the senseless decisions and heartless bureaucrats they'd railed against. But the feeling passed quickly as he thought of John. He smiled at Marie. "I've given up my career. My pride. I'd even give my life. I can choose to do that if I want to. Maybe I'm *supposed* to do that.

But Mary's right. I don't have the right to ask that little boy you're talking about to die. And I won't."

"How are you going to feel in a year?" Marie said. "Will your morals let you face yourself when he's dead and my Annette's off all these machines and medicines, and living her life again?"

The last sentence sent Rick's mind back to the visit to Annette's room, and the bags and syringes he'd seen in the trash. Methylprednisone and cyclosporin, in huge doses. It hadn't made sense. Now it hit him. He stood up to face Lana, Marie, and Phillippe. He wondered which of them knew the truth. But before he could speak, Marco's phone rang. He answered, then held his hand up, waving the room to silence as he listed intently. After a moment he stood looking at Rick and Mary in turn. He was biting his lip. "I have news you have to hear," he said. "I'm sorry."

He placed the phone on the table, speaker on. He said, "I'm with Rick and Mary now, Rhonda. Can you please repeat what you told me?"

The voice on the phone was tinny but clearly it was Rhonda Marsh. "I'm so sorry Rick and Mary," she began. "We've tried to reach you multiple times. John went into cardiac arrest about ninety minutes ago. We tried everything. But his heart. It was just too much for him to take. He passed away a few minutes ago."

Mary let out a guttural cry. Rick felt the air leave his lungs and the room seemed to close in around him. It seemed surreal; his mind could not process how this faint voice on this tiny device could be delivering such terrible news.

Mary's face contorted in rage. "You killed him," she screamed at Lana. "All of you. You killed my boy." She collapsed deeper into the chair, her shoulders shaking as sobs racked her body.

Rick wrapped his arms around her, containing his own rage and grief as he tried to comfort Mary. Lana sat stunned at the head of the table. Phillippe dropped his head into his hands. Marie just stared stoically across the table.

"Either you can kill us too or you can let us go home now, Lana." Rick said. Images tried to push into his mind: John, terrified, asking for his parents as the world turned dark around him; his body now on some gurney in a hospital morgue. Rick shoved them to the side for now, focusing on just moving, to get him and Mary out of this place and back to Detroit.

Lana looked dazed. But then she seemed to focus, even though the focus seemed to come from some desperate place inside her.

"We can still work this out," she said. "The plane. It's not ready." She said the words tentatively, trying to gather some rationale even as her mind tried to grasp the disintegration of her plan.

Rick snarled at her "We are going, now, Lana. With or without your help." He helped Mary to her feet and they started moving towards the door.

Lana looked at Anton. "Stop them. Or you're fired." The young man looked back and forth between Rick and Lana for a moment, then in a smooth motion drew a pistol out from under his jacket and pointed it at Rick.

Rick froze in disbelief. Marco took a slow, almost imperceptible step towards Anton, who flicked the barrel of the pistol in his direction for a moment. "Don't, Marco," he said.

"I brought you here," Marco said to Anton.

"Yeah, but she pays me," Anton retorted, nodding towards Lana.

"Everyone, just calm down," Lana said. The words hung ridiculously in the air. "I know this is terrible news, but we can still work something out. The money..."

Phillippe climbed slowly and a bit unsteadily to his feet, his empty glass in his hand. "Lana's right," he said, the two words running together in a quick slur. "There's got to be a way to work this out. Think about the money," he said generally in Rick and Mary's direction, waving at the house around him, "It's not a bad way to live. I got used to it." He made his way to the bar at the back of the room where Anton stood. Phillippe seemed oblivious to the man with the gun. He tossed some ice cubes in a glass.

"I don't need your help, Phillippe," Lana said. "If you hadn't made that donation to them, we wouldn't even be here."

"I know," Phillippe said. "I just wanted everyone to be okay." He picked up the bottle of whiskey, which was nearly empty, and poured the remainder into his glass. "But I can help. You all think I gave up my morals. I gave up my beliefs. For this!" He gestured again at the space around him, the whisky bottle waving carelessly in his hand. "For jet planes, and European vacations. For people calling me 'sir' just in the hopes of a bigger tip. For Annette. For Marie. I'll admit, it's not so bad," he said, weaving on his feet. "Like I said, you get used to it. After a bit, you kind of just expect it. Then you start thinking you deserve it."

"You're drunk. And you're making a scene," Lana said.

He put down his glass and said, "Like I said, you get used to it. But I guess I do still have some limits after all." Then, in a surprisingly quick motion, he spun to his right and smashed the whisky bottle against the side of Anton's head. Anton stumbled into the wall but stayed on his feet. Phillippe hit him again and this time the man crashed to the floor, the pistol skittering out of his hand.

Marco dove around the table and grabbed Phillippe's arm. Phillippe did not resist and dropped the bottle. Marco leaned over to check on Anton. Rick started to guide Mary towards the door. He didn't know where he was going but knew they had to get out of here.

"Jesus, Phillippe," was all Lana could say.

Rick started moving more quickly towards the door. He'd reached it and had his hand on the knob when Marie shouted, "Stop!"

Rick turned and saw Marie, now at the far end of the table, holding Anton's pistol with both hands. The weapon looked ridiculously large in her small hands. But it was still deadly. And it was pointed at Mary's back.

"You are not leaving. You will not do this to Annette," Marie said. "I'll kill you if you try."

Eighty

Dr. Mirchandani's body went into its final collapse only minutes after Esther had left KC and the ICU. He was rushed back into surgery. One team worked frantically to keep his body functioning, while another prepared to take out his heart and end whatever life he had left.

Fiona had signed off on the required forms, serving as medical proxy for Dr. Mirchandani. Now it was simply a race against time. Esther waited outside the surgical suite, checking her watch and wondering when Shreya Kim would arrive. It would all be a waste if the woman didn't get there fast enough.

Shreya arrived on the surgical floor only fifteen minutes after Esther had called her, and Esther met her there. A thin, twenty-something man with a scraggly goatee and ponytail was with her, carrying a bin full of sealed plastic bags.

"This is Freddy. He's the hardware tech," Shreya said, gesturing to him with her head. "He's got all the parts we have that have been sterilized. I didn't dare take anything else."

Esther had already rounded up a team of surgical nurses who were waiting to help. She directed Shreya and Freddy into their surgical scrubs and showed them how to wash up correctly.

"We need a pan," Shreya said, "big enough to hold the heart."

"And a drill," Freddy said, shooting an embarrassed look at Shreya Kim. "I forgot the drill."

"Freddy!" Shreya said. "We don't have time to go back."

Esther was horrified to think that, even with some of the world's best doctors working in the room next door, the whole plan now hung on a kid named Freddie who seemed to not be entirely with it. But she couldn't show that now. "No problem," Esther said. "Yours wouldn't have been sterile anyway."

"I'll call Ortho," one of the nurses said. "They have drills." Freddy looked confused.

"Orthopedic surgery," Esther said. "They're basically carpenters with medical degrees. They'll have whatever tools you need."

The team set to work on a table on the side of the room, near a power outlet. That operating table was set, too. It was more than big enough for a ten-year-old boy. Esther just hoped they'd get a chance to use it.

Eighty-One

"Marie, stop." Lana said, almost begging.

"Why, Mother? We've come this far. We can't weaken now. You should be the one telling *me* that. We can still make this work."

"But not with you in jail," Lana said. "Please."

"You'll have Annette," Marie said. "I don't mind. She can grow up with you. I think we both know you'd be fine with that anyway."

Rick saw the pained look flash briefly across Lana's face. Most people would have thought it was a reaction to her daughter's words. But Rick knew the truth.

"They don't know, do they." Rick said to Lana.

Lana's face became a mask as she tried to keep a thousand emotions from registering on the surface, hoping to prevent what she seemed to know was coming next.

"What don't I know?" Marie said, looking between Rick and her mother.

"Annette is dying," Rick said. "Isn't she, Lana?"

Marie bared her teeth at him but glanced at her mother. Lana did not move. Or deny Rick's claim.

Doubt crept onto Marie's face, seeing her mother's odd reaction. "You're wrong. She's just recovering," Marie said, but there was a hint of desperation in her voice. "It's a slow process. The doctors said so."

"I didn't get it at first," Rick said. "Methylprednisone and cyclosporin drip. In massive doses. The doctors are crashing her immune system." He met Marie's eyes. "Her body is rejecting the heart."

"You're no doctor. You don't know that." Marie said.

Rick smiled at her. But there was no humor in his gesture. "I've read everything there is to read on heart transplants, Marie," he said. "Believe me, I know."

Marie looked at her mother, who still refused to meet her gaze.

"That's impossible," Phillippe said. "The doctors wouldn't hide that."

"The masks? The plastic sheeting? That's not a normal recovery," Rick said. "I'm sure of it."

Marie turned to her mother. "He's lying, right?"

Lana stayed frozen.

"My God," Phillippe said, seeing Lana's reaction. "We had a right to know." Marco released him and moved over to tend to Anton.

"You two let me manage everything else in your life, Phillippe," Lana said, finally. "Why would this be any different?" Marie's eyes brightened. "The other boy. His heart," she said. "We can use that." Her eyes narrowed as something seemed to dawn on her. She turned to her mother, keeping the gun on Rick and Mary. Some sort of realization seemed to strike her. "Why didn't you do that already, Mother?" she said, her voice rising as she spoke. "You knew Annette was sick. Why did you offer it to *them* instead?"

"She made her calculation," Rick said. "Annette needed to take her chances with the heart she has regardless, so Lana knew she could use the other one to bribe us and save the company. Right, Lana?"

"It's too late for Annette," Lana said to Marie. "They can't do another transplant with any real chance of success. Either the doctors save her now, or they don't." She set her shoulders. "I had to try and save the company, too, Marie. It's our legacy. *Her* legacy."

"*Annette* is my legacy," Marie said. "Not the stupid company. How could you not even try?"

"What do you think of *that*, Marie?" Rick interjected. "The company matters more to your mother than you or your daughter."

Marie's eyes took on a wild glare. "No." she said, wheeling around and turning the gun on her mother.

Lana glared at her. "Put that stupid thing down, Marie."

"Maybe it's too late now. But you could have done it before," Marie said. "They could have already operated on Annette again." She pointed at Rick and Mary with her free hand. "You waited, to have a bargaining chip for *these* people."

Lana shook her head. "We talked about this, honey. I *wish* Annette was all I had to worry about. I did put her first."

"Annette could die, and you're worried about the *company*?" Marie said, her voice rising on the last word.

"Somebody has to be," Lana said.

"You made this a mess for her *and* the company," Marie said. "Now you're willing to risk Annette's life just to clean it up?" She snarled the words, her eyes growing darker.

"This *mess*?" Lana said. "I saved Anette, honey. There's still a chance. I did what I had to for her. And for you. You know that."

"You didn't save her. You're killing her," Marie hissed.

Lana's eyes flashed. "*I'm* killing her? Maybe you and Phillippe shouldn't have taken her on those stupid charity missions to God-knows-where when you should have been learning how to run the business. Then she wouldn't have gotten sick in the first place. You killed her when you got on that plane to Africa six months ago, Marie."

Marie's face had dissolved into a contorted mask of anger and despair. "You have to save her, Mother. You know she's everything to me."

Lana sighed at her daughter, a look that was half pity, half contempt. "You say that. And yet you couldn't even keep her safe on that stupid trip to Africa."

Marie screamed in rage, her voice drowned out instantly by the roar of the pistol. The bullet struck Lana in the right side of her chest. Her eyes registered a moment of surprise before the shock set in, and she fell to the floor. Marie dropped the gun in horror as she saw her mother collapse. Marco left Anton at the far end of the room and rushed over to Lana's side. He grabbed a cloth napkin from the table and shoved it into the wound.

"Call an ambulance," he shouted to the room in general. "It's really bad."

Eighty-Two

Esther slipped into the room where the two teams were working on Dr. Mirchandani.

"Five minutes," one of the nurses said.

"They need longer," Esther said.

"It doesn't work that way," one of the surgeons said, without looking up from the table. "It needs to come out now."

Esther hurried back to the other surgical room. The sound of a whirring drill met her as she entered the room.

"You got great tools here," Freddy said, balancing the drill in his hand.

"Just keep working," Shreya growled at him, as she connected a small black control unit to a set of wires.

"There's one more thing," Shreya said. "We don't have enough fluid."

"What does that mean?"

"The fluid that's pumped through the heart in the container. We have two liters. That's all that's been made. Usually, red blood cells from the donor would be suspended in the fluid. They carry oxygen to the heart while it's in the container. I measured the container and the tubing. Two liters isn't enough."

"What do we do?"

Shreya took in a breath. "I need Kunal's blood. Lots of it. Freddy's head shot up from his drilling work. "That won't work," he said. "Whole blood will coagulate. It will gum up the pump."

"The fluid we have will help thin it. It should work, for a while."

"How long is a while?" Esther said.

Shreya just shrugged. "Longer than the alternative, which is zero."

Esther rushed back into the other suite where Kunal's body lay. "We need his blood. Three liters at least."

"That would have been good to know ten minutes ago," the surgeon said. "There might not be enough time to get that much."

"Just try," was all Esther could think to say.

Within minutes, two IV lines were set up and blood was draining from Doctor Mirchandani's arteries and into storage bags on the floor. The two tubes were bleeding him to death even as a battery of machines worked to keep him alive a little bit longer, just so the waiting doctors could end his life in a matter of minutes anyway. "I'm sorry," Esther whispered to Kunal, shaken by the sight of the tubes, wires, and clamps attached all over his failing body.

"Don't be. He'd want us to do it, if it gives that kid a chance," the surgeon said quietly to her, even as he continued his work.

Two floors below, John Morrow was being prepped for surgery for the second time in 10 days. His chest was swabbed with disinfectant and a saline drip put in his arm. Those were things the hospital could do. But they would not put him under anesthetic until they had his parent's consent. That was the law, and Fiona Esperanza was not willing to violate it. Esther checked her phone again. Still no word from Mary or Rick. *Come on Mary,* Esther thought again. *Don't let all this be for nothing.*

Eighty-Three

The door to the library burst open and one of the staff looked in, drawn by the gunshot.

"Call an ambulance," Marco shouted, and the woman fumbled in her pocket for a cellphone.

"Come here, Phillippe," Marco said. Phillippe knelt next to Lana. "Hold the napkin tight against the wound. Don't let off the pressure. She'll bleed out if you do." Phillippe nodded dumbly but pressed his hand against the square of cloth. The crisp white napkin was already crimson, and blood still seeped around the edges of the wound.

Marco turned to the woman in the doorway. "And get the doctors from down the hall."

The woman rushed off, phone to her ear as she connected with the 911 operator.

Marco checked on Anton, who was struggling to his knees in the corner, shaking off the effects of the blows. Then he turned to Rick and Mary.

"Come on, we're going," he said. "If you're here when the police arrive, they'll keep you for questioning. It could be days."

He looked at Marie, who sat crumpled in a chair. "We're taking the plane," he said. She just nodded, staring at her mother on the floor, the carpet around Lana darkening from the spreading blood.

Marco led Rick and Mary out of the room. Two doctors rushed by them into the library, led by the woman who'd called 911. They carried armfuls of bandages and saline drips, not knowing for sure what to expect.

Halfway down the hall, Mary turned back. "We can't leave yet."

"We don't have time," Marco said. "It's the Cera residence. The police will come fast when they're called."

Mary ignored him and pushed her way back into the library, Rick and Marco chasing her. She strode over to the table and picked up Lana's cellphone, which lay ignored on the table. She held it up to Marie.

"You're going to tell them to let the little boy go."

Marie tore her eyes away from her mother and stared at Mary. "Why would I care what happens to him?" she said, her eyes wild with shock.

"Do you still care about your daughter?"

"Yes," Marie said.

"Then do it," Mary said. "And I promise not to come after you, for the heart or for anything. I can't tell you Annette will live. But if she does, she'll live in peace. At least from us." She looked over at Rick, who stood by the door. Rick nodded in agreement.

Marie seemed unable to process it all, her brain cycling back and forth between the image of her mother on the floor and Mary's words. She made no attempt to move.

"Do it!" Mary screamed at her, bringing her out of her shock. Marie stared at Mary blankly, but there was some recognition at least. Mary found the last number dialed on the phone and pushed the "Send" button. Then she shoved the phone towards Marie. "Now."

Marie finally came out of her reverie and sneered at Mary. "Sure. It doesn't matter. I can just call again tomorrow, and the surgery will be back on. For Annette. You'll never know."

"But I will," Phillippe said. He looked up from his spot on the floor, his hands still pressing the makeshift bandage against Lana's chest. "We won't do that. There's been enough misery already." He turned to Rick and Mary. "The boy will be fine. I promise."

"*Now* you finally get a spine?" Marie said to him bitterly. But she put the phone up to her ear. She identified herself and delivered the news to the man who answered. At the end, she simply said, "Tell Prince Nassir my mother appreciates his friendship," and hung up the phone.

"We need to go now," Marco said. Rick and Mary followed him at a jog through the house and out to a big black car in the driveway. Marco dove into the driver's side as Rick and Mary jumped in the back. Tires shrieked as Marco accelerated down the long driveway. They made it to the main road just as two police cars screamed past, heading towards the looming mansion they were leaving behind.

Marco drove with a skill she'd never seen in anyone before, never going much over the speed limit but somehow cutting through the building traffic like it wasn't even there.

"If you think this makes up for John, it doesn't," Mary said to him. "We'll never forgive you for that."

"You can blame me for a lot of things," Marco said, not taking his eyes off the road. "But not that."

"He wouldn't be dead if it weren't for you," Mary said.

"He's not dead *now*," Marco said.

"But we heard Rhonda," Rick said, once again feeling the world spin around him. "She said it."

"Yes, you heard her say that. But John's not dead. I just needed Lana to think he was. I'll tell you more later. Right now, we need to get back to Detroit, fast." Marco said. "And Mary, you need to call some woman named Esther."

Eighty-Four

Ani lay unconscious on the operating table in a surgical suite in Riyadh. He'd been that way for most of the trip from Yemen. Doctor Khalid was holding a scalpel over the boy's chest, lining up to make an identical incision to the one he'd made two weeks earlier for Annette. He paused the blade when a man in a sport coat thrust open the door and strode into the room.

"You can't be in here," Doctor Khalid shouted.

"It doesn't matter," the man said. "The surgery is not required. You can save your effort."

Doctor Khalid stared at him for a moment, then looked down at the boy on the table. "What do we do with him?"

The man in the sport coat shrugged. "We have a plane headed back to Yemen tomorrow. Clean him up and we'll send him back to his mother." He gestured at the knife hovering over Ani's chest. "Unless you want the practice," he said. "Nobody will care if you do." Then he turned and left the room.

The nurses stared at Doctor Khalid, awaiting his instructions. He looked at them in turn, then dropped the scalpel back in the pan. "Send him back to his mother," he said, to no one in particular. Then he followed the man in the sport coat out of the surgical suite, peeling off his latex gloves as he went.

In a similar surgical room in Detroit, Shreya and Freddie worked at a mad pace, connecting tubes and wires. Shreya powered up the control panel and took out her phone.

"You can't use that here," one of the nurses said.

"It's how we program the device," Shreya said. "We built an app for it." She started typing quickly on the tiny keypad, as casually as if she was texting a couple of friends about dinner. Esther watched her, suddenly feeling old.

"Okay," Shreya said. "It's ready."

"Will it work?" Esther said doubtfully, looking at the chaotic tangle of metal and plastic.

"There's only one way to know for sure," Freddy said.

Moments later a nurse backed through the swinging door into the room, holding a deep metal tray. Two of the doctors followed her, carrying the bags of blood. The nurse put the metal tray down and lifted Doctor Mirchandani's heart out of it, as if she was taking a pot roast out of a pan. "Where do I put it?" she said.

Shreya Kim seemed to gag a bit at the sight.

"You OK?" Esther said, watching Shreya's reaction.

"I think most people are gross enough on the outside," Shreya said. "Never mind the inside." But she took a breath and told the nurse where to place the heart and guided the two doctors on how to connect the right tubes to the main arteries and veins. As they worked, Freddy poured the blood into the holding canister along with the rest of the fluid. Once all the tasks were completed, Shreya took out her phone again.

"Here we go," she said, and typed in a command. Instantly the pump connected to the device started whirring.

The heart stirred gently as the fluid began moving through it. Shreya switched to a different screen that showed dials and bars. She studied it for a moment.

"I think it's working," she said breathlessly. "Holy shit, I think we did it."

Esther choked back tears of relief, watching the heart fill and empty slowly in the pan as the machinery pumped fluid through it. The nurse tented the pan with a sterile cloth. Then Esther felt her phone buzz in her rear pocket. She didn't recognize the number but moved out into the hallway to answer it anyway.

"Esther Williams," she said, out of habit.

"Esther, it's Mary," said the voice on the other end. This time Esther did start crying, even as she told Mary what had to happen next.

Eighty-Five

Mary finished the call with Esther and joyfully filled Rick in on the frantic effort happening in Detroit. She was still sniffling from the echoes of her grief and the almost numbing relief of finding out John was still alive. Based on what Esther had said, a hope they'd thought impossible was maybe coming true.

"I'm sorry," Marco said once she'd finished. "Having Rhonda tell you John was dead was the only way I could think of to get you out of there. Lana had to think there was no value in keeping you in Vancouver any longer. She figured if she could keep you long enough, you'd break down once you knew it was too late to save the other boy."

They drove the rest of the way to the airport in silence, except for Marco's call to the private jet terminal alerting the crew to their imminent arrival.

"Is the plane ready?" Rick said as they got close.

"It was always ready," Marco said. "That was just another stalling tactic from Lana." He kept glancing in the rearview mirror, half-expecting to see police lights bearing down on them, but instead all he saw was the usual sea of afternoon traffic.

Once the plane was in the air they collapsed into the elegant seats. It was only now, off the ground and putting Vancouver behind them, that they could start to relax.

"I got the gist of what's happening," Marco said. "But I thought your son's blood type was rare and that hearts for him were hard to come by."

"That's right," Rick said, quietly.

"So, where'd the heart come from?" Marco said. He seemed genuinely curious, and even excited at the news about John.

Rick paused a minute before answering, realizing Marco didn't know the final outcome of his encounter with Doctor Mirchandani. Esther had filled Mary in during the car ride to the airport.

"Doctor Mirchandani," Rick said. "The guy who you jumped in the alley."

Marco's face fell. "I didn't want that."

"We believe you," Mary said.

"He just wouldn't give up the computer," Marco said, mostly to himself.

"He never gave up on anything," Rick said. "Or anybody."

"He knew he was a match for John," Mary said. "But he never told us. Esther said he had a note added to his living will, just in case. But I'm sure he never thought it would come to this."

Marco nodded. Rick went to the back of the plane and rummaged around until he found two beers and a small bottle of wine. He brought them all to the front of the plane and opened them.

They drank in silence, watching the ground spool away six miles below. Marco pulled out his backpack, which was still under the seat from the morning's trip. He turned to

Mary. "Are you serious about what you said to Lana?" he said. "About not turning her and her family in for what they did?"

"Yes," Mary said. "If that what it takes to save that boy."

"I thought you wanted justice?" Marco asked, turning to Rick.

"I think there will be plenty of that," Rick said, thinking of Annette and the probably futile attempt to stop the organ rejection. "In its own way."

"Well, I have one more piece of justice for you," Marco said, rummaging through the backpack. He pulled out a stack of papers. "Since you're willing to agree to the gag order, I really suggest you sign the paperwork I'd shown you before. As an agent for the Cera family, I think I should get that confirmation in writing." He said, mock-seriously. "And you should get the five million dollars that goes along with it."

"We don't need the money," Mary said.

"Neither do the Ceras," Marco said. He pulled the small table out from its resting place next to the seat and found a pen in his bag. "The money's already been authorized by the board, at Lana's direction. It's just sitting in an account." He looked at Mary and tried a smile. "A deal's a deal, eh?"

"Will this cover the other deal, too? The one for the guys at the shop?" Rick said.

Marco nodded. "The lawyers know about that, too. It's not in here, but I know it'll get triggered when this paper-work goes in."

They signed the documents, and Marco returned them to his bag.

Rick and Mary fell asleep, the stress of the day catching up with them. Marco watched the giant lakes of Winnipeg give way to the freckled landscape of Wisconsin. Farms were outlined on the grasslands with small towns sprinkled between. Open space was everywhere. He wondered if his dad was out working the field of the family farm just below Big Quill Lake. And he wondered what would be waiting for him when they landed in Detroit. Rick and Mary might not speak about the entire scheme, but the Detroit police would now be investigating a murder, not just a robbery. He'd killed people in raids and gun battles. He'd had men die under his command. But what had happened to Doctor Mirchandani felt different. Nobody had ordered Marco to do that. The doctor had not volunteered to put himself in harm's way or chosen to make a living on the misery of others. Mirchandani's death might save John Morrow, but to Marco it was just a death all the same. And it was all on him.

He decided he needed to put that aside for now and complete the mission one more time. That meant getting Rick and Mary to the hospital. Then he'd worry about his own future.

Eighty-Six

The surgical team worked quickly and surely on John Morrow, while Dr. Mirchandani's heart stirred restlessly in the metal pan a few feet away. It had been two hours since the heart was connected to the pump system. Shreya had been monitoring the display regularly.

They had inserted a breathing tube down John's throat, cut an incision down his center and split his sternum in half, spreading open his chest. They'd peeled back the membrane covering the heart. Then they had connected his vessels to a heart lung bypass machine to keep his blood flowing and oxygenated. This process took almost an hour. They then examined his weakened heart, already reconfigured almost beyond recognition by two previous surgeries. "It's amazing this kept him alive," the surgeon said, looking at the lump of grayish red muscle. "Dr. Mirchandani was a miracle worker."

Shreya continued to monitor the makeshift container. Suddenly the numbers on her phone screen began to change. "The pump is starting to struggle," she said to the room at large. "It's gumming up from the blood."

"How long?" one of the doctors asked.

"I don't know," she said. She tried to make sense of the information on the display. "A few minutes? Half an hour?"

"Damn," the surgeon said quietly under his breath, but he continued to work smoothly and deliberately. They needed to leave the arteries and veins in such a shape that the new heart could be attached securely. It was a painstaking process.

After ensuring they had a plan, they began to remove the failing organ, leaving part of the left atrium in place to attach to the new heart.

They severed the remaining vessels and began to cut away the heart itself.

"The vital signs are dropping," Shreya said, her eyes glued to her phone screen. "The AionOne's not getting enough oxygen to the heart."

The surgeons completed the cuts and lifted out John's heart. As they placed it into a waiting tray, a warning tone sounded on Shreya's phone. "It's stopping," she said. "The pump is failing."

The surgeon spun around and began detaching the new heart from the tubes in the metal pan. "Somebody start a timer," he said.

The team began working even faster, relaying instructions and sharing information quietly but urgently. One of the surgical nurses shouted out the time in 30-second intervals.

"Five minutes," she said. The surgeon muttered under his breath. John's chest was smaller than the doctor's, and he needed to trim the atrial walls and atrial cuff of the new heart to ensure it would fit appropriately.

"Ten minutes," the nurse said as he made the final connections.

"How long can it go?" Shreya asked a nurse near the foot of the table.

"A healthy heart could go a few hours," the nurse said. "But with everything that one's been through? Who knows?" Once he was sure it would fit, the surgeon stitched rapidly, reconnecting veins and arteries, and securing the new heart to John's body.

"Fifteen minutes," the nurse said, worry creeping into her voice.

The surgeon finished his work. "Okay," he said. "Let's shock him."

A pair of small flat paddles were placed on either side of the heart.

"Clear," the head nurse shouted. There was a snapping sound as the heart received a pulse of electricity. Time froze in the room for a moment.

"Nothing," ones of the nurses said, watching the monitors.

"Clear," the head nurse said again, and a moment later the snapping sound cut through the air.

The line remained stubbornly flat, bisecting the display from left to right.

"Again," the surgeon said.

"Nothing," the nurse said after the procedure was repeated.

"Come on, Kunal," the surgeon said quietly. "Save this kid one more time."

Once again, the paddles were placed next to the heart and the shock was delivered. The snapping sound seemed louder than ever. After a split second, a beep filled the silence in the surgical chamber. Then another beep. The line on the monitor jumped and then jumped again.

"We have a heartbeat," the nurse said excitedly.

Everyone in the room cheered and whistled, the tension ebbing even as they continued to watch the displays. The surgeon attached fine wires to the heart; they'd use a pacemaker for a few days to be sure the heart stayed beating on its own.

They stitched John up, reassembling his body with thread and wire, his new heart working steadily in his bony chest.

Eighty-Seven

The Cera's jet settled onto the runway with a gentle bump. They were at the private terminal in a matter of minutes. Marco had Rick and Mary retrieve their passports. When the door opened, a young woman in a U.S. Customs jacket entered the cabin. She checked the names and passports against the list on her clipboard, welcomed the three to Detroit, and disappeared down the stairs.

One of the pilots came out of the cockpit.

"Is the car here?" Marco asked. He'd had the pilot radio ahead to the private terminal to be sure a car was available to get them to the hospital.

"Yes, all set."

"Let's go then," Marco said, slinging his bag over his shoulder.

"The police are here, too," The pilot said. "The tower gave me a heads-up."

Marco's face fell. He'd hoped the police in Vancouver would not piece things together so quickly. His mind was racing, trying to think of ways to get Rick and Mary out of the airport and over to John, and not taken down to a police precinct for questioning.

He wondered if they'd figured out his role in Dr. Mirchandani's death. In some ways that would be preferable, he thought. They'd just be looking for him.

As his mind was turning, one of the cops climbed the stairs and scanned the contents of the cabin. "Ok folks, grab your bags and follow me," he said.

"They don't need to come," Marco said to the cop, gesturing to Rick and Mary. "I'm the only one you need."

The cop gave Marco a strange look. "Of course they have to come," he said. "It's their kid, right?"

"Our kid? Is John okay?" Mary said.

The cop shrugged. "I don't know, ma'am. I was just told to escort you to the hospital as quick as we could. Seems the CEO there called in a favor for you with my boss." He looked at Marco and spoke with the dismissiveness only a big-city cop could muster, "Assuming it's okay with you, champ."

Marco just smiled and let the cop lead them all out of the plane.

They got to the hospital in ten minutes, speeding through intersections behind the lights of the police car. The wailing sirens and flashing lights reminded Rick of his trip in the back of the ambulance, strapped to the gurney, his cellphone buzzing against his leg. He realized with a shock that that had been less than two weeks earlier.

"Is there any way you can find out if they really let that boy go?" Mary asked.

"I will," Marco said.

"It's hard to imagine she can cover things up now though, with the police involved," Rick said.

"You'd be surprised what the Ceras can get away with. They're the biggest donor to local and national politics in Canada." Marco said. "But I'm guessing she'll have some other things to answer for, too, if she lives. And those will be much harder to explain."

Marco swung the car up against the curb at the front entrance.

"Do you want to come see John?" Mary asked him.

He shook his head. "I have some things to finish up," he said.

"I can't believe I'm saying this, but thank you," Mary said.

"I'm pretty sure I owe you the thanks." Marco said. "And good luck to John. I hope he has a wonderful life ahead of him."

"He's had a wonderful life already," Rick said, looking at Mary.

Rick and Mary climbed out of the car and the vehicle pulled smoothly away. They called Esther on the way, and she was in the lobby when they entered. She smiled from ear to ear when she saw them and wrapped them each in bear hugs.

"He's upstairs, sleeping," Esther said.

"It's done?" Rick said.

"Yes," Esther said.

"How did it go?"

"Just like we plan them," Esther said, rolling her eyes. "I'll tell you about that later. Come on, let's go see your son." She escorted them to the recovery room. They knew the doctors would probably keep John unconscious for another day or so, to give his body time to recover from the massive trauma of the heart transplant. He had a breathing tube covering his mouth and an IV tube in his arm, but otherwise he looked like nothing other than a sleeping 12-year-old boy.

"He looks just like he did when we left him," Mary said.

"It seems impossible."

"Everything went well?" Rick asked again. Esther was all smiles, but he could see the fatigue around her eyes.

"It was quite a day," Esther said carefully. "You know what John's body has been through. And Kunal's heart took quite a beating, too." Her voice caught a bit as she said her dead friend's name. "But the surgery was successful. The heart is beating on its own. We have a pacemaker in for now, just to help if needed." She took a breath and continued, "I know you know this, but John's condition...the condition of the heart...like I said, both were in rough shape. The surgery might only buy him a couple of years But maybe a lot more."

Rick reached out and took Mary's hand, squeezing it gently in comfort.

"It's okay. We'll make every one of them count for him. And we'll see what happens from there. After this week, it's hard to say anything is impossible."

Esther nodded, then looked quizzically at the two of them. "So, what happened up in Vancouver? Private jets, police escorts. A shooting? Seems like you two had quite a ride."

Rick and Mary glanced at each other. "It was quite a trip," Mary said. "But in the end, all the really important stuff happened here."

Eighty-Eight

After Marco left Rick and Mary at the hospital he headed back to his hotel. He'd kept his room and left most of his gear there.

Once in the room, he fired up his PC and logged into the CeraGlobal network. He'd wondered during the flight to Detroit what Lana could offer the Saudi Crown prince to get him to take that great a chance. Human rights were a big sticking point with western governments already. The royal family would not want to risk association with a plot to cut out a little boy's heart just for money or a better contract on some equipment.

His role for Lana meant he had access to the computer security systems and logs of every employee's online actions. He started running through the log files for Lana and after a few minutes confirmed what he'd suspected. He packaged up the log files and forwarded them to two of the network security analysts at CeraGlobal. And he forwarded a set to an old friend in the Canadian government.

He drove back to the airport and returned the rental car. He walked to the private jet terminal and handed the envelope containing the documents Rick and Mary had signed to the CeraGlobal pilot.

"You don't want to deliver them yourself?" the man said.

"Nope. You're flying back alone," Marco said.

Marco found a taxi and took it back to the Marriott at Renaissance Place. He packed up his gear and headed down to the hotel's lobby. On a sudden whim, he walked out into the central area of the massive tower complex which was home both to the Marriott and to GM's global headquarters. Curving ramps circled down from where he stood, leading to the building's main entrance on the ground floor. GM's flagship vehicles were displayed all along the ramps and in the lobby below. Visitors milled about, looking at the vehicles and the other artifacts of GM's history.

The back side of the building's lobby was a massive glass wall facing the Detroit River. Across the blue-black waves beyond the glass, he could see the taller buildings of Windsor, their lights beginning to shine as the daylight waned. Somewhere past those lights was Big Quill Lake. And even beyond that, somewhere, he still imagined a mountaintop with a secluded cabin. Far away from the wet, rotting earth of the jungle, and the memories that still festered from there. And far away from the petty schemes of the people and governments he'd dedicated his life to serving in one way or another.

He went to the street level and asked the bellman for a cab, which dropped him off at a different car rental office than the one he'd used earlier. He rented a small SUV, tossed his bags in the back, and ten minutes later was nosing into the tunnel under the river, towards Canada.

Eighty-Nine

Rick and Mary sat at one of the simple metal tables at the Metropolitan Hospital coffee shop. The sitting area sat next to the coffee shop that served the children's wing and had a view of the children's play area. The space was open and brightly lit, with a colored glass skylight that let beams of red, blue, and green sunlight stream in. It was not nearly as dramatic as the atrium at its sister hospital in Pontiac, but Rick decided he preferred the quiet and warmth enveloping the sitting area to the view he'd seen looking down from Rhonda's office.

They had fallen into a regular routine in the week since they'd returned from Vancouver. Rick would work in the mornings, then meet Mary at the hospital. John was back in his old hospital room. Other than containing fewer pieces of medical equipment, the only changes in the room had been the addition of a crumpled yellow get-well card, centered on the wall over the bed, and a white stuffed lion, still looking a bit worse for wear but keeping loyal watch on John from the corner of the room.

After sitting with John, they'd make sure at least one of them was home in time to meet David at the school bus.

Today was a day off from school, however, and David was in the play area a few dozen feet away from them.

The shop had been happy to give Rick whatever flexibility he wanted. As Marco had promised, Rick's boss gotten a call confirming they'd won the CeraGlobal contract, as long as they agreed to keep Rick involved in the business in whatever capacity he desired.

Mary sipped her coffee and sighed, looking at the news feed on her cellphone. "Lana Cera died today," she said to Rick. "Complications from an accidental shooting at the family home, the news says. There's nothing about Annette."

"Serves Lana right," Rick said.

Mary shrugged. "I don't know. We both tried to do the same thing she did, in our own ways. She just had more ways than we did. That sort of pain and fear. It makes everybody do things they never thought they would."

"Like want a divorce?" Rick said. The topic had been a silent, dark companion, both to their joy over John, and to their slow return to a more normal world over the past days.

Mary reached across the table and took Rick's hand. "John got a second chance to live his life now. I think maybe we got one, too," she said. "I don't know what that means. But for once we get a chance to live for something beyond the next hospital visit. At least for a while."

"What happens now? We split the money, and you just go find somebody new?"

Mary smiled ruefully. "That's the funny thing, Rick. Watching you in Vancouver. Even seeing you in that empty lot, in so much pain. I realized you didn't do any of it to prove anything to yourself. And I realized I don't really know you at all."

Rick smiled, too. "That's how I felt when I watched you take apart Marco at the restaurant." They sat in silence for a bit, watching the foot traffic walk by. "Maybe nobody marries the person they think they do," he said, finally.

Mary shrugged. "Maybe not. I do think we both deserve to find somebody new." She met Rick's eyes and spoke more slowly. "But I'm starting to wonder if maybe each of us already has. What we have isn't perfect. But I'm thinking it's something worth fighting for."

They sat back in a comfortable silence for a minute. "Oh goodness, I need to get back upstairs," Mary said suddenly, checking her watch.

Mary headed back toward the elevators. Rick decided he had time to grab another coffee, and a doughnut for David for the drive home. He collected David from the play area and they got in line at the coffee shop. Rick scanned the menu board as he waited. He laughed to himself that he still felt a pang of guilt at the prices, even though five million dollars had been deposited into their account a few days earlier.

The line at the counter was populated with hospital staff, visitors, and vendors. An older woman in front of Rick and David got distracted checking her phone just as the line moved forward. A stocky man in a business suit, seeing the opening, stepped from the aisle into the gap in front of the woman just as the counter clerked shouted "Next!" A few people in line around the man muttered under their breath, but the man ignored their displeasure and barked out his order.

David looked up at his dad, scowling. "People shouldn't skip the line like that," he said. "It's not fair they get away with it."

Rick tousled David's hair. "They don't always get away with it, champ," he said, smiling down at his son's upturned face.

"Not always," he repeated to himself, more quietly, as the line moved forward.

***